P9-BYE-685

Hunting down a terrorist...
Finding a war.

continued . . .

DEBT OF HONOR

It begins with the murder of an American woman
in the backstreets of Tokyo. It ends in war . . .

"A SHOCKER."   —*Entertainment Weekly*

THE HUNT FOR RED OCTOBER

The smash bestseller that launched Clancy's career—
the incredible search for a Soviet defector
and the nuclear submarine he commands . . .

"BREATHLESSLY EXCITING."   —*The Washington Post*

RED STORM RISING

The ultimate scenario for World War III—
the final battle for global control . . .

"THE ULTIMATE WAR GAME . . . BRILLIANT."
                                —*Newsweek*

PATRIOT GAMES

CIA analyst Jack Ryan stops an assassination—
and incurs the wrath of Irish terrorists . . .

"A HIGH PITCH OF EXCITEMENT."
                                —*The Wall Street Journal*

THE CARDINAL OF THE KREMLIN

The superpowers race for the ultimate Star Wars
missile defense system . . .

"*CARDINAL* EXCITES, ILLUMINATES . . . A REAL PAGE-TURNER."   — *Los Angeles Daily News*

CLEAR AND PRESENT DANGER

The killing of three U.S. officials in Colombia ignites the
American government's explosive, and top secret, response . . .

"A CRACKLING GOOD YARN."   — *The Washington Post*

THE SUM OF ALL FEARS

The disappearance of an Israeli nuclear weapon threatens the
balance of power in the Middle East — and around the world . . .

"CLANCY AT HIS BEST . . . NOT TO BE MISSED."
                                            — *The Dallas Morning News*

WITHOUT REMORSE

His code name is Mr. Clark. And his work for the CIA
is brilliant, cold-blooded, and efficient . . . but who is he really?

"HIGHLY ENTERTAINING."   — *The Wall Street Journal*

NOVELS BY TOM CLANCY

The Hunt for Red October
Red Storm Rising
Patriot Games
The Cardinal of the Kremlin
Clear and Present Danger
The Sum of All Fears
Without Remorse
Debt of Honor
Executive Orders
Rainbow Six
The Bear and the Dragon
Red Rabbit
The Teeth of the Tiger
Dead or Alive
(written with Grant Blackwood)

SSN: Strategies of Submarine Warfare

NONFICTION

Submarine: A Guided Tour Inside a Nuclear Warship
Armored Cav: A Guided Tour of an Armored Cavalry Regiment
Fighter Wing: A Guided Tour of an Air Force Combat Wing
Marine: A Guided Tour of a Marine Expeditionary Unit
Airborne: A Guided Tour of an Airborne Task Force
Carrier: A Guided Tour of an Aircraft Carrier
Special Forces: A Guided Tour of U.S. Army Special Forces

Into the Storm: A Study in Command
(written with General Fred Franks, Jr., Ret., and Tony Koltz)
Every Man a Tiger
(written with General Chuck Horner, Ret., and Tony Koltz)
Shadow Warriors: Inside the Special Forces
(written with General Carl Stiner, Ret., and Tony Koltz)
Battle Ready
(written with General Tony Zinni, Ret., and Tony Koltz)

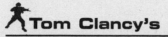

Tom Clancy's

ENDWAR™

THE HUNTED

WRITTEN BY

DAVID MICHAELS

BERKLEY BOOKS, NEW YORK

THE BERKLEY PUBLISHING GROUP
Published by the Penguin Group
Penguin Group (USA) Inc.
375 Hudson Street, New York, New York 10014, USA

Penguin Group (Canada), 90 Eglinton Avenue East, Suite 700, Toronto, Ontario M4P 2Y3, Canada
(a division of Pearson Penguin Canada Inc.)
Penguin Books Ltd., 80 Strand, London WC2R 0RL, England
Penguin Group Ireland, 25 St. Stephen's Green, Dublin 2, Ireland (a division of Penguin Books Ltd.)
Penguin Group (Australia), 250 Camberwell Road, Camberwell, Victoria 3124, Australia
(a division of Pearson Australia Group Pty. Ltd.)
Penguin Books India Pvt. Ltd., 11 Community Centre, Panchsheel Park, New Delhi—110 017, India
Penguin Group (NZ), 67 Apollo Drive, Rosedale, North Shore 0632, New Zealand
(a division of Pearson New Zealand Ltd.)
Penguin Books (South Africa) (Pty.) Ltd., 24 Sturdee Avenue, Rosebank, Johannesburg 2196,
South Africa

Penguin Books Ltd., Registered Offices: 80 Strand, London WC2R 0RL, England

TOM CLANCY'S ENDWAR™: THE HUNTED

A Berkley Book / published by arrangement with Ubisoft Ltd.

PRINTING HISTORY
Berkley premium edition / February 2011

Copyright © 2011 by Ubisoft Ltd.
EndWar, Ubisoft, and the Ubisoft logo are trademarks of Ubisoft in the U.S. and other countries.
Tom Clancy's EndWar © 2010 by Ubisoft Entertainment, S.A.
Cover art provided by Ubisoft Ltd.
Interior text design by Kristin del Rosario.

ISBN: 978-0-425-23771-7

BERKLEY®
Berkley Books are published by The Berkley Publishing Group,
a division of Penguin Group (USA) Inc.,
375 Hudson Street, New York, New York 10014.
BERKLEY® is a registered trademark of Penguin Group (USA) Inc.
The "B" design is a trademark of Penguin Group (USA) Inc.

PRINTED IN THE UNITED STATES OF AMERICA

10 9 8 7 6 5 4 3 2 1

ACKNOWLEDGMENTS

The author would like to thank a wonderful group of family members, friends, colleagues, and supporters. In particular, Mr. Tom Clancy and all of the folks at Ubisoft who created the EndWar game deserve my gratitude, as well as the following individuals:

Mr. Sam Strachman of Longtail Studios helped me create this story from the ground up, working from brainstorming to outlining to final draft manuscript. His contributions are greatly appreciated and invaluable.

Mr. James Ide served as our primary researcher and story expert. He scrutinized every page, relying on his extensive military background, his keen writing skills, and his commitment to this story to provide criticism, advice, and suggestions that greatly improved the manuscript.

Ms. Jackie Fiest graciously volunteered to serve as our first reader and provide her reactions and sharp eyes as a proofreader.

Mr. Tom Colgan is simply the keenest and most supportive

editor an author could have, and I'm fortunate to have worked with him on many projects.

Nancy, Lauren, and Kendall Telep know quite well why they are mentioned here.

I will kill the president of the Russian Federation.
I will bring down the motherland. And then I will
stand back and watch it all burn.

—VIKTORIA ANTSYFOROV, AKA "THE SNOW MAIDEN"

PROLOGUE

San Fernando Valley
Los Angeles, California
2009

Alexander Brent dropped into sixth gear and studied the digital head-up display glowing in his windshield:

116 mph and climbing.

The Corvette's short throw shifter felt warm, while the 505-horsepower LS7 engine roared its demand for more fuel and pinned him to the sport seat.

Streetlights and shop windows blurred by in a kaleidoscope of reds and blues and greens.

Taking his cue from the car, Brent jabbed his foot on the accelerator pedal, and the beast leapt forward across the rain-slick pavement, the scent of burning rubber still wafting up into the black leather cockpit.

Just a few minutes ago he'd come off the mark in a massive burnout, reaching sixty miles per hour in just 3.7 seconds. For a few heartbeats he'd lost control, the rear tires hopping, the back end swinging out until the traction control system engaged. He wasn't used to this. In fact, this was not him at all.

He tensed. Would he hit 120 . . . 130 mph down this municipal street? Would he dare go 150 mph? It was a Sunday night, 11:50 P.M., and there were still a few other vehicles on the road, although the sidewalks looked clear of pedestrians. How fast would his rage take him?

He kept a white-knuckled grip on the steering wheel with both hands. There was no more shifting to do; it was pedal to the metal, and the future would unfold.

He flicked his gaze to the right and saw Villanueva's door just a few feet away, both Corvettes neck and neck now, their Borla exhaust systems thundering as they raced up the four-lane road.

Carlos Villanueva was just eighteen, the same age as Brent, and they were seniors at Northridge Academy High. They had never spoken to each other until Brent had rolled into the school parking lot with his Corvette. Brent had inherited the Vette from an uncle who'd passed away, and from that day on Villanueva had been challenging Brent to a street race, going so far as to follow him, harass him at every intersection, cut him off, and even show up at Brent's doorstep, waiting for him to leave in the car. Villanueva had an older Vette, a yellow 2003 Z06 that he and his brother, Tomas, had heavily modified to boost the car's horsepower. They called Brent's car "the blue devil" and vowed to send him and the vehicle straight back to hell.

Villanueva's harassment was brutal, unrelenting, and he even enlisted his gang buddies to threaten Brent, telling him he'd better not drive the car unless he was willing to race. As Brent quickly learned, you can't hide a jet-stream-blue Corvette very well in traffic; it tends to stand out. The bullying became so fierce that for a while Brent stopped driving the car, opting to walk or hop on his bike to school.

Admittedly, an eighteen-year-old kid behind the wheel of a fifty-thousand-dollar sports car would draw some animosity and jealousy; in fact, his father, a successful city engineer with ties to local and state government, had warned him about that, but Brent had had no idea it would come to this.

Villanueva's bullying crossed the line on the night of Brent's senior prom. Brent had picked up his date and they'd had a great time, but then, on his way back to drop her off, Villanueva had shown up and had forced Brent onto the shoulder as they'd descended Laurel Canyon Boulevard's tortuous series of switchbacks and hairpin turns. Brent missed the guardrails by inches, pulled over, and bolted out of the car, only to watch as Villanueva flashed him the bird and squealed off.

"I can't take this anymore," he told his girlfriend.

"Then do something about it."

Two days later, as Brent was returning from a late movie, Villanueva pulled up beside him at a streetlight. Brent glanced over—and a mental switch was thrown.

Villanueva sat there, revving his engine, his evil eyes

sparkling, his shaven head and the tattoos spidering over his forearms suggesting he'd spent a lifetime in prison while he was really just a punk.

Brent had taken a long breath. Enough. He was going to dust this bastard once and for all. And when they were finished, maybe Villanueva would bow out like a man and stop the BS games. Maybe this fool would realize that driving a fast car did not make you a man.

Yet now, the faster they drove and the more they challenged each other, the more Brent realized that if he lost this race, he'd never live it down; Villanueva would never get off his back. The bullying would grow even worse because Brent would be the loser who got dusted. Winning meant he'd be free of this bastard forever.

Or so he'd thought.

As part of its modification package, Villanueva's Corvette was equipped with a nitrous oxide system, or NOS, that allowed the engine to burn more fuel and air. He suddenly boosted away, pulling a full car length ahead of Brent, who, seeing this, reacted with more acceleration. 121, 122, 123 mph . . .

There had been long stretches between intersections, but now they rocketed into a much busier part of town, with cross streets coming in five-second intervals.

A string of green lights gleamed overhead, but then a small commuter car pulled onto the road far ahead, blocking Villanueva's lane. The two lanes for oncoming traffic were empty, so Brent rolled the wheel, taking himself across the road, allowing Villanueva to take his lane so they could both pass the car. This was a tacit understanding between street racers that Brent knew about but had never practiced.

They whooshed past the unsuspecting driver, who saw only blue and yellow streaks from the corner of his eye and whose car shook violently from their passing.

In unison, Brent and Villanueva cut back into their lanes.

125 mph . . .

Brent's mouth fell open as he once more checked Villanueva's position: perfectly aligned with him.

The dotted yellow lines were a continuous ribbon, and the apartment buildings that walled in both sides of the road squeezed tighter as sheer acceleration made the road appear more narrow. Brent was now one with the machine, and he'd never felt anything more powerful and invigorating. There was no other adrenaline rush like it. At the same time, his shoulders knotted in terror because he knew just the slightest deviation in his course or sudden obstacle in his path could end it all. He drove along a cliff between pure terror and utter joy.

During the winter months in Los Angeles, when those precious rains most often occurred, a year's worth of oil would begin to bubble up through the pavement. So as they crossed the next intersection, Brent felt the rear wheels begin to drift, and he realized with a start that they'd hit a large patch of oil and blasted over it, but now their wide race tires had grown slick.

Villanueva must have felt it, too, because he suddenly course-corrected, shifting over toward a row of cars parked along the curb.

Brent began to lose his breath as both he and Villanueva began sliding even more rapidly, but then the yellow Vette jumped forward, the car's front end rising as Villanueva accelerated out of his slide, missing the parked cars by a side mirror's width, Brent estimated.

With a gasp, Brent shifted his wheel and missed the last car in the row by what could be a hairsbreadth.

Now Villanueva was squarely in the lead.

There wasn't much time. The first driver to cross La Bonita Avenue was the winner, and Brent figured they had only a half mile or less to go.

But these speeds were ridiculous, the whole idea that he'd succumbed to this insane.

He should abandon now. Cut his losses. Deal with Villanueva's crap. Just take his foot off the pedal and go home . . . with his tail between his legs.

But then Brent remembered the look on his prom date's face, how she, too, had been humiliated by Villanueva, and he considered all those days he'd cycled to school to avoid dealing with the guy. Was he supposed to be a victim all his life?

He booted the accelerator pedal, and his neck snapped back.

Villanueva held his position in the right lane as Brent came blasting up beside him, and then, taking in a deep breath and holding it, Brent stomped on the pedal. The engine's whine lifted, and the tailpipes rumbled even more loudly. He was almost afraid to check the HUD for his speed, and when he did, he thought, *This is it, I'll be arrested.*

131 mph . . .

No one would believe he'd gone that fast down a city street, and everyone would say what an utter fool he was, that he was no better than Villanueva, that he was endangering lives and belonged in jail. But first the police would confiscate his car and make him watch as they put it in the crusher. This was the well-advertised fate of cars used by street racers.

The string of lights ahead turned yellow.

Beyond them, a few cars rolled to stops, the drivers waiting for their green lights.

They would cross into Brent's path. Their timing was perfectly horrible.

Brent glanced over at Villanueva, who mouthed a curse and accelerated again.

Brent's heart was in his throat and sweat dappled his forehead. He could hardly breathe as one after another the lights turned red and Villanueva streaked toward them, his car blurring into a yellow sun impaled by crimson taillights.

Cars began to move across the intersection.

Villanueva would attempt to weave through them.

Something told Brent to check his rearview mirror, but nothing was back there, no police car or other vehicle, nothing—but then he noticed them: his eyes, bloodshot, heavy, and aching. He did not recognize himself.

A wide pothole rushed up, and Brent veered so sharply to avoid it that he bumped—ever so slightly—the rear quarter panel of Villanueva's car. The impact was so light that Brent knew there'd be no damage to his Vette, but at their speeds, the slightest shift of tires could be catastrophic.

And it was. Brent watched with a horrid fascination as the tap caused Villanueva to slide and lose control. The car broke into a spin that sent him into the oncoming lane.

Villanueva's pinwheeling came to a sudden halt as his back tire slammed into the curb and the momentum lifted the entire car into the air.

The yellow Vette now spiraled like an Indy racer that had just hit the wall.

Brent gaped as Villanueva's fate became even more apparent. The car was tumbling toward the massive concrete column of a streetlight.

And before Brent could pull in his next breath, the Vette struck the pillar, T-boning it so hard and fast that the entire vehicle split in two as glass, plastic, and shattered fiberglass rose in a debris cloud while the heavier sections plunged toward the pavement.

Before the rear half could hit the ground, it exploded in a fireball that consumed most of the street.

A half second later, the front end of the car came to a thudding halt and was swept up into the first fireball.

Three, two, one, and a second explosion tore through the front end, engulfing Villanueva in veils of black smoke backlit by the flames.

Brent jammed on the brakes, then downshifted to second, rolling up on the scene.

He was frozen, rapt, unable to fully process what he was seeing.

But with a chill and shudder, he realized he had to get out of there. He hit the gas . . .

The flames were painfully similar to the ones Brent watched now, at this moment, some seven years later, flashing across the flat-screen TV . . .

Forward Operations Base Cobra
Lashkar Gah, Afghanistan
2016

Brent stood in the base's rec room, watching with the rest of his Special Forces team as the nuclear explosions detonated in Iran and Saudi Arabia.

Indeed, those fireballs had just taken him back to that terrible moment when Carlos Villanueva had died on that rainy night. While his fellow Special Forces operators had been voicing their disbelief, Brent had remained there, stunned, reliving his senior year in high school, feeling it all again. That night had changed everything.

Everything.

"Hey, Captain? Captain Brent?"

Someone was yelling for him now, telling him to gather up his people, that the evac choppers were on the way . . .

But Brent was still in 2009, inside his Vette, crying as he sped down a side street, crying because he fervently believed that his life was over.

What would his parents think? His mother was an elementary school principal, a community leader who also worked for several charities. How would she feel about her only son being involved in a street race in which someone was killed?

If Brent hadn't challenged Villanueva, if he'd just continued to dismiss him, the kid would still be alive. He couldn't just say it was all Villanueva's fault, that he'd deserved to die . . . because Brent had been weak. Brent had, indeed, stooped to the kid's level. And because of that, the kid was dead.

The ride home had been the longest one of his life. He'd pulled the Vette into the garage, shut the door, as though he were being followed by someone who'd seen the accident, then dropped to his knees and vomited.

He remained there for five minutes, just drooling and breathing and trying to explain to the police in his head why he'd been racing and how sorry he was and that now, yes, his life was over . . . *Take me away* . . .

And his parents would stand there, crying, as he was escorted into the police car, the cop placing a hand on Brent's head so he wouldn't bang it as he took a seat inside, behind the wire separating them from him.

He was a dog. A street-racing dog headed to prison.

Brent rose and cleaned up the mess, then went to his room and lay there, afraid to shut his eyes because through that darkness would come the fire. Yet after a few more minutes and even with his eyes open, all he saw was the street, the cars, the Vette shattering into a million pieces.

The next day at school, everyone was talking about the car accident, but there wasn't a single witness who could—or would—identify the other car.

In fact, no one was coming forward with information because the media was reporting that Carlos Villanueva had ties to several gangs in the area, and that word *gang* scared everyone into silence.

Brent was called into a room at school and questioned with several other students who knew Villanueva. Brent assumed they'd ask him about Villanueva's bullying and that eventually he'd break down and confess to the race.

But the detectives seemed bored, going through the motions, and Brent wasn't the only kid harassed by Villanueva and his brother. Brent learned that other kids with fast cars both in his high school and in neighboring schools had also been challenged to street races. It seemed the police were already chalking this up to another foolish punk who'd been killed doing something stupid. The police had asked Brent what he'd been doing that night. He said he'd gone to a movie and then gone home—a half truth, to be sure. They even did a cursory inspection of his car, as they did with the other kids, but the Vette yielded no evidence about the crash.

During the weeks that followed, Brent's sorrow and guilt compelled him to learn more about Villanueva and his family. In moments of utter weakness he saw himself going over to their house and confessing to them what had happened, apologizing for his sins, and begging for their forgiveness. But it would never come to that, he knew.

And so he'd watched them from afar, and he read the memorial MySpace page set up by Tomas. There Brent learned that Villanueva was going into the Army after high school. Who knew what Villanueva would have done in the military? He might have gone to war and fought valiantly for the United States. He might have done so many better things, smarter things, than racing his stupid car. And for months Brent wondered about that, about the life he had taken from this world. He didn't have to agree to race. He didn't. He was smarter than that. But his actions had said he wasn't.

Some days he'd argue that Villanueva was a bastard, and he'd curse and tell himself he was a fool for feeling bad.

Other days he would cry.

His parents expected him to head off to college. For six months he did nothing but work a part-time job in a local supermarket, come home, and float in his pool like Dustin Hoffman in that old film, *The Graduate*. Tony, the produce manager, said Brent was one of his best clerks and that there was a real future in the supermarket business if Brent wanted it. A real future.

Brent would only shrug.

Brent's father had long talks with him about ambition and the value of a college education. Brent stayed up late at night, wrestling with the idea that he didn't deserve to live a good life because Carlos Villanueva would never have one and that Brent had ruined the lives of Carlos's parents and brother. Brent deserved to be punished—so deliberately ruining his own life was the only path.

But then one day while Brent was at a gas station, he watched a soldier get out of his car and prepare to fill up. Brent looked at the young man: high-and-tight crew cut, uniform starched to perfection, and right there he realized it wasn't too late for him.

"I want to join the Army."

His parents were shocked. His father argued that at the very least he should become an officer, that maybe, just maybe he could pull some strings and get Brent into West Point via a congressional appointment.

"Why do you want this so badly?" his mother had asked.

"I just do," he'd said.

"I wish I could understand this."

"Mom, this is what I need to do."

"Will you be happy?"

"Of course . . ."

Brent's father had come through, and West Point was a culture shock and a hundred times tougher than Brent had ever anticipated. There was the encouragement, camaraderie, and support, to be sure, but there was also the competition that drove his fellow cadets to extreme limits. There were many sleepless nights and moments when Brent was staring into the demonic eyes of an upperclassman and wanting to drop out . . .

But two things kept him there: the thought that he could live Carlos's life for him and the thought that he deserved to be punished for what he'd done, so when the pain and torment and stress came, he often welcomed them.

No surprise: Brent graduated at the *bottom* of his class.

And when that happens, you don't get your pick of duty stations.

He shipped out to Camp Casey, South Korea, and there he became a platoon leader in charge of four M1A1 tank crews and was part of First Tank, the more forward-deployed armor unit in Korea. If the North Koreans decided to invade, they'd be knocking on Brent's front door. He did that for a few years and made friends with several Special Forces operators who'd convinced him to give SF a try. So he'd applied to the Special Forces school. He was rejected twice before the third time was a charm.

He still had nightmares about the Robin Sage event that tested everything he'd learned as an SF operator . . .

But ultimately, he'd graduated, been promoted to captain, and been sent to Afghanistan to lead a Special Forces team near the tri-border area between Afghanistan, Pakistan, and Iran.

And now, as he finally dragged himself away from the TV to issue orders to his men, he sensed that his life was about to change just as it had on that fateful rainy night, both moments marked by swelling clouds of smoke and fire.

ONE

**Mumbai, Maharashtra, India
2021 (Present Day)**

For five years after the nuclear exchange between Iran and Saudi Arabia that killed six million and crippled the world's oil supply, Manoj Chopra had been having a recurring dream:

He was five years old, dashing through the slums of Mumbai, and being chased by three men with long, metallic wings extending from their backs and glistening in the sun. They said they were angels, but their skin was translucent, with flickering flames coursing beneath. They seemed to smile, yet their heads were like fire-filled globes devoid of real expressions. They seemed unaware of the heat and flames.

Their voices came in silky whispers, and they said they wanted to save him, but he wasn't sure if he could trust them, and he understood that if he got too close, he'd be burned.

So he ran. And they chased him down the alleys, across the trenches, the sewers, the garbage heaps, and the crowded city streets choked by businesspeople, tourists, and beggars.

He would turn down another street, and suddenly one would take flight and swoop overhead, then drop in front of him, fold his arms over his chest, and with wings extending, say, "You are a good boy, Manoj. You will always do the right thing. So come with us now."

"I'm afraid."

"Don't be."

"I want to come with you, but I can't."

"Why?"

"Because I have to stay here."

Chopra charged past the fiery angel and ducked into a small house, the same house that appeared repeatedly in the dream.

About a dozen women and children sat on the bare floor, all of them making bidis by placing tobacco inside small *tendu* leaves, then tightly rolling them. They would secure each bidi with thread, then move on to the next one, hoping to make more than a thousand in a single day.

One of the women was Chopra's mother. The two teenaged girls who sat beside her were his sisters, and all three were deeply in debt to the bidi contractors who loaned money at ridiculous interest rates in order to keep them enslaved. This had been Chopra's fate. In his youth, he had rolled thousands of bidis himself.

"Go away," his mother said. "I still love you."

"I can't."

"You can't stay here. Is this the life you want? Your father would have wanted better."

Chopra's father had been killed in a construction accident, leaving his family with bills and no medical insurance.

Chopra shook his head at his mother. "He's gone. He will never know about me and what I do."

"Go with them."

Chopra glanced back. In the doorway, framed by the afternoon light, stood one of the angels. He glowed in silhouette and extended a hand. For a moment, Chopra thought the angel had his father's face. He tensed and turned away as now a woman strode from the back of the room, along with an impeccably groomed man in a dark suit.

"He has, we believe, an eidetic memory," said the woman, whose face came into the light and whose hands were covered in chalk. She was one of Chopra's teachers from senior secondary school (high school).

The man, Mr. Sanjay Deol, was a top executive with Axis Bank and one of Chopra's mentors who had helped send him to the Judge Business School in Cambridge. Because of his gifts, because of his "value" and talent, Chopra had been able to do something rare in his world: escape his destiny.

"Yes, we know all about him," answered Deol. "He is the most remarkable mathematician we've ever seen— and he's so young."

"But what about them?" Chopra asked. "Can you save my family?"

Deol shook his head and turned away, metallic wings sprouting from his back.

And at that moment, as always happened, Chopra snapped awake and lay there in a pool of sweat.

"The dream is simple to interpret," said one of the half dozen therapists Chopra had consulted over the years. "You're feeling guilty about the deaths of all the men who supported you. The men who turned your life around. The men who gave you a life, as it were. They were your angels, and they burned in the Middle East holocaust."

Chopra was forty-seven years old now, and he knew better than to dismiss the dream as simple guilt. Something much deeper was simmering in his subconscious, and he was determined to uncover it.

He'd heard the axiom that all great athletes are always running away from something. So what was it, really? Was he trying to run away from his meager roots?

Chopra leaned back in his office chair and glanced up through the panoramic windows of his penthouse suite. The city lay before him: the choked streets, the towering buildings—some old and weather-worn, others newly constructed. He was quite literally at the top of his world.

He wanted for nothing. He could never spend all the money he had earned and saved. His mother and sisters had been rescued—by him, not by those creatures from his dreams.

And yet at forty-seven he had never married. Could he blame that on his physical appearance? Not solely. He was not an ugly man, he thought, but his short stature and considerable girth would never earn him a starring role in the latest Bollywood production. That he couldn't tolerate contact lenses and wore thick spectacles didn't help matters, either. However, his unwavering commitment to his work had most often interfered with his personal life. Because he had been taken from such squalor and been trained, educated, and placed in an environment of such ultra wealth, he felt he owed his mentors a remarkable return on their investment.

In fact, for the past ten years, he had abandoned all thoughts of dating and had simply begun working more than ever. After the nuclear strike, his job became exceedingly more urgent and complicated.

Chopra leaned forward and studied the computer screen. At the moment he was making a large money transfer from a sovereign wealth fund bank account belonging to the former nation of Dubai. Although most of Iran and Saudi Arabia had been leveled in the blasts, Dubai's infrastructure had been partially spared, although what was left of the country had been evacuated and even now, some five years later, it was still unsafe to be there, unprotected, for more than eight hours at a time.

Chopra was and continued to be the minister and custodian of Dubai's accounts, and this particular one was worth some ninety-two billion dollars.

How he had come to this position was yet another small miracle. After his mentors at Axis had financed his college education, he had graduated and gone to work for them, becoming one of their chief financial analysts by the time he was just twenty-six.

At thirty, he had been recruited by the Al Maktoum family of Dubai, who had ruled the country since 1833. They wanted him to manage their sovereign wealth fund and become one of the country's chief financial advisers. Chopra left Axis with his mentors' blessing because the bank continued to do much business with Dubai and other United Arab Emirates members. This was, as one of his American-raised mentors had put it, a marriage made in heaven.

Chopra found his work in Dubai both stimulating and rewarding. His employers treated him like royalty, paid him ridiculous sums of money, and encouraged him to be creative with their investments.

That creativity had continued—even after nuclear holocaust had effectively killed nearly all members of the family and left Chopra in a wasteland of grief.

With care and precision, he worked the computer's mouse and manipulated the funds. He was moving oil money into the green industry in an attempt to save the fund from more losses. A 400-billion-euro plan to power Europe with Sahara sunlight was finally getting off the ground after nearly twenty years of setbacks and debate, and Chopra saw a good future in that. His employers might be gone, but he deemed it his responsibility to manage their money—because he believed he had a moral and ethical responsibility to do so . . .

And because he believed that at least one heir to the empire was still alive.

Hussein Al Maktoum would be sixteen now. The boy and his three sisters had been, like Chopra, out of the country when the strikes had occurred. They had been wisely hidden away from those who would attempt to manipulate them and undermine what resources were left in the country.

Chopra had been sought by the other emirates to turn over the funds, but he had refused, instead saying that they belonged to the country's rightful heir, and until Hussein was found, Chopra alone had been legally entrusted to manage them. While the emirates plundered what was left of Dubai's other resources, Chopra kept the sovereign wealth fund in check—along with a considerable cache of gold and silver held within Dubai's subterranean vaults, gold that belonged not only to Dubai but to other surrounding nations. Chopra believed he was one of the last "living keys" who could gain access to those vaults.

For the past five years he'd wanted nothing more than to turn over this terrible burden he carried and deliver the codes, the funds, and the gold to the country's new leader. He was a man of fierce loyalty, and he would rather die than see these resources fall into the hands of evil men. If Hussein was still alive, he could rule now with the help of a regent or adviser who could be appointed by the emirates, or he himself could choose one from among other surviving relatives.

Indeed, there was a rumor that Sheikh Juma Al Maktoum, a family cousin, had become a warlord of sorts and occupied a few of the islands in the Strait of Hormuz, but Chopra's attempts to contact the man had repeatedly failed because of mistrust and Russian interference in the area.

Chopra finished the computer transaction and rose to fetch a glass of Merlot from his wet bar.

His cell phone rang, and the name on the screen was familiar: Harold Westerdale, a British private investigator whom Chopra had hired years ago to track down surviving members of the Al Maktoum family. Chopra hadn't heard from Westerdale in many months, so the call was, indeed, a surprise.

"I think I have him, Mr. Chopra," came the breathless voice. "I think I have him."

"You have Hussein?"

"Yes, I've got some decrypted communications between him and his sisters, as well as the staff he's been with since the attacks. They're using high-tech military satellite phones to call each other now. Hussein is in the Seychelles."

"Call me back in five minutes with all the details. I'm packing right now."

"Yes, sir."

Chopra rushed through the living room and into his bedroom. He'd been sitting there, making the transfer, reflecting on his life and what had happened to the Al

Maktoum family when, at that very moment, Westerdale—a man he'd not heard from in months—had called about a lead.

Perhaps there was, as Chopra's mother had once told him, a connection between people with like minds and pure hearts. Maybe there was a connection between himself and Hussein, that they were destined to meet again now. To Chopra, Hussein was still just a small boy playing with a radio control car inside one of the new palaces.

The Republic of the Seychelles was a group of islands off the east coast of Africa, and that was about all Chopra knew of the place. He'd have to get online and decide what to pack, but he vowed that he'd be en route to the airport within an hour.

His heart raced. This was the best lead they'd had since the beginning.

He would do it. Find Hussein. That was his purpose. He wasn't sure if he was now the man with the metallic wings, but he understood that this was the right thing, the honorable thing, the only thing he could do. His heart ached for closure.

He'd come a long way from his days spent rolling bidis, and as he entered middle age and could say he'd already enjoyed most of life's luxuries, there would be nothing more pleasing than to see this young man become the phoenix of his nation and rebuild it from the ashes even as the boy himself rose into manhood.

They would be Arthur and Merlin, and Chopra would do all in his power to help the boy sheikh—because there were others, particularly the Russian Federation, who wanted nothing more than to control Dubai, seize its remaining oil, decontaminate it, and profit from the sales. Their government had been eyeing the country like wolves in winter, but the time had finally come for Dubai to return to power and prominence.

Chopra stood a moment and closed his eyes. Maybe this was the true purpose of his life. To bolster a young man, to see a nation rise again. His eyes burned with tears, but then he reminded himself that his celebration was premature, that he hadn't located the young sheikh yet. Not yet. He wrenched a suitcase from his closet and tossed it on his bed. With trembling hands, he began to pack.

TWO

Montereau-Fault-Yonne, France

She was a woman of three names—but only one accurately identified her.

Her birth name was Viktoria Kolosov, the daughter of a schoolteacher and a car transporter from Vladivostok, Russia.

Her married name was Viktoria Antsyforov, wife of the late Nikolai Antsyforov, a physician ten years her senior.

Her code name was *Snegurochka*. The Snow Maiden.

She was thirty-seven and once described by a colleague as a "woman of sinister beauty."

But those days were gone.

The once long locks had been hacked off into a spiky punk cut. The once curvaceous body was now lean, raw muscle.

However, some things never changed: The man currently chasing her down the narrow cobblestone street would die slowly.

Painfully.

He would, as all the others had, meet only the Snow Maiden, because that's all she had left.

Snegurochka was the snow maiden in Russian folklore. In one tale she was the daughter of Spring and Frost. She fell in love with a shepherd, but when her heart warmed, she melted. In another narrative, falling in love transformed her into a mortal who would die. In a third story she was the daughter of an old couple who created her from snow. She leapt over a fire and melted.

Consequently, it was better to remain in the cold. Always the cold, where she could see her breath, where people warmed to her personality before she tore out their jugulars and walked away, feeling only the numbing chill.

And the cardinal rule: Never look back.

She rounded the next corner, pressed her back against the wall, then slipped the knife from her hip pocket and thumbed the button. The stiletto flashed out from its hilt and shimmered in the moonlight.

Drawing in a deep breath, she willed herself into a state of calm and waited for him. Oh, how she hated this, hated it more than anything.

She was always running now. Never pursuing. She loved the chase but despised being on the wrong end of it.

Who didn't want a piece of her?

That was a good question. She was valuable to everyone: the Americans, the Euros, the Russians, even the Green Brigade Transnational—the terrorist bastards she'd betrayed back in Canada. They wanted her because she'd used and murdered their leader, "Green Vox," a code name for the replaceable idiot in charge. She'd done an expert job of convincing them she was a bleeding-heart tree hugger who loved to blow stuff up.

The Americans wanted her because she was a former member of the *Glavnoje Razvedyvatel'noje Upravlenije* (GRU) and could open up the Russian Federation's entire intelligence community like a can of tuna.

The Euros wanted her for the same reason, and the Russians wanted her dead for screwing them over when they had tried to invade Canada to seize the oil sands. Plus, they didn't want her puking up all their secrets to their enemies.

She smiled bitterly. It was, after all, nice to be popular.

Where the hell was he? She dared not peek around the corner. He was waiting. So would she.

The Snow Maiden had come to France, risky though it was, to wish her cousin Andrei Eskov good luck with his final stage of the Tour de France. Andrei was riding for Katusha, the Russian Federation cycling team, and he was currently wearing the yellow jersey after twenty days of brutal racing, but his lead was only forty-three seconds, so there was a chance he would win the entire tour . . . or lose it. She had always had a fond place in her heart for Andrei, who as far back as she could remember loved to ride his bike up the hillside roads overlooking

Vladivostok. Twice he had taken her on spectacular rides, experiences she would never forget.

After a brief and somewhat tearful dinner together at the team's hotel restaurant, she had slipped off and returned to her own hotel. At about midnight, she hailed a cab for the airport. Before she could get out of town, another car had followed, she'd been attacked, her driver killed, and now she was on the run.

Her pursuer couldn't wait anymore and finally rounded the corner, his footfalls light, his breath audible.

She could even smell him—a faint mixture of cigarette smoke and leather.

In one fluid stroke, she buried the blade in his abdomen while simultaneously relieving him of his pistol with attached suppressor. He gasped and fell back against the wall, his breath reeking even more now. She tore off his woolen balaclava to reveal a blond-haired man, perhaps only eighteen or twenty.

"Who sent you?" she asked him in French. "You'll die anyway. Just tell me."

He cursed at her in Russian.

She grabbed the hilt of the knife still jutting from his abdomen, gritted her teeth, and drove it deeper into him. He gasped and clutched her hand.

She put the gun to his head. "Did Izotov send you? Are you working with Haussler?"

Before he could answer, a shot tore into the brick wall just over his shoulder.

With a start, she spun—just as another round sent a piece of the wall tumbling onto her back. She flinched, squinted against the shower of debris, and tried to steal a look at her attacker.

He was across the alley, but she only caught a glimpse before he ducked back behind the wall. He had cover. She was in the open.

Time to run. She yanked free her blade, used the guy's shoulder to close it, then raced away.

The cobblestones beneath her boots threatened to send her tumbling if she wasn't careful. Her ankle twisted slightly as she reached the end of the alley and turned right, heading down a broader street lined by dark storefronts. She kept low and repeatedly glanced over her shoulder.

Napoleon had fought one of his epic battles in Montereau-Fault-Yonne, and so it seemed she, too, might engage in a battle to the death. She had never imagined herself dying on the streets of a small French town. She'd always assumed the Russian government would catch up to her, throw her in a Siberian prison, torture her for months, and then, one night, her cell would fill with light, and there would be Nikolai, standing there, welcoming her to heaven. They would be together, finally . . . and forever.

Before their marriage he'd been assigned to treat the workers cleaning up the 70-MWe and 90-MWe pressurized-water training reactors in Paldiski, Estonia. He had been fresh out of medical school and had attended to her own brother Dimitri, who had suffered radiation poisoning while constructing the two-story concrete sarcophagus that now encased the two reactors. Officials and administrators had been grossly negligent, and the Snow Maiden had lost her brother first . . . her husband two years later, a delayed victim of the contamination.

At the moment Nikolai died, the true Snow Maiden had been born.

While standing at Nikolai's funeral, she had vowed revenge. She'd kept her husband's name to honor his work in the service of others and had set her sights on the GRU, the organization with the most power and freedom to move throughout the country and exact her revenge where and when she could. But first she would work her icy tendrils throughout the entire organization so that she could eventually choke them once and for all.

Thus, she clambered her way up the intelligence ladder with a vengeance, becoming one of the most effective and lethal officers the GRU had ever fielded. Her martial arts skills and marksmanship were awe-inspiring, as evidenced by the looks on her colleagues' faces when she competed against them. Her reputation grew, and she was eventually recruited by General Sergei Izotov himself to work missions on behalf of the director and the president.

She'd been asked to work alongside another man, Colonel Pavel Doletskaya, and together they had coordinated several attacks on selected European Federation targets, mostly information gathering and a few assassinations.

On the day she'd been promoted to colonel, she'd been called into Director Izotov's office, where he'd told her she was one of the most brilliant and trusted GRU officers in the history of the organization.

That remark was met by her shrug. "Is there something you need, sir?"

He'd gone on to say that a security leak involving Doletskaya had been exposed and that the Euros had alerted the Americans. Izotov needed her to go underground by staging her own death with the GRU's help. She would need to erase herself from the organization— all in the name of restoring the motherland to greatness.

Would she take the mission? Of course. By going underground she could more efficiently destroy the entire Russian Federation. They'd helped her set the fire in her apartment, plant the body, and even Doletskaya, with whom she'd been having an affair, was not privy to the plan. Izotov became her mentor from that point on, a father figure . . . and even a lover for a short time, though none of these men could ever replace Nikolai.

As part of her new mission, she'd forged a relationship with the Green Brigade Transnational because the Russians liked to use them as fall guys for certain operations against Europe and the United States. It was painfully simple to set up these fools, and they enjoyed claiming responsibility for acts that were, in truth, perpetrated by Russian or Russian-backed forces.

She had even made Izotov believe to the bitter end that she was with them, until she was able to blackmail him and the rest of the federation with some nukes in Canada. But then her other brother, Mikhail, had gone down with his submarine, *Romanov*, before he was able to help. That her plan had fallen apart didn't matter. She was still free and still working for her new employers, whose goals were similar to her own. There was, however, no rest for the weary, no walking without checking your back.

The Snow Maiden learned that Izotov had hired Heinrich Haussler, agent of the Bundesnachrichten-dienst (the German Federal Intelligence Service), to capture her, since most of their own best spies had failed (and been killed by her). Haussler was a double agent, and the Snow Maiden knew him well. If anyone could capture her, it was probably him. He was a crafty bastard who made few mistakes, so she was beginning to believe that these fools after her now were not working for him. The attack was too sloppy.

She dropped into the next alcove, finding herself huddled against the closed door of a bakery, and removed the small infrared camera from her coat pocket. She carried the credit-card-sized device wherever she went. Point and click and you had a picture of your environment with the heat sources illuminated. Forward-looking infrared radar in your pocket.

The second man was coming straight down the road, toward her, and she had to gamble that he hadn't seen her duck out of sight.

She pocketed the camera, waited, heard his footfalls grow louder, then braced herself.

Just as he passed, she balanced herself on one hand,

slid out her right leg, swung it around, and made contact with his ankles, her leg like a blade cutting him down.

As he dropped, she reached up and put a round in his gluteus maximus. He screamed, landed on his gut, and was about to roll over and fire when she dropped the gun, and, with both hands pushed up, she leapt on him, knocking him onto his back and latching both hands onto his wrist to release his weapon. She dug her nails into his skin and quickly pried free his gun, which clattered to the sidewalk. She shoved him back, grabbed the second gun, and trained it on him.

In Russian, she asked, "How is Vox these days? Or should I ask, *who* is Vox these days?"

The guy was panting through his balaclava. She tore it off and sighed.

She knew this guy. He wasn't working for Haussler. His name was Thor, and he was a member of the Green Brigade Transnational.

The attack might have been sloppy, but they'd come dangerously close and were getting better. She'd no idea they were on her back, and perhaps she was the one getting sloppy. How the hell had they found her? Haussler had contacts, resources . . . what did they have—

Unless Izotov had also employed them to catch her and they had access to the GRU's databases? This development wasn't good. Not good at all.

The guy raised his hands. "Nice girl," he purred in Russian.

She put a bullet between his eyes. His head bounced

off the pavement. She stood, stole a look around the street, then hustled off toward the taxi.

Within two minutes she reached the still-idling vehicle, tore the dead driver out of his seat, hopped in, and was about to throw the car in gear when her phone rang. She checked the screen: It was Patti. She had to take it. They spoke in English.

"Can I call you back?" she asked.

"You have two minutes."

"I've got a little problem right now."

"So do we. Two minutes."

She hung up and drove off, eventually heading north up Quai des Bordes along the river. She would continue northwest toward the airport.

Dr. Merpati "Patti" Sukarnoputri was an Indonesian physician and deputy director-general of the World Health Organization, United Nations, Geneva.

Patti was also a member of the *Ganjin* (pronounced gahn-jeen), the group that now employed the Snow Maiden.

Much of the Snow Maiden's knowledge of the *Ganjin* was sketchy, and her efforts to learn more about the group drew serious threats. She had concluded, though, that they were composed of a handful of academics and business professionals whose primary goal was to manipulate the superior powers during this time of war in an effort to benefit the People's Republic of China. Whether the Chinese government was aware of or endorsed their efforts remained to be seen, but the *Ganjin* paid the Snow Maiden quite handsomely so that by the time she was forty she would never have to work again. She would get out of the espionage business. She would continue donating money to cancer research and work with children afflicted with the disease. But she would not do this until she saw the federation—and all of its evil—seize up like an old man in cardiac arrest and then . . . flatline.

Once she was on the highway, she returned Patti's call. Security protocols were in place, and consequently, Patti was the only member of the *Ganjin* that the Snow Maiden had ever met. Patti was in her fifties and a cunning career woman who never appreciated the Snow Maiden's sarcasm.

"That was a minute and forty-seven seconds," the Snow Maiden said after Patti answered her phone. "Fast enough? Or am I fired?"

"Shut up and listen to me. I'll be at the airport waiting for you. I'll tell you where when you arrive."

They met at a Starbucks inside the main terminal. The Snow Maiden ordered a pumpkin spice frappuccino and told the cashier that Patti would pay for it.

The Snow Maiden always received her mission orders in person, and that was fine by her. Electronic listening and tracking devices had become so complicated that she never knew who was watching or listening. Nanobot technology had developed rapidly in the past decade, and it only took a light dusting for an enemy to be able to track her wherever she went. Countermeasures were necessary, and so they'd both gone into the ladies' room and "dusted off" before speaking.

"It's all on here," Patti said, handing the Snow Maiden a smartphone whose screen displayed a picture of an Indian man who resembled a professor or business professional.

"Who's this guy?"

"Manoj Chopra. He's a banker, a finance manager, a genius with investments. He was working for the royal family of Dubai before the war began. One of our people in Italy was tipped off to a transaction involving one of Dubai's sovereign wealth funds. We'd thought no one had access to them. The funds had been lying dormant since the bombs, but this recent activity has sparked interest."

"You want me to kill him?"

"Of course not. He'll get us into Dubai's vaults. Intel we were gathering before the war indicated Dubai was beginning to stockpile oil reserves. The locations of those secret reserves, along with the country's gold— and the gold of several other nations from the region— will be in one of those subterranean vaults, and Chopra is our key."

"You're positive he can get you in there?"

"He was one of the most trusted confidants of the royal family. He can get us in."

"All right, then. It's a simple kidnapping. Don't you have anything more interesting?"

"That's rather amusing coming from someone who almost lost her life because of carelessness."

The Snow Maiden smirked. "If you guys were watching me, why didn't you help?"

"We don't like to interfere. You know that. You're merely a subcontractor, but we've put a lot of faith in you, and your work thus far has been exemplary. I hope you're not too preoccupied."

She tensed. "Chopra's location is in here?" she asked, lifting the smartphone.

Patti nodded.

The Snow Maiden rose. "Then thanks for the drink. I'll call you when I have him."

THREE

The Liberator Sports Bar and Grill
Near Fort Bragg, North Carolina

Brent sat alone in a corner booth, sipping his draft beer and absently eyeing the flat screens suspended from the ceiling. Several football games, a car race, and a European soccer game barely earned his interest. The Liberator was a requisite hangout for Special Forces guys and those considered a step up from them—the men and women of Ghost Recon, an elite and highly classified group of warriors handpicked from the Special Forces ranks. Ghost Recon soldiers were issued the most cutting-edge, state-of-the-art technology, and it was a great honor to be selected for such an organization—even though you couldn't tell anyone about it, because the Ghosts didn't exist.

From 2016 on the day the nukes dropped to mid-2020, Brent had fought with various Special Forces teams, even traveling up to Canada to fight against invading Russian forces. His work there had gained him the attention of Ghost Recon's leadership, and, after dragging himself through an intense qualifications process and course, he'd been selected to train and lead a new Ghost Recon team.

But that glory was short-lived.

He and his new group had run a couple of small missions in Pakistan that had gone south because Brent was too used to fighting by the seat of his pants instead of sticking rigidly to a plan. He'd had that freedom in the regular Special Forces, and he wasn't always compelled to keep everyone in the communications loop, but the Ghosts were much more hardcore about their operations, not blindly following orders but executing them with surgical precision and with full disclosure and accountability on the battlefield. His newbie team had run a simple intelligence-gathering operation in the country of Georgia, and that, too, had wound up in the toilet because Brent had second-guessed the plan and had jumped the gun on the operation. He'd also failed to properly communicate with his superiors. Some things were better left in the field, and sometimes his superiors didn't need to see the uglier side of an operation. Unfortunately, the Ghosts' equipment had higher-ups breathing down Brent's neck 24/7, which really unnerved him, and he sometimes took out his frustration on his people.

As a consequence, Brent went through team members the way he went through beer, some requesting transfers, others simply getting dropped by him. Recent rumors had it that guys who couldn't hack it on other Ghost teams were being busted down and collected into a group of misfits to be led by Brent. They would get all the crap jobs like guarding oil tankers, or they'd get some of the most dangerous but least important jobs—since they were the most expendable group in the unit. They would act as "bait" while the other teams swept in and stole the glory. Ironically, even the military's most elite still had its bottom of the barrel, and though the Ghosts' least capable operators were arguably ten times more lethal than the average Joe, Brent's colleagues would never let him live down his mistakes and weaknesses.

And speaking of one such devil, "Schoolie," a master sergeant with no neck and a complexion as scarred as a crushed beer can, ambled over to Brent's table. They called him "Schoolie" because he dreamed of becoming a professor at the U.S. Army War College. Trouble was, he was too inept to ever get his degrees. He was an excellent warrior but more of a kinesthetic guy who did much better with physical tasks than mental ones.

The drunken oaf shook his head at Brent. "I know why you're sitting alone."

Brent just looked at him.

"They hate you," Schoolie went on. "You've put 'em back through Robin Sage like they were noobs. You're talking trash to them. So they hate you."

Brent took a long pull on his beer and thought about that. He had forced his entire team to go back through the Army's hellish and grueling Robin Sage training exercise, normally reserved for Special Forces candidates, not seasoned Ghost Recon warriors. Being forced to go back through the training was humiliating enough, but Brent had deemed it important and necessary because his current group was suffering from a severe lack of morale. He'd hoped that returning to the course might rekindle some of their "beginner spirit" in regard to combat operations. He'd been mistaken. His team had resented the training, though they were respectful enough to keep those feelings to themselves; however, their expressions said it all.

"Is there a punch line in here somewhere?" Brent finally asked Schoolie. "A sarcastic remark? Or are you auditioning to become my therapist?"

Schoolie grinned. "That's pretty good."

"Unless you're picking up my tab, you're dismissed."

"Your people won't even drink with you."

"They're not here yet. Get lost, before I pull rank and things get ugly."

Schoolie snorted. "They're right over there. They've been here for fifteen minutes. You haven't even noticed."

Brent rose slightly so he could look over a small wall between the booths. He realized with sagging shoulders that the bastard was right. His entire Ghost Recon team—all eight operators—had put together two tables on the other side of the bar. They were sitting around, drinking, joking, and getting ready to order.

"Look at that. Not a one of them came over here to say, 'Hey, Captain, why don't you join us?'" said Schoolie.

Brent dropped a few bills on the table, then stood, bracing himself to confront the group.

"I think you got a situation on your hands, Captain," said Schoolie.

Brent threw up a hand, ignoring the man.

Now Brent's cheeks began to warm. Yes, they hated him, all right. If they could pick up their game and jettison their bad attitudes, he wouldn't have to deal with this.

That he kept forgetting their names certainly contributed to their lack of respect. He'd made himself a cheat sheet just to keep track:

Lakota: my assistant. Native American. Wiseass.
Daugherty: the big guy with the tiny voice.
Copeland: the New York mafia guy. Medic.
Riggs: punk chick. Good shot.
Heston: Texas cowboy, movie nut.
Park: Korean guy, never talks.
Noboru: Japanese guy. Uncle was in NSA.
Schleck: string bean. Sniper. I like him.

Brent paused a moment, slipped the index card out of his pocket, stole a quick look at the list of names, then tucked it back into his pocket and slowly approached the table. They weren't just stereotypical soldiers; they were real people with real hopes and dreams. He knew that, but his job wasn't to stroke them—it was to whip their asses into shape while earning their loyalty and respect. Easier said than done for a man whose patience was already threadbare.

Conversations broke off, and all gazes fell upon him. He cleared his throat. "What's up?"

Lakota, who'd taken her hair out of the usual tight bun, looked rather attractive as she raked her fingers through her locks and said, "Captain, uh, I guess we all really need to talk."

"Yeah, about how much we suck," said Copeland in his New York drawl. "This is a weird place to be—back in noob school. I thought I was done wearing diapers."

Just when he'd thought they were respectful enough to keep their complaints to themselves—boom—here they came . . .

"Copeland, right?" Brent asked.

"Very good, sir."

"You're a good medic and a good machine gunner, but they sent you to me because you're a wiseass."

"That's what we heard about you, sir," said Lakota.

Brent grinned crookedly. "I want to clarify that. I've been doing this long enough to realize what works and what doesn't. That's all. I'll do my best to get the job done and keep you alive. That's why we're back here, back to the beginning. This is good. This keeps us humble and honest. I'm not trying to be anything I'm not. I've been skipped over for promotions. My record ain't that great. My personal life is nonexistent. But I like to think I got heart. And I'm betting you got heart, too."

"Sir, this might keep us honest, but I'd rather keep lying," said Riggs, wriggling her brows, her spiked hair hard as icicles. "We all know what you're trying to do, and we appreciate the idea, but the fact is we've all just had bad luck."

"Well, there you go. I appreciate that honesty," said Brent.

"And speaking of being honest, why don't you do the same with us, sir?" said Heston, his voice coming slowly, musically. "Luck or not, we're all close to getting busted out of here and sent back down to SF or the regular Army."

"That's not true," Brent said, tasting the lie. "Look, we get through this, you prove to me you're ready, and I'm sure something will come along that will . . ."

Brent didn't finish his sentence. His phone was vibrating in his pocket. The caller ID was blocked.

His people groaned as he answered. He held up a palm when he realized who was calling.

On the way over to the isolation chamber, Brent accessed the network on his smartphone and retrieved the declassified bio on Major Alice Dennison, tactical operations specialist, code name "Hammer."

When the Joint Strike Force had formed and had better organized all of the United States' military operations through concentrated global network systems, Dennison had become a key player. She'd been raised in a military family, with a father who'd been an Air Force pilot. She'd attended the Virginia Military Institute and had graduated with the class of 2004. Then she'd gone to the naval academy, received her BS in systems engineering, and had graduated summa cum laude. She'd been in U.S. naval intelligence and logistics and gone on to serve in the U.S. Naval Special Warfare Command. She had been selected by General Scott Mitchell himself to join the JSF.

Brent's eyes bugged out as he finished reading the screen. General Scott Mitchell was a former Ghost Recon operator, one of the organization's best, a living legend who now led the entire Joint Strike Force.

And Dennison had been recruited by him.

This was huge. Dennison was a *major* player with a record that made you hate how good she was.

Brent frowned. And then he *really* frowned.

Why the hell did Dennison want to talk to him, a scrubby-faced gunslinger with a tainted record?

They reached the base, and the isolation chamber wasn't a chamber at all but a heavily guarded Quonset hut near the nondescript cluster of small buildings that housed Ghost Recon command. There were no signs, no indication at all that some of the world's deadliest warriors were commanded from this post.

Inside, Brent took a seat before a sixty-inch screen, along with the rest of his team. They were instructed to wait there until Major Dennison called again.

At the back of the room sat two men, and Brent had to do a double take, pun intended, because they were, in fact, twins, one well dressed in slacks and expensive silk shirt, the other wearing jeans and a T-shirt that read MUCKY DUCK RESTAURANT, CAPTIVA ISLAND, FLORIDA. They were both at least six feet, perhaps slightly taller, as lean as Olympic swimmers, and although they both had the same length blond hair, the jeans guy wore his all shaggy and sticking out, while the slacks guy had gelled his back. They might be twins, but there was a definite and deliberate distinction between them that seemed more on the part of the sloppy guy than the neat one.

Brent smiled weakly at them. The jeans guy nodded. The slacks guy looked daggers and folded his arms over his chest.

"Hey, Captain, who're they?" asked Lakota in a near whisper.

Just then a burst of static and series of encryption code numbers scrolled across the screen for a few seconds until an image appeared. On the left was Major Alice Dennison, too pretty for her own good and remarkably young for her post. On the right was another woman, much older, with gray streaks through her medium-brown hair. Her narrow glasses suggested she was as much academic as she was intelligence officer.

Dennison cleared her throat. "Good afternoon, ladies and gentlemen. For those of you who don't know her, I want to introduce Anna Grimsdóttir, director of the NSA's Splinter Cell program. I know once you were promoted into Ghost Recon, you became aware of the Splinter Cell's existence, but I'm assuming most of you haven't met its director. Grim?"

"It's a pleasure," said Grimsdóttir, nodding politely.

Brent stiffened and began to slide back into his chair. He was a cut-to-the-chase kind of guy and couldn't wait to escape from the pleasantries. "*Hi, my name is Brent and I like piña coladas and blowing stuff up in the rain . . .*"

The next five minutes went like this:

Blah, blah, blah. Blah, blah, blah, until, finally, something important caught his attention—

". . . and you'll have two Splinter Cells attached to your team. The target will be Viktoria Antsyforov, aka the Snow Maiden. Her dossier will be available on the network. Suffice it to say that we want her alive if possible. You are, however, authorized to shoot to kill. But that's a last resort. This woman is former GRU and more valuable to us than you know."

Dennison gave them more details about the Snow Maiden's last known location and how they would be heading off to Europe within the next four hours.

They'd been formally introduced to the two Splinter Cells at the back of the room, George and Thomas Voeckler. George was the clean-cut one, Thomas the looser free spirit.

Brent had already decided to request full dossiers on the two spies, and he hoped Dennison would divulge that information. Bottom line: You wanted to know who had your back—and who might not.

As they left the room, Brent reached to shake George's hand.

The spy frowned and accepted the handshake. "Nice to meet you, Captain."

"It's not easy, I know," said Brent. "You guys are used to working alone."

"That's right," said Thomas. "I don't even like to work with my brother. And all this military talk gives me an upset stomach. We're spooks, not soldiers."

"I apologize for my brother," said George. "He suffered some head trauma as a child and he's never been—"

Thomas jabbed George in the ribs, then faced Brent. "Don't worry about us, GI Joe. Just give us a long leash, and we'll deliver that bitch on a silver platter." Thomas tossed his head back, hair flying, and for a moment, Brent wondered if the man was on drugs. No, just a little weird.

Back in their barracks, Brent gathered his team into a half circle. "You got your wish. No more training. Live fire now. Test of fire. Are we up for this?"

A few of them shrugged.

"Look, they gave us a good operation."

"Yeah, but something's not right," said Lakota. "They wouldn't give us something this important— unless they're making it seem important and it's really not . . . or maybe we're just part of some bigger plan and acting as cover . . . or bait. The spooks got the real work. We're just the bulldogs waiting outside to cover them when they leave."

"Not true. And don't get paranoid," said Brent. "Higher knows I've had some nice captures in Afghanistan, seven in all, and those ops went well. Maybe they figure me for a guy who can abduct people. I'm like a

UFO, so they gave us this. That make you feel better, Lakota?"

She shrugged. "A little."

Park, the Korean guy who never talked, widened his eyes and lifted his chin. "Captain, I don't think we should trust the spies."

Brent frowned. "What makes you say that?"

Heston cursed under his breath. "Captain, he never talks, but when he does, you should listen."

"Park?" Brent asked again.

"I don't mean to sound unprofessional, sir, but I do have some experience with the NSA through joint operations in the Helmand Province. They always have another agenda. And you heard what the director said about those CIA agents who went after the Snow Maiden. Two dead, two still missing."

"Well, we sure as hell ain't the CIA."

Park's tone grew more grave. "No, but those teams all had one thing in common—they had Splinter Cells attached to their units."

"Could be just a coincidence, but if you haven't learned this about me by now, here's a quick lesson—you need to earn my trust. And so will they."

"I'm not worried, sir. But you should be."

Brent sighed. "All right, everyone, let's pack up. Bring your civvies. We need to look like tourists. We finally get to insert with real cover. I always love it when they drop us into a city wearing unmarked fatigues—but we're not supposed to look like soldiers."

"Can I wear a dress and heels?" said Riggs.

That query was met by the hoots, hollers, and catcalls of all the men, save for Park.

"Calm down, wolves. Riggs, that sounds good. Just be ready to ditch the heels when I need you."

"You got it, sir."

"All right, on the ready line in twenty minutes."

They muttered behind him as he spun on his heel and left, heading back to the office to pick up their travel docs.

While en route, Schoolie caught him on the sidewalk. "Heard you're shipping out, got a big mission."

"Yeah, we're going to rescue your father from the backyard kiddie pool. He's been lying in it all day, getting drunk."

"How do you come up with this stuff?"

"You inspire me."

"Seriously, Brent, just wishing you good luck." Schoolie proffered his hand.

When Brent glanced down at that hand, he saw another one, darker skinned, and when he looked up, there was Carlos Villanueva, grinning. *All I want is a race. Just shake hands and tell me you'll race so I don't have to kick your ass.*

Brent blinked hard and faced Schoolie. "I'll shake when I get back. Don't want to jinx myself, okay?"

"Okay, Brent. I heard you were superstitious." Schoolie lowered his hand. "Make old Buzz proud."

"Roger that."

Schoolie had just referred to Major Harold "Buzz" Gordon, born March 17, 1955, and one of the first soldiers assigned to the Ghosts when they were formed in 1994. He'd gone on to become a lieutenant colonel and company commander, working extensively with Scott Mitchell. Buzz was now considered the "father" of Ghost Recon, while Mitchell was considered its greatest living Ghost. Brent hoped history wouldn't record him as the black sheep of the unit, but you had to do more than hope to change history . . . you had to *act*. And he would.

FOUR

Château de Menthon-Saint-Bernard
Lake Annecy, France

Brent and his Ghost Recon team, along with the Voeckler brothers, had traveled to a locale so spectacularly beautiful that it was hard to remember he was working. The juxtaposition between this part of France and some of Brent's old duty stations—little hellholes in Afghanistan draped in "moon dust"—was enough to weaken his knees.

The Château de Menthon-Saint-Bernard, a medieval castle built in the tenth century, towered some two hundred meters over Lake Annecy, the second-largest lake in France. The castle was like something out of a movie, with great stone walls, spires, and ornate turrets set against a verdant hillside. Walt Disney might have taken his inspiration from the place when he'd planned his Magic Kingdom castle because the environs had a distinct fairy-tale air. Behind the fortress's ancient walls were 105 rooms on four levels, and Brent presently stood in the main banquet area on the second floor, watching as partygoers slowly filtered in past the orchestra.

A banner hung across one wall. In Cyrillic it read, *Congratulations Team Katusha, victors of the 2021 Tour de France.* Despite the war, sporting events like the Tour de France, the Super Bowl, and the World Series forged on and were more popular than ever; however, the Americans, the Euros, and the Russians were all prone to banning certain groups from their international events. Brent had read in the papers how the Russians had threatened to pull the oil plug on the Euros, because the French were talking about banning the Russian team from the tour. Well, the French had bowed to the pressure, and the Russians had won, with their best rider, Andrei Eskov, claiming the yellow jersey as rider with the best time and another of their riders claiming the "king of the mountains" competition. The Russian had conquered the tour, and the French now wore their dismay like moth-eaten coats. Nathalie Perreau, the president of the European Federation, called the victory a travesty and insisted on more anti-doping checks for the Russian team. None of that mattered.

Now the team was celebrating its victory in a French castle that had been rented, no doubt, through extreme pressure on the French as the Russians continued dangling the keys to all their oil.

Admittedly, Brent was glad the Russians had won, otherwise he wouldn't be standing in a French castle.

It seemed that Andrei Eskov was the Snow Maiden's cousin, and there had been a shooting near Montereau-Fault-Yonne, a stop along the tour. One man had turned up dead and been identified as a member of the Green Brigade Transnational. Death always lay in the Snow Maiden's wake, and so Brent and his team had prepared their trap.

The others were in position outside the castle and in the surrounding hills, while he and George Voeckler were inside, with Voeckler posing as a guest and Brent as part of the French security team. Dennison had worked out this arrangement, and the security team, while sarcastic and aloof, were playing along as they repeatedly slipped outside for their cigarette breaks.

Brent's wireless earpiece buzzed. Lakota and the others reported the arrival of the next group and were scrutinizing every woman. Viktoria Antsyforov would be disguised with a wig, heavy makeup, who knew . . . The more Brent had read about the Snow Maiden, the more uneasy he'd become. Capturing her would be like trying to wrestle a Siberian tiger into a pair of handcuffs.

The Snow Maiden's profile had been supplied by a man named Pavel Doletskaya, a former colonel with the GRU who had worked with *and* slept with the woman. The colonel had been captured in Moscow, dragged back to Guantanamo and then to Tampa, and broken by Dennison and her people, who'd told him about how the Snow Maiden had faked her death. They now had a valuable ally feeding them secrets, and Doletskaya's information had been useful and comprehensive. That the Snow

Maiden had an intense hatred for her own country fascinated Brent; that she'd already killed dozens of people in her quest to bring down her homeland kept the lump in Brent's throat.

Brent's attention was drawn to the main entrance, illuminated by a pair of colossal bronze wall sconces atop which rose tall, slender flames. The cycling team had arrived, and as planned, they had come in full biking uniforms: colorful blue-and-red jerseys covered with their sponsors' logos, matching bib shorts, and even color-coordinated socks and sneakers. Their mechanics, coaches, drivers, and other support personnel wore team shirts and slacks, while the rest of the guests were suited up for this black-tie affair.

The waiters and waitresses began circulating with silver trays of hors d'oeuvres—stuffed mushrooms, fig and olive tapenade, and chutney baked Brie, according to one waiter. Voeckler, who'd been standing close to the main entrance, his gaze constantly scanning the growing crowd around the clusters of elegantly appointed tables, ambled over to Brent. "You see that woman there?"

Brent tensed and squinted across the room. The sun was beginning to set and the shadows had grown long, but he did see her, a real looker whose lithe form barely tented up her burgundy-colored dress. Her dark hair shimmered in the firelight.

"Is that her?" Brent asked with a gasp.

Voeckler sighed. "Soon as I nod at the orchestra leader, he'll get them to play for me, and I'll waltz with her."

"She looks way too thin. That's not her."

"No, Brent, of course that's not her. She's just the woman I'll dance with."

"So this is how you guys play, huh? Come to rich people's parties and dance with all the hot women? While me and my people eat dust and tiptoe around IEDs? Yep, there's a world of difference between the NSA and the United States Army."

"I thought you'd pull up my dossier."

"I did. I know you were a Force Recon Marine, a hardcore operator. I respect that. You got the track record. It's your brother I can't figure out."

"You and everyone else."

"So he only got in because he's your twin. Grim figured you'd have a perfect alibi with him."

"He's come a long way. He was a slacker his whole life. This is pretty amazing for him."

"Well, I hope babysitting your brother doesn't get in our way."

"I'm not babysitting him, Captain. I'm babysitting all of you."

"Whoa, I think you just hurt my feelings."

"All right, enough with the BS." Voeckler's tone hardened. "Now listen. If the Snow Maiden is here, we'll draw her out, just like a black widow from her web. The orchestra is going to play Tchaikovsky's Opus Number Twelve. It's her favorite."

"How do you know?"

Voeckler snorted. "Opus Twelve is called 'The Snow Maiden.'"

"Maybe she hasn't heard it."

"Oh, yes, she has. The NSA and Third Echelon like to do their own intel gathering, thank you. The report the JSF gave us is only fragmentary."

"Then I'd appreciate you sharing the rest with us."

"We will, soon as I get authorization."

Brent sighed in disgust over the politics. "Well, all right, Mr. Voeckler. It's your party for the time being."

"Just get my back, Captain. I might be a little distracted." Voeckler drifted off across the hardwood dance floor, toward his unsuspecting dance partner.

Meanwhile, Brent kept his gaze focused on Andrei Eskov, who'd taken a seat at the rectangular main table. All of the riders would be sitting in a row, facing the audience, not unlike the seating arrangement for a panel discussion. Perhaps each cyclist would be asked to speak, Brent wasn't sure, but at any rate he had a perfect and unobstructed view of the target's cousin, even though the room had grown crowded with dozens of guests now.

"Captain, it's Lakota. Is it okay if we order a pizza?"

Brent grinned inwardly—"ordering a pizza" was her way of saying no contacts or anything else worth reporting. "Still clear out there?"

"Good to go," she responded curtly.

A familiar face appeared at the doorway. Riggs. Now it was her turn to join the festivities. God, she looked stunning in her blue dress, matching purse, and heels. The spiky hair had been toned down and softened, and her makeup appeared delicate and expertly applied. She had a folder tucked under her arm as she sashayed across the room and homed in on Eskov. Okay, Brent was a man and couldn't help but gape at her cleavage, though as her commanding officer he did feel guilty about that. She reached Eskov, said hello, and asked for his autograph.

The young Russian was all too eager to comply, wearing a silly grin fueled by raging hormones. As Riggs continued to chat with him, the orchestra, numbering some thirty musicians, began Opus Number Twelve.

Voeckler took his lady onto the floor and began to waltz. They looked dramatic and stunning, and Brent frowned. Voeckler was taller and better looking and had a better job. He could pick up women with ease, and his organization seemed to have better intelligence than Brent's.

"Brent, Schleck here," began the team's sniper, positioned in the hills overlooking the castle. Schleck was a bird with long torso and pointy jaw, the "string bean" Brent had called him on his cheat sheet. But the bird ate like a pig and gained nothing. "Car just pulled up. Got three guys in tuxedoes getting out. Looks like the Mafia or the Secret Service. You hear anything about added security, Captain?"

"Negative. Stand by."

Brent slipped off toward the back of the room, where he discreetly donned his Cross-Com: an earpiece with integrated camera, microphone, and attached monocle that curved around his eye. He tapped a button on the earpiece and whispered, "Cross-Com activated."

Brent's monocle glowed with screens displaying his

uplink and downlink channels and icons representing his support elements, among other bits of data. These images were produced by a low-intensity laser projecting them through his pupil and onto his retina. The laser scanned horizontally and vertically using a coherent beam of light, and all data was refreshed every second to continually update him.

The system was connected via satellite to the entire Joint Strike Force's local- and wide-area networks (LAN/WAN) so that even President Becerra in the White House could see what he was doing and speak to him directly on the battlefield (not good, according to Brent). That level of Network Centric Warfare—all part of Ghost Recon's Integrated Warfighter System (IWS Version 9)—was just a leash of technology. But that's the way the game was played. Fortunately, the old tricks still worked: "Uh, sorry, command, uh, you're breaking up. What was that order? Oh, I think the signal is dropping . . ."

He issued a subtle voice command to bring up the camera built into Schleck's Cross-Com. Now he took in the scene from the sniper's point of view. "I see your boys, Schleck. What do you think?"

"I think I don't know what to think. Heads up, though."

"Roger that. They could be team security."

"Okay. Standing by."

Brent removed the Cross-Com and shoved it back into his inner jacket pocket, replacing that earpiece with the one issued to him by the French security force.

The guys Schleck had spotted now moved toward the security line and metal detector. They would have to pass through those checkpoints before they could get anywhere near the main banquet room. Schleck was just being paranoid, but you wanted your sniper to be hypersensitive to his surroundings.

Brent retuned his gaze to the banquet room.

Voeckler was now wooing the entire crowd with his dance moves; he could probably win a national contest, billing himself as the "dancing spy" after he retired. His partner was fully in lust with him, and again, Brent thought of murder.

Riggs was now surrounded by Eskov and two other cyclists, and if the Snow Maiden wanted to get near her cousin, she'd now have to rub shoulders with a very sexy Ghost Recon operator.

Once more Brent scrutinized the guests, focusing on each female. He assessed, dismissed, and moved on. He took a deep breath, and something ached deep down in his gut.

The first salvo of gunfire—originating somewhere outside near the security checkpoint—sent his head jerking back. The second drove him toward the wall and reaching for his pistol as the three men Schleck had spotted burst into the room, brandishing snub-nosed machine guns.

They opened fire.

With a gasp, Brent dove onto the floor and looked up, trying to get a bead on the shooters, but the party guests were scrambling in all directions, legs shifting and blocking his view. He had no time to check on Eskov, Riggs, or Voeckler and only seconds to try to stop these bastards.

Finally, Brent had a shot as a heavyset man took a bullet in the chest and tumbled, exposing the shooter behind him. All three men had donned green balaclavas, and one cried in French, "We are the Green Brigade Transnational! We are your doom!"

Brent took out the lead terrorist with a single head shot and was about to shift fire to the next guy when a wave of rounds exploded from the French security guys, so much fire that their wider shots were striking guests cowering just behind the terrorist.

Another terrorist flailed under all that fire, dropped his weapon, and thudded to the floor as the screams and groans lifted and the sulfur stench of gunfire overpowered the room.

The third guy suddenly ducked around a table and bolted, vanishing past the doorway.

"Lakota, we got fire, two Tangos down. I'm chasing a third. He might be coming your way!"

"Roger that. Lock and load. Schleck? Get ready!"

"Ready!" cried the sniper.

Brent stole a quick look back, trying to find Riggs and Voeckler, but he couldn't see them. He darted outside the hall and saw the thug bounding up a stone staircase just ten yards off to his left.

He scissored past dazed and frightened guests, reached the stairs, and took them two at a time, hearing the thumps of the terrorist above as the staircase jogged left. At the same time, he tugged out his Cross-Com and jammed it over his eye and ear.

On the next landing, Brent spotted the terrorist, who turned back and raised his pistol.

Brent fired a shot, missing the guy, even as the terrorist raised his machine gun. Brent dove back out of the guy's bead as rounds stitched into the stone behind him and ricocheted wildly. Dust swirled as Brent rolled back and squinted.

More footfalls. The thug was still ascending. Something crashed to the steps above, and as Brent rounded another corner, he saw his prey ripping art and tapestries from the wall and dropping them down across the stairs to block the path. Brent slid his way past a tattered painting, its frame splintering across the stone, and kept on.

Meanwhile, the security guard earpiece still jammed in Brent's other ear crackled with Lakota's voice. She had taken over the rest of the team, as she was trained to do, and they were collapsing back in on the castle; however, Schleck would remain in his perch for overwatch.

Brent reached what he believed was the fourth-floor landing, where he found a narrow door hanging open. He dodged past it, coming into one of the circular towers.

He glanced up at the spiral staircase constructed of heavy oak planks. Thud, thud, thud. His boy was heading up, and unless he'd grown wings or had some other escape plan on the roof, Brent figured he had him. You never run *up* into a building to escape—unless the chopper's up there waiting for you . . .

And that thought made Brent prick up his ears, listening for the *whomp-whomp* . . .

More gunfire rained down from somewhere above, and Brent crouched and returned fire, just to keep the bastard looking.

Then he resumed his charge upward, growing breathless now, the dress shoes hurting. He longed for his automatic rifle and a little Kevlar to catch stray rounds.

As he climbed, he popped out his near-empty magazine and slapped home a fresh one. Twenty steps later, a cool breeze filtered down toward him, and as he finally reached the top, he kept low, paused, saw the area was clear, then came into a small room whose single window hung wide open.

Brent spoke into the Cross-Com: "He's on the roof."

The window was barely wide enough to fit a person, and Brent resisted the temptation to stick his head out first to steal a look. The guy could be waiting just on the other side, out of sight and ready to blow Brent's head off.

Instead, Brent came at the window from a sharp angle, able to see if anyone was standing just beside the edge. Then he dodged across it and checked the other side. Satisfied he was clear, he leaned forward, pushed the window all the way open, and looked down.

He lost his breath. The guy had leapt some four meters to the angled roofline and was working his away across it toward the adjoining curtain wall. He would leap down just a couple of meters to run across the wall walk—a place from where ancient bowmen had lined up to defend their home and from where modern-day scum-bags ran to escape.

"I have a shot," said Schleck.

"Hold your fire," Brent snapped. "I think I got him, and we need some answers."

"He has a machine gun and you want to take him alive?" asked Schleck.

"Oh, I do love a challenge," Brent quipped.

Cursing, he hauled himself through the window, slid out his legs, hung on for dear life, held his breath . . .

And jumped.

He hit the next roofline solidly and turned back, lost his step, and fell onto his rump, nearly dropping his pistol. But at least he wasn't rolling off the roof. He got back up on his hands and knees to spy the thug leaping down to the wall.

Brent followed him, reached the edge of the roof, took aim, and fired, striking the thug in the right calf. The guy screamed, rolled back, fired a wild salvo, then kept on, now limping.

Gritting his teeth, Brent levered himself off the roof and jumped to the wall. Now he raced across the stone, the moonlight picking out the guy ahead, and for a moment, Brent thought he had another shot until he realized with a start what was happening.

The guy had reached the door to the next tower, but it was locked. Seeing he had no time to try shooting it open, he whirled back and brought his machine gun to bear.

Brent dropped to his gut as the guy opened fire from

about twenty meters away, but after only three shots that struck within a meter of Brent's head, the gun fell silent.

Knowing that either the guy's weapon had jammed or his magazine was empty, Brent launched to his feet.

The thug could have another weapon, but that didn't occur to Brent until after he began his charge. He cursed and was about to fire when the guy did something quite extraordinary:

He dropped his machine gun, raised his hands, and tore off his balaclava, revealing his short, black hair and chiseled jaw. If he was twenty-one, that was being generous.

"All right, don't move," Brent ordered in French.

The guy responded in French: "You're meaningless to me."

"You came here looking for her, didn't you."

As Brent neared the guy he suddenly raced to the wall—

"No, no, no!" screamed Brent as the thug simply threw himself off.

Brent darted to the wall and watched as the guy plummeted toward the mounds of weed-encrusted rocks below.

"Oh, man, Captain," called Schleck over the network. "He's on the ground. No movement yet."

"Of course he's not moving. He just took a god-damned nosedive off this castle." Brent winced. Everybody back home had just heard him say that.

And he might as well have cued her. Major Dennison appeared in Brent's HUD. "Captain, Voeckler reports from inside that Andrei Eskov was shot and killed. We're not sure if the Green Brigade Transnational thought the Snow Maiden would be here, but I'm certain they were targeting her cousin for payback. You're sitting in the middle of an international incident, and I want you out of there right now, lest the JSF be implicated in this mess."

Brent was already heading toward the tower door. "Ma'am, you'll get no argument from me. Would've been nice to take one of them alive—or at least question Eskov."

"Just get to the airport."

"Roger that."

Brent shot out the lock on the tower door. Still locked. He fired again. Still locked. He swore. Dead bolt, maybe. "Schleck, I'm stuck up here. You see another way out?"

"Sir, the blueprints are available via your Cross-Com."

"Schleck, I don't want to think right now. Just find me a way out!"

FIVE

Banyan Tree Seychelles Resort
Mahé Island
Republic of the Seychelles

The Banyan Tree Seychelles was a five-star resort situated on the southwestern coastline of Mahé and offering breathtaking views of the Indian Ocean. Chopra had reserved one of the sixty pool villas perched on the hillsides. The brochure had described the rooms as combining contemporary, colonial, and plantation décor with sweeping ceilings; large, open verandas; and ethnic woven textiles, and every villa was equipped with all the modern conveniences.

Although Chopra hadn't seen them yet, he'd read about the indigenous arts and crafts gallery, the spa, the health club, the library, the tennis courts, and the mountain-biking trails. Upon first glimpse, it was easy to see why this place was worthy of the young sheikh's presence.

Within an hour of his arrival, Chopra met up with Harold Westerdale in the Banyan Tree's La Varangue for an afternoon cocktail. The private investigator's tropical-print shirt was soaked, his short, gray hair plastered to his head. The breeze had died off, and stepping onto the veranda was like stepping into a loaf of warm bread. Chopra took the bar stool beside the man and ordered a drink while staring out into the turquoise waters.

"It's been a long search," Chopra muttered.

"And we've had a lot of false leads," the man grunted in return.

"But this time you're certain."

"I've already spoken to Warda. She knows you're coming. She's willing to meet with you."

"You made contact?"

"I did."

"You fool. They'll run now. We'll lose them."

"No, she's scheduled a meeting for later today."

Chopra recoiled in confusion. "Why aren't they scared? Why aren't they running? *They* scheduled a meeting? I'm confused . . ."

Westerdale pulled a handkerchief from his pocket and dragged it across his brow. "I don't know why they did this."

"You should've asked."

"It didn't occur to me. I guess I was too shocked."

"I don't like it."

"I don't like this place. Bloody hot here! Maybe the heat has gotten to this family."

Chopra shrugged.

Hussein Al Maktoum had three older sisters: Ara, Kalila, and Warda. Hussein's father, it seemed, had kept having children until he'd produced a son. Warda was the oldest of the group, twenty-four now, and the woman with whom Westerdale had made contact. They, like their brother, had done a remarkable job of hiding themselves from the powers that be via a well-trained and well-paid staff.

So what had changed? Maybe they were running out of money? Or perhaps the young sheikh had just grown tired of hiding? That seemed more likely. Was he aware of the dangers of revealing himself, especially now? The Russians would want to capture him, influence him, take control of the oil. There was already a huge price on his head as the sole heir to Dubai.

The more Chopra thought about it, the more tense he became. "I need to meet with Warda right now."

"They said no."

"Because now they're running, you fool. Why do I pay you? Where is she?"

"She said she would come down to my villa. We'll wait for them. Do as they say. I trust them."

Chopra stiffened in anger and glowered at his drink. He remembered an eighteen-year-old Warda arguing with her father over her extravagant spending on clothes and jewelry and her father's grief over the massive phone bills she was incurring by calling friends all over the world, all the time, at all hours. Chopra smiled inwardly; the family had more money than they could ever spend in a thousand lifetimes, but her father had been trying to teach her responsibility, and it seemed that their world of lavish homes and exotic cars had made it nearly impossible to do that, unless he became much more of a disciplinarian. Nevertheless, Warda's father was a push-over when it came to his daughters. They'd beg, and he'd give in.

Chopra took a sip of his drink and felt a little better. *Let the alcohol relax you*, he told himself. If it was meant to be, it would happen.

Across the bar sat a lean woman with short, dark hair. She wore a low-cut sundress, and when he looked at her, she averted her gaze and checked her watch. Women that beautiful were always waiting for someone—a man twice as handsome as Chopra, no doubt. He sighed and took a longer pull on his drink.

It was nearly sundown when Warda arrived at Chopra's villa. She was accompanied by a large black man whom she did not introduce and whose job was obvious. After exchanging a tearful hello, they sat on Chopra's veranda and spoke for a few minutes about the war, the bombs, the loss of her parents, and Chopra expressed his most sincere condolences. The children had been smuggled out of the country during the first indication that missiles might be launched. Their parents had been trying to escape not long after, but the sheikh's plane had been targeted by Iranian fighter jets and blown out of the sky.

Warda nodded and pulled back her long, black hair.

She was a painfully beautiful woman, a flower who'd sprouted up from the heaps of debris that was now her country. "My father trusted you very much, which is why I agreed to this meeting. He once told me he loved you like a brother. He told me he had never met a man as smart or as loyal as you. He told me I should marry you."

Chopra blushed. "That's rather shocking."

"Because of the age difference?"

"Because I'm a Hindu."

She nodded her understanding. "He'd had some wine. I think he meant that I should marry a man with your qualities."

"Well, I hope you find him."

"Given the way I must live my life now, that is very, very difficult."

Chopra nodded. "You've done a remarkable job of hiding. It's taken me this long to locate you—and all I want to do is help."

"There are so many who want to manipulate us, especially my brother."

"I need to speak to him."

"Why?"

"Because it's time for him to lead your country back from the ashes. I want to return to him what is his, and I want to help him rebuild your nation. It's the least I can do to thank your family for all you've done for me. That's all I want. I have no other motivation. I have all the money I could possibly need. This is not about that. This is about restoring a family, an ideal . . . a country."

Warda began to choke up. She grabbed his hand. "I believe you, Manoj. I believe you."

"Then take me to him."

"Unfortunately, he's not here."

Chopra sighed deeply in disappointment. "According to the information I had—"

"He was only here for a few days. A short holiday. He just returned to London. He's been attending a private prep school there, at my insistence. My other sisters have a place nearby."

"Excellent. He must continue his education."

"He doesn't exactly agree. I think you'll find him an interesting—and challenging—young man. That's all I can say about my brother. We disagree over many subjects."

"I understand. Well, then, can you give him my contact information? I'll leave for London in the morning." Chopra reached into his wallet and withdrew his card.

She rose and accepted the card. "I will. I'll have him call you. It was wonderful to see you again, Manoj. And I hope this dream of rebuilding our country comes to pass. I'm tired of hiding."

He glanced around. "It's not entirely unpleasant."

"No, but the company . . ." She glanced at her bodyguard and rolled her eyes.

He smiled wanly. "I see."

She offered to have dinner with him, but he declined. It would be a form of torture he could not endure. He left and returned to his villa, where he sat in the living room, computer balanced on his lap, and began the process of chartering a private jet back to London.

* * *

A short time later, Chopra had dinner with Westerdale and shared the good news. The Brit reminded Chopra of the bonus attached to his contract, and Chopra assured him that he'd receive it. Westerdale had been scanning the news, and by his second glass of wine he'd launched into one of his trademark tirades about world events.

Argentina's new offshore oil discoveries, with the aid of Russian technology, were a windfall of the highest magnitude for the Russian Federation. The thick ooze pumping out of the Argentine ocean bed wasn't the sweet crude of the Middle East, but in a world starving for oil, the industrial world's lifeblood, there'd be no difficulty passing the excessive refining costs on to the Europeans. So yes, Westerdale, said, the Russians had found yet another way to screw over the Brits. The new fields kept product moving through the world markets, filled Russia's coffers, and reduced the demands on Russia's own oil production and reserves.

The Russian Federation's growing financial power unnerved Westerdale and Chopra and increased Chopra's sense of urgency in helping the young sheikh put Dubai back on the map. The Russians had no idea how vast Dubai's secret reserves were, and Chopra wished he could see the look on President Kapalkin's face when some of his European clients began to turn away oil sales in favor of doing business with Dubai and the other emirates.

Westerdale and Chopra finished dinner, and as

Chopra was about to leave, he spotted that same woman again: lithe, muscular, short black hair. She was eating alone this time. Oh, how he wished he had the nerve to go over and speak to her. But he was leaving in the morning. And nothing would come of it, of course. She was probably a full head taller than him, and he was at least ten years her senior. He sighed as she took a phone call, then bid Westerdale a good evening. With a full belly and a renewed longing for female companionship, Chopra began the uphill hike for his villa.

The Snow Maiden could have abducted her prey within the first hour of his arrival in the Seychelles, but she planned to study him for a while. What was he doing here? What did he want? She wasn't foolish enough to blindly take orders from her employers. She was ever the opportunist.

Patti had said that Chopra was the key to getting them inside Dubai's vaults. The *Ganjin* wanted the locations of Dubai's secret oil reserves and the gold stored in one of the vaults. That was simple enough, but the Snow Maiden believed that Chopra was involved in something else that both intrigued and unsettled her.

She'd already dusted his villa with nanobots so she'd be able to track him; consequently, she would keep him on a leash for a while, let him wander, let him provide a few more answers that could prove useful. She'd been in the hills near his villa and had electronically observed and listened in on his meeting with the woman. She had learned via a surveillance photograph sent back to the *Ganjin* that the woman was Warda Al Maktoum, daughter of the royal family of Dubai. Now Chopra was heading back to London in the morning to continue his mission to restore the old Dubai. It was hard to fathom that he had no ulterior motives. Those kind of people rarely existed in the Snow Maiden's world. At once she admired and pitied him.

And she resisted the temptation to move in now. Let him go to London. Let him make contact with the young sheikh he'd been struggling to find all these years. And certainly any more information about him was better kept from the *Ganjin*.

She leaned back on the sofa of her own villa, staring at the signal superimposed over the satellite map on her computer. With a click she brought up views from the micro cameras she'd planted in his villa. Chopra was still there, preparing to settle down for the night. She would do the same. She'd already hacked into his computer and had his itinerary. She could relax for the moment. She closed her eyes, and they were there. Always there. Her husband. Her brothers.

And now her cousin Andrei.

He was too young and just a victim, and she was entirely responsible for his death. They killed him to hurt her, to demoralize her, to weaken her . . . so they could move in. But they had no idea what they had just done. Her rage was now a fiery maw that would consume them.

Oh, yes, she felt certain the Russians had hired the

Brigade. The terrorists had become too good at tracking her. Izotov was training and equipping them, letting them get their hands dirty while the smug bastard sat in his office and stuffed his face with gourmet food.

Revenge would not bring back the dead, of course. Revenge was foolish, she knew. So she no longer called it revenge. She called it justice—for the future generations of Russia. The richer her nation became, the more corrupt grew its leaders. It would end. It must end.

She was with Nikolai again, holding his hand while he lay in that hospital bed. The chemotherapy had turned him into a pale skeleton, but behind those sunken cheeks and hollow eyes was the man she loved.

"Don't cry," he'd told her.

"They did this to you."

"No, I did this to me. I chose. But it's okay. This life is only temporary, and we'll be together again."

"They knew this would happen. They didn't care. They sent my brother in there. And they sent you to clean up the mess."

"Don't be angry. You have a beautiful heart. Keep it warm for me."

She laid her head on his chest and cried.

The Snow Maiden took in a long breath and opened her eyes. Her wineglass was nearly empty. As she sat up and reached toward the bottle, the door to her villa smashed open and was split in two.

The man who appeared behind the shattering wood was a stocky German wearing a broad grin. That he had found her here was a testament to his tenacity because she'd been excruciatingly careful.

But here he was, nonetheless, Mr. Heinrich Haussler, old GRU colleague and double agent, new nemesis, with a suppressed pistol pointed at her head.

"Hello, Viktoria."

She snorted. "Hello, Heinrich. You could've knocked."

SIX

Banyan Tree Seychelles Resort
Mahé Island
Republic of the Seychelles

To say that Brent had grinned until it hurt would be an understatement. They'd sent him to a French paradise, where, well, the escargot had hit the fan, but then he'd learned they were sending him to a tropical paradise. The irony was killing him. He barely made enough money to vacation in these spots, yet he was getting all-expenses-paid trips courtesy of the American taxpayers. He hoped his dumb luck would continue.

Dennison had leaned hard on the captured Russian colonel, Pavel Doletskaya, and he knew enough about the Snow Maiden to offer small details that might betray her whereabouts. She traveled under assumed identities, of course, and had access to some of the best document-forging techniques in the world via her old GRU contacts and other unknown sources. She was also able to defy most electronic ID systems. But in the end, she was still human, still susceptible to human impulse, to weakness, to using her mother's initials as a prompt for devising her aliases—a tidbit only the Russian colonel would know. That eccentricity had led the NSA and Army intelligence to locating her in the Seychelles. Dennison herself had checked the airport security camera footage, and voilà, there she was, the Snow Maiden, wearing a tennis cap and shorts and carrying a sling bag. There was something haughty and audacious about her using commercial airliners. With all of her resources, Brent would have considered her moving about on private jets; perhaps she wasn't as well connected or well funded as others thought, or perhaps a private jet might have called too much attention to her.

Brent, the Splinter Cells, and the rest of his team were en route within an hour after receiving their first lead. And by the time they neared the island, they had pinpointed her exact location.

They infiltrated the resort via a borrowed yacht anchored offshore, and dressed in nondescript black fatigues and heavily armed, they were ready to take the Snow Maiden alive. The team was fanning out, about to set up full surveillance of her villa.

Brent was curious why she was here. Her cousin had just been killed, and the higher-ups assumed she'd remain in Europe to exact payback on the terrorists. Maybe she was linking up with someone on the island who could help.

As he and Lakota shifted through a dense forest

running parallel to the hillside trail, the call came in from Thomas Voeckler: "We've just run an infrared scan on the hillside. I don't believe this. It's loaded with targets. I just pulled up satellite. We have nine armed operators already in place. What the hell is this, Brent?"

"I'll find out." Brent crouched down and took a deep breath. "Ghost Team, this is Ghost Lead. Hold positions. Hammer, this is Ghost Lead, over."

"Go ahead, Ghost Lead," replied Dennison, her image appearing in the head-up display.

"Does the old cliché 'we've got company' mean anything to you right now?"

"Scanning."

Brent sighed in frustration. "Be nice if we knew who they were . . ."

"Not sure yet. Let's feel them out."

"Roger that. Ghost Team, split and shadow those other operators. I want you breathing down their necks, but don't engage. Not yet. Schleck, you hold back and get ready to do your thing. Get your bead on that front door, over."

"Roger that, Boss," replied Schleck. "Holy—" Schleck finished the curse and added, "A guy just broke down her front door. He's moving inside!"

Gunfire erupted across the hillside, all kinds of fire: single-shot, automatic, even the crack of a carbine. Brent began cycling through the camera views of his people as he sent Lakota off toward the Snow Maiden's villa about a hundred yards up the hill.

"Ghost Team, hold fire! Do not give up your positions! Let them give up theirs!"

"They just fired at a hotel security guard. He's down," reported Noboru.

"I think they have infrared on us," cried Daugherty. "Radar, satellite, the works! Might need to engage!"

Brent swore under his breath and cried, "Gun and run if you have to, but keep it moving!"

"He's right," Riggs chimed in. "I got one in my sights now. They've got headsets like ours."

Brent gritted his teeth and began cycling through the operator images piped in via his Cross-Com. He was trying to do the right thing as team leader: obtain as much information as possible before reacting to the situation.

Aw, hell. He took off running.

Chopra had been watching the highlights of a soccer game and was lifting the remote toward the set, about to turn it off. He'd set up his air travel to London and all had been well—until he'd heard the sound of gunfire coming from the hills near his villa. He immediately called Westerdale, who was already panicking and crying that they should "get the bloody hell out of there."

"We should just stay here and take cover," Chopra had argued.

"You fool. If they've come for Warda and take her, she'll talk. Then they'll come for you. The only way you can help Hussein is to save yourself!"

"All right."

Thankfully, Chopra had traveled light and his bag was already packed, except for his morning clothes. He gathered his belongings, flinched again at the sound of more gunshots, then, holding his breath, went running from his villa. He longed to go after Warda and prayed they wouldn't hurt her, but Westerdale was right: If Chopra didn't make contact with Hussein, then Dubai would never rise again and that would be a tragedy. As much as it pained him, he kept on toward Westerdale's villa. The pops and booms continued from the jungle above him.

The dimly lit trail took him to the main entrance and motorway, where two taxi drivers had climbed into their cars and were keeping low, their worried gazes turned up toward the hills. Between the damp stone and his own excitement, Chopra wound up slipping and falling as he neared the first car. He cried out, felt a throbbing in his elbow, but pulled himself back up and spotted Westerdale coming from a second path and hustling toward him.

The Brit waved and called out to Chopra.

Another exchange of gunfire thundered across the hills, stealing Chopra's breath.

He was dizzy by the time he fell into the backseat and the cabdriver sped away. He glanced over at Westerdale, who shook his head and said, "You're in over your head."

"I know. But this is the right thing to do," Chopra said, hardening his tone.

"You're an eccentric."

Chopra shook his head. "I just want what's right."

"Then go to London. Wait for his call. Hopefully she spoke to him before they attacked."

Chopra threw his head back against the seat, removed his glasses, and massaged his weary eyes. "You're staying here."

"I'm what?"

"You heard me. You're staying. I want to know about Warda. I want to know if she's safe."

Westerdale released a string of epithets, then demanded a larger bonus, and Chopra agreed.

The Snow Maiden mused that it was difficult to have tricks up her sleeve while wearing a short-sleeved shirt; however, she'd grown used to being chased and took nothing for granted. Her tricks were born of experience and electronics, and there was nothing magical about them. They were tools of the trade, and she knew how to use them.

So when Haussler rudely smashed in the Snow Maiden's door, said his hello, and thought he was about to hold her at gunpoint, the Snow Maiden simply raised her hands and rolled her wrist twice, and the transmitter in her custom-designed watch sent a signal to the detonator.

Three, two, one.

The resounding boom from the doorway sent Haussler ducking reflexively—and that's all the Snow Maiden needed: one simple diversion via an explosive she'd planted within the first hour of her arrival. In fact, she had booby-trapped the entire place—but for some reason the electronic surveillance warning system she had set up in the walkway had failed to alert her of Haussler's approach. The bastard had figured out a way to jam it. He was clever when it came to that.

Her sidearm, the one given to her by the taxicab driver who'd been bought by the *Ganjin*, was beneath the sofa pillow. She wrenched it out, was about to fire point-blank at Haussler, but he'd whirled to face a figure dressed in black who'd appeared in the shattered doorway.

The figure's face was covered by a balaclava, one eye shielded by an electronic monocle, a high-tech rifle balanced in the combatant's grip.

"Hold there!" she cried, and her distinctly feminine voice confirmed she was an English speaker, probably an American.

Haussler began to raise his arms—but abruptly dropped to his gut. He then rolled, about to fire at the woman in the doorway.

Seeing that, and strangely holding her own fire, the woman ducked back.

At the same time, the Snow Maiden fired two rounds that narrowly missed the woman. A heartbeat later the Snow Maiden was off the couch and lunging for the back door, on the other side of the small kitchen.

Haussler screamed after her, but more gunfire came from the living room as the woman must have turned back inside. The Snow Maiden snatched her sling bag from the counter, then tore open the door, rounds tearing into the frame beside her. She bounded outside, checked left and right, then sprinted into the forest behind the villa.

Brent arrived in the doorway, just behind Lakota, who reported that she'd seen a woman inside who could've been the Snow Maiden—but there'd been a man there, too. Dennison and her folks would already be searching for the man's identity since Lakota's Cross-Com had recorded images of the entire scene.

As the rest of his team chimed in, Brent rushed through the villa, falling in behind Lakota, who'd said that the woman had escaped out back, the man trailing her. They burst through the rear door, paused, and heard brush shifting in the forest.

"We've got two men who've just climbed into a taxi," reported Schleck. "Old guys. Probably just tourists running scared. All right, I've got satellite. Two runners in the jungle now, heading down toward the beachfront road. Watch it, though, Captain. Those other operators are coming around to cut us off."

"Good job, Schleck. Keep the play-by-play coming. I like your style."

"Roger that, Captain!"

"All right, Ghosts, pull up those other guys in your HUD. See if you can flank them while Lakota and I punch straight on through toward the beach. We're taking that main road around the resort."

The responses came in, and not a second after the last

one, a woman's scream came from the bungalow ahead. Brent rushed up to the small quarters, which were heavily draped in vines and foliage. He kept tight to the wall and hand-signaled for Lakota to head around the other side.

The Cross-Com automatically zoomed in on two heat sources around the corner: a big man lay on the ground, and hovering over him was another person, both glowing in a mottled orange-red. Brent hustled forward, came through the big fronds, then lifted his palm in truce.

She had long, dark hair, and though the light was faint, Brent thought she might be Middle Eastern. Her dress did not indicate that, though; she appeared very Western in a T-shirt and cutoff jeans. The heavyset man lying on his back wore an expensive suit, his white shirt stained deeply with blood. He might have been a heavyweight boxer in his day and might now be a hotel security guard, Brent wasn't sure. The young woman screamed again as he approached.

"It's okay. I'm not here to hurt you."

Gunfire raked along the ground, drawing up on the woman. Brent threw himself forward and hit the ground, shielding her from the salvo. He rolled up and returned fire into the woods as Lakota came around and added her triplet of fire to the fray. Brent's Cross-Com picked out three targets, outlines of each flashing in red, yet all three broke off suddenly, as though they knew they were being watched.

Just then Riggs and Copeland ran forward, out of

breath. Brent shouted for Riggs to stay with the girl, while Copeland dropped to the big man's side, sloughed off his medical pack, and checked for a pulse. None.

"He's already gone." Copeland frowned at the woman. "I'm sorry."

She bit her lip and began to cry.

"Do you speak English?" Brent asked her, realizing that should've been his first question.

"Yes."

"What's your name."

"Warda."

"All right, Warda, get back inside. Don't come out again."

"Are you working for Manoj?"

"Who?"

"Never mind."

"Come on," said Riggs, helping Warda to her feet. "You need to go."

"Get her in there, then get back to me," said Brent, tipping his head for Lakota to join him. "Wait a minute. Riggs? You stay with her." The woman knew something, and Brent decided he would question her later.

Riggs nodded. "On it, Captain."

Lakota cocked a brow. "Can you keep up with me?"

Brent snorted.

Suddenly, she was gone, bulleting down the road.

He cursed and charged after.

Fifty yards later, sweat was already pouring off his face. Lakota could run, he'd give her that, and she showed no signs of slowing. They darted by the main building, its light casting a faint glow over a jagged fence of palms, and then they followed the narrow road as it curved down again toward the beach. Brent was losing his breath. Lakota seemed comfortable, hardly panting. As she tried to kill him with her pace, he divided his attention between the road and his HUD, checking on the two figures and their escape.

"Captain, Lakota, hold up there. Take cover!" Schleck finished his warning a second before the tree line erupted with gunfire.

Targets flashed red in Brent's HUD, reticles zooming in on the red outlines.

Brent was down, and he and Lakota were thinking the same thing as rounds tore through the bushes on either side of them, splintering limbs and echoing loudly off the hills.

They reached into their web gear and withdrew one of their new L12-7 heat-seeking grenades shaped like small missiles.

"'Nades away!" he cried.

They lobbed their grenades, and within a second of leaving their hands small fins popped out, tiny engines ignited, and the devices' explosive payloads were about to be delivered on time, on target, strike three, you're out!

The grenades shot off toward the tree line with a whoosh, whoosh, boom-boom!

The gunfire dropped off to nothing.

"You got 'em," cried Schleck.

Lakota tugged down her balaclava and flashed him a smile. They high-fived and got back on their feet.

This time Brent took lead, but he felt her there, right on his back, and he wondered if she thought he was too slow. He'd show her the "old man" could still run and bounded off down the long, dark stretch, with the sounds of the breakers echoing in the distance.

Stones and scrub pockmarked the rugged dunes above the beach, and the Snow Maiden turned off the main road and ducked behind a row of larger, waist-high rocks, her tennis shoes quickly filling with sand. She wove through rows of tropical plants and coconut trees better known by the locals as *coco de mer*, found a ditch behind one particularly thick patch of hibiscus or something akin, and hunkered down there, unmoving, to catch her breath.

She swallowed. Damn. Haussler had come this close to capturing her. First France and now this. What was wrong with her? Was she, as Patti had suggested, getting too careless? Too tired? Too sick of it all?

Now Haussler would have all the GRU's toys at his disposal: infrared tracking, portable radar, nanobot trackers, you name it. He may have already dusted her with the 'bots. She could not rest for much longer.

Well, at least she'd tagged Chopra. All she had to do now was escape from the German. But who was the woman? Could she be an American member of the Green

Brigade? And if the Brigade was involved, why had they attacked Haussler? Then again, maybe the Russians had not told them about Haussler, so the right hand didn't know what the left hand was doing . . . perhaps the Euros and Americans had new teams after her now?

She checked her own radar and saw that Haussler had turned south up the main road running parallel with the beach. No, he had not dusted her. Not yet.

Her GPS map showed the Lazare Picault hotel lying to the north. From there she'd hail a taxi. There would be no flying off the island. Haussler already had the airport under his lock and key. As much as she dreaded needing the help, the Snow Maiden would need to call Patti to arrange for an exit by sea.

But one last task. From her sling bag she withdrew a battery-operated device that resembled a cell phone. She switched it on and plugged in her height and weight, and the device began to produce a heat source that would be detected by an IR sensor and draw attention. From a distance, the source could be mistaken for a person, although the closer you got, the more readily identifiable the unit became. She left the decoy in the bush and trotted off, nearly running straight into a tall man dressed in a plain green uniform. He had a rifle pointed at her chest.

The man spoke in Russian, obviously his native tongue. "He runs that way, I run this way. I get lucky. He doesn't."

"Oh, really?" she asked, the Russian rolling off her tongue and feeling like an old friend.

"He wants us to take you alive."

"You're Spetsnaz?" she asked.

"The best."

"But you work for Haussler? A German? Then you're just a dog."

He took a step forward. "Put your gun in the dirt."

"I like my gun right here, in my hand."

"Then I'm going to shoot you."

"I thought you were taking me alive."

"I'm going to shoot you in the leg. You have nice legs. Too bad."

He was in the middle of his grin when she shot him in the head so quickly that even she gasped.

His head snapped back, and he thudded to the ground. She seized his rifle, then swore through a chill. It was worse than she'd thought. Haussler had a team of Spetsnaz at his beck and call.

She took a deep breath.

And ran.

SEVEN

Banyan Tree Seychelles Resort
Mahé Island
Republic of the Seychelles

"It's coming from right there," said Lakota, pointing toward a narrow patch of shrubbery cutting across the back side of the dunes like a jagged scar.

They'd been drawing up slowly on the heat source in an attempt to ambush the operator lying in wait. The Cross-Com was still unable to ID friend or foe and superimpose a targeting reticle over the person.

As they drew closer, the signature got weird.

"Fire?" Brent guessed as they shifted farther up into the dunes, then crouched even lower as they neared the source, now glowing brilliantly in their HUDs.

"No, it's not fire," said Lakota. "No scent. No smoke. I think I know what we have here . . ." She moved ahead, leaned over, and picked up the device in her gloved hands.

Brent hurried up beside her. "Wow, decoy."

"Just to slow us down."

"Schleck?" Brent called. "Launch the drone."

"Roger that."

From his vantage point high in the hills, Schleck would activate and send airborne one of Ghost Recon's latest UAV6a Cypher drones, no larger than the size of a Frisbee and equipped with a comprehensive array of high-tech sensors, including chemical and radiation detection. Brent had been holding off on using the device because he never had much luck with them. They'd crash or get whacked by the enemy before he collected any usable data. His colleagues used them with great efficiency, but the gods of technology never smiled down on him. And worse, after each mission he'd have to answer for the cost. It didn't matter whether he was the operator or one of his people. He had no luck, but that excuse wasn't good enough for his superiors.

But what the hell; he'd take another gamble now . . .

"Drone away," announced Schleck.

As Brent and Lakota set out once more, following footprints that still held the slightest trace of a heat source, Schleck said the drone was closing on the enemy operators. There were, according to his count, six men remaining. Although the drone's little motor was relatively silent, Brent knew that if Schleck took the bird in too close, one or more of the bad guys would go duck hunting. He warned Schleck about that.

"Roger that, Captain. Got news on the primary target and pursuer. They've split up. One's heading north, the other south. Not sure who's who, though . . . Would you like me to follow one?"

"Not yet. Stay with the others and report back."

"You got it."

"There's a hotel to the north," said Lakota, reading something in her monocle, assumedly her GPS.

"North it is."

They followed the dunes, the heavy sand beginning to slow them. In the distance, lights from the next hotel glimmered, and it wasn't two minutes later when Brent heard a faint rush of air and knew what was happening.

"Get down!"

He grabbed Lakota by the back of her shirt collar and drove her onto her back, into the sand. The explosion tore into the dunes behind them.

"Captain, I'm sorry, I lost them for a minute. But now you got two guys on your six, one hundred meters out," said Schleck. "Cross-Com says that grenade was a Russian 99Z. These guys are packing the hot stuff."

Brent's head was still spinning from the drop and subsequent burst. Yet he and Lakota rolled over onto their bellies and propped up onto their elbows. Targeting reticles began to float across his HUD.

The enemy operators advanced, drawing up on the next dune. For a moment, Brent got a bead on one, his reticle flashing crimson. He squeezed off a salvo, but the guy dropped quickly back behind the rocks.

"They're trying to slow us down and keep us busy while they get the Snow Maiden," said Lakota.

Brent answered through a groan, "I know."

The second guy was shifting left in an attempt to flank, but Lakota was on him, tracking for a second until she fired three shots, and Brent watched the target fall.

"One more," she said, her voice coming in a near-purr, feline and deadly.

If he hadn't switched his gaze back to the rocks he would've missed sight of the first guy, hurling his next grenade.

Moments like this sometimes came at him in an almost underwater slowness.

But sometimes they came in a hypersensitive way, as though the world were suddenly being fast-forwarded, the contrast jacked up to ten, every sense tingling—which was how he viewed the battle zone now.

He shouted to Lakota and they bolted around the rocks to the next ditch, where, at the foot of a palm, they dropped again, like baseball players diving for home plate.

A rumbling concussion shook the ground. Within the next heartbeat, shattered stone began raining over them in a moment that seemed torn from the Book of Revelation. The 99Z wasn't quite as sophisticated as Ghost Recon's grenades, but the device did have a nasty by-product—if it didn't kill you, it dusted you with nanobot trackers so the next grenade could better lock on.

Knowing this, Brent burst up from his cover and ran directly at the rock face behind which stood their attacker.

This wasn't some foolhardy attempt at bravado, or some selfless act to earn himself a posthumous Medal of Honor.

Brent just knew how to kill this guy: Fight fire with fire.

He already had one of his own grenades in hand, so as the guy popped up to set free his next one, Brent's bomb was already in the air.

The light of that tiny engine streaking away like a frightened firefly was enough to make Brent gasp, "Yes."

It was the single-second moment of surprise that doomed the bad guy. He'd assumed he would finish his prey, came up, and realized he'd been had.

His mouth fell open before the missile-like grenade struck him dead-on in the chest. He exploded in a small conflagration, an arm tumbling here, a leg there.

"Come on!" hollered Lakota.

"On my way!" Brent answered, jogging back toward her.

"Captain, I just spotted the primary target," said Schleck. "I know you said stick with the bad guys, but I just put the drone in tight—and it's definitely her."

The Snow Maiden reached the short wrought-iron fence that marked the perimeter of the hotel grounds. To her right lay the long, circular drive leading up to the valet station and the taxis. To her left stood the entrance to a labyrinthine series of walkways between clusters of bungalows not unlike those found at her own hotel. It was all quite posh and welcoming.

She paused a second, panting, heard the curious hum from above, then glanced up. She cursed in Russian as she frowned at the tiny UFO marking her every move.

No, this wasn't Haussler's doing, was it? The Americans liked to play with these little surveillance robots, but so did the Euros.

She drew her suppressed pistol, steadied herself, and then with a quick twist of her torso she aimed up, expecting the drone to engage in some evasive maneuver.

It didn't.

She fired.

Only after she hit it dead-on did the thing veer left, its motor whining as though it'd been stripped of all grease. She took another shot, dead-on again, and the thing plunged unceremoniously behind the tree canopy. Thump. It crashed somewhere in the forest below. She gave a slight snort and sprinted up the driveway, toward the valet station.

There, she paid one taxicab driver to head to the airport, while she took another cab to make her rendezvous with Patti's people, whom she'd call en route.

The cabdriver was a lean, dark-haired man who seemed more rodent than human. He glanced back and gave her a salacious grin. In broken English, he asked, "Are you on vacation?"

She almost smiled.

By the time Brent and Lakota reached the Lazare Picault hotel, Schleck had already reported that two cars had left approximately five minutes prior. One was heading toward the airport; the other had taken the beach road northward and had then turned into a heavily wooded area, at which time the satellite had lost it. He'd added that the remaining operators had fallen back toward the coastline, collapsing on the head operator, who'd gone south.

"Ghost Lead, this is Hammer," called Dennison. "We've IDed the man in the Snow Maiden's villa as Heinrich Haussler. He's a German spy and double agent. He worked with the Snow Maiden at the GRU. We've reason to believe the GRU has hired him to capture her."

"Wonderful. So now we've got competition. Is he a secondary target? Can I take him out?"

"Absolutely. However, if you can take him alive, he'd be another valuable asset to us."

"Roger that. I'm thinking now she sent a decoy car over to the airport. She'd never go there, but now we've lost her in the forest up north. I don't have any choice. We need to head up there and engage in a ground search."

Brent ordered the rest of his team to pursue Haussler and his remaining men, save for Riggs, who was still holding watch over Warda. Meanwhile, he and Lakota slipped up behind one of the taxicab drivers at the hotel. Trembling over the sight of their weapons, the driver was more than happy to oblige.

They drove up the narrow road, the cab's headlights playing over nothing more than thick foliage to their left, more dunes to their right. Were it not for work, Brent would've had time to admire a spectacular sheet of stars.

Instead, he kept his attention on his HUD and the images coming in from the others' cameras. The foot chase down to the shoreline was going nowhere fast, and

Brent realized that Haussler and his men had such an appreciable lead that if they were making a water exit, they'd reach their craft well before his people could close the gap. Still, you never knew, so he kept the bulldogs running.

He and Lakota eventually ordered the driver to pull over along a secluded part of the road. They zipper-cuffed his wrists and ankles and left him sitting in the sand. Someone would pick him up by morning. Brent even gave him some cash for his trouble, which raised the driver's gap-toothed smile.

Brent and Lakota took off, reached the jungle near the Snow Maiden's last location, and spent the next thirty minutes combing the area. They did, in fact, find her cab—or rather it and its driver found them as it rumbled down a narrow road and nearly ran them over. Brent took aim at the driver and ordered him to stop. Then he wrenched the guy from his seat and demanded answers. His gerbil-like face tightened into a knot. "I dropped her off at the end of the trail. That's all I know. She paid me double."

"Where does the trail lead?" Lakota asked.

"There's a small boat launch."

Brent and Lakota raced back to their taxi and roared off up the trail. The path was barely wide enough for a car, and large fronds dragged across their roof and doors.

Within five minutes they swung to the right and simply ended at a tall stand of palms. Beyond them lay a meager dock rising crookedly against the dark sea.

Empty. They'd missed her.

And Dennison confirmed that. The Snow Maiden had left in a small boat and was met by a larger, high-speed cigar boat that was now streaking away south toward Madagascar. They could follow the boat until it reached the coast, but after that, there was no telling where she'd go. Dennison said she'd seek authority to access one of the JSF's space-based lasers to order a strike on the boat's engine.

Meanwhile, Brent and Lakota would return to the hotel to pick up Riggs and question the woman.

The Snow Maiden was on the phone with Patti, and she'd learned that the second decoy had gone off without a hitch. At the moment, she was lying in the taxicab's trunk. That close call with the Americans had left her breathless, but the cabbie had done his job and she would reward him handsomely, once they got back to the hotel.

Satellites and portable drones made your straightforward escapes all the more complicated, and the routes required stealth, cunning, doubling back, bribery, and whatever other incantations you could conjure up—including some low-tech trunk smuggling that made her feel like a drug runner or illegal border crosser.

Thus, when it came to escape, she had no ego. That she had foiled them was enough. The *how* never amounted to much anyway. You did what you had to do.

She opened the trunk's pass-through and called out to the driver, "Nice job!"

"It's okay. I'm not scared of them. I hope you do not lie to me. I want the rest of the money."

"You'll have it when we get back. You'd better spend it on your family—and not on hookers and booze."

"I will. I promise you."

She had no plans to double-cross the driver. She'd learned he had a family and two small daughters, even if he was lusting after his passengers. She would keep her word. She closed her eyes and remembered the promise she'd made to Nikolai at the moment of his passing: *I will avenge you.*

Chopra's plane wouldn't arrive for another ninety minutes, so he planned to spend the time at Seychelles International Airport, tucked discreetly away in a corner seat. All he could think about was Warda's safety and whether he really would reconnect with the young sheikh. He'd sent Westerdale back to the hotel, and the man had called to say that the police had cordoned off the place and he couldn't get close.

"And let me remind you, Manoj. You'd best retrieve some documentation—if you know what I mean. You cannot waltz into London as Manoj Chopra. You must assume they know who you are. And now they'll believe that if they get to you, they'll get to him."

Chopra sighed deeply. "You're right."

"We've worked together for a while, and I've actually grown fond of you, my friend. Please don't get yourself killed."

"I'll be careful."

At the first sign of local police activity, Brent had ordered Riggs to evac the Banyan Tree—and to take the woman Warda with her. Riggs said it was a bit more complicated than that. Warda had three other women who worked for her, as well as two other bodyguards.

"Bodyguards? Who the hell is she?"

"Somebody important, I guess."

"Well, get the whole party out of there," Brent had ordered.

Another report came in from Schleck regarding Haussler's team. They'd continued to flee south, where they'd boarded a few Zodiacs, taken them directly east, and then simply vanished.

"Say what?"

"The Zodiacs are empty and lying adrift," repeated Schleck.

"Submarine extraction?" Brent guessed.

"Or maybe the rapture," said Schleck. "But I think a sub is more likely."

The team rendezvoused back on their yacht—an eighty-two-foot luxury sailing vessel with a reduced crew of four borrowed from the JSF navy.

Once onboard, Brent was accosted by the Splinter Cells, who demanded to be present while he questioned Warda.

"Let me see if I can soften her up first," he told George.

"Captain, we're experts at interrogation."

"So am I."

"Then let's go."

Brent blocked the man's path. "Too many people will intimidate her."

"Then I'll do it," snapped George.

"We're back to me pulling rank?"

George frowned. "All right, Captain, but you're bound to share everything."

Brent tensed. "Of course."

He met up with the woman belowdecks and was relieved to speak with her alone. It wasn't that he didn't trust Dennison or the Splinter Cells; he didn't trust anyone, and as he'd told George, Warda might zip up with a bunch of hard-faced guys leering at her.

So he wore his best sympathetic look and offered her some tea. He apologized once more for the loss of her friend and bodyguard, then said slowly, "We came to Mahé looking for a woman."

"Can I ask who you are?"

He was impressed by the steel in her tone but kept his soft. "My name is Brent, and I guess it's kind of obvious that I work for the American military."

"Is this an interrogation? Have I been kidnapped?"

"Of course not. We're just here to talk, then you're

free to go, but given recent events, I think you should remain with us. We'll keep you safe."

She probed him with her gaze. "I hope so."

"Believe it."

"So what do you want from me?"

Brent leaned toward her. "You asked if I worked for Manoj. Who's he?"

She took a deep breath and closed her eyes. "I don't think I can say anything else."

"You have to trust me. I know that's not easy, but something's going on here. It's a lot bigger than you and I, and I'm sure you understand that."

"Oh, I understand. But maybe you don't understand how I've lived my life for the past five years. You have no idea. All of this is insane. This is not a life."

"We know who you are," Brent confessed. "And actually, I have orders to protect you at all costs. You want a life? We can give you a new one."

"Really?"

"Really."

"Then prove it to me. Give me your gun."

That drew out his frown. "Warda, I'm a soldier and a pretty good one. I do not give up my weapon. I'm sorry."

She mulled that over. "I guess I should respect that. And you did save me."

"Yeah, I remember that."

"So I'll tell you what you need, then you'll just kill me. Maybe staying quiet is what'll keep me alive."

He gazed deeply into her eyes. "I won't hurt you."

After a moment, she blushed and averted her gaze.

Brent rose and pulled a bottle of water from a small refrigerator. He offered her one, then took a seat and leaned back on the sofa as a knock came at the door. "Who is it?"

"Schleck, sir." The young sniper opened the door and stuck his head inside. "Dennison got a laser on that boat's engines. Nice little fires. If she's onboard, she's hiding below. We're heading over now."

"Excellent."

"What's happening?" asked Warda.

"We're after a woman who's very important to us."

"Will you kill her?"

"I don't want to."

"Why is she so important?"

Brent smiled, unable to tell her, of course. "She came to the Seychelles for a reason. Maybe the same reason you're here. Who's Manoj?"

She pursed her lips and studied him again, as though trying to decide if the color of his eyes made him trustworthy. His gaze grew more emphatic, and he began to nod. "Warda, please, there isn't much time."

"There never is. I used to say that to my father all the time. But he never believed me . . ."

Suddenly she told him everything: who Manoj was, his plans for her country, and the fact that her brother was set to be Dubai's next heir. She told him in rapid fire, as though slowing down would change her mind. He thought he should have recorded the conversation, that it all came at him so quickly he might forget a significant detail. He repeated it to himself: Manoj Chopra was heading to London to make contact with Hussein Al Maktoum, a young man he'd been searching for since the nuclear exchange.

The Snow Maiden was connected to the royal family and connected to Manoj Chopra and Dubai. It was no coincidence that all three were in the Seychelles . . . and Haussler, of course, had come for the party, charged with capturing the Snow Maiden.

Was the Snow Maiden after Warda? Or, perhaps, the young sheikh? Or maybe she was after Chopra, the finance man. He wanted to turn over the bank accounts to the sheikh.

Maybe she wanted the money? Interesting. She had to be working for another entity, but Dennison's intel had turned up nothing on that organization thus far.

After a long sip of water, Brent said, "So you'll come back to London with us—or if you'd like I can arrange to have you taken to the United States, along with your sisters. Maybe you could work things out with our government."

"I'll go to London to be with my sisters. That's where I belong."

"You'll need more protection—better than what you have. They'll use you to get to your brother."

"I know."

"Then let me help with that."

"Okay."

Muffled gunfire from above sent Brent's gaze toward the door.

"More trouble," Warda said.

"Stay here."

Brent rushed up to the deck, where he cried, "What do we got?" as gunfire ripped across the yacht and he dropped behind the gunwale.

"Couple of punks still on the cigar boat," said Lakota.

Brent stole a look out across the starboard bow, where the cigar boat was rising slowly on the waves.

"Gas 'em and board."

Lakota relayed the orders to Daugherty and Heston, who fired CS gas grenades that plopped into the cigar boat's cockpit, hissing and creating a thick column of smoke that sent the thugs leaping overboard. Brent asked the navy boys to bring the yacht up alongside the cigar boat, after which his people climbed onto the sleek craft.

"Sorry, Captain," said Daugherty after a minute's worth of searching. "Looks like another decoy."

EIGHT

Within twelve hours Brent and his team were onboard a V8-99 Sphinx, the next generation of V-TOL troop transport/fighters. According to the Sphinx's designers, many of the problems that had plagued the old V-22 Osprey had been solved, and this new bird was a composite of multiple designs and a complete retooling of that old aircraft.

Despite that, Brent held his breath during the takeoff. That this death trap didn't look much different from the old Osprey further unnerved him. There'd been one particular hard landing in the mountains of Afghanistan that had left him wearing his breakfast. Ah, the good old days . . .

With noise-canceling headphones pressed tightly to his ears and a small boom microphone at his lips, he stared down at the computer screen built into the seat ahead and positioned just above his knees. He said hello to Colonel Pavel Doletskaya.

The gray crew cut, barrel chest, and broad shoulders were stereotypical for a man who'd spent most of his life in the Russian military and intelligence services. A keen sense of competition and pride kept most of those individuals in top shape, more so as they got older because they wanted to prove they were still agile and transformed themselves into athletes comparable to colleagues half their age. That visage of power and prestige was, however, deflated by the baggy orange jumpsuit with a prisoner number emblazoned on his breast. Dennison sat beside him, and it appeared that the conference call was being held in the colonel's prison cell somewhere within JSF headquarters in Tampa. The room was windowless, with a small bunk positioned in one corner and a large stack of books piled ten or twelve high, as though Doletskaya were plowing daily through a ton of material. Access to electronic texts must have been forbidden or limited.

The old Russian cocked a brow. "Hello, Captain. It's my understanding that you came very close to capturing her."

Brent carefully measured his words and his tone. "Not close enough, sir, but I'm confident we'll bring her in."

"Pride cometh before the fall, Captain. You won't get her without my help."

Brent repressed a shrug. "I will say she's one of the best escape artists I've ever seen, except for a few *muhajadeen* I met while in the 'Stan. She knows how to misdirect and set up those decoys, that's for sure."

"Oh, I can assure you, Captain, she's much better than anyone you've ever met. You'll see."

"I hope I don't. We'll get her in London. What's she after? The boy? Maybe we can get two steps ahead and set up an ambush."

The Russian turned to Dennison and grinned darkly. "You've sent a butcher to capture an artist."

"No, I've sent an unconventional thinker. Now then, Captain Brent, we know that Chopra is trying to find Hussein. And we think the Snow Maiden may be after the boy as well. Find the boy and we find the Snow Maiden."

"It's that simple," Brent said sarcastically. "Now what about Warda? She give us anything else?"

"She won't tell us where her brother is, and I don't blame her, so we'll have to tail Chopra. We have to assume he's gone undercover as well, so it's going to take me a while to pick him up. Once we do, you'll need to move quickly."

"I understand, but that seems to preclude any chance of an ambush. We need to get ahead of them, not chase."

"In a perfect world, Captain," snapped Dennison. "At least the Voecklers will arrive in London ahead of you. They'll remain with Warda and her sisters until we pick up Chopra. I've worked out a deal with the Brits to provide a security force for Warda and her sisters, once we're gone."

Brent nodded and directed his gaze to Doletskaya. "Colonel, is there anything else you can tell me about our target? I mean something not in the files, something you think might help us catch her?"

The old colonel simpered. "If she's going to London, you might find her at a little pub called the Bread and Roses on Clapham Manor. It's run by a trades union council and associated with the Workers' Beer Company. They raise money for workers' rights causes. She always fought for the little guy, donated money to lots of causes, cancer research, and many others. She'll be in the big beer garden out back."

"Why didn't you tell us this sooner?" Dennison asked the colonel.

"It didn't occur to me until he asked."

Dennison shook her head in disgust. "Brent, I'll get some people there a-sap."

He nodded. "And I'll send two as soon as we land."

Doletskaya snorted. "Good luck."

"Sir, can I ask you something? You seem willing to help us capture her, but you doubt we will. She's just an individual on the run, and I don't care how many resources she has. Eventually, she'll make a mistake. And we'll bring her in."

Doletskaya's lips curled in amusement. "Captain, I've spent enough time with Viktoria to know there are few people in this world who can stop her. If by some miracle you do happen to accidentally capture her, I believe she will have surrendered and that it would have nothing to do with your skills. Her cunning is unmatched."

Brent returned a lopsided grin. "Thank you for the vote of confidence, sir."

Dennison told Brent to stand by while she spoke off camera with the colonel. He couldn't hear what they were saying, and after a moment, Dennison returned while the colonel was escorted out of the cell by two armed guards.

"Major, you really think that old man can help us?" Brent asked. "What if he's lying?"

"He's not. At least not entirely. He's already helped with a number of items and issues."

"It's my understanding that he had a relationship with the Snow Maiden. What makes you think he's not still working with her?"

Dennison smiled. "You're sharp, Captain, no matter what they say about you."

Brent grinned himself. "Are you setting him up?"

"Of course. We'll give him enough bait . . . see if he tries to contact her. That'll give us her location as well—and I know the Voecklers will continue questioning Warda. She still doesn't trust us, but if she'd just give in, we could end this quickly and set up that ambush."

"Can I ask you something? Once we capture the Snow Maiden, do you really think she'll talk?"

"I don't know. But it's clear she poses a major threat to the JSF and the Euros. She's even working against her own government—and that's what really scares me. Now Captain, I need for you to capture her in London. Do you understand what I'm saying?"

Brent shrugged. "Yeah."

He remembered the five-minute meeting he'd had

with her, just before they'd taken off. Her words were off the record, and they had stung:

"You've done some exceptional work in Special Forces and earned your recruitment into Ghost Recon. There's no denying that. You did a fine job up in Canada during the Russian invasion, but since then it's been downhill. I'm just saying that this operation has to go by the numbers—for both of us. I can't promise you what'll happen if you lose her in London. I just can't."

"Ma'am, what're you saying?"

"I'm saying there's no room for mistakes like failing to check that taxi. She slipped away once. That can't happen again."

"Otherwise, I'm gone."

"They were thinking about removing you from Ghost Recon before I brought you on board for this."

"Are you kidding me?"

"No. I'm taking a risk on you because I need someone who's got more at stake than just a mission. I'll be honest. I figure that if your whole career depends on capturing the Snow Maiden, you'll probably get the job done. Some of your colleagues have less to lose—but you've got it all."

"I don't believe this . . ."

"I'm sorry, Captain. They could even bust you down to the regular Army. I can make recommendations, but ultimately it'll be their call."

"So, if we don't get her in London, I'm done."

"Don't think of it that way. Think of it as your chance

to bring in the world's most dangerous woman and earn a reputation for yourself as one of Ghost Recon's top operators."

"So it's all or nothing."

Brent tensed as Dennison now nodded and said, "I'll be in touch once you're on the ground."

He returned the nod, and she abruptly broke the link.

All he could do was sit there, the seat straps feeling as though they were tightening like a boa curled around his shoulders and back, ready to suffocate him.

He'd dedicated his entire life to service. He'd tried his best to be a good soldier, a good man, and to atone for his sins. He'd tried to set the world right by taking another man's place. And now they were presenting the ultimatum, as though they'd seen through him, knew that his heart hadn't truly been in it from the beginning, that he'd joined the Army out of guilt, and that he wasn't destined to retire as a Ghost Recon operator. He couldn't fool them anymore. And now they were giving him enough rope to hang himself.

All right. You didn't get into Ghost Recon without rising to the top of SF, he told himself. He needed a stronger bond with his people. He needed them more than ever now, and he wondered how forthright he should be. *"If we don't get her in London, I'm done."* Would that inspire confidence in them, or would that place them under more pressure?

They needed to hear something. Once they landed, the operational tempo would pick up, and there'd be no time for idle chatter. He unbuckled and rose from his seat, turning back to face the group, seated in pairs down the long aisle.

"Ladies and gentlemen," he began.

They, like him, also wore headphones and microphones and were patched into the intercom, so they could hear each other over the tremendous booming of the Sphinx's engines.

"I just finished my briefing with Major Dennison. Although we had some complications in the Seychelles, she's confident we can get the Snow Maiden in London— and so am I."

Lakota raised her hand. "Sir, honestly, I think it'll be more difficult to get her now. Big city. So many places to hide. We haven't even dusted her. And we need to worry about Haussler's people on our back. I'm just thinking this whole op belongs to the NSA and not us."

"We're unconventional fighters. That means one minute we're spies, the next we're stand-up warriors. We think, move, shoot, communicate, adapt, and drink beer." He winked at the group and got a few quick chuckles.

Then he added, "I know you're worried about this. We need a win. But I want to tell you that I couldn't have been more impressed with your performance on Mahé."

Noboru lifted a finger and said, "Captain, I know we did a good job—based on the limited information we had—but the mission failed. Not sure how impressive that is."

Brent stared a moment into the Japanese man's frown, then quickly responded: "I wrote it up as, 'Due to circumstances beyond our control and limited intelligence, we arrived at the target location too late to run either an ambush or an effective blocking operation.' We couldn't control that. And I'm not focusing on losing the target. I'm talking about what we did do . . ."

"I thought we rocked the house," said Riggs, wriggling her brows at the others, even turning around so those behind her could see. "We took out nearly half that Spetsnaz team—and not a single one of us took a hit."

"Hoo-ah!" cried Heston.

"You're damned right we did good," said Brent. "Now we're going to drop into London and do it again. It's not the misses that count; it's the hits."

"So we're back to wearing civilian clothes, packing very light, and running tight surveillance," said Heston with his Texas drawl.

"I know you'd all prefer a stand-up fight. But you've been around long enough to know how it goes. I'm counting on every one of you to give one hundred and ten percent here." Brent lifted his voice. "Are you with me?"

They all cried in unison, "Sir, yes, sir!"

Brent held up a fist, shook it, then returned to his seat and closed his eyes. He was trembling.

About fifteen minutes before they were set to land, Lakota took the chair beside Brent. She motioned for him to turn on his intercom to channel three so they could talk privately.

"What's up?" he asked.

"I'll help you."

"That's nice," he said, unable to disguise his sarcasm. "I was kind of hoping for that."

"You know what I mean."

He gave her a look. "Uh, I don't."

"Rumors get around, and I'm sure your briefing with Dennison didn't go so well. Here's what I think. I think she told you if we fail in London, it's all over for us. They'll break up the team again, and as for you . . . I don't know . . . but she gave you the ultimatum, right?"

"What are you? A fortune-teller?"

"You're just like my ex-husband. Easy to read. When he was trying to tell me he wanted a divorce, I'd already had the papers drawn up."

"Ouch."

"For him, not for me."

"Sorry about that."

"I'm sorry you haven't asked about it. That's your problem, Captain. You need to be more nosy. You need to know us better. Pry. I mean, you haven't even hit on me."

"Are you crazy? I respect your privacy."

"We don't want it respected. Ask about our personal lives. There isn't a hell of a lot there anyway. This is pretty much all we got. But ask."

Brent shrugged. "Well, I guess I shouldn't be telling you this, but you're right. I'm hanging on by a thread here."

"And like I said, we'll help. You were good back on the island. I'm proud to serve with you. We just need to get her in London."

Brent took in a long breath. "Yes, we do."

She was about to get up, but he stopped her. "Thanks. I can't do it without you . . . or them. I know that."

She winked. "Tell them."

By the time Lakota made it back to her seat, their pilot was on the intercom, his voice tense. "Sorry, guys, but we've just been diverted to RAF Lakenheath."

"Why's that?" asked Brent.

"It doesn't sound good," answered the pilot.

"What's happening?" Brent demanded.

"The Russians have some heavy troop transports en route."

"They're coming here? They're crazy."

"I thought the same thing. I don't know if it's an occupying force or what, and they've got fighters in the air. The Brits are worried about shooting them down because of collateral damage. Hold on a second. We've been locked! We've been locked!"

Suddenly, the Sphinx banked hard right, and Brent felt his stomach slam into his ribs.

"Oh my God," gasped the pilot. "Brace for impact!"

NINE

Sandhurst, England

Warda had told Chopra that according to her father's wishes, Hussein would be given lessons in all the major subjects by officers from the Royal Military Academy at Sandhurst, commonly known as Sandhurst. These officers would tutor the boy at a small, nondescript home on the outskirts of the town, where he would reside for nine months out of the year. The tutoring had begun last year, when Hussein had turned fifteen. Prior to that he'd been moved every few months and instructed by a select few teachers who traveled with him. The boy's father had wanted him to be formally trained and educated, and he'd always had great respect and admiration for the British education system and for its military officers; thus, he'd left specific instructions for Hussein's preparations to become a well-rounded individual.

The e-mails and videos from her father were difficult to read and watch, and Warda had spent many days crying over them. It seemed that in the months prior to the nuclear exchange, tensions had grown so high that her father had actually been planning for his own death and preparing as much as he could for the survival of his country. However, most of his wishes had been thrown by the wayside when, for the most part, the people who would have enacted them had also been killed during that fateful and horrible day.

With Westerdale's help, Chopra had obtained excellent documentation and two things to alter his appearance: He'd bought a much thicker pair of plastic frames instead of his usual ultralight titanium glasses, and he had shaven his head completely bald. He typically wore a short, conservative haircut, his salt-and-pepper locks parted to one side and held in place with a squirt of hair spray. Now he was bald with thicker glasses and resembled an overage punk rocker or insecure artist type. Looking in the mirror proved unsettling.

Westerdale had also reported that Warda was now in the hands of the Americans, which was, for the most part, not a bad stroke of luck. He doubted they would hold her against her wishes and suggested that Chopra share this news with Hussein or Hussein's people so that they might attempt to locate her.

Chopra arrived at London Heathrow Airport and caught a black cab out to Shepperton, where he changed cabs again, then headed down to Windlesham and did likewise once more, all in an effort to thwart anyone trying to tail him. He instructed the last driver to pull up outside the Premier Inn, where at such time a nondescript sedan was waiting for him. He paid the driver and climbed into the other car.

Ironically, he recognized the sedan's driver, a white-haired man named John Southland, an American who had been working for the Al Maktoum family for decades as a professional mechanic and driver.

"Mr. Chopra, it's been a long time," said Southland.

"Much too long," answered Chopra, growing a bit misty-eyed. "I thought you'd been killed."

"They sent me away early with the children. I urged them to come, but they insisted on staying. He thought if he evacuated he would be deemed a coward by the people. And he paid for that with his life. But we are still here and have been with the children ever since."

"And how many others?"

"Just four of us. And two more with the sisters. They have an apartment nearby."

"You've done an excellent job of protecting them."

"We didn't do it alone. And I've heard that everything could change now. We are understandably concerned."

Chopra took a long breath. "I have what is rightfully his. And he, under the guidance of a regent, can now assume leadership of the country."

"The Americans are calling Dubai the Wild West. No rule, with refugees moving in and out, and radiation still a problem. You are handing him a garbage heap."

"No. Dubai will rise again. This needs to happen."

"The Russians will not be happy."

"That's why we must protect him."

"I'm confused, Manoj. It's not even your country."

"You're wrong. I wouldn't have a life if it weren't for them. I'm a man of two countries. Hussein will rebuild his nation, our nation."

Southland chuckled under his breath. "You'll have fun convincing him of that."

"Oh, really?"

"You'll see. He's not the boy you remember."

They fell silent as Southland took them to the Owls-moor section of Sandhurst and turned down Horsham Road to park beside a four-bedroom detached house similar to an American townhome. These were mod-est quarters for the young sheikh, but that was part of remaining subtle and keeping a lower profile here in Europe. Time spent away in places like the Seychelles was obviously another matter.

As he climbed out of the car, Chopra frowned over the deep thrumming that emanated from the house, and as he followed Southland toward the side-entrance door, the thrumming became a distinctly deep and steady pulse.

"He likes to listen to his music in the morning," said Southland.

"What about headphones?" asked Chopra.

Southland rolled his eyes. "Oh, we've tried . . ."

Once inside, Chopra winced at the booming and shouting coming from an upstairs bedroom. He wasn't sure if they called it rap or hip-hop or had invented some new term, but the sounds were headache-producing, the language unabashed.

They moved into the kitchen area, where seated around the table were two men and a woman, again all of them middle-aged and familiar to Chopra. The leaner man and the woman were private tutors, and the other, more stocky man was one of the family's personal body-guards. Chopra had forgotten his name but remembered that he'd retired from the Saudi Ministry of Defense and Aviation.

He greeted them, but they were, in a word, cold, barely glancing up from their toast and cereal, which smelled wonderful since all he'd had was bitter airport coffee.

"I'm sorry," said Southland. "We don't quite agree with what's happening here."

"Why is that?" asked Chopra.

"Because he's not ready for such responsibility," said the woman.

Chopra glanced at her emphatically. "He's sixteen. We all know the story of Sheikh Maktoum bin Buti."

Southland snorted. "We're living in much different times."

"History repeats itself," said Chopra. "He, too, will rise back to power."

"Maktoum bin Buti was very young, yes, but he was courageous. Hussein is a product of the computer age, bloated with information and blinded by his own desires for stimulus and pleasure."

This eloquent argument had come from the female teacher, and her surname finally came to Chopra: Werner. Mrs. Werner, a British college professor who'd been swept up out of graduate school to work exclusively with Hussein and his sisters.

"I didn't come to debate this," said Chopra. "I need to speak with him. I need to remind him of who he is and what I've been protecting for all these years."

"You're an idealist, Chopra," Werner said, staring up at him over the rim of her glasses. "And I hope you've braced yourself for disappointment."

"You're making him out to be a monster. He's a sixteen-year-old boy."

The volume on the stereo upstairs suddenly spiked, and Southland lifted his voice like an irate father. "Hussein, that is much too loud!"

The volume increased further.

After a deep breath, Chopra headed for the staircase. He wound his way up to the first landing, and the music became so loud that he thought his eyes would begin to tear. He found the nearest bedroom door at the top and gave a loud knock.

No answer. He knocked again, much more loudly, and when the door swung open, Chopra took one look and remained there, aghast . . .

The Snow Maiden had just finished launching her own surveillance drone, which separated into four distinct modules, each sensor no larger than her thumb and attaching itself to the house. She'd just finished listening to Chopra speak to the boy's staff, and she decided that she would move soon to catch them all in one place, when they were most vulnerable.

She was crouched behind Southland's car as the man came outside to fetch the newspaper.

She took a deep breath and reached out with all of her senses.

If someone had been electronically monitoring her heart rate and respiration, the numbers would've barely risen. By the time she'd joined the GRU, she'd stopped counting the number of people she had killed. If you asked her, "Do you remember that night in Cairo when you had to take out that man just before he got in the cab?" she would squint into that memory. The kills had become routine—an ugly word when it came to death—but she hoped they'd remain that way. Without emotion or guilt to cloud her judgment or delay her performance, she could operate efficiently, robotically even. No drama—just the elimination of obstacles.

She got to work.

The neighbors would be heading out soon, and she scanned the doorways before acting.

Clear.

After a barely appreciable thump, Southland collapsed from a perfectly timed and executed head shot. She dragged his body behind the car and left it there, out of sight from the street or adjacent doorways. She fetched the newspaper and held it up in front of her face as she entered the side door.

"What the hell are they reporting on now?" came a man's voice. Ah, yes, the bodyguard.

She lowered the paper, and in its place came her suppressed pistol. The bodyguard swallowed her first round. The teachers met her entrance with wide eyes and open mouths, as though they were hungry, too. She shrugged. Her gaze lifted to the ceiling. Indeed, the boy's music helped muffle any sign of commotion.

Two more shots. The male teacher snapped back, then fell forward into his bowl of cereal. The other fell sideways off her chair. The Snow Maiden neared the table and snatched up a piece of the woman's toast. Peach jam. Yummy.

Her phone vibrated. She checked the screen: a message from Patti. *You'd better move. You've got trouble.*

The missile struck the port-side engine, and the explosion sent the Sphinx banking hard and losing altitude. As the others swore and screamed, Brent thought, *Well, all that worrying over my career was a waste of time. And the engineers who designed this contraption probably haven't addressed the old autorotation issue that I'd been hearing about, so we're dead.*

But then the aircraft leveled off and the pilot got on the horn to say he had control.

That was the only good news.

In a voice tense and breathless he added that they were still coming down hard and fast and losing hydraulic fluid. Belly flopping like a five-hundred-pound man into an inflatable pool might be the best that he could do.

Brent checked one of the windows, a new addition to the Sphinx, and noted their angle of descent and the farmers' fields splayed out before them. A pair of fighter jets raced by before he could identify them. He wanted to ask the pilot if he had any more information, but thought better of it. Let the guy focus on landing.

"Who's praying with me?" cried Heston. "I'm not ready to meet Jesus, and I say we tell him that!"

"Get in crash positions," ordered Brent. "Remember your training."

As he listened to Heston's prayer and leaned forward to place his head between his legs to, of course, kiss his butt good-bye, the Sphinx turned again, as though riding on broken rails like an old mining car. The shuddering began at the back of the aircraft and worked its way forward, as though a fault line were opening in the steel deck.

The pilot shouted something, his voice now burred by frustration. Brent strained to hear him, but the intercom cut off into static as the stench of jet fuel began filtering into the cabin. Oh, that was not good.

"Masks on!" Brent shouted above the din.

They fished out the O_2 masks from their packs and slid them over their faces. These were not attached to the Sphinx but self-contained and man-portable units that Brent always carried when he flew the not-so-friendly skies. The oxygen flow came immediately and cleared the stench of fuel. Brent dug his fingers into his palms and kept seeing fireballs—a Corvette exploding, nuclear mushroom clouds rising, as Dennison's voice came in a whisper, *"It's over. You're finished."*

The Sphinx dropped as though hitting another air pocket, and the straps dug into Brent's shoulders. His stomach now greeted his ears. The engines shifted pitch, whining now like lawn mowers burning pure alcohol. A sudden clunk from the deck indicated that the pilot was lowering the gear, but a redundant clunking alarmed Brent. He remembered that hydraulic leak. He chanced a quick look up at the window. The port engine was on fire, trailing smoke, but the drone suggested the rotor was still functional.

It would be fitting, Brent thought, if he died in a ball of flames as Villanueva had. His death would be the other bookend. Maybe that was his fate, and he was just walking toward the open door.

Another dip that made him feel weightless, and the panic rose from his gut and burned. The Sphinx now sounded like a freight train that was derailing and plunging over a cliff.

Place your tray tables in the upright position.

And prepare for "landing."

When drunks get in car accidents many of them walk away because at the time of impact, their bodies are fully relaxed. They take the hit and conform more naturally to the trauma. Those who tense up and have white-knuckled grips at the moment of impact tend to be the worst off. Brent knew that. He'd talked to medics, seen crash victims, been told about relaxing into an impact.

So part of him said, *Clear your mind and let it happen*, that if he could imagine himself as a rag doll he could better survive the impact.

His more logical side argued that he was about to die and a death grip on the seat or straps was the only response. Fight or flight. You can't deny instinct, deny nature.

Brent's ex-girlfriend had been right; he should have left the Army as she'd wanted. Somer had spent three years trying to convince him, while he'd fallen deeply in love with her. She was in love with him, too, but not in love with his career. He'd kept saying, "You knew this going in. If you couldn't marry a soldier, why'd you get involved in the first place?"

"I got involved with a man who happened to be a soldier."

And she'd just cried and wondered why she had.

Their three years together—really eighteen months since he'd spent the other half deployed—had taught Brent one sad and rather trite lesson: Don't get involved. It wasn't worth it. He admired those colleagues who could maintain families despite the challenges; he just wasn't one of them because the time and distance turned him cold and he couldn't switch on his feelings just like that. And if he'd just listened to Somer, he'd be at home in California, probably working some day job that didn't thrill him, but he'd be with her; they'd have a small house or apartment, a couple of kids, and on the weekends they'd buy ice cream cones at the galleria. Was that such a terrible life?

Now he would die like a filthy dog, probably burned alive as the jet fuel washed over him and the flames licked their way up his spine.

Damn, why was he being such a pessimist? The team needed him now, despite the fact that their lives were in the hands of the pilots, and there wasn't a damned thing they could do about that—except remain hopeful instead of resigning themselves to death.

He took a long breath, then shouted at the top of his lungs: "All right, everybody! We're Ghost Recon! We don't die in crashes! The runway comes to us!"

"Hoo-ah!" they cried, a bit halfheartedly.

"I can't hear you!"

This time they shouted with everything they had, and just the sheer volume of their voices made it easier to pretend they were still in control.

Sheikh Hussein Al Maktoum glared at Chopra as he tossed his long, curly hair out of his eyes. Then the boy returned the baseball cap to his head and positioned it so the brim jutted cockily to one side.

The oversized black T-shirt that said GANG WARZ in purple text, the hoop earring in one ear, and the large gold necklaces he wore were not quite as surprising as the black tattoo of barbed wire running across the young man's forearm.

He was a Muslim. Tattoos were forbidden, or at least Chopra understood that they were. Hopefully the tattoo was not real, a decal that would wash away.

"You're not from Sandhurst," Hussein hollered, his accent distinctly British.

"Turn down the music!" cried Chopra. "I need to speak with you! You don't remember me?"

Hussein made a face, pushed open the door, and allowed Chopra to enter.

To say the boy was a pack rat wildly understated it.

Stacks of movies, books, and video games rose along nearly every wall, forming a mottled wainscot of spines and rising in testament to a young life spent consuming all that was commercial and, in Chopra's humble opinion, all that was deplorable about society.

Framed posters on the wall depicted more of the boy's thug heroes: shirtless men making obscene gestures while scantily clad women clutched their waists and knelt at their sides to pay homage. At least three flat-screen TVs hung from the upper walls, and every conceivable game console on the market sat on the floor below them: elaborate headsets encrusted with a spaghetti of wires along with high-tech gloves and a rug of some sort that was also wired to an antenna.

In the far corner of this teenager's nest stood a small refrigerator beside which was a shelf loaded with junk food: chips, crackers, cookies, and assorted candy. Those dietary choices certainly accounted for the young sheikh's puffy cheeks and the paunch he attempted to hide beneath his baggy shirt and jeans. Chopra also noted the boy's expensive sneakers made in Vietnam of some space-age fluorescent material that shimmered like blue-green algae.

Now wearing a deeper frown, Hussein sauntered over

to a tiny box on one shelf and suddenly lowered the music with a remote he snatched off the top, but even as he turned back to face Chopra, he was mouthing the words of the song.

"Hussein, you don't remember me?" Chopra repeated.

"Maybe. Like maybe you worked with my father or something. What do you want, old man? Are you one of the new tutors? You don't look like an officer."

Chopra motioned to a pair of overstuffed leather recliners from where Hussein played his video games. "Please sit. We have a lot to discuss. You don't know how long I've been waiting for this moment."

"Frankly, I don't care. I'm hungry. And the two dolts who tutor me will be here soon. I don't have time for this. I'm hungry!"

"Hussein, listen to me. I hold the keys to helping you rebuild your country. But it's up to you. Do you understand what I'm saying?"

He stood there a moment, scrutinizing Chopra. Then something occurred to him and he burst into laughter. "What the hell? Is Southy playing a joke on me?" He moved toward the door and lifted his voice. "Southy! What the hell is this?"

"Hussein, please sit down."

The boy's face screwed up into a knot. "Old man, I have no clue what you want, but this isn't funny anymore. Get out of my room." He cocked a thumb toward the doorway. "And tell those bastards downstairs they'd best have my breakfast ready!"

Chopra lowered his head and sighed deeply, and when he looked up, a woman stood behind the young sheikh—

The same woman Chopra had seen in the Seychelles. Short, dark hair. Lean, muscular. Penetrating eyes. Jeans and tight-fitting leather jacket.

Wearing a smug expression, she held a pistol with large suppressor to the back of the boy's head.

"Hussein, don't move," gasped Chopra.

But the boy whirled to face the woman. "Who the hell are you?" He glanced at the gun. "And what is this? How dare you wave that piece in my face? How dare you!"

Chopra nearly fainted as Hussein slapped away the woman's pistol and shouted, "Southy, what in bloody hell is going on here! Who are these freaks? You're going to pay for this charade! I'm telling you right now! This is the last time you play a joke on me!"

But even as he finished, the woman seized him by the neck, slammed the door behind her, and forced him into the room and toward the recliner beside Chopra.

Though her weapon sent a chill through him, Chopra rose immediately from his chair and shouted, "You will not hurt him! Do you hear me?"

"You sit down!" she screamed.

Then she jammed her pistol into Hussein's head and spoke between her teeth. "Now listen to me carefully, little boy. Your friends are all dead. And you're going to do exactly as I say, if you want to stay alive." She spoke English with a Russian accent, an accent that took Chopra's breath away. God, the Russians were already on to them.

"This isn't a joke?" Hussein asked, his voice cracking.

The woman widened her eyes. "Do I look like I'm joking?"

"Who are you? What do you want?" Chopra demanded.

Slowly, she removed her weapon from Hussein's head, and then she suddenly backhanded Chopra, her leather glove dragging across his cheek. His glasses flew across the room and he groaned, his own palm going reflexively for the pain.

"Quiet, old man. I do all the talking now. You want to know who I am? Well, they call me the Snow Maiden."

TEN

**Joint Strike Force V8-99 Sphinx
En Route to London**

The Sphinx jolted forward as the pilot decreased power to both engines and Brent began a mental countdown, believing he could estimate their altitude.

Who was he fooling? He was counting just to keep his mind off their impending doom. Smoke obscured all view through the window, but it seemed they would hit the ground at any second. They weren't kidding when they said the waiting was the hardest part. Something buffeted the Sphinx, and he wondered if they'd just taken some fire or hit a downdraft.

Whether they had actually reached RAF Lakenheath remained to be seen. Any solid ground would do for now. He was rooting for the pilot the way he rooted for the Dodgers: with balled fists and pure fury, even when the team was down by ten runs and most fans had already left after the seventh inning. Brent would shove his fourth Dodger dog into his mouth, rise, and with a mouth full of mustard, relish, and hot dog, scream, "Come on, you bums, score a freaking run!"

Their forward momentum began to decrease as the bird pitched forward and descended even more. Brent thought of stealing one more glance through the window to see if the smoke had cleared, but that thought was lost on a terrific boom resounding from the cockpit.

The racket swept over the craft.

And Brent realized they'd struck the ground and were scraping forward because the gear had not fully lowered and locked into place.

That boom had been the gear snapping off.

They began to fishtail like a sports car driver accelerating too hard—and Brent was too familiar with that sensation.

Thrown right, then left, he tightened his grip on the seat rails as the fuselage floor buckled beneath his boots. The cacophony of the impact was muffled only by the sound of his panting into the oxygen mask.

At once a massive crack opened in the deck, and a large piece of the landing gear—one of the wheel arms—burst up into the hold, severed hydraulic lines dancing like bleeding snakes as the nails-on-chalkboard scraping continued.

Brent glanced over at his people, expecting them to be praying some more or cursing or screaming or doing something that would indicate that they were railing against their fate—or at the very least, afraid to die. But there was none of that now. They eyed each other and nodded. They'd had good lives. Done good work. Made a difference. And screw it, if today was the day, they would take it like warriors. Just take it.

In that moment, as he seemed to hang there between worlds, between life and a sudden and horrific death, he never felt more proud of a team. He took a deep breath.

If I'm going to die, then bring it. I'm in good company.

And then, quite suddenly . . .

It was over.

The Sphinx burrowed itself into the earth and came to a sudden halt, lying there, somewhere, creaking, the engines still groaning but winding down—as opposed to Brent's heart, which jackhammered in his chest.

His ears betrayed him for a moment. The world went muffled, almost silent.

And then it hit: the fear of fire and explosion. And the racket returned, the volume on ten. "On your feet! On your feet!" he cried. "Lakota, blow the exit door! Everybody evac right now! Right now!"

Brent unbuckled from his seat and rose, counting off his people as Lakota worked the release mechanism on the side door and the hatch yawned open.

The pilot and co-pilot hustled through the cabin and joined the group. The co-pilot was nursing her left arm but seemed otherwise okay. Everyone was on the ready line to pile out, everyone except the quiet man, Park. Brent saw him still seated in his chair and unmoving. He raced past the line as the others shifted out. He got to

Park, found him unconscious, felt his neck for a carotid pulse and got one. Brent wasn't sure if the fumes had gotten to him or something else, but he unstrapped the guy and took him up in a fireman's carry. With his knees buckling, he turned for the doorway—

To find a wall of flames blocking his path.

With a gasp, he realized the fire wasn't coming from inside the Sphinx.

The words slipped from his mouth. "Oh my God . . ."

Their hot landing and even hotter exhaust had set fire to the brown grass field outside. It was midsummer, and parts of the U.K. had been suffering a record drought. The others had made it out seconds before the ground beneath them burst into flames.

Brent's worst nightmares regarding an explosion would not play out. He wouldn't die in a crash and fireball like Villanueva had. He'd die in a grass fire created by the ninety-three-million-dollar taxicab in which he'd been a passenger.

You call that a blaze of glory? Aw, if he died, he'd go to customer service with his receipt for a life well lived and ask God for a refund. He deserved a much more dramatic death.

Then again, he was assuming he'd go upstairs instead of downstairs, where the fires of hell would be fueled by the gas tanks of a million burning Corvettes.

He lowered Park to the deck, his gaze sweeping the compartment for a fire extinguisher.

There! On the wall ahead, near the entrance to the cockpit. He darted for the long red cylinder and tugged it free from its rubberized holder. Smoke now billowed into the hold and burned his eyes. He pulled the extinguisher's pin as he swung around toward the flames.

The air raid sirens came as a muffled hum from somewhere outside, beyond the boy's room, and the Snow Maiden paused a moment to prick up her ears and listen.

Patti had warned her about trouble—but nothing quite as dramatic. Were the Russians making a move? She'd expected the Americans or Haussler to show up . . .

"Is the city under attack?" asked Chopra.

"Those sirens go off a lot," said the boy. "Usually just a warning."

The Snow Maiden cocked a brow. "Not this time."

"How do you know?" the boy asked.

"I know. Both of you—up. We're leaving."

"Where are we going?" Chopra demanded.

It didn't matter if he knew, so she just told him the truth. "Geneva."

"Geneva? Why there?"

"I know a good restaurant for lunch. Now quiet. Let's move." She motioned with her pistol toward the door.

"I'm not going anywhere," said Hussein, rubbing his neck. "You can't kidnap me. That's ridiculous. That's probably not even a real gun."

She grinned. "You're right. This is ridiculous. And I have no use for you, so . . ." She moved toward him, raised the pistol, and felt pretty comfortable about putting a bullet in his head.

"Please," cried Chopra. "You have no idea who . . . I mean, he's just . . . he's a boy. There's no need to kill him. Hussein, you will come with us!"

The kid snorted. "Yeah, right."

Chopra began to lose his breath. "Hussein, we'll go with her now."

"You heard me, old man. I'm staying."

The Snow Maiden couldn't believe what she was hearing from this little punk bastard. She walked up to him, smiled, then quickly punched him in the face so hard that he fell back onto the floor. Then she fired a round not three inches from his kneecap. The bullet burrowed into the floor. "Now get up. You're coming!"

He looked at her, at the gun, then began shaking and struggling to his feet. Chopra went to him, and together they ambled to the door.

She predicted they would gasp when they viewed the carnage she had wrought in the kitchen.

They gasped.

And she needed no further demonstration that she was a woman of her word, that she would kill them if they didn't cooperate.

She'd parked her rental car around the corner but decided on the spot that they would take Southland's sedan and make at least one more car exchange that she'd arrange with Patti. She dug into the dead man's pocket, tugged out his keys, and ordered Chopra and the boy into the car, with Chopra at the wheel. She and the boy climbed into the backseat.

"Just get us out of here. Now," she ordered. "South, toward Dover."

He started the car and pulled out. She kept the pistol aimed at the back of his head and flicked her gaze to the boy. "All right, I want to know everything."

Before Chopra could answer, engines roared overhead, and she leaned down to watch a squadron of fighter planes streaking away.

"Something's happening," said Chopra. "Something very big and very bad."

"What do you want with us?" asked Hussein.

She rolled her eyes at him. "You're just baggage."

"You want him?" The boy sounded confused.

"Chopra, why don't you tell him about the secrets you carry? You're one of the last keys left. Maybe the only one. From what I've read, the boy's father was very paranoid that way, and there were very few who knew."

The boy snorted. "What're you talking about?"

"Come on, Chopra, tell him why I've come," she urged the old man.

"She's here because the Russians want what is left of Dubai for their own. They think they can decontaminate the oil and gain even more control over the European market. But they're overzealous fools, and they'll suffer another defeat—even worse than their invasion of Canada."

"You think I'm working for the Russians?" she asked, almost chuckling. "No worries there, old man. Those days are long gone. Long gone."

"Then who are your employers, and what do they want?"

"We know about the secret reserves. We know about the gold. And you'll get us into the vault."

"So you've come to rob Dubai of what little it has left? That won't happen. Dubai will rise again. And I'll die before I see you inside the vault."

She took a long breath. "You'll come around. A man like you does not respond well to torture."

"He's not the only one who can get you into the vault."

"Shut up, boy, you're bluffing."

"What I mean to say is yes, there aren't many who can get you inside, but once you're in, he can't give you the locations to the oil reserves, the ones my father kept secret. He doesn't know the password, and he wouldn't pass the DNA scan. Only someone with my family's blood can give you what you want. I've been there. My father was very careful about this. He taught me a lot. I know exactly what to do. I've never forgotten."

"This is a good story to help keep you alive, huh?" she asked. "You want me to think you're valuable. That's pretty clever for a little boy who knows more about video games than the real world."

"He's more valuable to our world than you know," snapped Chopra.

"To be frank, I agree," she answered, probably stunning him, though she couldn't see his expression. "Let Dubai return to the world's economy. In fact, I'd like to see the emirates return to power and undermine the

Russian economy. I'd like to see Mother Russia fall to her knees. But I still want the gold and the locations of the oil reserves."

"I'm willing to negotiate," said Hussein.

"No, you're not!" cried Chopra. "There's no negotiation with this . . . this terrorist!"

"Shut up, old man, does it look like we have a choice here?" shouted Hussein. "Now listen to me, Snow Maiden, or whatever your name is, he can get you the gold but not the oil. I'll give you the locations, but you're going to split that gold with me."

She marveled over the boy's naïveté and actually found it as charming as it was pathetic. "Okay," she said quickly. "I'm willing to do that."

"Very well, then. We have a deal."

"There's no deal, Hussein. You don't know who she's working with. We're not giving her anything. And that gold doesn't belong to you. It belongs to your country and to the other nations who've made deposits."

"If you don't deal with me, then you'll both die," she told them. "And Dubai will perish with you. At least if you work with me there's a chance the country will return to power. I have friends who can help. We have the same goals, just different methods of achieving them."

"Are you listening to her, Chopra? I'm sixteen. I'm not going to die. Now you work for me, old man. You take orders from me! And this is what we're going to do!"

"Don't make this mistake," Chopra said. "Let me

talk to you alone. Let me tell you about what your father really wanted. Let me share with you my own dreams for our country."

"*Our* country?"

"Yes. Ours."

"You're from India."

"But my heart is in Dubai, with you. Don't make this deal with the devil. You haven't given me a chance to speak with you, to express your father's wishes, to share with you all the things—all the dreams—he shared with me."

The Snow Maiden grinned darkly at the boy. "He's quite dramatic. This is, in the end, nothing more than business. And we both know that."

"Dubai will never rise again," said Hussein. "It's nuked. It's dead. Just a contaminated junkyard."

"Please, Hussein, you can't think that way," said Chopra. "You must listen to me!"

"All I can do now is take some of that gold and try to build a future for myself and my sisters. And that's exactly what I'm going to do. Do you hear me, Chopra?"

"No, you're wrong. This is wrong! Please, Hussein, I'm begging you . . ."

"No more talk, old man," said the Snow Maiden. "The young sheikh has made up his mind."

Brent sprayed himself a tight path through the burning grass, then tossed the extinguisher down to Heston, who seized it and continued hosing down the hatch area.

With his eyes tearing heavily, Brent hoisted the still-unconscious Park over his shoulders and, with Lakota's help, climbed out of the Sphinx and began running through the foam-covered path paralleled on both sides by rising flames. Brent could do little more than run half-blind, the footfalls and screams and pounding of his heart driving him on as once more images of fireballs swelled in his mind's eye. Oh, yes, there in his mind, the images were quite clear.

That blaze of glory he sought was suddenly not far out of reach. He realized the grass fire would ignite the fumes inside the Sphinx's ruptured fuel tanks. And within a few more seconds twin booms resounded behind him, followed by a concussion that swept him off his feet. He smashed into the ground, and Park went tumbling off his back.

Copeland was at his side as he hit the ground. Brent rolled over and rubbed his eyes. "I'm good. It's Park! It's Park!"

"Roger that, sir, I got him."

As the medic began to examine Park, Brent sat and his vision began to clear. He was trying to catch his breath but almost lost it again as he took in his surroundings.

The landscape had contorted into a postapocalyptic charcoal painting, with a ribbon of mottled white separating two fields of unrelenting fire. Those fields swept out toward a greater curtain of flames beneath which lay the shattered remains of the Sphinx, its rotors tipped forward into the dirt but still rotating like a pair of massive grass edgers. The fuselage had split in two and was bathed in orange and blue beneath the faint shadow of the wings, one intact, the other hanging half off at an improbable angle. A mound of still-settling earth completely obscured the aircraft's nose, where yet another dust cloud was still rising into the air.

And above it all hung a morning sky filling steadily with wide columns of black smoke, while smaller ones corkscrewed upward on the periphery of the crash site.

Lakota was muttering a roll call to herself, while the pilot and co-pilot were just behind Brent, talking with the tower and their superiors on portable radios.

Brent coughed, cleared his throat, and activated his Cross-Com. "Hammer, this is Ghost Lead, over."

Dennison appeared in a data box in one corner of his HUD. "Ghost Lead, this is Hammer. We've got evac transports en route. ETA should be ten minutes."

"Roger that. I've got a man down and a sky busier than A'stan on a weekday. What the hell's going on?"

"The Russians know she's in London, Brent. They're dropping in ground troops. Could be a full battalion."

"They're fools. We'll cut 'em off. And they won't damage the infrastructure, not when the Brits are buying all their oil."

"We know that. And they know we know. This is just a diversion. We haven't picked up Haussler yet, but we know he's there somewhere. We finally got the sister to talk, and we have the location of the boy. He's near Sandhurst. GPS coordinates uploading now but we can't get our satellites in close for a look. The Russians are jamming us. You'll proceed there immediately.

The Voecklers will rendezvous, but they'll get there first."

"Roger that."

"Now, if you'll excuse me, I've got a little problem in London."

"Yes, you do . . ."

Brent blinked hard to clear his vision, then regarded Copeland, who was holding an oxygen mask up to Park's face. Park was conscious and breathing steadily.

"He'll be all right. Might be a little high for a while," said the medic. "Fumes got to him before he could mask up."

"Thanks, bro. Good job. I mean it."

"Thank you, sir. You sure you're all right? Looks like you could use a little more oxygen."

"No, no, I'm good. I've just never liked flying."

Copeland cracked a smile. "Me neither, sir. And I hate landing even more."

Brent gave a little snort and shook his head at the burning field. Then he turned back.

Clouds of dust rose in the distance like small dust devils, and Lakota, who'd lifted a pair of binoculars to her face, cried, "Here come our rides! Get ready to saddle up!"

She then jogged over to Brent. "Saw the new GPS on our target."

"Yep."

"You think she's still there?"

Brent took a long breath. "Without eyes in the sky? All we can do is hope—and get our asses in gear."

* * *

The Brits had sent out a pair of Huskies that resembled the JSF's HMMWV or "Hummer" but were smaller, so the team had been forced to pile into the small flat-beds. The vehicles were normally crewed by four, but these had only a driver and gunner manning a big fifty-caliber out back. Brent rode shotgun in one truck, Lakota in the other.

While en route to Sandhurst, Dennison told Brent that the helicopter transports she'd secured were now unavailable, so they were forced to take the Huskies all the way down to Sandhurst, at least a two-hour drive through rolling countryside.

He reminded Dennison of the crash landing and lack of satellite and helicopter support, that these were circumstances beyond his control and that the time delay might result in loss of the target.

"I understand that, Captain. But you have your orders. And your mission. Hammer out."

She didn't want to hear it. And if the op went south again, he would take the fall. She'd already gone to bat for him and couldn't do any more.

So now he could play it two ways: be the stressed-out maniac barking at his people . . . or remain cool, calm, and collected, a man already resigned to his fate who stared into the sun as it was about to explode and said, *"No problem, people. Let's get to work."*

He leaned over to the driver. "We need to be there yesterday."

"Right. Tell your folks out back to hang on. There's nothing I like more than breaking the speed limit!"

Brent smiled. "You and me both! Go for it!" He then passed word back to the others as the Husky leapt forward with a roar and subsequent vibration working up through the reinforced floor.

After a burst of static, George Voeckler appeared in Brent's HUD: "Ghost Lead, this is Romulus, over."

"Go ahead, Romulus."

"We should be at the target coordinates in about thirty minutes. Suggest we move in immediately and try to secure the target, over."

The word *Negative* was about to escape Brent's lips, and he was certain that George expected him to deny the request and order him to set up an observation post and wait for them.

But it was all about timing, not ego, and the Russian attack had no doubt alerted the Snow Maiden. She was a fool if she wasn't already on the move, and they needed to check out the leads quickly and efficiently.

"Romulus, I want you guys all over that location. You get in there and try to take her alive. But if not, you know what to do. No delays."

George appeared a little flabbergasted, his face shimmering a bit in the HUD, but then his voice came steadily. "Roger that, Captain."

"And keep the channel open. I want full access to your cameras."

"Will do. Romulus out."

As he settled deeper into the seat, Brent wondered if

they hadn't given him the Snow Maiden job as a way to ditch a troublemaker. They were always two steps behind her, and the more he failed, the easier it was for them to bust him down and out.

Now he was just being paranoid, and he wasn't the biggest troublemaker in the group. They'd given him the job because they knew he wouldn't play it by the book. Never did.

He got back on the Cross-Com, called Dennison, and asked to speak directly to Warda if he could. He waited. Five minutes later he had the woman on the line. His focus was on the vehicles owned by her brother's staff. She didn't know tag numbers but had a general idea of style and color. He asked Dennison to relay these details to the local authorities. She said she was right on it.

Suddenly, a fist was rapping on the cab's back window. It was Daugherty, looking wide-eyed and pointing above them.

Brent thrust his head out the open side window as two helicopters swept overhead, one of them decidedly Russian, the other an AH-80 Blackfoot American gunship firing on the Russian bird, the rounds and tracers missing as the Russian swept down toward the field.

And then more rotors drew closer, and with an immediate roar one more Russian bird appeared, a gunship itself, and fired on the American chopper, all of it happening not more than five hundred meters ahead, the first Russian helicopter descending to less than a hundred meters above the road. It was, in a word, surreal to see Russian Federation military aircraft flying over the U.K. and being engaged by Americans. Even their driver remarked on the audacity of it all. Obviously, JSF forces had been called in to assist, but now it seemed that the lone American bird could use some help.

"Can you tell your gunners to put some fire up there to help him out?"

"Negative!"

"Why the hell not?"

"Because—you dumb Yank—that'll draw fire on us! And because I'd have to call for authorization."

"Authorization? We're not sitting here to watch that pilot die! You get some fire on those enemy birds!"

"No, I won't! The Russians are his problem, not ours. And you've got a mission, right?"

Brent gritted his teeth. A fellow combatant needed him. "Ghost Team, this is Ghost Lead. Relieve those gunners of duty, at gunpoint if necessary. Heston? Daugherty? I want you on those fifties. Lay down some fire on those Russian birds right now!"

"Captain, you'll get us killed!" hollered the driver.

Brent glared at him. "If I do, I'll make sure you die first."

ELEVEN

Ghost Recon Team
En Route to Sandhurst

"Captain, don't let them fire," said Lakota from the other Husky. "Check it out. We're rolling up on another neighborhood. Collateral damage."

Brent couldn't deny the fact that civilians could be injured or killed should one of those choppers go down into the homes. Of course, the Russians didn't care if the American gunship crashed into a residential neighborhood; they just wanted that aircraft out of the sky.

And it was true that firing on them would no doubt draw a response. Those Russian choppers, identified in Brent's HUD as KA-65 Howlers, noted as being one of the most armed and armored helicopters in existence, could tear their little trucks to shreds in all of ten seconds. And it was Brent's job to reach Sandhurst.

He cursed and hollered into his boom mike: "All

right, stay on the guns but hold fire for now. Be ready in case they turn on us."

"Thanks, Captain."

"Now that's the sane choice," said the driver.

"Shut up, Brit. That pilot's going to die. We'll honor him with our silence. And is that as fast as you can go?"

The driver swore under his breath and accelerated even as in the far distance, Brent watched the American gunship get double-teamed by the two Russian helicopters, while yet another Russian chopper, a troop transport, followed behind. A missile flew, and within a breath the American bird vanished inside an orb of white light. Below that orb, in an eerie slow motion, debris appeared and began tumbling down toward the rooftops of residential homes. The two choppers broke formation and wheeled back around to the north, while the third troop transport continued southward, ahead of them.

The driver got on his radio and called in his report, while Brent was interrupted by word from George Voeckler: They were just a couple of minutes away from the target location.

Brent issued a voice command to his Cross-Com, bringing up camera images from both George and Thomas Voeckler in separate windows of the HUD. He took a deep breath and waited as their car raced up a narrow suburban street.

"Looks like a police checkpoint," said Chopra, his mouth going cotton as he eased on the brakes.

The barricade lay about two blocks ahead as they were passing through the rural village of Flexford, according to the car's GPS. The Snow Maiden had ordered him to keep off the main highways, and this was the first barrier they'd come across. It was comprised of two police "smart" cars parked at forty-five-degree angles on either side of fluorescent red cones spanning the road.

The roadblock appeared about as dangerous and imposing as a little old man armed with a water pistol, and Chopra doubted it would pose much trouble to the woman in his backseat.

"All right, calm down," said the Snow Maiden. "Drive right up and speak to them."

"What do I tell them?" asked Chopra.

"The truth."

"Excuse me?"

"I said the truth."

He wasn't sure what this crazy woman had in mind, but he decided he would do just that.

As he drew closer, he saw two bobbies armed only with short, wooden truncheons. The Snow Maiden, he suspected, could dispatch both of them with barely an effort.

"Chopra, don't do anything stupid," said Hussein. "Just hand over your identity and tell them we're going to Dover. The truth. Just like she said."

He looked back at the Snow Maiden, who nodded.

With a deep breath he brought the car to a stop before the cones and tapped the button to lower his window. One bobby came up to him as the other went around the other side of the car. They were both middle-aged men, a little thick around the center, and setting up this roadblock was probably the most exciting thing that had happened to them in weeks.

"Good morning, sir. Your identification, please?"

Chopra had already withdrawn his wallet and was about to hand over his ID when a thump made him flinch. The bobby fell back, away from the car.

She'd shot him right over Chopra's shoulder.

Before he hit the ground, the Snow Maiden wrenched open her door and ran around the other side, toward the second bobby, who'd ducked at the sight of seeing his partner drop.

The Snow Maiden's gun went off twice more. She reentered the car and slammed the door. "Go. There'll be another car waiting for us in Chilworth."

Chopra threw the car in gear and floored it, crashing through the cones and leaving the bodies of the two men behind. He glanced at them in the rearview mirror, then raised his voice. "You see, Hussein? You see who you're dealing with? A thug. A murderer. Nothing more. And when she's done with us, we'll be shot like dogs, just like them."

"You didn't have to kill them," Hussein told the Snow Maiden.

"No, I didn't. I wanted to."

"You really are just a killer."

She gave a big snort. "And it's all for my own entertainment pleasure—not yours."

*   *   *

Brent didn't realize that he was clutching the seat with both hands until a sudden bump broke his grip. George and Thomas had just left their cars and were charging up on the house, and he was watching it all in his HUD, the images piped in from the trident goggles worn by each Splinter Cell. The two spies found the body of a man lying at the far end of the driveway, near the side door. At that point, they split up, with George taking the side entrance and Thomas falling back to hold off in the yard, in case anyone tried to bolt as George entered.

No, Brent wasn't fond of a single operator entering the house and attempting to clear room after room, but this was the best they could do, and posting Thomas outside to tag potential runners was a smart move. Bringing in a team of local police to back them up would've been too obvious and noisy; however, sending in George was, admittedly, not conducive to the Splinter Cell's health. Then again he'd served in the Marines and had been well trained. You had to give him the benefit of the doubt.

The images came in from George's goggles.

Bodies in the kitchen. Damn.

"You seeing this, Captain?" George asked.

"She was there," said Brent. "We might be late. Now all we do is follow the trail of bodies . . ."

Thomas began cursing over the channel until his words turned into a warning: "Russian chopper landing in the street! Troops coming out! George, get out of there!"

With a start, Brent realized that troop transport they'd just seen had been en route to Sandhurst.

George rushed to the window, and Brent saw what the spy saw: At least a dozen darkly clad soldiers—Spetsnaz troops—were hopping down from the chopper, and the last man out was their old German friend from the Seychelles, that blond-haired bastard Heinrich Haussler.

"Hammer, this is Ghost Lead. The Voecklers are on the target zone but so are the Russians, along with Haussler. We're too far out right now. We need some CAS for them, if you got it."

"Negative, Ghost Lead. Close Air Support unavailable. They're all tied up in London."

"Then some kind of evac. Anything!"

"Negative."

Brent swore and switched channels. "Romulus, this is Ghost Lead. You're on your own for now."

"Just another day in paradise." George bounded up the staircase.

"George, I'm coming in," said Thomas.

"No, you fall back, out of sight. You come in here, you're done, you hear me? I'll get out. *Do not give* up your location. Just do what I say."

Brent could barely contain himself as he witnessed George's escape. At the top of the stairs, the Splinter Cell turned right, then left, then rushed toward a door and slammed it open with a fist. He stopped. Looked back. Listened.

The troops were entering downstairs.

He rushed forward, through what had to be a teenager's

room loaded with games and movies. He reached the window and tugged it open, and then he was all about his portable scaling tools, wrenching them from his web gear. He fired a zip line across to the next house, and the "sticky mount" stuck like superglue to the side.

He climbed through the window and was sliding down the line with a whirr and hiss.

It was impossibly frustrating not to be there and lend a hand. Brent reached reflexively for his sidearm to take out the Spetsnaz troops as he imagined them storming into the bedroom only seconds after George got out.

But all Brent could do was watch George gliding down toward the next house as gunfire suddenly punched holes in the wooden siding ahead of him.

Before George reached the house he fired another line at a shed lying across the backyard. The sticky mount struck the sloping roofline. George grabbed that line in one hand, and then he fired a third shot. Line number three attached itself to the roof of the current building. Using the shed line as a guide, he released the first line, gripped the second, then swung around, out of the enemy line of fire. It was a brilliant piece of maneuvering that left Brent awestruck.

Once around the next house, he slid down the rope and hit the ground hard, lost his balance, and tumbled.

"Thomas, fall back even more. Get over that fence and wait there for me. I think there's a shed."

"Roger that."

George was up on his feet now, running at full tilt

along the row of apartments. He ducked behind a pair of parked cars and paused.

The spy's own labored breathing raised Brent's pulse, and it was getting even harder to watch.

Meanwhile, Thomas scaled the fence his brother had mentioned, dropped behind, and spotted a small utility shed. He bounded for the shed, wrenched open the door, and stepped inside between pieces of lawn and landscaping equipment. He quietly closed the door and stood there, staring through the dust-covered window and just breathing. "I'm inside the shed," he reported. "Hidden pretty good."

"I see that. Stay there," said George.

Brent longed to pull up a close-in satellite view of the area so he could tell George where the troops were moving. The team had nothing, though, technology rendered useless by more technology. They would rely now on their good old-fashioned wits to escape.

Thomas remained in the shed, staring through that dusty window at the second story of the apartment. He could see Russian troops appearing in the window from where George had escaped. They were tearing up the house, while one remained there, sweeping the yard with his scoped rifle.

With an audible shiver, Thomas swore again as the Russians shouted to each other on the other side of the fence.

Brent could barely breathe now as he checked the images coming in from George's goggles. "George, just get some cover like your brother and wait for us."

"That's the plan," said the spy. "That's the plan." He burst up from the parked cars.

From around the corner of the next apartment building came two Spetsnaz troops—Grim Reapers dressed in black uniforms and web gear, with black helmets and balaclavas concealing their identities.

They were but fifty meters away.

George dropped to the ground and shot one guy in the face with his pistol, while the other ducked and George did likewise. Gunfire struck the cars behind him as he jogged around and sought cover once more.

Brent wanted to scream at the Splinter Cell, tell him not to remain there in a standoff while that Russian troop called for backup. But George was a seasoned veteran and didn't need Brent pointing out the obvious.

In fact, George did something remarkable again. He suddenly broke cover and darted to the building, even as the trooper, who'd sought refuge behind the corner, eased out for another look, the top of his helmet jutting out.

While the Russian's gaze was reaching out toward the car, George came at him from the side, sliding an arm around the man's head while raising a combat dagger high in his free hand.

George plunged the knife deep into the man's neck, just north of his clavicle, then George grabbed the hilt and got to work. To say that George opened up the man's head like a Pez dispenser would be understating the point, and Brent had a front-row seat to all the carnage. He grimaced.

George dropped the body and shifted to the front side of the apartment. He hunkered down beside a row of shrubs and stole a look out at the helicopter sitting in the field across the street.

Oh, no, Brent thought. *I hope he's not thinking what I'm thinking . . .*

Two civilians had come out of the homes, one holding a kitchen knife, the other an antique-looking pistol. They were a husband-and-wife team, white-haired, wizened, and wild, and they waved and shouted as two troops who'd been stationed just outside the helicopter drifted toward them.

"No, don't do it," Brent muttered aloud.

It was over before it started. One Russian shot both the man and the woman execution style, boom-boom. And George just sat there and gasped. Then George cleared his throat and said, "Thomas, stay in the shed."

"I will."

George sighed into his microphone. "They must've found our car by now. We can't get out on foot or by car if they still got that bird."

"George, don't even think about it," said Thomas.

"George, just dig in and do not do anything," said Brent. "That's an order!"

"Too late."

"Voeckler!" Brent cried. "What're you doing?"

The image coming in from George's trident goggles grew so shaky that Brent couldn't see anything.

But he could hear the man breathing. Faster. And faster. Panting now.

* * *

The Snow Maiden let out a faint snort as she glanced sidelong at Hussein. The boy was staring out the window, looking bored and about to fall asleep as they continued on toward Dover.

Chopra was droning on and on about what the boy's father had wanted for him, and the old man's cadence and tone had become yet another form of white noise, like the wind buffeting the car, the engine's hum, and the steady vibration of the tires on the pavement.

Even the Snow Maiden herself was beginning to drift off, barely listening, reminding herself that if she didn't keep her guard up, the sixteen-year-old next to her could launch a surprise.

Abruptly, her cell phone rang. "You'll be met at Dover," said Patti. "They know you're coming."

"Excellent. Thank you."

"I'll see you in Geneva. Excellent work, as always."

"You might want to call Izotov and thank him as well."

Patti laughed. "I'm sure he'd appreciate that."

The Russians—in their attempt to capture her—had inadvertently helped her escape. It seemed they might come in handy now, and she thought about manipulating them to her benefit in the near future.

For just the briefest of moments, though, she took herself back to the tiny town of Banff, just off the Trans-Canada Highway, seventy-eight miles west of Calgary. She was with Green Vox, that terrorist leader whose identity was kept a secret so that he could "live forever" through any number of followers assuming his role. Together, they had chosen Banff so they would be upwind from the nuclear fallout, once she had detonated the nukes. But the entire operation had been foiled by the Americans. No matter. She'd had other plans.

"I am Snegurochka. What did you expect?" she'd asked the terrorist.

"Viktoria, what are you doing?"

"Did you *really* think I was working with you?"

His mouth had fallen open. "You can't be serious."

She'd grinned and aimed the gun at him.

Vox's eyes had widened. "Go ahead, kill me. Green Vox will return. He always does."

She shot him between those eyes.

"Yes," she said, staring down at his body. "You always come back—and always as a man. What a pity."

Now as she sat in the car, she realized that an aching fear had brought on the memory. She was worried about whether the Green Brigade Transnational had given up on their quest for revenge. Perhaps her work in France had reminded them of the futility of getting too close to her.

The Americans and the Russians were so predictable, but these bastards . . . they were the wild cards and could appear at any time. And as she'd speculated, they could be getting leads from Izotov, who'd perhaps hired them as mercenaries in addition to his "official" efforts involving Haussler and the Spetsnaz troops. Izotov was a clever one who could be feeding information to the terrorists that he wasn't sharing with Haussler. He might even be playing them against each other and would reward only the victors. She knew him all too well, knew that all he cared about were end results and that people were disposable, people like her husband and brothers.

In the Snow Maiden's Russia, loyalty was a spring flower that wilted far too quickly without water.

"We're almost out of gas," Chopra said, wrenching her from her thoughts.

"Then you'll stop at the next petrol station."

"I don't have cash, and if we use cards they will find us."

"Exactly."

"Please don't kill anyone else."

She took a deep breath. "If they cooperate, I won't. But I make no promises."

"How did you get to be so deplorable?"

She attempted to speak softly and not through her teeth. "I used to think they made me who I am. But I've always had a choice. So I choose to be this way."

"Why?"

She let the question hang for a moment, then said, "Because I will never become their victim."

"How would you become their victim? And who are they?"

"Doesn't matter."

"What happened to you? I'm sure you were a little girl once. A sweet child."

She closed her eyes for a moment. "Yes. Once . . ."

* * *

Brent wanted to close his eyes, but he couldn't help himself. He was as much horrified and fascinated by George Voeckler's insanity . . . or bravery—the line between them was often indistinct.

The Russian pilot and co-pilot were in the cockpit of that enemy chopper and could effortlessly lift their 12.7-millimeter four-barrel machine gun, bringing it to bear. But George Voeckler knew that as well, which was why he jogged along the front of the apartments, keeping low and breaking cover only at the last second to run at the chopper, rear back, and hurl his grenade, one of six "Ghost Recon specials" given to him by Brent.

Just as the pilot swung his gun around, the fins and engine on George's L12-7 activated, and the tiny missile streaked into the open bay door.

The whish was followed immediately by a muffled explosion that echoed strangely louder from inside the chopper.

The explosion was clearly not enough to destroy the bird, but the pilot and co-pilot had to be seriously injured, Brent thought. Thick smoke poured from the open bay door, yet the rotors kept on spinning.

A moment later, one man jumped out, staggered onto the ground, and fell. The other pilot never appeared.

As expected, the explosion drew the attention of the rest of the Russian troops, and even as George began hightailing it back out of there, the camera images making Brent dizzy, the window showing his input went blank for a second.

Gunfire boomed.

And then that "blank screen" turned out to be the pavement as the camera was raised, and it appeared someone was holding George's trident goggles.

Haussler's smug face panned into view. "Hello, hello, Americans! I see you, too, have come hunting. Until we meet again." Haussler dropped the goggles, and he might've stomped on them because the signal cut off.

Thomas screamed into his microphone, and Brent got on his channel. "Don't you move. You stay there. I've lost one man, and I won't lose another, do you hear me, Thomas?"

"No way. I'm going!"

"If you go, you die, and you die like a fool. That's not what your brother wants. Do what he said. Stay there! We're coming for you!"

Brent regarded the driver. "You need to get us there, now!"

The driver gritted his teeth and accelerated even more, as Thomas once more announced that he was going after his brother.

Brent wondered what he would do were he in that shed and his own brother had just been killed. Hiding there would feel like an act of cowardice. He should face his brother's killers. So he understood, in part, how Thomas felt, but remaining wasn't being a coward; it was being smart, and Brent so much as told the man that. "Just stay there, buddy. Stay there."

"I'm not leaving him there." Thomas lapsed into a string of curses.

"Just listen to me, bro. You got a whole squad of troops out there. And just you. I need you alive. You hear what I am saying? I need you to stay there. That's all you have to do. Just sit tight. We'll get George. He's not going to lie there for long. Just believe me, all right?"

Thomas kept swearing. "This is not the way it was supposed to happen. I'm the one who should've died! I'm the loser, not him! I'm the loser."

"Just calm down. We're on our way."

TWELVE

Brent had assumed that Haussler and his Spetsnaz team would call for immediate evac. Their chopper had been damaged, the pilots injured or killed.

But the Russians weren't going anywhere.

As a matter of fact, they were digging in around the target house, setting up defensive positions, and pretty much taking their time. A team inside was tearing the place to shreds in search of the Snow Maiden or any evidence that would lead to her location.

Much to Brent's chagrin, Thomas did leave the shed, but only after the troops turned more attention back on the house. He'd made a successful break.

Now he was at his brother's side. The Russians had stripped George of all of his gear but had left the body there. They couldn't operate George's Cross-Com or

OPSAT or any of his other communications devices, but the Russians loved to reverse-engineer anything they could get their hands on.

As Thomas held his brother in his arms, Brent urged the man to take cover, reminding him that the Ghosts would be there in less than ten minutes.

"I don't care," said Thomas. "I don't care anymore."

Brent was at a loss. You could train operators time and again on how to deal with death and that you could never, ever afford a breakdown in the field. You owed it to yourself, your people, and your country to remain strong—and alive—because there would be plenty of time, far too much time, to grieve later. Everyone knew that. Everyone believed in it. But you never knew how you'd react if death was staring you in the face and it was your turn to feel the cold chill close, so very, very close . . .

Nevertheless, this Thomas Voeckler guy had been an enigma from the beginning, and his dossier raised many unanswered questions, which in turn had raised Brent's brows:

Thomas had attended Florida State University and had majored in psychology. At that time he'd had no desire to rise above slackerdom, let alone join the military like his brother had. He'd changed majors three times and had finally wound up with an English degree, which he did nothing with for ten years. When he wasn't taking, dropping, or flunking out of graduate courses, he'd been, in no particular order, a pizza delivery guy, an apartment building maintenance man, a clerk at a local video store, and an attendant at a state park where he rented canoes. He'd volunteered at a local library and at the local animal shelter on Captiva Island, Florida. He built houses for Habitat for Humanity. He fed homeless people during the holidays, even when he was only a paycheck or two away from being homeless himself.

This was not the profile of one of America's most cunning and lethal covert operatives.

Meanwhile, his brother moved up quickly through the ranks and had made a name for himself in the Marines and in Force Recon. George was a textbook operator, exactly the kind of man you'd expect to find in Third Echelon.

When Thomas had been recruited by Grimsdóttir, he'd initially declined, admitting he was not cut out for this kind of work. She'd offered him a six-figure salary to entice him, and though Thomas finally agreed, he'd flunked out of the training program three times before receiving a provisional pass. He was no man of action, as evidenced by several broken bones and other assorted injuries during past operations.

But he was, as Grimsdóttir had carefully noted in his record, meant to serve as his brother's primary alibi and not necessarily his field partner. Third Echelon had been experimenting for years with team operations: large groups, small groups, and pairs, but the implication in Thomas's dossier was that he should be a human mannequin, meant to stand around and look pretty but do nothing. George was to keep him on a tight leash.

Unfortunately, that was now Brent's job.

"Thomas, it's time to go," Brent told him for the nth time, checking his HUD for maps of the area. "Take Copperfield Avenue northeast toward the woods. Shooting you the grid points now. Go around past the academy, and just keep moving through. We'll link up with you there."

"I'm taking George with me."

"We'll come back for him. I promise. You *cannot* afford to be captured."

"I'm not leaving my brother!"

Brent wanted to scream, but didn't. "You need to go."

Thomas hesitated.

"Voeckler, I'm warning you . . ."

"I know! I know!"

Brent hardened his voice. "Then . . . get out of there. Run! Right . . . now . . ."

"We can't run. We need to make them pay."

"We will. Later."

"I need your word!"

"Jesus, dude, you got it. Just go!"

"All right. You watch this . . ."

Thomas's tone was beginning to harden, too, and that was a relief. Brent needed him angry enough to stay alive so he could exact revenge. There would come a time.

After a deep breath audible through his microphone, the Splinter Cell took off in an impressive sprint, but not before shouting erupted behind him, along with gunfire.

"They've tagged you!" cried Brent.

Thomas cursed and bolted even faster down the

street, suddenly ducking behind a row of parked cars. He glanced over his shoulder.

Three Spetsnaz troops charged after him.

Manoj Chopra pulled into the petrol filling station. There were no other cars.

The Snow Maiden instructed Chopra to shut off the engine and hand her the keys. She took them and said, "Everybody out."

"Please, no violence," Chopra said.

She didn't answer.

They went into the small convenience store, where two old men stood behind the counter.

Without a word, the Snow Maiden raised her pistol, even as Chopra gasped.

The men barely had time to widen their eyes before they were tumbling to the floor.

It all happened too quickly for Chopra to fully comprehend. That someone could kill in such a cool and casual manner woke a hard shudder across his shoulders.

Hussein seemed less surprised this time, glancing up at her and asking in an eerily calm voice, "Can I get a drink before we leave?"

"Get me one, too," she said. "Some juice."

"Okay."

"Are we this cavalier about murder?" shouted Chopra.

The Snow Maiden rolled her eyes, crossed around the counter, and began working one of the touch-screen computers to activate the filling pump.

"If you're hungry or thirsty, better shop now," she told him.

Chopra eyed the men lying behind the counter. He had no thirst, no appetite. Blood pooled around their bodies.

"I thought you promised not to kill," he said.

"I did not," she spat back. "I said I make no promises. Let's go."

Chopra just stared at her. "You're a monster. And if I didn't have something you wanted, you would've killed me already."

"What's your point?"

"My point is that balance will return, once you are gone from this world. Balance will return."

She shrugged. "Get yourself some cookies, and get back in the car. Hussein? Have you ever pumped gasoline?"

"You must be joking," said the young sheikh, handing her a bottle of juice.

She popped the cap. "There's a first time for everything."

Brent wasn't sure how many now, four or five maybe, but they were on Thomas's tail, gaining on him as he reached the heavily wooded perimeter of the Royal Military Academy. Because the Russians had full control of the target area, this was at best a rescue operation of his remaining operator. They could engage in a stand-up fight against the Russians, but for what? He no longer believed they'd gain much from searching the house, and the Russians might have already secured evidence that indicated the Snow Maiden had been there.

Brent repressed a chill. Was his career already over? The Snow Maiden was gone.

Only for now, he convinced himself. Dennison was working in coordination with a dozen other agencies, and Brent had just learned that the Russian jamming had stopped, so eyes in the sky were busy probing every inch of the U.K. for their target.

Time wasn't just of the essence; it was everything now. If she got out of the U.K., he feared she could more easily drop off the grid. She no doubt had many contacts in Europe she'd made over the years, friends who owed her favors. She'd left herself much more vulnerable to link up with Chopra and Hussein. If she had both of them now, she need only disappear.

"Hammer, this is Ghost Lead. Anything, over?"

"Still searching, Ghost Lead . . ."

"Roger, still waiting." He winced over his sarcastic tone. There it was—the stress beginning to unravel him.

He took a deep breath and glanced over at the driver, who returned the gaze. "What, Yank? Not fast enough for you?"

"You're good. It's nothing."

Brent and his team were but five minutes from reaching the northeast perimeter of the forest when Dennison called.

He'd thought he was being glib about following the

trail of bodies to locate the Snow Maiden, but Dennison and her allies had been doing just that:

Flexford. Roadblock. Two dead cops.

The Snow Maiden had gone south, then had turned east and was now, perhaps, en route toward the coast to cross the English Channel and head into Europe. At least that was Dennison's theory. The town of Dover was a major ferry port and about ninety kilometers away.

"There will be at least two or three obvious escape points," Brent told Dennison. "And she'll have decoys, just like the Seychelles."

"We can't expect anything less."

"Right, so we need to track every vehicle between here and the coast," he said, his voice growing more emphatic.

"Brent, that's a huge search and a massive amount of data. The government's declared martial law, but there's a mad dash to the coast now, with thousands of cars on the road, and you know she could've changed vehicles."

"But maybe she didn't."

"I'll do what I can. Hammer out."

Brent blinked hard and studied the terrain map and live satellite overlay in his HUD. Six Spetsnaz troops, identified as red blips, were closing in on the green blip, Thomas, who was still beating a serpentine path through the forest. The images streaming in from his goggles were blurry, jittery, but clearly noted his effort.

"Lakota, keep Thomas updated, over?"

"Roger, I'm on it," she said, then immediately began speaking to the Splinter Cell, feeding him data on the

Russians behind him so that he could concentrate on moving and communicating without splitting his attention between the course ahead and his own HUD. She would guide him directly toward their location.

The team came to a fork in the road, with the forest dead ahead, and Brent instructed both drivers to pull over and wait for them.

In silence the Ghosts dismounted from both trucks and expertly fanned out in a split-team formation, Lakota leading one group, he taking the other.

"Schleck, when we draw in, I need a sentinel, over."

"Just say the word," came the sniper's immediate reply.

"Riggs, you, too," Brent added.

"Hope I don't break a nail," she said with a snort.

"All right, Ghosts, listen up. We'll flank, cross, and top down, with the package running a TD right up the middle."

"You read my mind," said Lakota.

Brent jogged with the fear and enthusiasm of a first-year cadet at West Point, threading through stands of large oaks and booting his way across a carpet of dirt and leaves. The air was much cooler and slightly damper.

Heston, Park, and Noboru fanned out to the left, while Lakota, Daugherty, and Copeland shifted right. The plan was simple: Guide Thomas through the center of their flanking positions, toward the trucks. Once he passed, they would squeeze the belt on the approaching Spetsnaz and catch them in a crossfire—which was, in fact, a diversion that would allow Riggs and Schleck—the sentinels positioned in the trees—to shoot them from their over-head snipers' perches.

How much of that plan survived the first enemy contact was a question they had no time to pose—

Because in less than two minutes they'd have their answer.

Lakota cursed.

"What?" Brent asked.

"Check southern perimeter. Got some armed officers from Sandhurst moving into the woods. They must've spotted the Russians."

Brent saw them, too. "Aw, man . . ."

"I know," she said.

"Cross-Com, this is Ghost Lead," Brent called into his mike, activating the Cross-Com's new artificial-intelligence feedback control.

"Go ahead, Ghost Lead," came the automated voice of a tactical computer aboard a satellite hurtling some 220,000 miles over Brent's head.

"Lock on to foes. All others in the area are IDed as friendlies, over."

"Roger. Foes locked. Friendlies identified. Four additional combatants moving into operational zone. Are these the contacts you wish IDed as friendlies, over?"

"Roger!"

"Designating."

At least Brent's people wouldn't misidentify those officers from the academy; they would appear as green blips in the team's HUDs. However, those academy personnel could easily mistake a Ghost Recon troop for a

Russian—after all, both groups wore nondescript black, with only the design of their helmets being different, along with their communications devices. The Russians had a headset resembling a pair of sunglasses, whereas the Cross-Com was monocle-based.

Of course, you had to think like a young military man whose country was being invaded: Any guy with a gun who didn't look like British military was an enemy. Shoot first. Apologize later.

Brent notified the rest of the team about the academy officers as he and the other group advanced toward their flanking zones. Their jobs were threefold now: rescue Thomas, ensure that the Brits did not interfere, and try to shield those officers from the Russians. If they had to neutralize one of the Brits, they would do so with less-than-lethal fire, and his team members carried an assortment of such weapons.

Amazingly, the initial plan was still in place despite one unforeseen complication.

He grinned darkly to himself and jogged on behind Heston, Park, and Noboru. They reached their positions, and he sent his three men ahead while he dropped behind a pair of trees and listened as Lakota instructed Thomas to begin turning northwest along a line that would take him directly between them.

"Riggs, Schleck, you up there?"

"Almost," said Schleck, his voice tense.

"What's the delay?"

"Sorry, Ghost Lead," said Riggs. "My fault. I needed his help. I'm up now."

"And so am I," Schleck reported.

"Stand by . . ."

Brent lost his breath as he eyed the HUD and saw the Russians closing in on Thomas, coming within thirty meters. Automatic weapons fire broke the still, damp quiet.

That fire had come from the Russians, and through Thomas's goggles Brent noted the trees splintering on Thomas's right side.

At nearly the same time, more gunfire echoed from the south—this from the academy officers who were closing in behind the Russians.

Not good. One of their stray rounds could catch Thomas.

Brent watched now as two Russians broke off from the chase to circle back on the Brits.

He broke from his cover and ran parallel behind Heston, Noboru, and Park. "Ghost Team, I'm heading south after those two break-off guys. Once Thomas is through the gap, Lakota, you put the snipers to work, over?"

"Roger that," she replied.

"Keep running, Thomas, you're almost there," Brent cried.

Only the Splinter Cell's panting came through the mike. He was at his top pace now, his heart rate in the red zone, and he was probably scared as hell as another salvo of gunfire boomed.

Brent ducked and cut through another twenty meters of forest when, off to his right, about fifty meters away, he spotted Thomas dashing forward. Then he saw the Russians. He was tempted to draw fire away, but he knew his people were in place. He kept on toward the two troops that had doubled back.

"Ghost Lead, this is Hammer," called Dennison. "I think we've got her!"

The Snow Maiden was gritting her teeth as they reached a wall of traffic on the outskirts of Ashford. They were only about thirty or so kilometers away from Dover and she had kept them on the smaller country roads, but now there was a mass exodus toward the coast and Europe. Chopra turned on the radio, and a newscaster reported chaos at the coast. The citizenry feared that Russia was launching a massive ground invasion of the country.

Chopra slumped toward the steering wheel. "There's nothing else we can do but sit here. The traffic must be backed up all the way to the coast."

"This is a brilliant escape plan you have," said Hussein. "I guess you hadn't thought of this."

"Shut up, both of you," she snapped. She took a deep breath, closed her eyes, and cleared her head.

Then she got on her smartphone and searched for the business she had in mind. "Get out of the car," she cried.

"Right here?" asked Chopra. "We're just leaving it right here?"

"Get out!"

They complied, and she hid her gun beneath her jacket as others began to follow suit, stepping out from their cars to stretch and have a look down the narrow road.

She ordered them forward toward the next corner, then made them begin to jog. The old man protested. She barked back. He ran for a block until he was winded.

Within fifteen more minutes they reached the shop.

"Oh, you can't be serious," Chopra said, his mouth opening in awe.

"You're damned right I am."

"I don't want to watch," he said.

"That's all right, you can close your eyes," she said.

They stepped into the bicycle shop, and she took care of the owner and his two technicians. They picked out hybrid bicycles with straight handlebars and rode out the back door. They took the alley up to the main road and began moving parallel with the long line of gridlocked cars. Riding the bike got her choked up. Andrei had won the Tour de France, only to be executed because of her. Perhaps his ghost had whispered the idea in her ear: *"You're not far from the coast, just a few hours by bike . . ."*

For some reason, the hair stood on the back of her neck and she felt compelled to glance skyward.

THIRTEEN

Forest near Royal Military Academy
Sandhurst

Brent's HUD was lit up like a Christmas tree.

No, it better resembled the lights of Times Square, New York, with enough color and flash to make him blink hard and imagine an elaborate advertisement—WWIII sponsored by your favorite cola or sports shoe.

He looked again and realized he didn't fully comprehend what the computer was showing him. A data bar below indicated the obvious:

Target acquired.

Guidance system nominal.

"Do you wish to neutralize the target?"

Okay, he got it now. His race to this part of the forest had stolen his breath and blurred his vision. Data overload wasn't uncommon.

As he gained back control of his breathing, the computer's voice purred in his ear, repeating the question, and with a sudden rush and shiver his senses connected with his brain and he saw it all:

The trees ahead—

The pair of Russians beginning to fire on the four officers from Sandhurst who'd spread out along a slight depression—

And the wire frame targeting vector superimposed over it all that fed him the round's projected trajectory, replete with scrolling numbers that marked precise angles and distances.

Old-schoolers argued that this was more information than Brent ever needed, but it was impressive nonetheless. The real and virtual worlds had blended into a battlefield of mathematical relationships and ever-fluctuating calculations based on thousands of variables.

He took the shot.

The round that exploded from his rifle's XL7 underslung grenade launcher was an advanced prototype of a Less Than Lethal (LTL) weapon developed by the NSA and engineers at Third Echelon. Based upon the old "sticky shocker" that rendered targets unconscious via an electrical impulse, the new LTL Track-Shock was a homing dart that used heat, infrared, and acoustical means to locate the target's heart and deliver the shock with surgical precision, increasing or decreasing current as required to render the target unconscious without killing him.

These weren't your grandmother's tranquilizer darts to bring down wild elephants. And your grandmother would keel over from a heart attack if she knew how much each round cost her and the rest of the taxpayers . . .

The Track-Shock sped away, trailing a single ribbon of thin smoke. It banked, turned, and wove through the trees as though it were being steered by an alcoholic cabdriver on the last hour of an all-night bender.

But the round knew exactly what it was doing, and it sewed a remarkable if not chaotic course through the forest, only swooping down at the very last second to strike one of the officers dead-on in the chest. The man was racked by electricity for a second, shaking violently and involuntarily before he simply collapsed.

"Target temporarily neutralized. ETA to consciousness approximately eleven minutes. Warning clock initiated."

It had been a while since Brent had played with LTL ammo. He wasn't used to his targets coming back from the "dead" like zombies, but it was nice to have a computer that reminded you when the zombie clock ran out.

Without wasting another second, he loaded another round and lifted the rifle. "Computer, acquire target."

"Stand by. Target acquired."

The HUD no longer resembled a skyline of neon billboards. The second officer was there, at the end of the round's trajectory, and what had once been a dizzying kaleidoscope was now a perfect math equation within a fluctuating grid.

The launcher thumped. The round shot hungrily away, and that eerie smoke trail stitched the trees together for a moment before the second man shook like he'd been playing golf during a lightning storm.

Nice.

As expected, the other two Brits, noting that their brothers in arms had been "taken out" (and Brent was certain they assumed their friends were dead), broke from their positions and rushed off to the east.

What they didn't realize was that the pair of Russians had done likewise.

Those dumb-ass Brits were now rushing directly toward the Russians.

This was the part where Brent came in.

He swung around and started tracking back toward those Spetsnaz troopers, when—

"Ghost Lead, this is Hammer. Repeat, we've located her. Are you there, over?"

Brent had barely heard Dennison call the first time and had been so swept up into the moment that only now did he realize he hadn't responded to her, which was damned ironic—since his entire career was now riding on her intel.

"Hammer, this is Ghost Lead, stand by!"

"Brent, I need you out of there."

"I need me out of here. I understand. Where is she? At that bar the colonel told us about?"

"Negative."

"All right. Stand by."

Brent raced through the woods, foliage dragging across his arms and legs until he spotted the two Brits about forty meters to his right, with the Russians charging toward them another forty or so meters out (36.57 according to the tactical computer, but Brent ignored that detail at the moment, understandably so).

The one troop to the far left darted behind a pair of trees and dropped down to one knee, while the second forged on, cutting loose with two salvos meant to draw fire on him, while his buddy cut down the unsuspecting Brits from his more concealed vantage point.

This was a rather unoriginal gambit that made Brent snort. He reached into his web gear, drew his favorite model grenade, and let the bird fly home to poop on the Russian crouched behind the trees.

As the Brits opened fire on the first troop, the second one exploded in a flash of light backfilled by a shower of blood.

Both of those British officers dressed in digital pattern khakis turned in unison to spot Brent, just as he swung around, lifted his rifle, and fired on the second Russian, who'd dropped to the leaf-covered forest.

Brent was pretty sure he'd missed the guy, so he knifed off as though he had a 500-horsepower engine in his gut, covering the gap between him and his prey in all of a half dozen heartbeats.

When he arrived, the guy was gone.

He spun around, crouched. Looked up.

Son of a—

Brent glanced beyond the small clearing to the stand of trees from where the trooper had emerged, the Russian's rifle aimed squarely at Brent.

Only the troop's eyes were visible, his mouth covered

by his balaclava. But if eyes could smile menacingly, his did so.

A flurry of gunfire boomed in the distance.

That sound was enough to distract the troop, and all Brent needed was that fraction of a second, that mere flick of the Russian's glance.

He fired at the guy while falling backward, knowing the troop would return fire simultaneously, and yes, Brent's instincts paid off. The trooper's rounds punched the air no more than three or four inches above Brent's chest as he hit the ground. On impact, Brent glanced up, never losing control of his rifle, and fired again, riddling the soldier with a full salvo. If the guy wore Dragon Skin or other forms of Kevlar, Brent's rounds had found the seams. The troop did not move.

Brent sighed deeply.

"Who are you?" screamed one of the Brits, rushing up behind Brent. He was long-limbed and gaunt-faced, with a nasty set of crooked yellow teeth.

In truth, the Brit hadn't been that polite. He'd prefaced his question with a string of epithets that might've impressed the devil himself—and what kind of British hospitality was this? The guy held his rifle high and aimed it at Brent's head.

The Brit's partner ran up beside him. This guy was shorter, with a slight paunch and jet-black crew cut. Neither man was older than thirty, both still a tad baby-faced.

"Do you speak English, comrade?" cried the second guy.

"Don't you mean Yank?" Brent asked.

"You're an American?" cried the first guy. "You're lucky you're not dead."

"Then I guess this is my lucky day," Brent answered, wearing a silly grin.

"Oh, a wiseass, huh?"

"Go back to your buddies. They'll be waking up soon. We got it from here."

"Who's *we*?" asked the shorter guy.

"No one, really. Just a bunch of ghosts." With a groan, Brent hauled himself to his feet.

The first guy's eyes swelled. "You tell your Yank friends that the British government will be lodging a formal complaint regarding your unauthorized actions here. In this regard, you are trespassers!"

Brent shrugged. "We won't be staying long. See ya." With that, he turned and raced away, stealing one last look at the dumbfounded men. "Lakota, how we doing?"

"Awesome, Boss. Dropped the Russians. Thomas is back with us. Suggest we collapse on the trucks. Inbound rotary aircraft, still unidentified . . ."

"Gotcha. On my way!"

The bike was old and rusty, the rear fender barely attached, the handlebars loose, the chain grinding as Chopra pedaled through the rut-laden street. The other kids stared at him in envy. This bicycle had been the last thing his father had given him before he'd been killed, and so in Chopra's young mind the bike had become the man. He would park it near his small bed and stare at it, well into the night.

He turned the corner and headed down into the alley, where he would meet his old boss who would give him the list of deliveries. The front basket would be filled with bidis, and Chopra would make his stops and collect the money. It was a lot of responsibility for a twelve-year-old.

When Chopra reached their usual meeting place, the old man was lying on the ground, bleeding from a gaping wound to his forehead. The boxes of bidis were empty. Chopra got off his bike, rushed to the man, and tried to comfort him, but he was scared that the people who had attacked the old man might still be around. He got back on his bike, raced home, and told his mother, begging her to send help. She did.

The next morning, Chopra returned to the alley, hoping the old man had recovered and the deliveries would happen as usual. The old man was gone, the empty boxes still lying there. Before Chopra could climb back on his bike, he was stopped by two boys a few years older than himself. They'd been watching him from across the street, half hidden in the shadows of laundry lines crisscrossing the alley in a thick canopy of multicolored fabric.

The larger one with bushy eyebrows glanced at Chopra's bike. "It's mine now," he said evenly.

"What are you talking about?" asked Chopra.

"Your bike."

"You're not taking it," said Chopra, lifting his voice

and seeing his father smiling and saying, *"Take good care of it. Don't let anyone borrow it."*

The boy shifted up to Chopra and stared down at him. He was a full head taller, his eyes narrowing. "What are you going to do anyway?"

Chopra took a deep breath. His mouth went dry. "You can't have my bike."

"I'm doing you a favor. You're just making the old man rich. You can't work for him anymore. Do something else."

"You know I can't."

"Then you'll never be anything in this world, so it doesn't matter if I take the bike or not." He started away from Chopra and grabbed the bike's handlebars.

His friend came up behind them. "Can you ride me?"

"Sure," said the boy. "Climb on."

The second boy balanced himself on the rear wheel's bolts while the first took a seat.

"You can't take it!" shouted Chopra, reaching toward them.

The first boy turned and shoved Chopra away. "Don't do anything. I don't want to hurt you."

Chopra reared back, ready to punch the boy in the face, but suddenly he was on the ground, the dust coming up into his face. The other kid had hopped down and shoved him.

With tears in his eyes, Chopra watched as his bicycle vanished down the alley.

"Change of plans," said the Snow Maiden, riding up beside Chopra.

They were still pushing along the embankment, passing the rows of gridlocked cars, with Hussein keeping close behind them.

"Are you listening to me?" she asked.

Chopra glanced at her. She was riding through that old alley in Mumbai, and then the alley dematerialized into the narrow country road. "What did you say?"

"I told you we have a change of plans. We're not going to Dover anymore. We're heading to Folkestone. We'll be met there. It's farther south than Dover and closer to us. Now let's pick up the pace. Come on."

Chopra was already sweating profusely in the summer heat and humidity. He took a deep breath, wondering what those boys had ever done with his bike. He'd never seen it again, and in truth he'd never forgiven himself for allowing them to steal it. His father would not have approved.

But he'd shown them, right? He'd risen from the dirt, the ashes, the same way Dubai would in time. He refused to let this woman take that away, and he silently vowed that she wouldn't. No matter what he had to do. He glanced back at the young sheikh, who rolled his eyes and said, "When can we stop? I'm absolutely dying of thirst!"

"You have become an expert at complaining."

"Shut up, old man."

"You must learn to respect your elders."

"Get me a drink—or at least get her to get me a drink . . ."

Chopra braced himself. *Patience. Patience.*

*   *   *

Brent loved how politics affected military operations.

When he'd earlier needed Close Air Support, he couldn't get the time of day, but now, after Dennison had had some time to throw her weight around and negotiate her way up and down the pipeline, an old UH-60 Blackhawk came whomping toward them. They'd be picked up and whisked at high speed back into the chase.

The Snow Maiden, Chopra, and Hussein were on bicycles and riding toward the coast.

Dennison had had to repeat that.

Bicycles? There was the Snow Maiden's connection to the Tour de France, the cousin who'd been murdered. But bicycles?

Dennison had explained that all the roads had been flooded with people trying to flee to the coast and cross over to France. The Snow Maiden's escape was actually quite clever and much faster than any attempt by car.

A keen-eyed intelligence analyst with his face glued to a satellite feed had, however, picked up the group of three pedaling southward.

Easy prey? Hardly.

Worse, getting back in the air wouldn't go by the numbers, as Lakota confirmed. "Our ride's got a Russian on his tail. Looks like another Howler."

"All right, you talk in our ride, and I'll get us to put some fire on that Howler," Brent said, still jogging through the forest.

He reached the road and the pair of trucks where the

others had already climbed aboard and were waiting for him. He signaled to both drivers: *Take us back up the road*, to where a large clearing would serve as the landing zone.

They tore off, the engines revving, Brent's driver cursing under his breath, a habit it seemed. It took just five minutes to reach the zone, where Brent ordered his team to fan out, away from the trucks—all but Daugherty and Heston. He put those operators on the fifty-caliber guns. Then he told the two British drivers and gunners that they didn't have to stay, that his men would take out that Howler, and thank you very much for allowing us to borrow your nice toys.

"You think I can stand here and turn over my equipment to a Yank? Hell no!" hollered Brent's driver. He ordered his gunners back to their weapons.

"I'm sorry, but I'm not giving you a choice."

"Bloody hell, I know that. So rest assured, we'll get the job done. You put your boys on the bird as well. We're in the fight now."

Brent snorted. "Not worried about drawing fire?"

"I think *they* should be," said the driver, tipping his head toward the oncoming choppers. "Let's go hunting."

Finally, Brent smiled. "Thanks."

"Yeah, yeah, just get ready."

Brent jogged away as his people set up along a slight mound, all lying prone, weapons trained at the two dark blips appearing over the distant tree line. The team had packed relatively light, not expecting to face armor or aircraft, and Brent longed for a nice Zeus, a fire-and-forget missile launcher that would certainly give the Russians pause—much more so than a pair of fifty-caliber guns.

Brent dropped down beside Thomas, who'd been given a rifle by Lakota. His gaze was fixed through the scope.

"How you doing?" Brent asked, shifting awkwardly onto his elbows.

"Just fine. How are you?" Thomas snapped.

"Look, I'm sorry."

"No, you're just a guy trying to save his half-ass career, and I'm just a guy who doesn't belong here. Never did. Never will."

"Dennison knows your brother's there. She'll send a recovery team."

"He always knew he'd die out here. I have a detailed list of instructions of what to do. He wrote them for me. This is no surprise."

"Like I said, I'm sorry."

Thomas's tone grew even nastier. "You know why I finally joined the NSA? Because my father came to me, told me he wanted me to protect George. He said George took too many risks. I needed to watch out for him. And stupid me believed my father. What a crock. I found out later that George told my father what to say—just to get me on board. But I keep thinking that maybe it wasn't a lie. Maybe it was true. I was supposed to keep an eye on George because I'm the sane one, not the warmonger. And I failed. I let my brother die."

"Survivor guilt is natural. I promise we'll talk about this later. I promise." Brent cleared his throat and opened up a channel to the team. "Ghosts, this is Ghost Lead. Stand by. Here they come!"

The Blackhawk swooped down to within a meter of the treetops, with the Howler trailing. That the Russians hadn't already blown the transport from the sky bothered Brent. They were holding fire. What the hell?

Maybe they wanted something—or someone—on board. They'd been given orders to track and observe. Interesting . . .

"Hammer, this is Ghost Lead. The Russians aren't firing at our bird."

"Ghost Lead, just take out that Howler. Now!"

Brent glanced up at Lakota, waved her over. She rushed to his side and dropped down. He switched off the audio on his Cross-Com. "This is weird."

"I know."

"Talk to that Blackhawk pilot. See if he's carrying any precious cargo or VIPs."

"Dennison will hear."

"I don't care. Just do it."

Lakota called the pilot, who said he wasn't at liberty to discuss such issues. That was pilot code for *I got precious cargo but I can't tell you.*

Otherwise, he would've just said *nope.*

"All right, let's get that bird onto the ground, then we'll find out what the hell's going on here," Brent said.

The Blackhawk drew closer, then, under Lakota's guidance and on her count, suddenly banked hard to the left, exposing the Howler behind it.

"All right, fire, fire, fire!" Brent shouted.

The two Brits manning the fifties cut loose with a massive barrage, every third round a tracer that shimmered like laser bolts across green crowns of trees. It seemed now that two fire-lit wires were attached to the helicopter as it climbed and rolled against the onslaught. The wires fluctuated and wanted to drag the chopper down.

Below, both gunners adjusted fire until their rounds were drumming along the fuselage's thick armor plates. It was awe-inspiring to see an aircraft take that many rounds from the fifties and from the rest of Brent's people. The thing still remained aloft, seemingly undamaged.

"Damn, I don't think we can touch her," shouted Lakota.

"Oh, no!" cried one of the gunners, breaking off fire. "We've pissed him off now! He's coming around!" The man abandoned his gun, jumped from the truck, and began running.

As the Blackhawk thumped overhead and swept behind them, the Howler pitched forward, coming to bear on one of the trucks. White-hot flashes came from its rocket pods.

Before Brent could open his mouth in an order to fall back, the first truck lifted off the ground and burst into a dome of fire whose heat and blast wave sent Brent sliding backward.

Smoke swirled in the rotor wash and dropped on them like a woolen blanket as the din of gunfire rose.

Brent coughed. His eyes burned. He could barely see the images piped in from the Cross-Com. And then the smoke thinned.

The second gunner kept firing on the chopper, a fountain of brass casings rising at his side. Brent screamed for the guy to get out of there, but he doubted the man had heard him. The Brit seemed unfazed by the helicopter coming around to finish him off.

Brent hollered again as the rocket pods flashed like cameras and twin smoke trails slashed the air between the chopper and the truck.

But that gunner never released his weapon and fired until the explosion swallowed him.

FOURTEEN

**Clearing near Royal Military Academy
Sandhurst**

Knowing that Dennison was observing everything on the battlefield, Brent did not report the loss of the fifty-caliber guns or that the Russians were about to finish his team.

Those facts were obvious.

As was the fact that he needed immediate air support. He and his Ghosts were firing slingshots at an armored Goliath, and a break back for the woods would leave them vulnerable.

Only a few seconds after he'd called for help—his senses overloaded by the fires, the secondary explosions, the deafening din of rotors and rotor wash—did a new window open in his HUD to reveal a praying mantis or rather a fighter pilot wearing an alien-like helmet with attached oxygen line. A complex grid of flashing data displays was reflected brilliantly across the pilot's tinted faceplate.

"Ghost Lead, this is Siren, Joint Strike Fighter Support, over."

"Siren, this is Ghost Lead, our target is—"

"Relax, Captain. I have your target. Tell your people to take cover, over."

"Roger that!" Somewhere amid all the racket came the faint hiss of a jet.

Brent hollered for incoming, and they all dug deeper into the mound. Brent craned his neck up, studied the sky, and waited.

Finally, the whoosh of the F-35's Pratt & Whitney engine boomed louder than the chopper's.

The F-35 Joint Strike Fighter was a Short Take-Off and Vertical Landing (STOVL) aircraft that had often provided Close Air Support to Brent's operations in Afghanistan. Pilots could keep their jets hidden in the mountains and launch vertically on a moment's notice. Some of his operators referred to the fighters as helicopters on steroids, and Brent was well accustomed to working with their highly capable if sometimes immodest pilots. Small world, too, because he knew this particular fighter jockey, and she was one of the best.

Major Stephanie Halverson had fought bravely enough during the Russian invasion of Canada to earn the attention of the president of the United States, along with the admiration of everyone in the JSF. She'd been shot down, nearly captured behind enemy lines, and rescued by a stalwart Force Recon Marine unit, who'd plucked her from the waters of a frozen lake whose ice had given way.

Word was in Afghanistan that if you had Siren on your back, the enemy didn't stand a chance—and you stood a greater chance of coming home alive.

All of Brent's people had been trained as air force combat controllers, though Lakota was the most accomplished among them. At the moment, though, Siren didn't need any help. Brent watched from her point of view as she targeted the Howler and unleashed the dogs: a pair of wingtip-mounted AIM-9X Sidewinder missiles.

That the missiles used a passive IR target-acquisition system to home in on the Howler's infrared emissions was a trivial detail.

That they would utterly destroy the enemy aircraft was all you needed to know.

And now it was time to stop, hold your breath, and look up at the fireworks show.

And that's exactly what Brent did.

The twin flashes came, burning magnesium bright, and from the jet's wings came fate in all its destructive glory.

The Howler tore apart not a second after the Sidewinders struck their one-two punch. Flaming debris formed the petals of a brilliant flower before all of it came crashing down just thirty meters away, the entire field trembling, secondary explosions resounding, debris pinwheeling in all directions like razor-sharp throwing stars tossed by ninja warriors.

Brent waved his people away, lest they be sliced apart

or caught in the flames. His Ghosts needed no more coaxing and sprinted for the trees.

"Ghost Lead, this is Siren, is there anything else I can do for you today, over?"

"Yeah, you can finally surrender your phone number."

Although Halverson's face was hidden by her faceplate, Brent guessed that she smiled. "Always a pleasure, Ghost Lead. Siren out."

The team, along with the surviving Brits, rallied back to the edge of the field where they'd entered as the Blackhawk settled down into a landing.

"You can ride with us if you want," Brent told the driver.

"My people are on the way. Thanks for that," the guy said, glancing at the burning Howler.

Brent gestured toward one of the shattered trucks. "I'm sorry about your gunner."

The driver made a face. "Me, too. Glad you got us a little help, otherwise we would've joined him."

Brent nodded.

"All right, everyone, let's load," shouted Lakota.

Brent shook hands with the driver, a sobering moment to be sure, and then he and the others climbed aboard the Blackhawk. He was the last inside and searched the bay area for any surprising faces. Just the pilot, co-pilot, and two door gunners, about as nondescript a bunch as you could get.

He wanted to express his puzzlement to Lakota, but the bay was much too loud to do any talking. They lifted off and forged onward, toward the coast.

No precious cargo? No VIPs? Why hadn't the Russians fired at the Blackhawk?

The answer came within seconds. Dennison appeared in his HUD. "Ghost Lead, we've intercepted communication from Haussler and his team. They had direct contact with that Howler. They're trying to track us again, but we cut the line."

"I thought maybe we were carrying VIPs," Brent said, lifting his voice above the helicopter's engines.

"Negative. Well, actually, from Haussler's standpoint, *you* are the VIPs. He'll let you do all the work and show up at the last second to claim the prize. I've got a gunship keeping him busy right now, but that asset won't be mine for much longer. Brits are all tied up, too. I think our German buddy's going to slip away again, damn it."

"Roger that."

"But take a look at this," said Dennison, her image switching to a streaming satellite video of a hovercraft racing across the channel. A text box indicated that the craft was bound for Folkestone Harbor, with an ETA of just six minutes. The image then zoomed in to show three people on bicycles heading down the narrow, shop-lined Old High Street, en route to the linkup with that hovercraft.

"We have her now," Brent said, trying to control his pulse. "If she gets on that ship, that's it. Done deal. Much easier to isolate and control."

"I agree. I'm instructing your pilot to hold off. We want her to board, get out into the channel, and then I'm calling in a laser strike on the hovercraft's engines. Once she's dead in the water, you move in."

"Sounds familiar and perfect. Only this time she's going to be on board. Standing by."

Brent glanced around at the rest of his team. "Get fast ropes ready! We're back in the hunt!"

"Roger that," said Lakota, then she began issuing orders to the others.

So the Snow Maiden wasn't so clever after all. She'd had her fun back in the Seychelles, but now she'd run out of time and terrain. Brent could already feel the zipper cuffs tightening around her wrists. He moved in front of her, got into her face, and said, *"You're not an easy woman to find."*

And she would just glower at him with bloodshot eyes, resigned to her capture.

Oh, were it that easy.

Taking a deep breath, Brent continued to watch the satellite feed. The three cyclists neared the end of the road and disappeared into the alcove of a restaurant identified by the Cross-Com's AI as "Fat Sam's."

"What? They're stopping for an early lunch?" Brent asked Dennison.

"Probably holding back until the hovercraft gets through the harbor."

"She's obviously in contact with someone. Can you intercept?" he asked.

"We've been trying. New form of encryption. Hard to break. Cutting-edge stuff, say the geeks back here. But they always say that, right?"

Just then the Blackhawk pilot began to wheel around and reported, "In our holding pattern."

Below lay the leathery brown stretches of sandy beach and the Folkestone pier jutting out like a slightly bent arm serving as the end of a railway line.

After another minute, the three cyclists appeared, heading along Harbour Street toward the hovercraft, just now entering and blasting seamlessly up the concrete hoverport lying near the railroad tracks. They were all holding to-go cups and had probably stopped for a quick drink.

The cyclists rode a bit faster now, reached the hoverport, set down their bikes, and raced up a small gangway set in place by two crew members.

Brent watched them like a hawk perched on a branch and studying a mouse who'd come up on his hind legs to sniff the air. The swoop and attack were already racing through his mind.

Lakota reported that the team was ready to drop on both ropes.

He nodded, then faced one of the door gunners. He tapped his Cross-Com, indicating that the man should open his intercom channel. He did. "Once she's disabled, there's a good chance we'll take some fire."

"Don't worry, Captain. When people shoot at me, I always return the favor." The guy wriggled his brows.

Brent slapped a palm on his shoulders. "I like your style."

The hovercraft was a newly designed, high-speed model with hybrid engines, according to Brent's HUD. With a crew of five and about a hundred passengers, it wasn't the largest ferry around but arguably the swiftest, able to cross the channel in less than twenty minutes. A few decades prior, hovercraft travel had all but ceased and was only returning in the past few years with a new company, new technology, and a new influx of international businesspeople trying to navigate around chaotic relationships strained by the war.

The craft powered up and slid backward off the hoverport, turned tail, and headed swiftly out of the harbor.

"Hammer, this is Ghost Lead, she's heading out."

"We'll give them about ten minutes to move farther off shore. I've already got laser strike authorization and controllers on standby."

"Roger that." Brent switched channels and asked the pilot about their fuel. They would have enough to complete the mission but probably not enough to get back to base. He could put down somewhere else, though, and had several smaller facilities in mind.

And so they circled, watching as the hovercraft moved farther away.

After several minutes, Dennison appeared: "Laser strike in five, four, three, two—"

Sparks arced high from the hovercraft's stern, and Brent knew the lasers had done their job. Smoke began billowing, and the broad wake behind the craft began to fade.

"Ghost Lead, this is Hammer! Move in!"

"Roger that." Brent waved his gloved hand in the air. "Ready on the ropes!"

As the chopper pilot throttled up and took them out and over the English Channel, Brent flexed his fingers and mentally prepared for the descent. The ropes were specially braided, and their gloves were designed of a Kevlar-Nomex outer shell that quickly absorbed the high heat they'd generate while sliding down. Fast-roping wasn't easy, wasn't safe, but it sure as hell was, ahem, *fast*. Grab the rope and slide. Three-meter gaps between operators. And you'd better not get any second thoughts. You loved the adrenaline rush but loathed the idea of being the guy in the middle, with operators sliding above and below you.

The Blackhawk banked around the still-billowing smoke and descended.

Both door gunners swung their 7.62-millimeter machine guns to bear on the hovercraft, and Brent came up behind one, clutching a wall rung for balance.

"Get ready for incoming," said the pilot. "Here we go." He brought the chopper in lower, slowing, pitching the nose up a bit until they glided not fifteen meters above the deck.

The gunners kept panning with their guns. Civilians who'd been outside on the deck began rushing back into the enclosed bay, while crew members were throwing up their hands, confused.

Brent listened in as the pilot spoke to the hovercraft's captain, telling him to prepare to be boarded.

"Keep your eyes on all sides of this boat," said Lakota. "She could slip off and try to make a swim for it."

"Is it really a boat?" asked Riggs. "I mean technically—"

"Just watch it!" Lakota ordered.

The captain lodged his protests but was allowing them to board. Brent issued the orders.

Without hesitation the ropes dropped and thumped on the bobbing deck.

"Go, go, go!" hollered Brent.

And drop they did, rifles slung over their backs, gloved hands clutching those ropes, balanced between life and serious injury.

Brent was the last one down, his people already moving forward, rifles raised to begin clearing the deck.

The civilians were understandably shaken, but this was wartime and many were already settling in, realizing that the boarding and search operation was a necessary evil. If they sat quietly and didn't intervene, they'd be fine, especially since they'd been told that "an American boarding party" had arrived.

As the others went below to continue the search, Brent ordered Park and Noboru to circulate through the passengers with photographs of the Snow Maiden. Within a minute, a few said they'd seen a woman who looked like her heading back to one of the rear restrooms.

After hearing that report, Brent charged toward the stern, went down a narrow flight of stairs, and found the hatch to the restroom locked. He rapped, called. Nothing. He ordered Daugherty and Heston to join him, and Heston grabbed a small prying tool from his web gear and busted open the hatch.

What the hell?

"Captain, did they do this?" asked Heston.

"No, someone else," said Daugherty.

A short, dark-skinned man, a teenaged boy, and a woman with spiked hair were all piled into the small room. The boy had a gunshot wound to the chest. The man had been shot in the head. Heston moved in, reached down, and turned the woman's head, revealing a bloody mess. As he did so, the short black wig slipped off, revealing blond hair pulled into a tight bun.

Decoys.

Brent took a step back and began screaming the word *No!* over and over.

He screamed so loud that even the chopper pilot could have heard him.

The Snow Maiden had to give Patti credit for her assistance and organizational skills. She'd set up the entire decoy run, right down to having the decoys themselves murdered at the last minute so they couldn't be tortured into confessing. Now there was only one man on board the hovercraft who worked for the *Ganjin*, and he was just a simple, unassuming passenger, a potbellied, gray-haired old codger more interested in the news flashing across his smartphone's display than in some boarding party search of his hovercraft.

For the moment, she, Chopra, and Hussein were being driven far away from Fat Sam's by a taxi driver who'd been paid to take them up to Dover, their original destination. From there, Patti had arranged transport across the channel by private yacht, but that would not happen until nightfall. They would spend the day at the West Bank Guest House, south of Dover, where Patti had made all the arrangements, no questions asked.

Once they reached the house, the driver said he'd already been paid and left. They entered into a main foyer/reception area, where a heavyset woman with shimmering white hair showed them to a room. Chopra and Hussein remained strangely silent, until she closed the door and faced them. "I want to thank you for your cooperation thus far. This could be much more difficult. You've made the right choice."

"I'm starving. When do we eat?" demanded Hussein.

"Relax, you'll get fed," she shot back.

"We're not going to Geneva," said Chopra. "We're not leaving this room."

She sighed deeply for effect and pointed at Hussein. "You've obviously been looking for him, and I've been looking for you. So now that we've all found each other, why can't we just live happily ever after?"

"I don't appreciate your sarcasm. This is a grave matter. But I guess you aren't much more than an evil person."

"You think I'm evil? How do you know that?"

"I've seen it."

"The murders?"

Chopra shrugged. "Of course."

"They were obstacles. There were no evil intentions in my heart when I killed them, only a job to do."

"And being that cold is not evil?"

"There are those who are much colder than I am. Trust me. Much colder. You don't know evil. If I had the time, I would show it to you."

Hussein took a deep breath and strode over to her.

"You need us. So you won't kill us, so really, we're calling the shots. The gun doesn't really mean anything because you won't use it. You can't. I can open the window and start shouting."

"You could," she told him. "And you're right, I won't kill you. But I can make you feel pain." With that she drew her silenced pistol and aimed it at the boy's leg. "Care to find out?"

"No, no, no," he said, backing away and bending over, as though he'd been struck by a softball in the groin.

"Okay, then do me a favor. Sit down at the desk. And Chopra, you sit there, and you explain to this spoiled brat why he needs to lead his country. He wasn't listening the first time. Tell him again."

Chopra scowled. "Another sick game? You want us to entertain you?"

She shook her head. "What you're telling him is the truth, and I agree with it. I admire your ambition and loyalty to him and his family. There aren't many people like you in this world, a world controlled by greed and corruption. And I'm no different. I only want the money and the oil-reserve locations. But his nation will recover. And he needs to lead it. He can help the emirates rise up against Russia."

"You can't be serious," he said.

She holstered her pistol beneath her coat. "I am. Believe me. I am."

Just then the room's phone rang, and they all looked at each other. Holding her breath, the Snow Maiden answered, and her heart sank as the man on the other end said, "Is this Viktoria Antsyforov?"

She slammed the receiver down and raced to the window. "Come on, we're leaving!" she shouted.

With the latch thrown, she shoved up the window and was about to climb out when gunfire pummeled the wall beside her, splintering the wooden shingles. She caught the briefest glimpse of a man standing near a small car, aiming an automatic rifle. His green balaclava concealed most of his face. He'd intentionally worn green to send her a message.

FIFTEEN

West Bank Guest House
South of Dover

The Snow Maiden hit the floor and crawled across the room as Chopra wrenched open the door, placing himself between Hussein and the incoming fire.

She screamed for them to go, and she was just behind, bolting up to slam the door after herself but not before something thumped on the wood.

Oh, no . . .

She hollered again for them to move.

And just as she reached the staircase, the room exploded behind her, the concussion knocking her down the stairs and crashing into Chopra and Hussein, who tumbled themselves as shouts and screams rose from below.

Her pistol slipped from her holster as she tried to pull herself up from the tangled mess of the old man and kid.

Before she could sit up, Hussein had her gun and pointed it at her. "Now you work for me. Just like him," the kid said, flicking a glance at Chopra, who was just sitting up and straightening his glasses.

A crash came from the other side of the house, and after a few loud footfalls, the man wearing the green balaclava rushed into the doorway, turned, and spotted them.

"Shoot him!" she cried as she reached for her second micro pistol tucked into an ankle holster. She had a third gun and a couple of knives as well—a switchblade and a small, sheathed neck knife that hung from a piece of paracord.

Remarkably—perhaps even miraculously—the kid got off the first shot, striking the terrorist thug in the shoulder. The guy's first salvo went wide as he took the hit, and then another ripped across the ceiling, sending plaster tumbling down onto their heads.

The Snow Maiden squinted through all the dust and finished him with two more shots—much to the kid's surprise. She gave him a look: *You think I carry only one gun?* Then she bolted off the stairs and grabbed the thug's rifle, searched his pockets, and found a set of keys.

"Shoot me or come along," she told Hussein. "Because this bastard's not working alone."

"They'll kill the sheikh!" cried Chopra. "We must protect him!"

"They're after me. You're excess baggage, and those guys travel light. So yeah—they'll kill the kid." She rushed to Hussein and thrust out her hand. "Give me back the gun."

"I think I'll just—"

The kid didn't get to finish. She ripped the pistol from his hand in one deft movement, and he'd screamed as she'd bent his trigger finger.

"Out now!"

They complied, and once clear of the stairwell, they charged out a back door, leaving the house staff lying on the floor behind sofas or beneath tables.

She told them to hold there, just outside, where she called Patti, who told her she was clear to go for the thug's car.

Taking a long breath and holding it, she made her break, racing around the house, weaving between bushes, traversing a small stone path, then wrenching open a wrought-iron gate to race across a brown patch of grass toward where the thug had parked his car. She fervently believed he was not working alone and felt a pang of fear over trusting Patti, who no doubt was watching via hacked satellite transmissions.

As she crossed the grass, the gunfire came in from across the street.

She dove onto her belly near an old oak, then elbowed her way behind it. Using the camera function on her cell phone, she kept tightly behind the trunk and slowly moved the camera out until she could see the street in the tiny screen: Two men had set up behind the row of parked cars.

The shuffling of feet from behind made her whirl

back. Chopra and the kid had joined her. "I told you to hold back there!"

"The house is on fire," cried Chopra.

He wasn't kidding. The stench had already grown unbearable, and the staff members were rushing out into the yard, screaming and talking on phones. Sirens began to sound in the distance.

"You have the keys to that car?" asked Chopra. "Give them to me. I'll be ready to get us out of here."

"Sure, I'll trust you with those," she said. "Come on." She rose and fired some covering shots to drive the men down as she ran from the tree to the car, just ten meters. The thugs returned fire, the rounds booming and ricocheting as she threw herself behind the back wheel. Chopra and Hussein charged up and crouched behind her. The old man could barely catch his breath, and the kid wasn't faring much better. This was probably more exercise than they'd had in a year.

With a pop and hiss both tires on the opposite side of the car went flat.

"There goes our ride," said Hussein.

The Snow Maiden cursed, looked back at Chopra, and handed him the car keys.

"Thanks a lot," he spat.

Two thugs. No escape plan. And Patti's intel was obviously worthless.

She closed her eyes for just a moment. Took a breath. All right, she'd been in worse situations. Time to go on the offensive.

* * *

The Blackhawk could not land on the hovercraft and didn't have enough fuel left to engage in a slow, one-by-one extraction of Brent's team via the hoist.

So Brent had no choice but to cut loose the pilot. The hovercraft was equipped with two small Zodiacs for emergencies, so he and the others would launch them and head back to Dover, where Dennison said she'd have them picked up.

"Wait, getting something else now," she told Brent, showing him streaming video from a house near Dover that was now on fire. "Reports of an explosion and gunfire. Not sure if it's related."

"It has to be," said Brent, watching as his people prepared the two Zodiacs for launch. "Can you get me some ground transport once we reach the harbor?"

"I'm on it. But don't get your hopes up, Brent. This could just be something else. Looters? Who knows . . ."

"They pulled a switch at the restaurant, so they didn't get very far, I'm telling you."

"I'll see if there's any other air support available. If we can get another chopper over there, we might have a shot."

Chopra flinched as another bullet burrowed into the car and sparks flew somewhere above him. He crouched tightly near the rear wheel, keeping Hussein close to his side. He draped an arm around the boy, who threw the arm off, saying, "You're not my father. And that's creepy."

"Who are they?" Chopra asked the Snow Maiden, whose expression had formed a tight knot of intense thought. "Did you hear me?" he added, raising his voice.

"Stay here. Don't move," she said, then shifted around the car, out of sight.

"We can make our break now," Hussein said. "We'll run back to the house. Hear that? The fire department's coming."

"We're staying here," said Chopra. "And if those guys out there are her enemies, they might be our friends."

"You know, you got a point," said Hussein.

"Finally, you're willing to listen to the old man."

Hussein snorted. "For now."

"Your father was a great man."

"That was random."

"You can be as great . . ."

A fresh spate of gunfire made Chopra lean out from behind the car.

He gasped.

The Snow Maiden had darted across the street, drawing the fire of one man while the other ducked back behind his car. She made it all the way across without being struck, or at least it felt so, and then she dropped onto her belly and glanced ahead, where she spotted a pair of legs.

She propped up the rifle, held her breath, and fired

a three-round burst, striking the man in the ankle. He cried out, went down, and that's when she rushed up, around the car, and ran straight at him.

He looked at her and began to bring around his gun, only the eyes showing beneath his green balaclava.

Her rounds drummed evenly across his chest, forming a perforated slash mark, and he flailed back like a leaf in the wind. She ran by, searching for the other guy, the kill as instantaneous and robotic as that.

She was taking a hell of a risk, all right, betting that the kid and the old man would be too scared to take off. Her attention was now divided between the car across the street and the row in front of her.

Then she saw it, movement just head. The tiniest portion of a green balaclava showed above the trunk of an old Mercedes. She threw herself beside the nearest car, rifle at the ready.

"Hey, fool," she shouted in Russian. "Tell Green Vox to stop wasting my time."

"You've already told him," the thug replied. He'd chosen to speak in English but his accent was thick and familiar; South American, she knew. "I'm Green Vox!"

"Sure, whatever. It doesn't matter. But let me ask you—how'd you find me?"

"You're sloppy. You're just very sloppy."

She gritted her teeth. "Izotov's helping you, Nestes. Isn't he?"

"Do you want to talk now or embrace in death?"

"That's dramatic. Unfortunately your death won't be. It's all very routine."

"I'm glad you remember me . . ." Surprisingly, he shifted out from behind the car, rifle pointed skyward. He wrenched off his mask to reveal a bearded face and piercing blue eyes.

Jose Nestes (not his real name) was a drug lord from Colombia who had joined the Green Brigade Transnational in an attempt to form a splinter group he called "the Forgotten Army." Nestes's dream was to lead a terrorist organization large enough to undermine the efforts of the superpowers themselves. He claimed to have brought together several of the world's most notorious terror organizations, including Hezbollah and the Taliban.

But Green Vox—or at least the original one the Snow Maiden had worked with—had rejected this idea, in favor of his ecological agenda. He fancied himself as more of a noble terrorist trying to save the planet than a crime lord trying to undermine the global economy, a goal that in and of itself seemed rather laughable to her.

Yet Nestes, if he was being honest, had somehow seized the Green Brigade's reins and was, quite possibly, steering the group in another direction.

"I want to make a deal with you," he said. "You know I'm serious, because you could kill me right now. We don't have time to discuss details. But we need to talk."

"If you wanted to make a deal, then why didn't you just drop by for tea?"

"Can you blame me for trying to kill you? There's a bounty on your head. A huge one. Didn't you know that?"

"You're right. We don't have time for this." She rose and started toward him, lifting her rifle.

He brought his rifle down and aimed at her. She should've shot him, but his offer sounded strangely intriguing, so here they were now, in a standoff.

"I guess we both die," he said.

"Yeah, but you die first, and I always get the last word."

The Snow Maiden's cell phone began to ring. She cursed.

"That wouldn't be Patti calling, would it?"

She froze.

In shock.

If you knew about the *Ganjin*, then you were in the *Ganjin*—or you didn't live long.

"Who're you working for?" she demanded.

"For you now."

"I don't believe it."

"There are those who don't appreciate your service and would rather terminate your employment."

"What the hell does that mean?" she asked. "You're just playing a little game. And I'm not biting."

The fire trucks' sirens resounded loudly as they turned the corner and barreled down the road.

She tossed a look to them, then summarily shot Nestes. He staggered back and fell to the ground. She bent down over him.

"You just made a big mistake," he gasped. "I could have helped you . . ."

With a chill, she rose, ran across the street, and

screamed for the old man and kid to get in the car. She jumped into the driver's seat and fired up the engine, and they tore away from the curb, riding on two flat tires.

In all her years of covert intelligence work and trade-craft, she had never made a more sloppy or pathetic escape. Maybe they were all correct. She had lost her edge.

Or maybe there were just too many forces working against her this time: the Americans, the Brits, the Russians, the terrorists, and now . . .

What the hell had Nestes been talking about? Were there enemies within the *Ganjin* that wanted her killed?

If they managed to get the hell out of the U.K., then she and Patti were going to have a very long talk. She glanced quickly at her phone; indeed, Patti had been try-ing to contact her.

Brent's team arrived at the docks near Dover. Dennison confirmed that the Snow Maiden, along with Chopra and Hussein, had been at the West Bank Guest House, now ravaged by flames. They'd left, heading northeast up Folkestone Road, but they had lost sight of them at Dover Towne Centre, where a massive traffic jam still blocked all roads.

Brent and his Ghosts jogged the short distance to that business center, broke off in pairs, fanned out, and conducted an exhaustive search of a three-block radius. They found the Snow Maiden's car, two wheels shot up, parked along a dense greenbelt near Priory Hill. She'd obviously broken out of the traffic jam and driven right through the woods, judging from the extensive damage to the vehicle, the tracks, and the gaping lines in the pavement from the rims.

Dennison tried to enlist the aid of the local authorities, but the request had been denied because they had their hands full with the massive crowds at the docks.

All Brent and his Ghosts had to do now was find the three people amid near-rioting crowds flooding toward the coastline.

Brent stationed Riggs and Schleck up on two of the highest buildings, where they'd maintain surveillance on the docks via Schleck's drone.

Splinter Cell Thomas, still bleary-eyed and distraught over the loss of his brother, volunteered to coordinate with Third Echelon and was communicating directly with them to gain more intel.

They spent the remainder of the day searching in vain, and as night fell, Brent stood near a roundabout opposite the harbor. "Hammer, you got anything? Anything at all?"

"Negative, Ghost Lead. Negative . . ."

He checked in with Thomas. The NSA had nothing either.

"She'll turn up again," said Lakota, drawing up to Brent's side. "She might lay low here for a day or two, but I'll bet she'll cross into Europe. They'll keep eyes in the sky focused on this route, and they'll pick her up."

Brent sighed. "They'll disguise themselves and slip

out in the middle of the night. And we can't stay here forever."

"What're you saying?"

"I'm saying that . . . at least for me . . . this is the end of the line. Before the night's over, Dennison will call me back with orders to pull out."

"We can't give up."

"They want results. And we didn't provide them. They'll bring in fresh meat to get the job done. But hey, I had a good run. The Ghosts are number one, that's for sure. At least I had a chance to play with you guys . . ."

Lakota shook her head. "I won't let that happen. All right, you were a little too hardcore by taking us back to Robin Sage, but you've been an excellent captain, sir. I would serve with you anytime, anywhere."

"Thanks." He smiled wanly. "But I'm done here."

She frowned. "You shouldn't be taking this so well."

"I'm not. It's all an act. After you leave, I'll curse. I'll break something. I'll get an ulcer, and my eyeballs will explode from my head."

"Now that I can believe. But please, sir, if she pulls us off, you have to argue. You have to fight."

"Trust me, I will, but I've been around long enough to know how these things go. The unit on the ground takes the responsibility for the loss."

"That's not always true. We're only as good as the intel they provide. If they keep putting us two steps behind and can't provide the assets, how can they hold us accountable?"

"Dennison went out on a limb for me. I owed her results. Simple as that."

"Let me talk to her."

"Forget it." Brent extended his hand. "It's been an honor and a pleasure."

"No, I won't take your hand. I won't. It's not over."

Brent shrugged, lowered the hand, and stared out across the harbor, where crowded ferries and dozens of private craft thrummed toward the French coastline.

SIXTEEN

Geneva
Forty-eight Hours Later

After abandoning their car in the park, the Snow Maiden, Chopra, and Hussein had fled to the equipment storage room of a nearby tennis club. They'd hidden there until nightfall, at which time they were met by their old taxi driver, who brought changes of clothing and took them to the docks to link up with a yacht bound for Calais. Patti had arranged it all.

Though the crowds had thinned somewhat, there were still enough evacuees to create a wonderful diversion. Getting lost among them was not difficult, and the ball caps and coats certainly helped. She knew that dozens of electronic eyes were focused on them, so they'd kept to the crowds. Moreover, they weren't the only ones boarding the yacht. A group of about fifteen others did so as well, all part of the guise. The *Ganjin*, it seemed, had a much larger network and sphere of influence than even the Snow Maiden had imagined. And that unnerved her.

The rest of the full-day road trip from Calais to Geneva unfolded uneventfully, though she imagined that Chopra and Hussein were plotting an escape. They occasionally glanced at each other, and when it became a little too obvious, the Snow Maiden addressed their unspoken communication outright: "If you run, I shoot you in the legs. Believe me—most gunshot wounds hurt. It's not like TV or the movies. It's serious pain. And I'll still drag you to Dubai. It's not worth it."

"Don't you ever sleep?" Hussein had asked her.

"My record is seventy-two hours."

When they were just an hour away from Geneva, the Snow Maiden had called Patti and once again had asked what was going on with Nestes—and how did he know about the *Ganjin*? Patti said it was "complicated" and that she wasn't prepared to discuss the matter at the present time.

Because of her reticence, the Snow Maiden decided to drop off the grid for a while. There were a few people she could call to follow up on Nestes's actions, but Patti would, of course, be privy to those conversations.

When they arrived in Geneva, she spoke with the owner of a coffee shop where a friend, Heidi Lautens, stopped every morning. Heidi lived in an apartment near the Rhone River and was a professor at the University IFM Geneva, an international business school where she taught economics. Her husband, Aldo, had also been a professor and operative working for the GRU for more than ten years. He'd been killed in a terrorist attack in Paris while on an assignment for the Russian government, an assignment that the Snow Maiden had planned. That was just a year before the war, and because the Snow Maiden had worked closely with the man, she felt responsible to help his widow, despite the GRU's insistence that she not make contact. Consequently, the Snow Maiden was vague regarding the details of Aldo's death and only identified herself as one of Aldo's research assistants. Izotov himself had learned of this security breach and had threatened her if she continued offering assistance. She'd threatened him. It was the *humanitarian* thing to do, a word, she'd said, the Russian government had never understood. If they didn't allow her to help, a security breach unlike any they had ever experienced would occur. Izotov had snickered, "Your soft heart will get you killed."

During the last few years, the Snow Maiden had kept in touch with Heidi and had even visited to have lunch with her several times. They'd had a lot in common and e-mailed each other a few times per month. Heidi was like the sister the Snow Maiden had never had and truly the only "real" female friend she'd ever had.

The trouble was, the Snow Maiden had never been honest with Heidi, but that was part of the Snow Maiden's protection, her armor, and she'd always known that having a friend in Geneva who was in her debt would someday prove invaluable.

At the Snow Maiden's request, the coffee shop owner

contacted Heidi, who came to the shop and went into a back room, where a table had been set up for them. The Snow Maiden had, of course, paid the shop owner handsomely for this small luxury.

Heidi wore her hair a bit shorter than the Snow Maiden had remembered, and her new "academic" plastic-framed glasses reminded the Snow Maiden of the woman's devotion to scholarship.

They spoke in English, as was Heidi's wont. She was more than a little surprised. "Viktoria, I didn't know you were in Geneva! It's so good to see you! But why are you back here? Why all the secrecy?"

Chopra and Hussein were seated nearby and watching, and their uneasy expressions caught Heidi's attention. "Are they your friends?"

"No, we are not," said Chopra.

The Snow Maiden looked fire in the old man's direction. "Please . . ."

"Viktoria, what's going on?"

"I'm wondering if we can stay with you for the night."

"We? You mean them as well?"

"Yes, I'll explain everything, and I'll take care of your rent for the rest of the year."

Heidi shifted in her seat. "This is, uh, quite strange. You drop in unannounced with these people. Can't you get a hotel?"

"No, I can't right now. It's complicated. I just need you to trust me. And we need to talk."

"You know I don't have much room."

"We'll sleep on the floor. I just need this right now, and I can explain everything once we're up there."

"I was about to have dinner. I don't have enough food for us all."

The Snow Maiden grinned. "Don't worry about that. I'll take care of everything."

"Viktoria, what's wrong? What's going on? You're scaring me."

The Snow Maiden reached across the table and clutched both of Heidi's hands. "You can trust me."

Brent had bought himself a little condo just thirty minutes away from Fort Bragg. In fact, the place was almost paid off, and the resale value wasn't bad, despite the ever-fluctuating market. Most folks who lived in his complex were military, and demand for such housing remained high. A condo was the way to go for a single military man: no lawn to worry about mowing, no building maintenance to perform, but the HOA fees would eventually bankrupt him, he knew.

He was on his way home after heading down to central Florida to see George Voeckler's parents. They lived in a small retirement home in The Villages, and it was with great sorrow and resignation that he expressed his condolences in person. The NSA had already sent representatives to notify them of George's death, but Thomas had beaten even them to the punch. He'd called his parents while en route back to the States, and as expected, neither Frank nor Regina Voeckler had taken the news very well.

Thomas had not been present during Brent's visit. Regina had said he'd gone off to his time-share on Captiva Island. The Voecklers were exceedingly proud of their two boys and made a point of telling Brent about the great influence George had been on Thomas. They feared that without George's continued guidance, Thomas might slip back into a depression and into his "old ways." He'd already been talking about quitting the NSA job when he'd come home. Regina had taken Brent's hand and had begged him to talk to Thomas. Brent said that he would.

But for now, he needed to get back home for a meeting with Lieutenant Colonel Susan Grey, DCO, 1st Bn, 5th Special Forces Group, a long title for a woman short on patience. Grey was a lean, athletic woman with short blond hair who seemed demure before she smiled and ate you for breakfast. She headed up Ghost Recon and had not endorsed Dennison's selection of Brent to lead the Snow Maiden mission. She would remind him of that, and the meeting would, of course, determine his future in the military, if there was one at all.

As he'd suspected, the team had been pulled off the hunt and sent back home, and were about to be reassigned. Lakota's eyes had burned when she resignedly had taken his hand at the airport.

Brent did something stupid and said that now that they weren't working together, he'd like to take her out and buy her a beer.

"You mean a date?" she'd asked.

"I don't know what I mean."

"Well, when you figure that out, give me a call." She'd given him a curt nod and walked away.

Oh, yes, he was quite an operator when it came to the ladies . . .

It was late afternoon when he got back home and he was too tired to cook, so he drove down to the Liberator for a burger and a drink or two. He sat alone in his usual booth, and Schoolie, the big boy with the scarred face, drifted over and slid into the seat opposite him. "Back from Europe."

Brent made a face. "I know why you're here, and I'm not talking."

"You don't have to. I got some scuttlebutt."

"We're friends now? Sharing secrets? I thought you wanted to bust my chops."

"Well, that, too."

"Then why are you talking like my buddy?"

"I'm still your buddy, Brent. But when I offered my hand before the mission, you should've taken it. You jinxed yourself."

"Okay, whatever."

"Look, let me tell you what's going on . . ." Schoolie leaned in closer and scratched his stubbly jowls.

Brent rubbed his eyes, leaned back, and sighed deeply.

Schoolie's tone grew emphatic. "Word is they've just assigned a new team to your old operation."

"Yeah, so?"

"I'm on the new team. We just got briefed. You didn't hear this from me—but they found her again."

Brent nodded. "We knew she'd turn up."

Schoolie winced, took a deep breath, and said, "This isn't the kind of stuff we should be doing."

"It's a different war now."

He snorted. "Yeah, I don't like it."

"So why're you telling me this?"

"Because I know you, Brent. You won't take this lying down."

Brent accepted his beer from the waitress and, after a long pull, said, "Maybe I will."

"Why don't you talk to Dennison? I'll drive you down to the comm center."

"I need a chauffeur?"

"You parked on the grass again, and they just towed your car. You didn't learn your lesson from the last time?" Schoolie tipped his head toward the front windows, where a tow truck was just leaving with Brent's car hanging from the back.

Brent burst up from the table, cursed, and started toward the door.

"Get it later," said Schoolie. "Come on, I'll take you for that call. See if you can have a little video chat. Do it now before your meeting with Grey."

"Yeah, I came back here to call down to Florida, where I just was . . ." he said wearily. "Maybe I should've dropped in on Dennison while I was there."

"Maybe. Have a seat, finish your beer and your dinner. Then we'll go."

Brent complied, and Schoolie tried to probe him for what had happened on the mission. Brent gave him the look that said even asking was breaking the law. That Schoolie had mentioned his own assignment was certainly a violation, not one Brent would ever report, but a violation nonetheless.

"Why are you trying to help me?" Brent said, after taking his last sip of beer.

Schoolie averted his gaze. "This is going to sound stupid."

"I figured."

"Seriously, I've served under a lot of people. I'd be honored to work with you. I'd like to see Boleman out and you in. I'd like to see that happen."

Captain Jay Boleman was a few years younger than Brent and regarded as one of the top three team leaders in the entire organization. Unfortunately, his skill was equaled by his arrogance.

Brent grinned broadly. "So you'd rather work for a junkyard dog than a greyhound, is that what you're saying?"

"Jay's an ass. We both know it. Anyway, I thought I'd help you out."

"Okay. Thanks."

They left the Liberator and went to the comm center for a secure line. Brent made the call to Tampa, only to be told that Dennison was gone for the day and that if the matter wasn't urgent that he should try again at 0800. He cupped the receiver.

"I guess you'll have to call her tomorrow," said Schoolie.

Brent swore to himself. "The meeting's tomorrow. I need to talk to her now."

So he told them the matter was urgent, and they patched him through to Dennison's home via an encrypted signal.

"She's going to be pissed," said Schoolie.

"Frankly, fat boy, I don't give a damn."

"Captain Brent?" Dennison began, tugging her robe more tightly around her shoulders. She had a quart of rocky road ice cream in her hand with a spoon jutting from it.

"Major, we need to talk."

"Look, Brent, there's no more discussion. If you take issue with what's happened, you need to bring that up to Colonel Grey. I shouldn't have to remind a career officer about the chain of command."

"Colonel Grey and I have different perceptions regarding my After Action Report."

"What does that mean?"

"It means I was removed from the mission before being allowed to finish it."

"I see you've had time to think. And in your case, that's dangerous. Look, I'm sure they'll have a place for you. I've heard a lot of great things about your skill as a trainer. You'd be excellent at the JFK School."

"Someday, yes. But not now."

Dennison glanced at her ice cream. "Is there anything else?"

"Don't give this to Boleman. It's mine. Let me finish it. I was close. Very close."

"I'm sorry, Brent, but it's too late for that. This call is over."

"How did you find her?"

"I'm tired, Captain."

"I'm just asking."

She sighed. "Doletskaya gave us a list of her contacts, and a name came up in Geneva. We had some eyes on that zone and spotted her. We'd tried to bait her, even had him leave messages. She either didn't get them or wasn't taking the bait. But the analysts picked her up right away. The NSA's already got people moving in."

"She'll be long gone."

"We need to figure out where she's going."

Brent assumed his best poker face. "I know where she's going."

"Oh, really?"

"Ma'am, I need to finish what I started."

"Good night, Captain."

She abruptly ended the link.

Brent turned back toward Schoolie, who was now engulfed by a fiery car crash, the flames rising up his body and burning him into a skeleton whose bones turned black.

Brent blinked.

"Damn . . ." Schoolie said, glancing away. "Tomorrow you're busted out of the Ghosts. Ah, it's not so bad."

Brent looked incredulously at him. "You think I'm going to let that happen?"

"What do you mean?"

Brent cocked a brow. "You *know* what I mean."

"Aw, no, you're crazy."

Brent widened his eyes. "Am I?"

*   *   *

The Snow Maiden spotted the man on the rooftop of the building across the street, so she, Heidi, and the others ducked back into the coffee shop.

"What's going on now?" cried Heidi. "I thought we were going to the market, then my apartment."

"I'm sorry. I'm sorry about coming here," said the Snow Maiden. "It was a mistake. I need a car right now."

"You know I don't own a car."

She looked to the coffee shop owner. "Him. Tell him I need to borrow his."

Heidi did so, and although the Snow Maiden couldn't hear what they were saying, the shop owner's expression was enough. The Snow Maiden crossed to the counter, waved the man into the back room, then drew her pistol, put it to his head. "Keys. Now."

He fished into his pockets. She took the keys, then motioned for Chopra and Hussein to head out the back door.

In the alley, they found the man's little Kia. She ordered Hussein into the trunk, told Chopra to lie across the backseat, and gave the keys to Heidi. "You need to drive."

Heidi was beginning to hyperventilate. "Viktoria!"

"Stay with me, and I'm going to tell you what's going on. Okay? I need your help."

Heidi fought for breath, took the keys, and climbed into the car.

"We need someplace secure. Maybe at the university?" the Snow Maiden asked.

"Okay, okay."

As they pulled out, she called Patti. "Unexpected friends here. Are they yours?"

"Yes, they are," said Patti. "And you should be thankful. The Americans sent operatives. We took care of them for you. Don't try to drop off the grid again, are we clear?"

"We are," she said through gritted teeth.

"Meet me tomorrow at eight A.M. Café Gavoroche. I'm sending you the map now."

"All right."

"Now there's no need to rush off just yet, if you'd like to spend some time with your friend."

"I'm afraid the evening's already been ruined . . ." She hung up and told Heidi to turn the car around; they were going back to Heidi's apartment.

Hussein began pounding on the trunk partition. "I want out of here! Right now!"

Chopra sat up. "I assume our little clandestine exit has been canceled?"

"Quiet," the Snow Maiden told him.

Heidi suddenly pulled over to the curb. "I need to know what's going on right now. I'm sure Hans back at the coffee shop has called the police."

"You're right. So maybe we're not going back to your place," said the Snow Maiden. "You can check us into a hotel. That'll work now."

"I'm not doing anything."

"Heidi, I never told you this, but Aldo was working for the CIA. That's why he was killed. And the same men who tried to kill him are trying to kill me."

"No, that's not true."

"Come with me, and I'll explain. I'll tell you everything. Just help us get a room."

"I don't even know who you are."

"I want to tell you. I really do. But it's important that you just do as I say. All right?"

"No, no, I won't do this, I can't," cried Heidi. "I don't know if you're a criminal or a prostitute or who you are!" She reached for the door handle and opened the door.

The Snow Maiden bit her lower lip, drew her pistol—

And as Chopra shouted, "No!"

—she killed her old friend.

SEVENTEEN

Brent sat in the reception area outside General Scott Mitchell's office. Mitchell was the man, head of the entire JSF. You couldn't go any further up the ladder.

And you didn't get a meeting with a guy like that by just whining that you disagreed with a superior's decision.

You got a meeting by showing . . . audacity. A word much in the news during the past year or so.

So Brent had made the call and had informed the general's staff that he wanted to strike a bargain.

The general had initially declined, but his curiosity won out when he learned that Grey had denied Brent permission to go over her head, and Brent retorted that he wasn't seeking permission; this was just a courtesy call advising her of his intentions.

Dozens of framed wartime photographs of Mitchell

in action covered the walls, and as Brent studied them, he began to understand the enormity of what he was doing, the enormity of this man's position.

Who in the hell was Brent to try cutting a deal for another chance? The mere act was going to incite every officer above him: most notably Grey and Dennison.

Moreover, Mitchell had been a Ghost Recon legend, arguably the unit's greatest living officer. Many of the techniques, tactics, and procedures that Brent had learned had been developed by Mitchell himself during his own time at the JFK School. Brent wasn't even sure if he could speak intelligently let alone make a persuasive argument once he faced the man in the flesh.

And worse, he'd have to do that on two hours of sleep. He'd spent most of the night arranging to get his butt back to Tampa, and as he checked his watch, he expected his cell phone to ring at any—

There it was, ringing. After a long sigh, he answered.

"Captain Brent, this is Colonel Grey's office. It's oh eight ten, and we're wondering where you are."

Brent tossed his head back, closed his eyes, and saw himself standing before a general court-martial. No, his punishment wouldn't be that severe, of course, but his imagination always took him straight to hell first.

"Captain Brent? Are you there?"

"Ah, yes, I'm here, here as in I'm at MacDill AFB for a meeting with General Mitchell."

"Uh, all right, I'll inform the colonel."

"Thanks."

As Brent hung up, he pictured Grey's face when she got the news. Heat waves would billow from her brow.

"Captain?"

Brent rose and was escorted into the general's office by Mitchell's assistant.

The general had divided the room into two areas: a rather regal-looking work zone with rich dark furniture, bookcases, and unit flags hung from the walls, the other area a high-tech observation post with a cocoon of monitors displaying battlefield operations. The station was, in effect, a miniature version of the JSF's more elaborate command center. Mitchell was seated at that station, wearing virtual-reality gloves and manipulating holographic data bars that only he could see via his VR glasses. His fingers flicked right and left, and he made the O shape with index and thumb several times to close open windows. He suddenly wrenched off the glasses and gloves and bolted from the seat as though it were on fire.

"All right, all right . . ." he muttered, clearing his thoughts aloud.

The general sported a snowy white crew cut that complemented his angular jaw. Brent guessed he spent as much time in the gym as he did in the VR chair, and an unmistakable twinkle in his eye seemed infectious.

"Captain Brent, you're a persistent man," said the general, taking Brent's hand in his own. "That much I admire. The rest of your record looks inconsistent. You, son, have been on a roller coaster ride instead of a career ladder."

"I just take it as it comes, sir."

Mitchell hardened his gaze. "So what the hell's the matter with you?"

"Sir?"

"Forgive my candor. Dennison tells me she pulled the plug on your mission. And Grey doesn't want you on it. You've come here to ask for a second chance in the guise of some deal regarding a low-life warlord in Afghanistan that you want to hand over to me."

"Sir, I've had sources there for years, and I'm finally calling in all my favors."

"At a rather convenient time."

"Sayyaf has links to China and the Russian Federation. There's a rumor that he's in bed with the Green Brigade, too. He's a piece we need to take off the board."

"And you're handing him to me in exchange for another chance to go after the Snow Maiden."

"What would you do?"

"I wouldn't come in here and insult my boss's intelligence."

Brent glanced away and smiled. "Sir, in the grand scheme of things, I'm just a little guy. I know that. And at my level, this is the best I got. The deal might be insulting, but you'll have Sayyaf."

"So Brent comes first, country second."

"I never wanted it to be this way. I hate the politics. I really do. But I'm asking for a lot, so I give something in return."

"So this has been your ace in the hole in case we screw you over, huh? Keep a little piece of the pie to yourself, and give it back when the time is right."

"No, sir. I wish I were that smart. When they pulled me off the mission, I started thinking about my options. Then I made a few calls."

Mitchell sighed very deeply for effect. "You want me to take this deal and overstep my officers."

Brent opened his mouth—but the general spoke before he could: "And you want me to take your intelligence on good faith and place more Americans in harm's way."

Brent glanced toward the window. The general's tone had come as a challenge, and Brent knew if he backed down now, there was no second chance. The general was probing, looking to see if he had any fight left in him. Well, he sure as hell did.

"Sir, can I ask you a question? Why'd you join the Army?"

Mitchell grinned, as though over some private joke. "You know the answer to that as well as I—because they forced you to read my bio."

"I don't mean the facts, sir. I mean the *feeling*."

"To be in control, right? To feel some power. To put forth that power in a way that yields a tangible and desirable result. Hell, that sounds so academic. Maybe we all got into this because it just makes us feel good. We want to do the right thing for our families and our country."

"That's not my story, sir. I got into this to try to be somebody I'm not. I did it out of guilt. I thought I could make things right. I learned a lot. And maybe I'm not the most qualified Ghost for this job, but you can bet I'm the most persistent. I'm disciplined, and I never forget what I want."

Mitchell crossed around his ornate desk and plopped down hard into the leather chair. He leaned back, pillowing his head in his hands.

"The idea that you've been withholding intelligence from us doesn't just strike a nerve, Captain. It makes me want to squeeze your neck until your face turns blue."

"With all due respect, sir, there's a difference between delaying my report and withholding it."

"Semantics. Your intentions are clear."

Brent knew he'd regret it, but he raised his voice. "Sir, I just want to fight another day. That's it. You've been the fall guy yourself, so you know what I'm talking about. Once a Ghost, always a Ghost. We know how this pans out."

The intercom beeped, followed by a voice. "Sir, I have Colonel Grey on vid channel three."

"Sir, don't take that call," said Brent.

"Why not?"

"Because she'll tell you I'm incapable and insubordinate."

"And you're late for a meeting with her," added the general. "So you're right, she doesn't have to tell me how insubordinate you are. I'm witnessing it firsthand."

"I just want to fight."

Mitchell told his assistant that he'd return the call. Then he faced Brent and sighed. "Why do I bet on you?"

"Sir, we lost a good man out there, and I'd like to take his brother, my team, and one other sergeant. You give me those people, and I'll get this Snow Maiden for you."

"You didn't answer my question. Why do I bet on

you—when you've already failed? And don't tell me it's because I'll get the warlord. I don't give a crap about him right now."

"We weren't allowed to finish what we started."

"So pulling the plug on you was premature?"

"Absolutely, sir."

"Even after repeated failures? Maybe we cut our losses with you. Why don't you just back off? Start training the new guys, be the voice of experience. Get back to Robin Sage. I did it for years and found it very rewarding."

"Because it can't end like this. I got into the Army for the wrong reasons. I need to finish for the right ones."

"So if I cut you loose, it's with the understanding that if we don't get results, you'll be moving on to something else."

"I accept that, sir."

"So you're highly motivated."

"I always have been, sir. I just need good intel. It's hard to catch up with someone when your intel keeps you two steps behind."

Mitchell took in another long breath, then scratched his abdomen, reminding Brent of the unique scar he had there, a scar shaped like a Chinese character. Brent had read all about the general's exploits in the Philippines before he'd been recruited into Ghost Recon. Mitchell had been stabbed with an exotic sword and had, it seemed, developed an unconscious habit of scratching the old wound. Brent had a few scars himself, and yes, they sometimes itched and drove him mad. "You're putting me in a difficult position," he finally said.

"Yes, sir."

The general thought a moment and grimaced. "They've already given the mission to Boleman. He's one of the best operators we've got."

"I'm sure he'll get over it, sir."

"He's highly motivated, too."

"Yes, sir. Ask him if he knows where Sayyaf is . . ."

Mitchell smirked, then got into Brent's face. "You're a real con artist, huh?"

"No, sir."

Mitchell widened his eyes. "Tell you what. I'll put you back out there. I'll expect to have Sayyaf in custody within twenty-four hours."

"My intel is good."

The general actually swore under his breath. "They're going to question this decision, but here I am, God help me, giving you one more shot. Last one. All or nothing. Hail Mary pass. Do you read me?"

"Yes, sir."

"And you're right. Boleman won't take the risks you will. He's too worried about his next promotion. You strike me as the kind of guy who doesn't give a crap about that."

"Born in the mud, die in the mud, sir."

"You won't be getting credit for Sayyaf's capture. Nothing."

"I don't care, sir."

Mitchell smiled, then rose. "Make no mistake, if she gets away, your field days will be over. I will say that teaching at the JFK was some of the most rewarding work I've done."

"I'll probably wind up there either way, sir. Hopefully later and not sooner."

Mitchell came across his desk. Brent wondered if he would extend his hand in a shake. He didn't. "You're dismissed."

Brent snapped to and saluted. "Thank you, sir. And sir, one last favor?"

Mitchell returned the salute. "Are you kidding me, Captain?"

"Major Dennison and Colonel Grey—"

"I'll talk to them. But you sure as hell better prove me right."

"Or I'll die trying."

The general gave a curt nod. "Very well."

Brent practically ran outside to the parking lot and got immediately on the phone with Schoolie. "Saddle up, fat boy, but don't tell Boleman yet."

"Holy . . . you did it?"

"I just need to call one more player."

The Mucky Duck was a neighborhood pub and restaurant located in the heart of Captiva Island. Its owners had adopted a bright green duck as a mascot/logo, and the place had become a tradition for vacationers since 1976.

Brent found Thomas Voeckler seated at one of the sun-worn picnic tables located right on the beach. Voeckler enjoyed the shade of a large umbrella with a Corona beer logo and was nursing one of the same while staring across the Gulf of Mexico. In the far distance, the dorsal fins of passing dolphins rose above the waves, and a salty tang clung heavily to the air. It was easy to see why the man found this retreat to his liking.

With his own beer in hand, Brent arrived at the table and sat opposite the Splinter Cell, part of him wishing he could spend a few weeks on the island.

Thomas noticed him and frowned deeply. "Aw, dude, you drove all the way here? You're wasting your time. I told you on the phone I'm done."

"You have to look me in the eye and say that."

Voeckler turned, looked him in the eye. "I'm done."

"Okay," said Brent, pretending to rise.

"And you're leaving now?"

"I got my answer." Brent started away.

"So what makes you think you can catch her this time?"

"I feel pretty good about it."

He gave a little snort. "You sound like my brother."

Brent returned to the table and took a seat. "You think he'd want to see you lying on your ass, getting drunk, not finishing the job?"

"He doesn't care anymore. Because he's dead."

"What're you, an atheist?"

"I am now."

"Well, I like to think that he's watching us and trying to give me some words that'll bring you around."

Thomas's grin turned sarcastic. "Good luck with that."

"I talked to Grim. She gave me her blessing. She'd like to see you get back in the saddle, too."

"I'll bet she would. I'm money, and I'm being wasted right now. That's how they think."

"Hey, they spent a lot of money on you. Time to give them a return on their investment."

"They've already been paid—with my brother's life."

"All right, I won't argue with you. I know what you feel like. You don't have to heal, but you have to go on."

"Why?"

Brent pursed his lips. "To better remember him. To respect him and what he believed in."

"All that honor and duty crap. It's all lost on me. And why do you even care? You feeling guilty?"

"Oh, I'm an expert at that. I'm just looking at you and thinking this guy's in the same boat I was. And it's a little boat, taking on water, and there's a big shark, and we're both thinking we need a bigger boat."

Thomas almost smiled.

"Come on, it'll keep your mind off it."

Thomas thought a moment, and then his expression brightened. "I guess if I go with you, I might get killed. Then I wouldn't be lying around here, feeling sorry for myself."

Brent chuckled under his breath. "Exactly."

"Then why the hell didn't you tell me that in the first place?" Thomas rose. "You're buying us beers for the road."

"You got it."

"So where does the wild-goose chase take us next?"

"Dubai," said Brent.

"That place is nuked out."

"It's not as bad as you think."

"Why there?"

"She's got the heir to the country and the chief money man. This ain't rocket science. Dennison tells me there are bank vaults intact."

"So she went after the kid and the banker so she could go rob a bank?"

"You know, sometimes we make life more complicated than it really is. Maybe it's always been a bank heist. And she just needed help."

"We get her and some of the people she's working for, and maybe we open up something a lot bigger."

"Exactly."

As Brent ordered more beers to go, Thomas asked, "So how did you get us back on the job?"

"I handed them Sayyaf."

"Are you kidding me? Third Echelon's been trying to nail him for years."

"I know."

"How?"

"Long story. I'll tell you on the plane."

Thomas was still aghast. "That's a story I want to hear."

"Not my proudest moment."

"What makes you say that?"

Brent paid the cashier and headed out, leaving Thomas's question hang.

EIGHTEEN

Just when Chopra thought the Snow Maiden was showing some kindness and humility, she'd remind him of
what she really was.

After brutally gunning down a woman who was pur-
portedly her friend, and after dumping her body in an
alley and seizing another car by gunpoint, they drove
about ten kilometers up to the small town of Versoix,
where they were met by two men who took the car and
ushered them into yet another, and a driver took them
to a small hotel, where they had already been checked in.
The Snow Maiden said her friends had arranged it all.

Now Chopra sat in the hotel room, palming sweat
from his forehead and rubbing his tired eyes. He still had
Heidi's blood on his left shirtsleeve. He was listening to
the Snow Maiden speak on the phone while Hussein sat

in a chair, watching a movie on the television. Chopra had been reading the tourist literature, something about a festival going on all week, sponsored by Favarger, a famous manufacturer of Swiss chocolate.

Abruptly, the Snow Maiden marched into the room and said, "I need to ask some questions about the gold and the vault."

"How much longer do you think we'll cooperate?" Chopra asked.

The woman rolled her eyes. "I'll shoot you in the leg or the arm, and you'll come around."

"I won't. I'm ready. Shoot me." He took a deep breath, closed his eyes.

Chopra tried to imagine himself a martyr for his cause, but all he saw was a frightened boy who'd allowed his bicycle to be stolen.

"What do you need to know?" asked Hussein, muting the television.

"We're assuming the main vault is located in the old Multi Commodities Centre."

"Yeah, it's there," said Hussein. "Almas Tower. There are a lot of other ones, too. It's easy to get confused."

"Exactly how much gold?"

"That I don't know. Chopra?"

Chopra spoke through his teeth. "Hussein, our country needs us. We cannot go along with this anymore."

"I'm ordering you. You work for me. You do what I say. I'm the sheikh. Tell her."

Chopra took a deep breath.

The Snow Maiden drew her silenced pistol and jammed it into his bicep. "This will hurt."

"Chopra, you stupid old man, tell her!" cried Hussein.

After a few more breaths, Chopra lowered his head in defeat. He was too weak, too fearful of the pain. He was a coward, and he cursed himself for that.

Her voice came through a hiss. "Tell me about the gold."

"Tell her!" Hussein cried again.

Chopra answered, but he would not face her. "There are between five hundred and seven hundred gold bars."

"How much do they weigh?"

"A lot. Four hundred troy ounces each."

"In kilos?"

"About twelve each or twenty-seven pounds each. Heavy. There's silver there as well. Each bar is worth nearly half a million U.S. dollars."

"So we'll obviously need trucks. Heavy moving equipment."

He glowered at her. "Obviously. And you'll need friends to move all that gold, friends you're willing to keep alive and not throw away like garbage."

"Shut up."

"Why did you kill her? She seemed like a sweet woman. An innocent. And you just shot her."

"You want to know why I killed her? Because I was starting to like her. Now tell me about the security system."

"Go on the Web. I'm sure you can learn all you need to know . . ."

She jabbed the pistol deeper into his arm.

"It's the usual. Very complex biometrics: iris patterns, fingerprints, facial readers, blood vessel authentication, and blood flow sensors, all combined with traditional password protection and token codes. The live finger-print authentication alone includes four biological markers of pulse, blood pressure, body temperature, and the capillary patterns in the skin to verify fingerprints by analyzing ridges of the print as well as the depth of the valleys between the ridges."

"I've bypassed those systems."

"Not these. You can't make a photocopy of someone's thumb and use it. Or even a gel copy. These are quite literally the best in the world."

"Which is where you come in."

"Well, you should know the Al Maktoum family wouldn't simply rely on those measures alone. The sheikh was an eccentric." Chopra smiled darkly.

"What are you saying?"

"I'm saying you should expect the unexpected."

"No, I'll expect you to get us inside."

Even as he'd spoken, Chopra was already formulating a ruse, but he could not put forth the plan without the young sheikh's help—and therein was his greatest challenge.

"He'll get us in," said Hussein. "And I'll get you the data on the oil reserves, but only if you get me something to eat."

"So you'll give away your nation's assets—all for one meal."

The boy shrugged. "Half the gold and one meal. I'm starving."

"I've already ordered," said the Snow Maiden. "And new clothes will be here shortly. You'll both shower and change."

"What you're attempting is quite huge," said Chopra. "And have you considered the radiation? Exposure has been limited to less than eight hours without full NBC suits."

"Who do you think you're dealing with here?"

"I don't know. I ask. You never answer. Why don't you tell me? Are you terrorists?"

She chuckled. "Hardly."

"Then what is your purpose?"

"Well, that's philosophical, isn't it?"

Chopra stiffened. "I don't want to talk to you anymore."

"Then you can just listen," she said, taking a seat across from him. "When I was a little girl, my father told my brothers and me a story about an old woman who lived in our town, and she was tired and old and couldn't afford to eat, so she would go into the market and steal some bread or soup, or people would give her a handout. She got caught stealing some potatoes one day, and they hauled her off to jail. And my father never saw her again."

The Snow Maiden just sat there, staring through him, reliving the moment.

"Was she put to death?" asked Chopra.

"I don't know. I don't think my father knew, but he

never trusted the government after that. And he taught us to be afraid of the police."

"Why does this bother you?"

"Because one day, I'll be that woman, and they'll lock me away because I stole some potatoes, and that will be my life."

"I'm here to change that young man, to make him recognize that he was not born to live an ordinary life. He will change. It's never too late."

The Snow Maiden just looked at him, as though yearning for change herself.

Thirty-six hours later, Brent, his team, Thomas Voeckler, and Schoolie rendezvoused with the USS *Florida* in the Gulf of Oman, fifty miles south of the strait. The small-boat personnel transfer between their cruiser, USS *Gettysburg* CG-64, and the Virginia-class nuclear submarine took place at 0300. All boarded the nuclear submarine and were issued thermoluminescent dosimeters worn on their belts. The units, about the size of a deck of cards, measured their total radiation dosage while onboard and were worn at all times. This wasn't the first time Brent had taken a ride aboard one of the JSF Navy's finest, but Thomas was new to it all, so the others took turns ribbing him over his naïveté and hundred questions.

They were all given a refresher course in life aboard a submarine, and Brent had been escorted to the captain's stateroom by the ship's XO.

Commander Jonathan Andreas was seated at a fold-out desk, working the touchpad of a small computer. Andreas, who couldn't be much older than Brent and had salt-and-pepper hair, gestured to a chair. "Have a seat, Captain."

"Thank you, sir."

"Our lockout trunk is good for nine, so you'll have to lock out in two evolutions. My SEAL chiefs will provide the training to your newbies. They'll also deliver all of your heavier gear, including your combat suits, with our wet vehicle. You've seen one of the SDVs in action, I assume?"

Brent nodded. The older-model SEAL Delivery Vehicle was a torpedo-shaped craft that cut through the ocean at six knots and expedited the transfer of a team's worth of gear. Brent was thankful for the help. Anything they could do to decrease their infiltration time was welcome. Two full evolutions of the lockout trunk was going to slow them down already, and it was his intention to establish an effective web of observation posts in and around Dubai before the Snow Maiden arrived. It all sounded excellent in theory. It always did.

The lockout drills were performed quickly, with each group standing inside the trunk in rising water, exiting the submarine, and reentering. There was some concern over Thomas's ability to remain calm, but the Splinter Cell went through the motions quite admirably. Afterward, Brent congratulated the man and said his brother would have been proud. Thomas agreed.

Lakota brushed past Brent in the confined passageway

outside his stateroom and asked if he'd ever had sex onboard a submarine.

He stood there, dumbfounded, speechless, shocked even . . .

And then just as quickly, she sang, "Kidding . . ." and started away.

"That's sexual harassment," he said.

She glanced back salaciously. "So?"

"I could write you up for that."

"Before or after?"

She rounded the corner, gone.

"Damn," he muttered. If insubordination didn't get him busted out of the Army, temptation like that would.

"Captain?" called the ship's XO. "We have Major Dennison for you. She's got updated intelligence on your target. If you'll follow me . . ."

"Does it sound good?" Brent asked.

"There's a lot of activity at your infiltration point. And there's been some Russian sub movement. We might even have a shadow. You boys come with a lot of baggage."

"Yeah. It is what it is."

The meeting with Patti was canceled, and that same morning a private jet belonging to the *Ganjin* flew the Snow Maiden, Hussein, and Chopra from Geneva to Fujairah, one of the seven oil-rich emirates that made up the old United Arab Emirates. Fujairah was located on the Gulf of Oman, about an hour's car ride directly

east of Dubai. They were put up in the Hilton Fujairah Resort, where they were to remain until Patti called
and was ready with the trucks and team that would head
west.

Without notice, a knock came at the door. The Snow
Maiden drew her weapon, asked who it was. Room service. She checked the peephole.

Two men stood there: one wearing a hotel uniform
and pushing a cart that carried food and bags of clothing. The other guy wore a long overcoat and had the
dark but graying hair and pale skin of an Eastern European. She guessed he was about fifty.

She opened the door, keeping her weapon hidden
behind her back, and allowed the cart pusher to enter.

The other man immediately said, "Viktoria, come
with me."

"Oh, yeah?" she asked, raising her pistol to his forehead. "Maybe you should come with me."

"I'm in the room next door. He'll keep an eye on
Chopra and the boy."

"Who the hell are you?"

"A colleague of Patti's. Lower that weapon. Right
now."

The Snow Maiden thought a second—he knew who
she was, knew about Chopra, and knew Patti. She lowered the gun but remained tense and ready. "Answer my
question."

"I will. Come on," he said.

She followed him to the next room, where inside,
seated at the desk near the window, Patti smoked a

cigarette and sipped a cup of tea. "Sit down, Viktoria. And please keep your mouth closed and listen."

"That would be wise," added the other man.

"This is Igany Fedorovich," Patti began. "He's director of SinoRus Group oil exploration. They have headquarters on Sakhalin Island. That's just north of Japan."

"And he's a member of the *Ganjin*," added the Snow Maiden.

"Of course."

Fedorovich looked at the Snow Maiden and put a finger across his lips.

Patti continued, "What I'm about to tell you, very few people in this world have heard. And if they learn that you know who they are, you will be a target."

The Snow Maiden smirked; tell her something she didn't know. Everyone already wanted her dead. Take a number.

"*Ganjin* as a concept was born many years ago, back in the 1970s, during the fall of the Communist regime. The movement was the precursor in China toward capitalistic individualism and enabled the beehive mentality of Chinese society to restructure into many hives. The concept also prompted Xu Liangyu and Isaac Eisenstein, two classmates at Harvard, to consider how the concept could be used to gain control of the world's natural and socioeconomic resources."

The Snow Maiden yawned. "Kill me now before this history lesson continues."

"Quiet," snapped Patti. "You need to understand this."

"Why?"

"Because you're part of it."

"I quit. You're here. You got the old man and the kid, who by the way is a spoiled punk who would sell his own mother to the devil. I'm done. You do the rest. I want to be paid right now."

"You'll do as we say—otherwise, you'll receive nothing."

The Snow Maiden raised her pistol at Patti's head. "Payment now. Electronically as usual."

Ignoring the pistol, Patti forged on: "Liangyu and Eisenstein were joined by myself, Igany here, and Dominico DiNezzo, who's president of the Vatican Bank and the man who discovered the existence of Mr. Manoj Chopra. We called ourselves the Committee of Five, members of the *Ganjin*, a network that extends over the entire globe. We've influenced this war in ways you can't imagine, and all for the benefit of the People's Republic of China, a nation we once believed would win this war and become the world's only remaining superpower."

"So I've been working for China."

"Indirectly, yes."

"What's wrong, then? I can hear it in your voice."

Fedorovich moved in beside Patti. "The committee has split. Patti and I do not agree with the *Ganjin*'s new direction."

"They no longer support China?" asked the Snow Maiden.

"They've linked with the Green Brigade Transnational. They've extended their network into South America. They're being heavily influenced by those factions, and many of our resources within China have turned their

backs on us because they will not endorse those relationships. The Chinese have very careful and thoughtful
plans to seize control of the Russian Federation, but these
South American factions can undermine those plans."

"So that's how Nestes knew who you were," said the
Snow Maiden.

Patti nodded. "I gave him orders to protect you against
attack, but he double-crossed me, then tried to play a different card with you. I'm glad you saw through him."

"He just knew too much. So I killed him."

"Exactly."

"So what now?"

"We're breaking off from the *Ganjin*. We plan to
form a new international health organization. We're getting out of the business of war and into the business of
peace. And Dubai's gold and oil reserves will help fund
our efforts."

"You already work for the World Health Organization."

She closed her eyes. "We are as corrupt and unman-
ageable as the *Ganjin* itself."

The Snow Maiden shrugged. "Look, this is all very
admirable, but I still haven't been paid."

"We'll offer an additional advance on services rendered," said Fedorovich. "But what we're really offering, Viktoria, is something more—a seat as director of
intelligence."

"You're going to screw over the *Ganjin*, and you're
going to use me to do it. And you don't think they'll be
mad about that?"

"No, I don't," said Patti. "They won't live long enough to get upset."

The Snow Maiden laughed. "This is insane."

"Viktoria, this entire operation has been run entirely through me. They have no idea that you've located Chopra and are here. I've misdirected them from the beginning."

She turned away from both of them, feeling a chill run up her spine. "I can't trust you. Why did I think I could?"

"We assumed you'd feel this way, which is why we thought we'd make a peace offering."

"The money . . ."

"And him," added Patti.

The Snow Maiden turned to face Patti. "Him?"

"Colonel Pavel Doletskaya, a man who loves you more than anything in this world. He's being held at MacDill Air Force Base in Tampa, Florida."

"I thought you said a peace offering—what are you going to do? Use him to blackmail me into this? Go ahead, kill him! I don't care! Do it!"

Fedorovich put a hand on her shoulder. "On the contrary, Viktoria. Within six hours, he'll be a free man."

"Impossible."

"We have a sleeper on the inside," said Patti. "This individual has been a project for many years and is now a high-ranking mole in the Joint Strike Force. Pavel will be at your side very soon."

NINETEEN

USS *Florida* **SSN-805**
Virginia-Class Nuclear Submarine
Persian Gulf

Brent and his team were just south of Abu Musa, part of a six-island archipelago near the entrance to the Strait of Hormuz. Iran had once established a special weapons facility there, but it had been destroyed hours before the nuclear exchange with Saudi Arabia.

Commander Andreas had suggested they take advantage of the littoral capabilities of his Virginia-class sub. The Persian Gulf had a maximum depth of ninety meters and an average depth of fifty meters. *Florida* measured 15.85 meters from the bottom of her keel to the tip of her sail, and thus she could get in tight to the coast while using her electronic "big ear" to help Brent with situational awareness.

Once in position, Brent thanked Andreas and issued orders for his group to begin lockout. The first group left the sub and assisted the SEAL chiefs in their efforts to store the load-out bags aboard the delivery vehicle. Those bags included the combat suits, helmets, weapons, liquid fuel and batteries for the suits, and other communications and intelligence-gathering equipment.

Brent, Lakota, and four others from the group, including Schoolie and Thomas, entered the lockout chamber in their wet suits, with their Draeger LAR-Vs buckled to their chests. The Draegers were closed-circuit breathing systems sans the telltale bubbles of conventional scuba gear and were standard issue for "black" operations. Even Thomas had taken a course on their operation as part of his Splinter Cell training. Once sealed, the chamber began flooding with cold seawater.

Dennison's update regarding the target zone had been brief, and the Snow Maiden had yet to be sighted within the heavily observed five-kilometer perimeter. However, Dennison had once more confirmed that the woman had been in Geneva, as evidenced by the dead operatives in her wake. The major had then turned her attention to Dubai itself, where satellite streams picked up a large militia force. Those well-armed combatants patrolled the streets for eight or so hours at a time, then retreated in boats to the offshore islands, where radiation levels were a bit lower. The patrols were replaced by secondary groups, but for about eight hours each day, usually during nine A.M. to five P.M., the city remained empty.

Much of Dubai's infrastructure was still intact following the nuclear exchange between its neighbors, including the Burj Dubai or "Dubai Tower," once the tallest human-made structure ever built at 2,684 feet before it was supplanted by the Chinese "Tower to the Sun," completed in 2019.

Yet another super skyscraper in the area, the Almas Tower, was of greater interest to Brent because it housed the country's main vault, a subterranean affair newly renovated in 2018 to include sophisticated biometric security measures. If the Snow Maiden was coming to Dubai for the money, then the Multi Commodities Centre vault should be her main target.

The militia's commander was also aware of what lay beneath his feet, as the patrols were heaviest near the Jumeirah Lakes Towers area, particularly around Almas. How the Snow Maiden intended to bypass those forces remained to be seen. Brent and his people would have their work cut out for them, if they were to remain undetected—at least initially. The real trick would be to cash in on what Special Forces did best: linking up with and recruiting locals to their cause. If he could turn this militia into allies, then the Snow Maiden wouldn't stand a chance of escape.

But what if they were wrong about this woman? What if she wasn't coming to Dubai? They would lay an elaborate trap for nothing, and Brent wouldn't just be out of Ghost Recon; he'd be regarded as a fool and fall guy by his colleagues. Once again, his career was in the hands of the intel they'd received. Good, bad, or ugly. And in the end, his fellow operators would remember only that the mission had failed, not the true reasons why.

He reassured himself that this had to be the Snow Maiden's plan: The kid and the money man could get her into the vault, and that was her goal. What else could she possibly want with them? Both were connected to Dubai. There was no reason to believe the money had been moved—no records of such movement. The country had been sitting in a radioactive vacuum for years, and the intel indicated that prior attempts to gain access to the main vault by the leaders of the remaining emirates had failed.

During the submarine ride, Brent had read up on "living keys" and other security techniques. It seemed clever and reasonable that Dubai's leaders would employ the most sophisticated measures available to them, but they hadn't anticipated losing so many of their "living keys" in one fell swoop.

Now the Snow Maiden had found some of those keys.

Worse, she wasn't operating alone, and whatever faction was behind her could be extremely powerful, perhaps backed by the Russians, the Chinese, or maybe even a clandestine group within the JSF or European Federation. For all Brent knew he could be an unwitting participant in the flushing out of a mole.

Brent shoved the rebreather into his mouth as the water rose above his neck and filled the trunk. The others lifted their thumbs. After a muffled clunk, the door swung open, and they swam into a long tunnel of ocean dimly lit by the delivery vehicle's red lights.

Once everyone was linked up with the craft, the SEAL chiefs shut the lights and set course for the marina.

Sometimes the SEAL pilot and co-pilot were part of the combat team, but in this case, after dropping off the Ghosts, they'd return to the sub. Andreas had warned Brent that Russian subs were sniffing for them, so he'd best have an alternate extraction plan in case *Florida* got caught up in that cat-and-mouse game. As "on-scene" commander, Brent would make that call. The USS *Independence*, a futuristic-looking assault transport with a trimaran hull, was also operating in the Gulf of Oman area and could be called on if they needed her. Farther out was the USS *Dwight D. Eisenhower* Carrier Strike Group.

The team's course would take them around the Palm Jumeirah, one of three artificial islands shaped like a palm tree with long fronds once serving as beachfront property for hundreds of homes now deserted. These islands were as surrealistic and improbable as many other parts of Dubai, where architectural ambitions had been fueled by magnificent wealth. The most elaborate of all projects had been known as "The World," an archipelago of three hundred human-made islands meant to resemble the land masses of Earth. The project had been abandoned, the islands now eroding back into the sea.

Once they skirted those areas, the SEALS would head into the marina and follow the canals toward the city proper. Lakota kept in touch via hand signals and closely monitored the radiation levels. Brent had already picked out several underground locations, subbasements and parking garages within the nearby Gold and Silver Towers that he believed would afford them some protection between observation shifts. Even with their suits, Brent was taking no chances by keeping anyone exposed for more than eight hours. He'd studied the blueprints of both buildings and would put Schleck on the roof of one, Riggs on the roof of the other. Those snipers would be rotated out with the rest of the team.

Within thirty minutes they had slid through the central canal and reached the Nuran Dubai Marina bridge. With the delivery vehicle still submerged, the team began to ascend, breaking the surface beneath the bridge and hidden from satellite view. Local time was 0924. They transferred the waterproof load-out bags to the concrete underpass, and then, with all the gear unloaded, Brent cut loose the SEALs with a hand signal.

"Better suit up now," said Lakota, consulting her wrist-mounted radiation detector.

Without a word, the group began the process, with Schoolie giving Thomas a hand because he'd practiced donning the Natick 9V Exoskeleton combat suit only a few times. The suits were a flexible and modular armor system, offered NBC protection (which certainly made them a necessity in Dubai), yet still allowed a remarkable range of motion. Brent had once listened to a trainer spend more than an hour discussing the suit's capabilities—including ballistic and blast protection and integrated data gloves for hand gesture interface with the Cross-Com, which was now part of the fully sealed combat helmet (no monocle or earpiece was required). The suits also had climate systems and user-specific operation modes with voice and facial recognition so enemies couldn't exploit them—but the bottom line, as Brent reminded his people, was that no amount of technological magic could replace the fervor of the human heart.

"Captain, there's a problem," said Lakota, over a private channel.

Brent winced. The volume on his communications system was much too high. He issued a verbal command to lower it, then responded, "What's up?"

"It's Schoolie," she said, gesturing across the way to the back of the group. Thomas, Schleck, and Park had surrounded the man and were working on his helmet. "He can't get a good seal."

Brent cursed. "He really wanted to come along, too."

"Either he sits this out, or we keep him in the basement as security."

Brent shifted through the group and faced Schoolie. "How we doing, bro?"

Schoolie shook his head and bore his teeth. "Don't send me back. This is just my luck."

"We can keep you with the gear. You need to stay below ground and to avoid full exposure."

"Brent, I've got an idea," said Thomas. "After I set up my sticky cams, we let Schoolie run them. That frees me up to focus on communications intel."

"What do you think?" Brent asked Schoolie.

"Beats sitting on the bench," said the big man.

Brent nodded to Thomas. "Let's do it." Then he whirled to regard the rest of the team. "Everyone else good to go?"

As they nodded, raised their thumbs, or shook their

fists, a circle of avatars representing each Ghost appeared in Brent's HUD, with his own positioned in the center. All but one of the figures showed green suits, fully online, fully functional. Schoolie's avatar showed a flashing red line at the helmet seal, as expected. Beside each avatar floated data bars that included vital signs, weapons carried, ammo, and the combatant's current GPS position, among other details.

With the flick of his gloved index finger, Brent minimized the report to the HUD's margin and returned to the "home" image of scanning the battlefield for potential threats.

They broke into four teams:

Brent, Daugherty, Noboru, and Thomas were Alpha team.

Lakota, Copeland, Heston, and Park made up Bravo.

The sniper team was always known as Charlie and was staffed by Riggs and Schleck.

Delta team or the "base" team was actually a one-man show. Schoolie would still have a chance to do his part.

Brent's team led the others up along the embankment. They wove their way between the marina buildings, wary of contacts and keeping tight to the walls.

The suit's 360-degree sensors and three-dimensional audio queuing heightened Brent's situational awareness, and the results of seeing what was behind him and sensing the depth of sounds around him was so effective that he couldn't help but smile. The taxpayers had sure bought him some nice toys.

Within five minutes they reached the pedestrian

footbridge spanning Sheikh Zayed Road. The concrete walls afforded some cover, so they crouched down and hustled across. Working their way on foot to the Gold and Silver Towers some 0.75 kilometers away was unavoidable, and doing so in broad daylight seemed surrealistic, but as Dennison had mentioned, the patrols had vanished like insects fleeing the light of day.

The team left the bridge and descended another concrete access way toward the Lake Terrace Tower, a forty-floor office building standing in the shadow of the much more massive Almas Tower.

"We have solar-powered surveillance cameras all over the place," said Thomas. "Sensors picked up their motors first, but now I've locked on to their broadcasts."

"Roger that, me, too," said Lakota.

"Hold up," Brent ordered. They strung out along a footwall beside the valet parking entrance to the Lake Terrace Tower. "Everybody sight a camera. The system will tell you if you're doubling up. I want eleven knocked out on my mark. Stand by . . ."

They raised their rifles, and Brent waited until the computer confirmed that each one of his people had sighted a different surveillance camera.

"Uh, Ghost Lead, this is Remus," called Thomas, using his call sign and reminding Brent of George, who'd gone by the other Roman twin, Romulus. "I have an idea."

"Not right now. Stand by, everyone."

There were four more cameras in their path toward the Gold and Silver Towers, but knocking out this many in one fell swoop would speed up the infiltration.

"Locked on," called Lakota.

Brent took a long breath. "In three, two, one. Fire!"

Eleven suppressed rounds sliced the air, and the flashing red dots superimposed over Brent's HUD all went gray, nearly in unison.

"Wow, that's one for the textbooks," cried Lakota.

Brent gasped. "You're damned right it is."

"Uh, Ghost Lead?" called Thomas again. "I could have jammed those video signals in about ten seconds. They're using old-school technology, and it's not even encrypted."

"Don't ruin my moment," said Brent with a laugh. "But all right, then. Jam the rest. And keep them jammed."

"You got it, Boss."

Brent rose. "Let's move out!"

As they bolted off, Brent told the computer to issue him verbal warnings regarding the proximity of enemies in the zone. The computer began to issue those reports, and as expected, two vehicles were inbound from another office building about a kilometer northeast of their position, ETA five minutes or less. Those men had probably sought shelter underground.

"Hustle up, people, they're coming to check on their camera problem . . ."

"Got 'em, too," said Lakota.

Chopra had tried to persuade the young sheikh to go along with his plan, but the boy had refused, and now it seemed inevitable that the country's assets would be surrendered to a thug—unless Chopra was willing to sacrifice himself. It might come to that. Did he have the courage? Would that be the ultimate repayment for being rescued from the slums? But if he stood up to her, and she shot him, the boy could only get her into the computers inside the vault, not the vault itself. He'd be useless. She'd kill him.

"Listen to me," he had whispered to Hussein while the Snow Maiden had been out of the room and they were being watched by a man posing as a hotel employee. "I'll tell her that if your vital signs are broken while inside the vault, the entire area is rigged to detonate."

"Is this true? Did my father tell you this?"

"No, but telling her the vault might explode could be the only way to save your life—after you give her what she wants."

"I thought you didn't want me to do that."

"Now you might have to. I think if we go against her, she'll kill us both and walk away, without getting anything. I think that's in her nature."

"Why?"

"Because she's a sociopath."

The boy snorted. "You mean a psycho?"

"I mean she no longer has a conscience. And she's working for others, so she might not care."

"Can I tell you something stupid?" The boy lowered his voice even more. "I feel horrible about what happened to everyone back home. But my life was so boring. And this is really exciting."

Chopra took a deep breath. "You understand this is real."

"Duh."

"You're not watching this on TV. You saw the people she killed."

"Yes, I did."

"Then you *should* find this horrifying."

"I know." He thought a moment. "So you're right. We have to give her what she wants."

Chopra widened his eyes. "And then what? What reason would she have to keep us alive?"

"I don't know."

"Listen to me again. I'm telling her if she kills you, the vault will explode. And you'll go along with that."

"I don't think she wants me to die."

"Don't believe anything she says."

"If you lie, I'll tell her," said Hussein.

"Why have you taken her side?"

"Because . . . I don't know. I think maybe she can help me."

"And I can't?"

"As a prisoner like me? No."

Chopra hardened his tone. "She's come to rob our country."

Hussein shook his head. "*My* country."

"And you'll let her get away with that?"

"I don't know."

"Once we get her inside, she'll keep us alive until she moves out all the gold and you give her the locations of the oil reserves. After we get out of the building, she'll kill us. So during her operation is when we must make our move. I know the vault very well. And the tunnels."

"If you run, I'm not sure I'll go with you," said Hussein.

"Then you'll die. And your father's dream will die with you."

For a moment, Chopra had thought he'd seen tears begin to form in the boy's eyes . . .

Now Chopra sat in the hotel, staring at the sleeping boy and listening to the Snow Maiden speak softly into her cell phone. He looked to the window, thought of throwing himself through the glass and plunging to the street below. It was a reckless thought brought on by self-pity. He closed his eyes, and there, in the darkness, he saw the first of the three angels with long metal wings and fire running beneath their skins.

"She is afraid. And you need to exploit that," said one of the men, his voice echoing.

"How?"

"You know how."

"No, I don't! Tell me!"

"She's only a little girl." The angel smiled and vanished, and Chopra opened his eyes to find the boy staring at him.

"You were talking," he said. "You woke me up."

Brent and his people reached the Gold Tower parking garage entrance exactly twenty-one seconds before the trucks arrived. He, Lakota, and Schleck remained at the entrance to observe while the others fell back to defensive positions deeper within the facility. The vehicles weren't military at all but a pair of Mercedes SUVs, and out hopped a pair of men from each. They wore conventional MOPP 4 gear that made them resemble old-school combatants. MOPP stood for Mission Oriented Protective Posture and Brent couldn't remember what the hell the four stood for, but had read about how confining, restrictive, and nearly impossible it was to operate with all that junk hanging from your face and limbs.

He used the helmet's camera to zoom in as the men pointed up at the damaged cameras mounted to the buildings. They glanced around, as though suddenly suspicious, then fell back to their vehicles.

"We need to make contact with these guys," he told Lakota.

"Take us to your leader," she responded in a mock alien voice.

"Exactly."

"I'll work with Voeckler."

"All right." Brent made a circle motion with his finger, brought up his roster, and tapped on the avatars of Schleck and Riggs. "Hey, guys. You're cleared to head up top. Riggs, you stay here, and Schleck, you head next door. Let me know if you have any problems getting up there."

"If the backup generators are down, it'll be a long walk up to the roof," said the sniper.

"Just keep me posted."

Brent shifted to Thomas's avatar and tapped on it. "Mr. Voeckler, you'll be accompanied by Copeland and Daugherty. Get your sticky cams in place, then hand over command to Schoolie."

"I'm on it," said the Splinter Cell.

"And then, while you're working on communications, I've got another job for you. You'll recon that entire vault. Alone. You're a spy. Do what spies do. Why? Because I don't trust blueprints. I trust you."

Thomas's tone grew more enthusiastic. "Nice. I won't let you down."

"No, you won't. All right, Bravo and Delta teams, down to level four. On your HUDs. You'll set up the tents. Couple million tons of concrete and glass should help us from glowing green."

"Ghost Lead, this is Riggs. Backup generators are down over here. Going to be a long morning, and this ain't no stairway to heaven, over."

Brent patched into her camera and saw the endless flight of stairs hanging overhead, the ceiling lost in the distant shadows. "You're a true warrior."

"I know that." She groaned. "Could be worse. I could be wearing heels."

Brent remembered her appearance at the cycle team victory party back in France, and he wished she hadn't reminded him of how breathtaking she'd looked.

Schleck checked in and jarred Brent back to reality. He was walking up as well.

And then, before Brent could issue another order or make another observation of their operational zone, a priority message flashed in his HUD, origin Ghost Recon Command, Fort Bragg. The data box opened to show Colonel Susan Grey. Then another box opened, part of a conference communication, and suddenly Brent was staring at both his immediate superior and General Scott Mitchell, who spoke curtly.

"Captain, listen carefully. There's been an unprecedented security breach on our end—and we believe it may have a direct impact on your mission."

TWENTY

Fujairah
Gulf of Oman

The Snow Maiden finished her phone conversation with Patti and plopped down on the bed. "We'll be here for a while," she told Chopra and the boy.

"Why?"

"No more questions." She took a deep breath and wanted to close her eyes, but she couldn't. She stared at the pistol, lying a few inches from her hand.

They saw it, too, but they only sat there, watching.

"I guess I should say thank you." Her voice cracked as she spoke, a rare sign of weakness.

"For what?" asked Chopra, furrowing his brow.

"You could have made this a lot more difficult."

He snorted. "We should have."

"Those people you work for," began Hussein. "You'll give them all the money?"

"I said no more questions."

"You started the conversation," said Hussein.

She grinned crookedly. "So I did."

"They get the gold, the oil reserves, everything?" asked the boy.

"That's what they think."

"You have another plan?"

She took a deep breath. "I have lots of plans."

In fact, she had considered stealing the gold for herself, but once again engaging in an operation that complex and pulling it off at the last moment was improbable, to say the least. Then again, you never knew how the radioactive winds of fate could blow . . .

Patti had indicated that a militia force was occupying the city. The Snow Maiden had told her that she had no plans to infiltrate a heavily fortified building with an old man and a boy. Patti had said that she and Fedorovich had already put plans in motion that would allow the Snow Maiden's convoy and twelve-man "work team" (in reality a Chinese special forces team) to arrive at the vault site without facing resistance.

"How?" she'd asked.

"Your old friend Haussler."

"Excuse me?"

"He's coming with his Spetsnaz force. We've tipped him off."

"Are you insane?"

"No. Izotov hired him to bring you in. The militia is Haussler's problem, too. He can't come after you with them in the way."

"So now what?"

Patti had laughed under her breath. "As expected, Haussler called for help, a diversion, so he could follow you. Now here's where it gets interesting. Izotov knows that if he sends in his own forces, the JSF will respond in kind. He doesn't want to do that . . . so he's called on the Euros."

"The Euros?"

"Yes, they have two Enforcers Corps companies airborne and they'll be in Dubai by nightfall, along with air support."

"How did he manage that?"

"He threatened to pull the plug on their oil supply, so they'll do what he says. The Euros will attack the militia north of the tower and keep them preoccupied while you slip in and empty the vault. Initially, the JSF won't interfere because the Euros are their allies. There will be a lot of saber rattling, but not much else from them."

"What about Haussler? I'll still have him on my back."

"No, you won't. I told you the *Ganjin* has climbed into bed with the Green Brigade. Well, I've arranged for them to cut off Haussler before he reaches the city. I have about forty combatants already in place. He'll be coming up from the south, following the main coastal road. They'll take him out."

"And if they don't?"

"Then the Euros will."

"You've turned this into a nightmare."

"I thought you'd enjoy the challenge."

"You thought wrong."

"Well, you know what you have to do, and I suspect I'll be calling with some good news. You can make plans for your reunion with Colonel Doletskaya."

"That's not a bribe. He doesn't even know I'm still alive. And when he finds out, he won't want to see me."

"Oh, he knows very well you're still alive, and the Americans have been leaning hard on him for information. In fact, he's become quite the security risk."

"So you're not rescuing him for me. It's for yourselves."

"It's for everyone."

The Snow Maiden had snorted and ended the call.

"I have to go to the bathroom," said Chopra, rising from his chair, his expression asking the question.

She nodded and watched as he moved past the bed, behind her, toward the bathroom. Her hand remained on the bed, away from the pistol.

A mistake.

He came in from behind her, dropping his full weight on her back and trapping her there.

Then he reached across the bed, nearly getting his hand on the pistol before she slammed her elbow into his arm.

He gasped in pain as the weapon flew off the bed and thumped onto the carpet.

"Hussein, get the gun!" cried Chopra.

Brent had thought that after multiple tours in Afghanistan he'd seen it all—police selling drugs out of their stations, soldiers using their armor breastplates as grills to cook steaks over an open fire. His world was utterly absurd, yet the insanity had begun to feel familiar and comfortable. Expect chaos and suddenly everything is normal, despite the gasps and wide eyes from outsiders.

But maybe he had *not* seen it all. He certainly hadn't seen *this* coming.

Surveillance video along with detailed hardcopy and electronic documentation had allowed Major Alice Dennison to make a "prisoner transfer" of Colonel Pavel Doletskaya.

She had transferred him, all right.

Straight to the unknown.

They were both MIA.

"My God, General, is she a traitor?" asked Brent.

"We don't know anything else yet, but since Doletskaya is connected to the Snow Maiden, I wanted you updated. From this point on, you'll be working with Colonel Grey instead of Dennison. I'll be checking in from time to time myself. This is a strange and disturbing turn of events. I handpicked her myself to join the JSF."

"Roger that, sir. I'll add Dennison and Doletskaya to our friend-or-foe cues."

"That's already been done," said Grey. "We have no reason to believe that she'd head to your location, but a rendezvous between the Snow Maiden and Doletskaya could occur in the near future."

"Yeah, in jail," added Brent.

"Now, Captain," the general began, narrowing his gaze. "We know what you're up against. Just remember: The Germans have a saying—*feel the cloth*. It comes from the days when men used to fight shoulder-to-shoulder and you could feel your buddy's arm rubbing against yours. It gave you courage. It reminded you that you weren't alone. Just go out there and feel the cloth. We're here to back you up in any way we can."

"Thank you, sir. Our infiltration was successful. I expect that if the target arrives, she'll be either terminated or in our custody."

"Excellent."

The general ended his link, leaving Brent to face Colonel Grey, whose deep scowl transformed her into an angry bird about to sink her talons into his flesh. Remarkably, she abandoned the cutting remarks and criticism and got down to business. "Brent, I'm taking into account that you might have received bad intel from Major Dennison and that she no doubt tipped off our enemies, but now more than ever we need results. I see you've placed snipers on the roof and have a perimeter around the tower."

"Observation posts out to about a kilometer from the vault. And I've got Voeckler moving down to recon the entrance. Schoolie's still patched into Voeckler's sticky cams."

"We're looking at those cams as well. I've also been following Lakota. Still no contact with the militia."

"She's working on that, and she tells me she's an excellent translator."

Most of his team had received extensive language training, but with the Cross-Com and intelligence teams monitoring back home, they could receive rapid-fire

translations as they spoke with locals without having
to attach a translator to the team. This was a welcome
improvement in the last few years. Many of the transla-
tors Brent had used in Afghanistan turned out to be spies
or were branded as traitors by locals and targeted for
execution; consequently, they required extra protection.

Dubai, however, was unique in that before the war,
more than eighty-five percent of its inhabitants were for-
eign born. Arabs, Indians, and Pakistanis were the largest groups, but people flocked to the country from all
over the world, so they really weren't sure who they'd
find and what language they'd speak.

"Once we link up with the militia, we'll see who's
running the show," Brent went on. "Do we have any better estimates on the size and composition of this force?"

"Not very big. Battalion-sized force. Maybe a thousand if they're lucky. Poorly equipped. Any armor they
had was probably looted years ago. Looks pretty ragtag,
probably just some remaining troops from the country's
old defense force and displaced persons. The emirates
only had about sixty-five thousand to begin with. We've
had some sketchy intel in the past, but this group has
been largely ignored, written off as survivors in a radio-
logical zone. There's a lot of movement in and out of
Kish Island right here," she said, switching her image to
a topo map of the area.

Kish was about 120 miles northwest of Dubai, across
the Gulf. Before the war it had been touted as a con-
sumer's paradise because of its free-trade zone. Now it
was a bombed-out junkyard.

"All right, we'll keep an eye on that place, too. And those guys might be poorly armed, but they've got numbers. Time to make some new friends."

"Good luck with that, Brent. You'll need it. Because we're going to pin a medal on your ass or boot it. Either way, when this is over, you and I will sit down and have a nice, long talk about the way you handled this."

He took a deep breath. "Understood."

Her eyes narrowed. "Good luck."

Bang, he ended the call.

Well, there it was. Even if he brought in the Snow Maiden, Grey would still burn him for going over her head. So it didn't matter anymore, really. He wasn't supposed to be here for himself, right? He was here to complete the mission, which in turn was vital to the security and stability of his country. That's the promise he'd made. That's the promise he'd keep, career be damned.

But just to show her how good he was, he'd capture the Snow Maiden, drag her kicking and screaming all the way back to Fort Bragg, and dump her in Grey's lap.

"Ghost Lead, this is Lakota. We've made contact."

Well, that didn't take long, he thought. "On my way."

Nice thing about the suits. Both her location and a suggested route were already superimposed in his HUD.

He followed the glowing yellow line (or yellow brick road, as they liked to quip) to her location between the towers, where she, Park, and Heston were standing beside two militants who'd been wearing MOPP gear but had removed their heavy face masks.

Brent was surprised to find that both heavily bearded

men spoke Pashto (which he understood) and had migrated down from southern Afghanistan. They said they were being paid a small wage by a man they referred to as Sheikh Juma, who had (unsurprisingly) established a camp on Kish Island from where he directed his operations. They'd called Juma, who'd said he was willing to meet with Brent. Juma said that since the Iranian holocaust, as he called it, they rarely received visitors from Russia, Europe, or the United States.

Lakota said it was a two-to-three-hour boat ride to Kish, and Brent was concerned that the Snow Maiden might arrive while they were gone. He asked the men to see if Juma could come over to see them, but Juma refused. This was, Brent knew, part of the "power game" of negotiations, and if Brent wanted anything out of Juma he needed to play along.

"All right," Brent said. "Tell him we're coming out to see him. Copeland? Daugherty? You guys are in charge of your teams. Lakota and I are going out to Kish Island. Schleck, Riggs? Keep eyes on."

The snipers acknowledged.

"I want to be back before nightfall," Brent told Lakota.

She nodded. "All we can do is try."

They climbed into in the militia guys' battered SUV and drove toward the coast.

Chopra could not believe the power that lay within the Snow Maiden's arms. She threw him off as though he were weightless. He sailed off the bed, toward the back wall, as she dove for the pistol lying on the floor.

Hussein just sat there, frozen. He could have reached the gun before she did.

The Snow Maiden snatched up the pistol, then came around and back toward Chopra, her eyes fiery as she reared back and pistol-whipped him at the base of his neck. His glasses flew off, so he didn't see the second blow coming, only felt the sudden pain in his cheek. Had that been a fist or a boot? He wasn't sure. The blood came warm and salty into his mouth. He slid down the wall and slammed onto his rump.

Hussein screamed for her to stop, but the Snow Maiden shouted more loudly, "Just when I was thanking you for making it easy, you do this?"

"Don't hit him anymore! Please!" the boy cried again.

"Are you serious?" she asked. "You don't care about him. You didn't care about your country, your father, your family. You don't give a damn about anything but yourself. You're a selfish little bastard, and maybe, after you give me what I want, I'll cut off your head and put it on a stick outside the vault. What do you think of that?"

"I think you're a crazy bitch."

"Then you should've gotten my gun. You're a little boy. A fool. That's what you are. You've thrown away everything your family stood for so you could be a pig watching movies and playing games all day. If your parents could see you now, they would vomit."

Chopra reached out, fumbled across the carpet, and

found his glasses. He slipped them on, but they'd been bent and the nosepiece dug in sharply. He removed them, made an adjustment, then pushed back against the wall, trying to stand. His cheek was already swelling, and his neck throbbed and ached. He began to feel nauseated himself as he swallowed back more blood.

"You can take me to the vault," he told the Snow Maiden. "But I won't let you in. I won't."

"You will," she said confidently. "Because I know how much you care about him. And I'll torture him slowly, right in front of you, if you don't do what I say." She raised a brow. "I won't remind you of this again. I'll just do it."

Chopra looked fire at her.

Hussein just stared.

"You're not a sheikh," she said, turning back to the boy. "You'll never be."

Chopra glanced at Hussein, the gears obviously turning in his youthful head.

There was no deal to strike with the Snow Maiden. The boy should understand that by now. They had but one goal: escape. Chopra wasn't sure how else to convince the boy.

Brent wished he could have sent Lakota and Daugherty over to Kish Island to meet with Juma, but he knew how these warlord/militia leader types operated. First, Juma would not respect Lakota's authority because she was a woman. Second, Juma would feel slighted because

Brent had sent his underlings instead of coming himself. You had to show face to save face. What Juma lacked in numbers and technological superiority, he made up for in demands of dignity and respect. Brent was certain he would hear phrases like "We are a proud people" and "The invaders who come to rob our land will be executed."

While riding aboard the small and agonizingly slow fishing boat, he contacted Grey and had her tap Ghost Recon's intelligence sources to positively identify Juma. Grey said once they had an image of his face they could do so immediately.

They reached the east side of the island and were met at the dock by a security force of six men, all wearing MOPP gear. They climbed into two trucks and were driven out to the postwar remnants of the Dariush Grand Hotel, once a 125-million-dollar five-star affair with more than two hundred guest rooms. Cross-Com data indicated the place had been built to resemble Persepolis, a city of ancient Iranian civilization and the ceremonial capital of the Persian Empire.

Now the hotel's once-magnificent grand columns and towering archways that reminded Brent more of ancient Rome than Persia lay in piles of rubble through which they threaded, finding what had once been an ornate marble stairway framed by rubble and leading down into the shadows.

Two of the security men fired up torches, which made Lakota glance strangely at Brent. He assumed they'd at least have flashlights powered by solar cells or other conventional batteries, but they clearly had limited resources.

In the eerie and flickering torchlight, Brent noted that the walls, once adorned by ornate murals of gardens and waterfalls, had been scorched black by terrible fires, and as they descended farther, Brent experienced the enormity of what had happened in this region. They had been far from ground zero, but there had been an unrelenting shower of conventional bombing prior to the nuclear exchange. Kish, though not a primary military target, had been flattened as an economic blow, because it had been one of the most popular tourist destinations and helped bolster the Iranian economy.

They continued on, winding their way through a labyrinth of bombed-out hallways intersected by fallen walls and doors blasted off their hinges. Once they had descended two more flights of stairs that had been sloppily repaired with bricks and thick mortar, they finally reached an open area that might have been a small ballroom or conference room, Brent wasn't sure. Giant chandeliers hung like twinkling mother ships from the ceiling but remained dark. The room was in fact lit by dozens of candles.

Two unmasked men stood at the entrance, both clutching AK-47s. They allowed the group to pass. Several large writing tables laden with maps, charts, and all kinds of papers lay directly ahead, along with books, thousands of books rising in piles like the Manhattan skyline against a horizon of more massive bookshelves lining the back wall.

Seated behind the broadest desk, a hand-carved piece of furniture as gaudy as Brent had ever seen, was a large man who had to be Juma. He had his boots kicked up, his face half-hidden behind a thick, graying beard as his stubby finger ran down the margin of a report in his hand. A pair of bifocals had slipped down to the tip of his leathery nose. Brent found it a bit ironic that the warlord still managed his forces via hardcopy documents; that was about as old-school as it got. Ghost Recon had been paperless for as long as Brent could remember.

Juma glanced up from his report. "Ah, finally!"

He immediately rose and shuffled around the desk to greet them. He was a large man, at least three hundred pounds, dressed in nondescript military fatigues and a traditional Arab headdress that might've been called a turban or something else, Brent guessed, because he'd never spent much time this far south. Surprisingly enough, Juma proffered his hand and said, "You must be Captain Brent of the JSF."

He spoke perfect English with a British accent and had either spent time in the U.K. or, perhaps, been educated there. Brent didn't have to wait long for the answers. Abruptly, a data box opened in his HUD, and information on the man scrolled downward as Grey had promised. Juma's face had been analyzed by the teams back home, who updated Brent with more than he'd ever need to know. Juma was a cousin of the Al Maktoum family, not directly in line to lead but a highly educated businessman once intimately involved with the country's oil exports. That he had become the leader of a militia was not too surprising, given his graduate degree education and skills.

"I see they're feeding you the gossip on me," said Juma, indicating the little flashes of light he detected in Brent's faceplate. "You can take off your helmets here."

"Thank you. I'm sorry, but how would you like to be addressed?"

The man grinned. "Juma would be fine."

Brent removed his helmet, which clicked and hissed as he raised it over his head. "All right. I'm Alex."

"Alexander the Great," said Juma with a grin.

"No, just a soldier here to help. And most people just call me Brent." He turned. "This is my second in command, Sergeant Lakota."

Lakota removed her helmet and shook out her hair. "It's a pleasure to meet you, sir."

He issued a polite if not perfunctory grin at Lakota but refocused his attention on Brent. "First we eat, drink, then talk."

"Excellent," said Brent.

Lakota looked at him, a bit weary. They didn't have time for this, but refusing the invitation would be an insult.

As they followed Juma toward a door near the back, Brent nodded at Lakota, who was donning her Cross-Com headset and earpiece so they remained in contact with the team and the network. As they walked, she spoke softly: "I'm having a hard time connecting to Grey now. WAN uplink temporarily unavailable."

"That's weird. Keep trying," said Brent.

"I don't like this, sir."

Brent gave her a sobering look. "I'll check back at the towers, see if LAN's operational." He did so, and the team reported back in sans any comm problems.

"Brent, I've finished my reconnaissance of the entrance-way to the vault, and I've picked out some ambush points, if you want to take a look," said Voeckler.

"Busy now, but I will. Run them by the others. Mean-time, stand by. I'll be in touch."

TWENTY-ONE

Town of Al Malaiha
About Seventy-five Kilometers from Dubai

The Snow Maiden yawned as the headlights reached out into the darkness, toward the squalid desert town rising in the distance. They were heading south on Highway 55, pushing through vast stretches of nothingness. She thought she saw an oil refinery off to their right, but the shadows and dust had collected into curtains of gloom.

Patti had procured four Renault medium-sized cargo trucks with a telecom service's yellow logo splashed across the sides. These trucks were not uncommon and wouldn't draw much attention to themselves.

The other three trucks were driven by members of her team, only one of whom, a Captain Chen Yi, actually spoke a little Russian. Her Chinese was poor, and they'd tested their English on each other with only marginal success. Patti had sworn that every man had been handpicked by herself and Fedorovich and that all could be trusted. The Snow Maiden had grinned to herself over that joke.

Her cell phone rang: It was Patti. She answered curtly.

The woman replied, "I have someone who wants to talk to you. Hold on."

After a moment, a man's voice, somewhat filtered by static, came through. "Viktoria, is that you?"

She almost drove off the road. "Pavel?"

"Viktoria, it's me."

"I don't know what to say."

"They're taking me to meet you, so you don't have to say anything right now. I know what you did. I know why you did it. And nothing matters anymore. I just want to see you."

A hollow aching woke in her chest. She was actually speaking to him, to Colonel Pavel Doletskaya, formerly of the GRU, a man she had hurt more than any other in this world, she thought. "I'm so sorry. About everything."

About more than she could ever tell him   about leading him on, staging her death with Izotov's help, dropping off the grid, and turning their relationship into a lie. He was the only one who had touched her after her husband's death. Pavel wasn't an expendable tool. He meant something, and the *Ganjin* knew that. He was supposed to be a bonus payment for her.

Or a source of blackmail. She would have to be ready for that, prepared to watch him die.

"Don't worry, Viktoria. I have always been here. It's not too late for us. If you will have me . . ."

She began to choke up.

"Viktoria? Are you still there?"

She summoned the strength and coldness back into her voice as she imagined Patti slashing his throat and the blood pooling at his knees. "I can't talk right now. But as you say, we'll meet. Take care, Pavel."

Chopra was seated beside her, with Hussein next to him across the long bench. "Is everything okay?" asked the old man.

"Shut up."

The boy asked, "Are you sad?"

"Not a word from either of you."

"What about that?" Hussein added, pointing toward the windshield.

Hearing Pavel's voice had taken her years and kilometers away, back to her work with him, back to their affair, to the moments lying in bed with him, moments so tender and so clear that she'd failed to see the roadblock looming ahead.

She radioed to Chen Yi, who in turn called back to the other drivers. Then she alerted Patti. "You didn't tell me about a roadblock."

"They must have observation posts. You've been tagged. We didn't count on this."

"Some old SUVs, maybe twenty armed soldiers."

"We can't afford any more delays," said Patti. "The Euros are on their way. Haussler is moving toward his trap. You've got your own troops. Deal with it."

The Snow Maiden cursed, then called to Chen Yi and

told him to be ready. She mashed the accelerator pedal, and the truck lurched forward.

"They're going to shoot us!" cried Hussein.

The kid's appreciation of the obvious was not lost on her. As they barreled toward the roadblock, the soldiers lifted their rifles and took up defensive positions alongside the cars. She braced herself.

And not three heartbeats later, the hailstorm of fire began, incoming rounds pinging along the truck, sparks dancing over the hood and side panels as she throttled up even more and both Chopra and the boy hollered for her to pull over.

And then, resigning to the situation, she spun the wheel, pulling off the road, as the other three trucks roared by, now taking the brunt of all those rounds. Her truck bounced violently over ruts and through small dunes.

Not a second after the last truck blew by, she cut the wheel again, bringing them into the draft of the last vehicle and keeping tight on that driver's wheels. They had a temporary shield, but they still had to pass those combatants.

The lead truck blasted through the SUVs blocking the road, knocking one onto its side, the other sideways. Steel and glass groaned and shattered while tires screeched across the pavement.

Then the next two trucks hammered through the gap, taking fire from both sides as though going through a car wash using bullets instead of water. At the same time, all that glass rained like diamonds glistening in the headlights.

She took in a long breath. Held it.

Now it was their turn.

They thundered into the opening, past the cars lying askew, gunfire riddling the side of their truck.

Just a second more . . . a second . . .

But in that second the window beside Hussein shattered and Chopra let out a scream.

She breathed, cursed again, turned, and the stench of gas immediately filled the cabin.

A glance to one of the side mirrors showed a string of winking lights—muzzle flashes to be sure—and the thumping continued, punching holes in the back of the truck.

Next came a crack and loud bang, then a steady hissing as the driver's-side rear tire went flat.

Before she could clear the second truck, a dull thud came from beneath the hood, and flames licked up toward the windshield.

You didn't need auto-mechanic training to conclude that the fuel line had been hit and had now ignited.

And you didn't need a driver's safety lesson to realize that if you didn't abandon the truck, you'd die in the fire, the explosion, or both.

With Chopra and the kid still hollering, she swung once more to the side of the road, booted the brake pedal, and brought the truck to a rattling halt.

The gunfire continued, AKs popping, triplets of fire ricocheting off metal or stitching across the asphalt.

"Get out!" she ordered the kid. "I'll get him!"

"I've been hit in the side," said Chopra. "I can feel the blood. Terrible pain."

"I don't care. Come on!" she cried, wrenching open her door, seizing him by the arm, and dragging him out of the cab as he shrieked and shuddered.

They hit the sand, and, as more gunfire suddenly woke around the truck, Chen Yi's vehicle stopped short just ahead. The rear door rolled open, and three of his men jumped out and began firing a barrage that suppressed the incoming fire. The Snow Maiden glanced out to the roadblock, where the soldiers there began shifting positions and returning fire.

"We need a doctor," shouted Hussein.

The kid's power of observation was astounding.

The Snow Maiden brought Chopra around the burning truck, using it as temporary shield while guiding him back and away, with more thick smoke pouring from beneath the hood.

They dropped into the deeper sand along the embankment. Chopra continued wincing.

"One of those men is a medic," she told the boy. "In the back truck, in the cab. Go get him."

Hussein remained a moment, his gaze torn between the incoming gunfire and the trucks up the road.

"I'm bleeding a lot," said Chopra. "Please, Hussein. I need help . . ."

The Snow Maiden put pressure on Chopra's wound. "Either you get the medic or he dies," she told Hussein. "And if he dies, we don't get into the vault. Then I'll have no use for you, right?"

Hussein swallowed. His eyes welled up.

She could almost see the tug and pull of his thoughts.

With a start, he darted away, carrying his flabby little body toward the trucks.

It was about time the kid showed some courage. He'd obviously been raised by cowards and fools, and she was probably the best influence he'd ever had. Without her, he'd been stuck in his pathetic hole.

Two of Chen Yi's men from the lead truck sprinted past them carrying shoulder-mounted weapons. The Snow Maiden did not recognize that ordnance, but she quipped that the weapons were no doubt Chinese knock-offs of something engineered by the Americans, Russians, or Euros.

The two soldiers got down on one knee, balanced the cylindrical launchers, and nearly in unison fired not one, not two, but three rockets in a single trigger pull.

It all happened in a gasp.

The road between Chen Yi's men and the roadblock lit up in a surreal fireworks display of green-blue rocket engines. Smoke trails extended like powdery threads to sew up the air for a second before a cacophony of explosions rose from the SUVs being used for cover. Soldiers were hurled into the air by the massive detonations, and multiple fireballs swelled beneath them, casting a blinding glow that had the Snow Maiden shielding her eyes as the heat wave struck and pushed over them.

Chen Yi ran up behind the men, barking orders in Chinese. They retreated to the trucks as Hussein returned with the medic and Chen Yi approached with them.

"Please help him," said Hussein.

The medic, a middle-aged man with a snake's eyes, produced a pair of shears and got to work exposing Chopra's wound.

"He has to work in the truck," said Chen Yi. "We have to move him now."

The medic yelled something in Chinese to Chen Yi.

"I don't care," Chen Yi answered.

"We have to move him," the Snow Maiden echoed. She batted away the medic's hand. "We'll get him into the back and you work on him there."

"Not good to move," said the medic in broken Russian.

"No time!" snapped the Snow Maiden. "We're moving him right now!"

"I can go," said Chopra, glancing back to Hussein. "Thank you. Thank you for getting him."

The boy looked scared. Really scared.

"All right," said the Snow Maiden. "Here we go!" She and Chen Yi helped Chopra back to his feet.

And that's when the old man fainted.

Brent and Lakota had sat on the floor, sipping tea and eating rice, beans, and a lamb dish that Brent had found a bit too spicy for his tastes, but he'd eaten it nonetheless. Juma was, as expected, a gracious and painfully ceremonial host who spent several hours discussing his family's history, his commitment to restoring Dubai back to power, and the extensive needs of his militia. It was clear to him that the JSF had arrived to strike a deal of sorts, and he was not shy in making his demands. Ironically, he never asked why Brent and his team were in the country. He'd assumed that it was all about him, as a man in his position might be wont to do.

The conversation had then drifted to Brent and Lakota, and he'd asked them pointed questions about their lives in the United States, why they'd joined the military, and what thoughts they had about the war and when it all might end.

Both were noncommittal in their responses, trying to feed the man what he wanted to hear. Ironically, he called them out on that, and Brent had been forced to apologize. For the better part of two minutes, Brent went on a rant of everything he thought was wrong about the war and the military.

Juma had grinned. "Now that is the truth!"

Finally, growing weary of any more delays, and believing they had indulged Juma enough, Brent got down to business. "We're actually here because we're after a woman who might have access to your vaults. She's captured a man named Manoj Chopra."

Juma's mouth fell open. "Chopra? I thought he was dead. I thought the Russians were using his name to try to contact me. Maybe that was him all along. We could never verify . . ."

"She has Chopra, and she also has Hussein, son of the late sheikh and heir to Dubai."

"My cousin. We all thought he was dead. I heard rumors of his sisters being alive. Why didn't you tell me this immediately?" Juma glanced around the room, his thoughts obviously racing, his eyes widening.

Brent winced. "I didn't want to offend you or dismiss your hospitality."

Juma rose quickly to his feet. "Who is this woman you're after?"

"We can brief you, provide all the intelligence we have, but we need a commitment. We brought in a small team to fly under the radar. We need your militia."

"Of course, you have it!"

"All right, then—"

Brent didn't finish his sentence.

What felt like an earthquake rocked the entire room, dust trickling down from the ceiling, the floor feeling as though it were about to buckle. A bookcase behind Juma began shaking, the books spilling to the floor.

One of Juma's men came charging into the room. "Sir, gunships! Troops! We're under attack!"

"Get to the big guns!"

As Brent and Lakota donned their helmets and sealed their suits, Juma bounded after his men, seizing a rifle propped up near the doorway.

When they reached the bombed-out entrance, they spotted a pair of gunships arcing across the night sky.

Brent's camera zoomed in and the computer immediately identified the aircraft. Data windows opened along the margins of his display. They were looking at a pair of PAH-6 Cheetahs, the main attack helicopter of the European Federation. They were dark, sleek, futuristic-looking birds that boasted hydrogen-powered turbo shafts, shrouded tail rotors, and HOT-3 optically tracked laser-guided missiles with tandem warheads to minimize collateral damage.

A rotating three-dimensional image with engine cutaways glowed alongside the windows, but Brent didn't need the virtual picture—the real-life picture was clear enough. The gunships streaked through the night as though riding on rails, suggesting they could outmaneuver anything thrown at them. Brent had seen these choppers only a few times during joint operations with the Euros, and he'd certainly never found himself poised beneath their gunners' sights.

"What the hell are the Euros doing here?" shouted Lakota.

"Good question!" Brent cried. "But the damn uplink is still down. Try hailing those birds."

"On it," she replied.

"He's coming around," hollered Juma, pointing at the sky and ushering them back behind a pair of fallen columns as the recoil-less autocannons on both choppers came alive, hundreds of rounds of caseless ammunition pounding into the ground as the militiamen scrambled for cover. Juma had said he had about two hundred in Dubai at the moment, two hundred on the island, and the rest scattered across the other islands and in the mid-desert areas. It seemed the Euros were intent on exterminating this piece of Juma's network. "Come on!" the man cried.

"Sir, Voeckler says the WAN uplink's not down—it's

being jammed," reported Lakota. "Can't get through. And no response from those pilots."

Brent ducked behind the rocks and called up his roster. He tapped Daugherty. Their suits used the most sophisticated encryption technology on the planet, and that paid off because the LAN still worked and Daugherty answered the call. "I'm here, Ghost Lead."

"Euros have some gunships here over the island," Brent reported.

"Just going to call you. Troop transports landing about five clicks north of the tower. They're deploying. Got a few heavy lifters dropping some armor. Not sure how many dismounts yet. Captain, what is this? The Euros got our backs now?"

"I don't know. But they're attacking the militia, which in my book makes them the enemy."

"Sir, are you ordering us to attack them?"

"Negative, but you'll return fire if fired upon."

"Roger that."

Brent grabbed Lakota by the arm. "We need to get back."

She'd been listening in and nodded.

A strange whirring and fluctuating hiss grew louder and was amplified by the suit's sensors. Brent craned his head in time to watch the entire entrance to the compound—piles of rubble, really—explode into more fountains of rock and other jagged debris as the gunship's pilot cut loose another missile, effectively sealing off the main entrance to Juma's base.

Two pickup trucks rolled into view with fifty-caliber machine guns mounted in their flatbeds. The men behind those fifties swung the barrels around and, howling at the gunships, directed their fire skyward as brass casings jingled and arced over the sides. Every third round was a tracer, slashing red hot against the night, and both men adjusted their fire, doing what they could to counterattack an overwhelming and technologically superior force. The engines, screams, and gunfire rose in a blaring crescendo as the gunners kept firing. Brent remembered what had happened to the two trucks in Sandhurst, and he doubted this situation would end any better.

As expected, the Cheetahs responded in kind, diving boldly and directly into the onslaught, their pilots launching missiles at each of the pickup trucks.

Brent couldn't take his eyes off the scene as the gunners tried to bail out before those missiles struck, but they were too late, both enveloped by fireballs, as were the drivers.

"What are they doing?" Juma demanded. "I thought you Americans were allied with them!"

"So did I!" Brent retorted.

And as quickly as the attack began, it ended, with both birds turning tail and heading southeast toward Dubai.

"Why are they leaving?" asked Lakota.

"I don't know," muttered Brent. "Call Daugherty."

She did. Brent told Juma they needed transport back to the vault and a contingent of men to come with them.

"I'll lead them myself."

One of Juma's lieutenants came dashing up with a cell phone and thrust it into Juma's hand. The conversation went quickly, and when it was finished, Juma said, "Some of my men attacked a convoy near Al Malaiha. Three trucks are still headed south. Also, there's been another skirmish south of Dubai, along the coast. I don't know what that's about. My men did not recognize any of the forces there. Can you contact your people?"

Brent frowned. He tried to call Grey himself. Still no uplink. "We're being jammed. And until my people can stop it, I'm cut off from back home."

Juma nodded. "Very well. To the docks."

As they jogged off, Brent called back to Riggs and Schleck, who were still up on the rooftops. He warned them of the convoy.

"No worries, Boss. We're on it," said Riggs.

The Snow Maiden's group was down to three trucks, and they would have to make the gold fit or leave some bricks behind, unless Patti could somehow arrange for a replacement. She sat in the back, trying to keep the flashlight steady as the medic gave her somber looks. He'd already started an IV on Chopra, but he didn't seem very pleased with that and muttered to himself in Chinese.

Chopra's breathing had grown shallow and wheezy. Though the medic didn't say it (he probably couldn't say it in Russian), the Snow Maiden guessed that the bullet had pierced Chopra's lung and chest cavity and that he was bleeding internally.

If the old bastard could live long enough to get them into the vault, she'd be okay. *Just keep him alive*, she kept screaming to herself. Part of her wanted the stubborn old bastard to die; yet she pitied the man because he had put such faith and belief in a punk kid who would ultimately break his heart.

She checked her watch. They were less than twenty minutes away now, and Chen Yi called her to say that he saw flashes, smoke, and fires in the distance.

She grinned. The Europeans had arrived.

Hussein sat across from them, his back pressed against the truck wall, fingers wrapped around a leather rung attached to the wall and used for strapping down cargo. "I want to tell you something," he began, raising his voice above the shimmying truck.

"What?" she said, grimacing.

"You have to keep us alive. The vault is rigged. We're both living keys. If we die while inside, the explosions will kill everyone and destroy the gold. My father was careful about these things. He explained everything to me. Showed me everything."

"Nice try, kid. We've studied the vault. We know exactly how it was constructed and what security measures are in place."

"You think you do."

She snorted. "We'll see." She glanced down at Chopra, still wheezing, and then at the medic, who was listening to Chopra's chest through a stethoscope and plugging numbers into a touchpad medical device that was providing an ultrasound-like image of Chopra's lungs.

"Bullet here," said the medic. "I find it. Not good."

"I need him alive for another half hour. Can you do that?"

"Not sure," said the medic.

She glanced back at the kid, just as a tear slipped from one of his eyes.

"So now you're finally scared," she said.

"I'm not scared." He dragged a hand across his face. "I'm not . . ."

"You should be."

"Are you really going to kill us?"

"I don't want you to die. I want you to lead your country. I told you that. But if you get in my way, then you know what'll happen. It's as simple as that."

Chopra began coughing loudly, and then he was choking, spitting up blood all over his shirt, over the medic, and the truck floor.

The Snow Maiden screamed at the medic, who rifled through his bag, produced a needle, and punched it into Chopra's ribs. He did something to the needle, and air whistled through. Chopra gasped and was beginning to calm. He caught a breath, then another.

"He bleeds bad. Not much time," said the medic.

"How long?" she demanded.

The medic shrugged.

"Don't let him die," pleaded Hussein.

Chopra reached out toward the boy, who just gaped at the bloody hand.

* * *

A flotilla of about thirty boats left Kish Island, and Juma was able to take Brent and Lakota back in a high-speed cigar boat procured from some Iranian drug dealers just after the nuclear exchange. It was, Juma had said, his personal ride.

Tensions were expectedly high, and Brent was somewhat baffled because the choppers did not return to attack; it seemed they were being lured toward Dubai.

As they neared the city—the skyscrapers like monoliths, black and dead—lightning, like flashes of combat, backlit the clouds about twenty miles north, somewhere near the airport, Brent estimated.

But up there, on the Gold and Silver Towers respectively, were Brent's eyes and ears, his own low-tech satellite feed in the form of snipers Schleck and Riggs.

"They've got about ten Badgers rolling south from the airport area, but real slow," said Schleck. "Real slow. Weird. They're taking fire from the militia, but their response so far has been limited."

The European Federation's AMZ-26 Badger was a hybrid-powered, eight-wheeled troop transport equipped with a Spanish-made thirty-millimeter dual-feed chain gun that fired seven hundred rounds per minute. Another variant came with a special multipurpose TOW missile system capable of engaging both ground and air targets.

However, the most notable and dreaded feature of the vehicle was its high-powered microwave emitter, capable of dispersing groups of infantry with a less-than-lethal dose of microwaves producing the sensation of being burned alive.

Brent had never seen the results of the lethal setting, but he'd heard about them. Horrific.

"We need to cut them off before they get near the vault. In fact, I want that place to look dead, so if our girl is with that convoy, she walks right in—then we got her."

"Roger that. No sign of the convoy yet. Wait a minute. Hold on. Whoa, whoa, whoa. Take a look, Captain . . ."

A camera window opened in Brent's HUD. Three trucks with lights off drove northwest up 1st Road, heading directly toward the Gold and Silver Towers.

"That's got to be her," Brent said. "Heads up, everyone, this is Ghost Lead. Three trucks inbound. Do not make contact. Just observe, roger?"

Alpha and Bravo teams checked in, and Schoolie, who was still deep in the parking garage, acknowledged that he had the trucks on Voeckler's sticky cams.

"Man," added Schoolie. "Looks like they're headed right for me. Wait a minute. They are! Coming down into this parking garage!" He cursed.

"Schoolie, hide the gear and get to cover," Brent ordered. "Do not engage. Observe only. Just like at the bar back home. Sit tight and watch."

TWENTY-TWO

Silver Tower
Business District, Dubai

Chopra chased the boys down the street, lost them in a crowd at the next intersection, then launched himself into the air, soaring like a bird as metallic wings sprouted from his back. He circled the crowd, spotted the boys once again, then swooped down and ripped the first one off his bike.

The second looked up as Chopra plucked him from the bike and tossed him to the ground as the bike crashed into a pair of steel garbage cans near the edge of the alley. Chopra landed in front of the boys, who were still lying on their rumps. They backed away, stunned.

"My father gave me this bike. You shouldn't have taken it. You have no idea what it means to me."

"Chopra? Chopra?"

He opened his eyes, saw a face half draped in darkness. The image grew more distinct . . . Hussein.

"We're here now. We have to get you up," the boy said.

Where were they? He remembered being shot, the pain, the truck, something about not having much time.

And then he remembered.

He was dying.

"Chopra, they're going to move you."

His mouth tasted foul, his lips dry and cracked with something. He licked them. Salty. Blood. The shooting pain and hissing from his chest would not go away. His fingers and toes were beginning to go numb.

Loud engines whined somewhere outside the truck. Chopra leaned his head to the right and spotted something quite surreal: Three forklifts powered by natural gas drove in a line past the truck and toward a long tunnel, their tiny headlights barely pushing back the darkness.

A fourth forklift stopped behind the truck, this one driven by the Snow Maiden herself. She hopped out and climbed up into the truck. "We're going to move you into the seat next to me," she told Chopra.

Hussein came around, and together they lifted him to a standing position. The world tilted strangely on its axis, and they caught him before he fell.

Brent was climbing into an old Jeep Wrangler driven by one of Juma's men when Schoolie called him. "Brent, I'm looking at her right now. I heard them come down here. There must be a tunnel that runs from this tower to the vault. They got forklifts. She's got about a dozen guys. They look Chinese. Military. They're heading over there. Take a look."

He finished taking a seat, then focused on his HUD, where he saw the Snow Maiden and the boy helping the old man into the seat of one of the forklifts.

"Schoolie, you are way too close. Get out of there. Wait for us."

"Aren't you going to thank me? You got confirmation. The target is here. I can move on her right now."

"Negative!"

"It's just them. Her team's already gone ahead. I can take her out right now."

Brent shifted his tone. Dramatically. "Get out of there. If she spots you—"

It had been the smallest reflection, so small in fact that the average person would not have seen it, but someone like the Snow Maiden, who had trained herself over the years to be hyperaware of her surroundings, picked it up in her peripheral vision. A trio of thick water and sewer pipes as fat around as a man spanned from the concrete floor to the ceiling in one corner of the sublevel, and it was there that she saw him, crouched behind one, his elbow partially visible, along with a wedge-shaped segment of his helmet.

Who was he? She'd find out before she killed him. "Wait here," she told Hussein.

"I could run away," he said.

She looked at him. "I run fast." Then she slipped off,

away from the truck, hugging the wall behind them. Chen Yi had given her a combat vest and web gear whose pockets hung heavy with grenades. She reached the corner of the garage opposite the pipes and tugged free a grenade.

"Don't move!" came a shout from behind the pipes.

An American. Damn, they'd caught up to her. It seemed Patti had done nothing to thwart their efforts.

"Who are you?" she cried in English.

"I'm the guy who's going to capture you! Stand down!"

She squinted toward the pipes as he came around with his rifle trained on her.

"Okay, okay," she said.

Then she pulled the pin on her grenade, let it fly, and threw herself forward, onto the concrete.

He fired, the rounds striking near her arm and leg as she kept rolling, knowing that his targeting computer would have to keep recalculating if she just kept moving.

She thought he'd be faster, but he wasn't. As he charged away from the pipes, trying to keep tight to the long, concrete wall, the grenade exploded in a magnesium-white flash, echoing in great thunderclaps down the tunnel and throughout the rest of the garage.

The pipes immediately ruptured, water whooshing and jetting as the soldier in the high-tech combat suit dove to the floor.

She found it odd that he wasn't wearing a helmet. Her bullet didn't care either way. It left her pistol and nicked the back of his head. A close shot but not a kill. His hand went up to the wound.

Holding her breath, she took off, but a massive puddle

now separated her and the soldier. She could barely keep her footing and wound up throwing herself down, onto her gut, and sliding across the wet concrete, firing three times at the soldier as he tried to turn and bring his rifle around.

She caught him in the arm, the abdomen, and the hand, but his armor held true.

He was a breath away from firing when she adjusted her aim and finally shot him in the head, the blood spraying across the back wall.

Gasping for breath, she rose, rushed to him, leaned down and pulled the blood-covered headset off, slipped it on, and tried to see what he saw.

"Unauthorized user," came a voice in her ear. "Shutting down . . ." She ripped off the headset and threw it across the floor.

Hussein was still waiting for her. She hurried to him and was joined by a trio of Chen Yi's men, who'd no doubt heard the explosion.

They helped load Chopra into the lift. She radioed to Chen Yi and told him what had happened. They needed to move the cargo trucks to the secondary tunnel. He agreed. The Snow Maiden climbed into the driver's seat and threw the lift in gear.

Meanwhile, behind her, the three men jumped into the trucks and followed her down the tunnel.

The original plan had been to extract the gold from the main vault beneath the Almas Tower and move it underground to the Silver Tower. From there, they'd make their aboveground exit to escape. Now the Americans were aware of that. They'd have to move directly up from Almas.

She called Patti, updated her on the situation. The woman told her not to worry, that the Euros were doing, as she put it, a splendid job.

Schoolie's avatar flashed red with a warning that he had no vital signs. A secondary message indicated that his communications and command had been locked down because of unauthorized use.

As Lakota threw the Jeep in gear, Brent called up to Schleck and Riggs. "Get to the Silver Tower, fourth level. We've lost Schoolie. She's got to be down there."

"Roger that," answered Schleck.

Poor Schoolie. How many times had he busted Brent's chops, only to beg for a place on this mission? The irony could not be more bitter.

"Look at that! They're cutting us off!" cried Lakota.

Two of the gunships had returned from the airport area to launch missiles on the bridges spanning the canal. There were four bridges in all, and they were targeting three, blasting away gaping sections that fell in an eerie slow motion toward the bubbling white water. Brent called up the map and nodded in understanding: They were not striking the bridge directly opposite the Almas Tower.

"Check it out," he told Lakota, sharing his HUD map with her.

"I see it."

The Euros were either creating an escape route for the Snow Maiden or attempting to funnel Juma's forces into a single approach. Perhaps both, Brent thought with a deep sigh.

He stole a quick glance at the camera images captured by Schleck and Riggs; they were still rushing down the stairs.

Then he switched to the other teams, who had moved about a kilometer up Sheikh Zayed Road and maintained their observation posts, along with several squads of Juma's men. Copeland was zooming in with his camera to reveal a dozen or so of Juma's men rushing onto the main highway to launch rocket-propelled grenades at a pair of oncoming Badgers. Just as the militiamen launched, the entire group dispersed in all directions; it was the strangest retreat Brent had ever seen—nothing orderly about it, as though each man were crawling with ants.

Then it dawned on him.

The Euros were using their microwave weapon, and Brent's stomach turned as the men fell to the ground, swelling like balloons as the water and blood in their bodies came to a boil and their skin began to separate like sausages being overcooked.

"Captain, are you seeing this?" asked Copeland.

"Yeah." Brent grunted. "I see it. Alpha? Bravo? Keep tight. Fall back on the tower. Do not engage. Do not get tagged. Go now!"

His people charged off, along with squads of militiamen in tow.

* * *

Chen Yi's team had placed wireless surveillance cameras the size of golf balls throughout the tunnel area and approach to the main vault. One of his men was monitoring those cameras via a notebook computer.

They reached an intersection where four tunnels met, and in the center lay a thick, tubular shaft within which sat a broad cargo elevator with heavy steel gates. This was how they got the gold into the vault, and this, the Snow Maiden grinned, was exactly how it was coming out.

The three truck drivers parked behind her, and Chen Yi ordered them to remain there on guard.

She leaned over to Chopra. "You need to get the elevator open for us. Just do it. Or I'll shoot the kid."

Two of Chen Yi's men carried Chopra from the forklift's wide seat and toward the elevator's control panel. Chopra looked weakly at her, then back at Hussein, who cried, "Just do it, old man! We have no choice!"

Chopra placed his hand on the scanner pad. Nothing. Without power to trickle-charge the backup batteries, they'd eventually lost their charge.

"There's no way in. The emergency generator is down in the vault," he said.

The Snow Maiden tore the lower panel off the biometric scanner station, exposing the batteries.

"How much power do I need?" she demanded.

"Twenty-four volts DC," he told her.

She ordered Chen Yi's men to pull two batteries from

the forklifts, wire them in series, and connect them in place of the panel's existing battery cables.

A moment after he touched it, the pad lit from beneath and light wiped across the screen. The status display showed *READING . . . AUTHENTICATING . . .* And then—

WELCOME, MANOJ CHOPRA.

The wide doors slid open.

"You did the right thing," the Snow Maiden told him, as Chen's people carried him back to the lift. Only two forklifts at a time could fit in the elevator, so the Snow Maiden's and one other entered first.

They descended for a full thirty seconds until the elevator stopped with a series of hard clunks and thuds. The cagelike doors creaked open. They drove into another access tunnel about forty meters long, only their forklift lights illuminating the way.

Next came security checkpoint number two: another pair of wide, blastproof doors beside which sat an empty security desk whose monitors flashed a message about being in standby mode since they'd just been powered up via the other terminal.

"I'm sorry, you have to get out again," Hussein said to Chopra.

This time the medic came rushing over and shouted at Chen Yi's other men as they carried the old man toward the interface panel. The medic was not pleased with all the moving of his patient.

Now Chopra had to place both hands on a glass-top counter and stare directly into a screen that showed a digitized and lifelike image of him, basically his avatar. A female computer voice, speaking in English with a British accent, instructed him not to blink.

A light shone directly into one of his eyes, and then the computer said, "Please state your name."

Chopra took a deep breath.

"Please state your name."

The Snow Maiden raised her pistol, put it to Hussein's head, then looked at him expectantly.

"Manoj Chopra."

"Identity recognized. Welcome, Mr. Chopra. It appears you are experiencing a medical emergency. Should I call for medical assistance?"

"No."

"Very well, then. Access is granted."

The broad metallic doors slid open, and without delay they drove the forklifts through them, down yet one more tunnel that terminated at a wall of thick titanium bars, not unlike a prison. This was a conventional barrier opened with either a set of four keys or another set of biometric measures.

And just beyond the bars, about twenty meters away, was the final barrier between them and all that gold: a circular door three meters in diameter and framed in gleaming steel. It reminded the Snow Maiden of a hatch to one of the bomb shelters beneath a few of the military bases in Siberia.

Chen Yi rushed up to the Snow Maiden. "Two soldiers moving down the tunnel. I want to lock the doors."

"We can't," she told him. "We'd need the old man

to get them back open. Everything has to stay open and remain open."

"Then we must move quickly."

"I will tell my men to suit up."

"You do that." She took hold of Chopra's arm. "We're almost finished, old man," she reassured him as they carried him up to the next panel.

He put his hand on the scanner, but then his head lolled to one side and his eyes rolled back in his head.

"Medic!" screamed the Snow Maiden. "Medic!"

Lakota turned sharply down Jumeirah Beach Road, a thoroughfare running parallel to the wider highway and leading toward the remaining bridge's on-ramp. A pair of residential towers known as the Jewel loomed over them, the sky still flickering from explosions across the canal.

The roar of helicopters had Brent looking up, just as Lakota turned sharply, nearly tossing him out of the Jeep because the vehicle had no doors and wearing a seat belt was the last thing on his mind.

"The Cheetahs are back," she sang, her tone dark and sarcastic.

No one needed the warning, and that was her nerves talking, he understood. He wanted to scream himself.

Cannon fire from one chopper tore a jagged line across their hood—

And that's when he and Lakota simultaneously bailed out, hitting the asphalt and rolling, as the Jeep glided on and crashed into the concrete guard wall.

Behind them, Juma's SUV, a dust-covered Cadillac with more dents than a carnival bumper car and whose rear hatch had been removed, veered out of the cannon fire and came to a screeching halt beside them.

A back door swung open, and there was Juma, waving a hand and shouting, "Get in!"

Meanwhile, one of his men had hopped down from the tailgate and shouldered a Javelin missile launcher, a newer surface-to-air model developed by the Brits.

Brent did a double take. "Where'd you get that?" he shouted as he climbed into the SUV.

"We have a few toys," answered the warlord.

The militiaman fired the missile, which arrowed skyward and locked on to one of the choppers. He wasted no time lugging the heavy launcher back to the SUV.

Brent peered up past the open window and held his breath.

The Cheetah's tail rotor took the brunt of the impact, and once the flash and fire had subsided, the chopper began to rotate violently, its tail rotor sheared off, hydraulic and fuel lines hanging down like leaking veins.

The bird sailed over their heads, and Brent turned back to watch as the Cheetah collided with one of the towers in a spectacular explosion of fireballs filled with showering glass.

"Holy—"

Lakota's curse was drowned out as the main rotor sliced away at the building before snapping, one blade whipping end over end across the road not three meters behind them.

As they swung right, turning up toward the bridge proper, the man behind the wheel hit the brakes so hard that Brent, Juma, and Lakota all collided with the front seats.

Before Brent could look up to see what hell was happening, Daugherty was hailing him. "Ghost Lead, two Badgers have pushed through and are setting up a barricade on the other side of the bridge. They're cutting you off, sir!"

"Ghost Lead, it's Schleck. Riggs and I are down in the tunnel. We found Schoolie, sir."

"I can see that," Brent answered, checking their camera broadcasts in his HUD.

"She was here, all right. They've set up some cameras, so we're being watched right now. Voeckler called me, and he's already on his way. He'll jam the cameras and clear the path, sir."

"Roger that, get him on it. In the meantime, I need some fire on those Badgers blocking my way. Daugherty? Copeland? Talk to me."

The boy was at Chopra's side, holding his hand now, as the medic tried to bring the old man back to consciousness. Chopra lay on his back, still unmoving, his chest barely rising and falling.

Unable to stand the frustration any longer, the Snow Maiden grabbed the boy's wrist and dragged him up and away, moving toward the scanner. "If you're a living key, then open the gate."

She slapped the boy's palm on the reader.

"Identity not recognized," came the computer's voice.

She glowered at him. "Were you lying?"

The boy repositioned his palm on the reader. "No," he said. "But I told you, I don't have access to the vault, only to the computers inside. Chopra's the only one who can get us in there. I told you that!"

With a pair of keystrokes on the touchpad, the Snow Maiden reset the reader. "Try it one more time."

He did. Nothing.

She cursed, then shifted away from him back toward the medic. "Lift him up. I need his hand on that scanner right now!"

"Not good to move him!"

"Lift him up!"

Chen Yi rushed over to the soldier monitoring the surveillance cameras, then came back to the Snow Maiden. "They've jammed the cameras. They're coming."

They propped the unconscious Chopra up and dragged him to the scanner, and the Snow Maiden worked his palm.

But then Chopra began to wake up. He lifted his head and glanced over at the Snow Maiden, and in that moment, as the computer sensed his consciousness, the gate began to slide open on heavy rollers.

Not three seconds later, he fainted again.

"You can't get into the vault," said Hussein. "Unless he wakes up."

"Come on, you old bastard," she muttered to him in Russian. "Just one more door."

* * *

"Sir, if you draw any closer, they'll hit you with the microwave. Don't do it, sir," said Daugherty.

"Roger that," answered Brent, and then he regarded Lakota. "We're getting out." He tapped Juma on the shoulder. "Tell your driver to stay here for now. Radio the rest of your troops. Tell them to fall back on the Almas Tower. The Euros landed north to divert your people away. Pretty simple diversion, so let's bring 'em all back here."

"I agree, Brent," said Juma.

Brent and Lakota hopped out of the SUV and crossed to the tailgate, where several hard cases containing more Javelin missiles had been stored. The militiaman who'd taken down the chopper was wide-eyed and breathless, still overjoyed by his excellent shot and ready to fire again. Brent and Lakota would oblige him.

"Captain, I've got some news for you," began Copeland.

"Not now," snapped Brent. "I'll be right with you."

"I think you need to see this," insisted Copeland.

Before Brent could refocus his attention on his HUD, twin flashes of light came from across the canal, from somewhere along the main highway south of the bridge.

And then he saw them: two missiles arcing high in the sky and suddenly dropping straight down toward the pair of Badgers on the other side of the bridge.

Lakota was swearing in surprise as the missiles struck a one-two punch to the armored vehicles, both of which lifted off the ground and blew apart, as though they'd been detonated from within.

"Cavalry's arrived," she said, now dumbfounded.

Secondary explosions lifted more debris in the air as the popcorn popping of ammo cooking off rose through the echoing booms.

More pieces of the Badgers rocketed back up through the smoke trails left by the missiles, and Brent waved a fist in the air and turned toward the origin of the fire.

It seemed Grey had somehow cut through the jamming and had called in the reinforcements—or Juma had yet another surprise up his warlord's sleeve.

"Thank you, whoever you are." Brent zoomed in and saw a convoy of six armored vehicles, BTR-12 Cockroaches, along with a man standing in the turret-top cupola of a T-100 Ogre tank rumbling in the lead.

Brent's jaw went slack.

"Ghost Lead, are you there?" called Copeland. "They just took out the Badgers, but they're heading our way."

Brent turned toward Lakota, and she said the name before he could:

"Haussler."

TWENTY-THREE

Almas Tower
Business District, Dubai

Brent zoomed in once more on the convoy trundling toward the tower. There were no more epithets to express his feelings; he'd exhausted them all.

Haussler's group was the same force Juma's men had reported moving up from the south. The German and his cronies had encountered some resistance, but not from Juma's people. That Haussler did not wear a combat suit or other radiation protection suggested his plans were brief: capture the Snow Maiden and go home.

Gee, that plan sounded strangely familiar.

"They're Russians," Brent finally said, glancing toward Juma. "Why didn't your guys recognize them?"

"There were no reports of armor. They must have picked up the vehicles farther north."

"If he's trying to keep low-key, he's failing miserably,"

said Lakota. "He should've picked up some local armor or just something less conspicuous."

"Maybe he doesn't care, and neither do the Russians. They're trying to capture a rogue, one of their own, and we already know that. They don't have anything to hide right now, do they?"

Lakota shrugged. "I bet Grey saw them coming, but she couldn't tip us off."

"That's about all she could do without turning this into an even bigger fiasco," said Brent.

"We have to wait now," Juma warned. "After they pass, we can go. If they spot us, we will be sitting dogs."

"Ducks," said Lakota.

The warlord frowned at her. "That's what I said."

Chen Yi tugged at the Snow Maiden's shoulder as she leaned over and watched the medic trying to revive Chopra.

"The Americans are in the tunnels," said the special forces captain. "Three so far. They just jammed the cameras."

She wrenched around and grabbed him by the neck. "Tell your men to kill them!" Then she shoved him back and away.

He glowered at her for a moment, glanced down at his sidearm, then put a hand to his earpiece, his expression shifting. "You need to suit up." He lifted his head at Chopra and Hussein. "My men will help them, too . . ."

"We open the vault first!" she cried.

He muttered something in Chinese and rushed off.

Chopra stirred, his eyes fluttering open. She yelled at the medic, ordering him to lift Chopra and carry him to the final access panel built into the wall beside the main vault door.

Gunfire began booming in the distance.

"They're coming," gasped Hussein.

Chopra saw the boy ascending to the throne like an angel, wings spread as he turned to face the crowds and then, finally, inevitably, as perfect and correct as the moment could be, he took a seat on the golden chair and smiled, all of the hope in his heart spreading out in waves across the millions who'd gathered, their faces stretching into the farthest reaches of the desert, their voices a steady hum, like an electrical current coursing through the universe.

And his father was there, too, standing beside the bike he'd given Chopra. "Your life has been remarkable, and I am very proud of you."

His mother and sisters were there, beckoning, even as an evil woman growled in his ear, "Wake up, old man. One more door. Come on. This is it!"

Computer voices.

His hand on something.

A light in his eye.

A prick to his finger.

And then the comforting thump of his heartbeat and the words *I am still here* echoing. Abruptly, the heavy clunking of the vault door jarred him as the ground began to shake.

He told himself he was submitting to her, if only to keep the boy alive. "Hussein?" he called. "Hussein?"

The armored transport drivers working with Haussler's Spetsnaz team maneuvered all four BTRs into blocking positions of the tower's four parking-garage entrances. They placed the tank on the main road facing north, toward Juma's oncoming forces, and the main gun had already boomed twice, those rounds targeting Juma's forces, as best Brent could tell without the satellite uplink.

Strangely enough, the BTRs had anti-aircraft guns, but not one of them was shooting at the European choppers, and that fact gave Brent pause.

Why would the Russians not target the Euros . . . unless they were now working together? And if they were, who had arranged that temporary alliance—even after Haussler had taken out those Badgers?

The Russians did have the European economy under their thumb, so perhaps this was blackmail or coercion of sorts. Whatever the case, the fact remained that Brent had to get past both of those forces to reach his target.

He, Lakota, and Juma crossed the bridge over the canal, but as they turned onto one of the side roads to reach the main highway, incoming fire ripped up the road in front of them. Ah, the BTRs weren't targeting the choppers; no, they were targeting them.

Juma's driver floored it as the Javelin missile guy considered firing his rocket while still hanging out the back of the SUV. Lakota hollered at the maniac: The back blast would kill them all—but he kept trying to swing out and shift the weapon so the blast would be directed outside.

"Hold fire for now, you fool!" shouted Brent.

He wasn't sure the man understood English, but Brent's tone and expression were hopefully enough.

"Ghost Lead, this is Schleck," called the sniper.

Brent immediately saw Schleck's point of view; it appeared he was pinned down, stealing glimpses around a corner. Ahead lay a long, dark tunnel. As Schleck leaned forward, gunfire sparked along the wall, driving him back.

"I see it, Schleck. Start gassing them out, but you move in slow. Buy us some time. They're sealing off the main tower entrances."

"Get around them and go in through the Silver Tower," said Schleck. "We'll flush them toward that exit. Grid test shows they've restored power to the vault security system down here."

"Okay, that's the plan, buddy. Flush them toward the Silver Tower. You hang in there. We're on our way."

"Brent, it's me," said Voeckler, his camera image appearing now in Brent's HUD. He was behind Riggs. Gunfire boomed in the background. "I'm jamming these local cameras, but I just busted through the encryption being used by the Euros outside. They want to engage the Russian troops, but they've just been ordered to hold fire."

"Surprise, surprise. Keep listening. You hear anything I need to know about, you call me a-sap. And while you're at it, see if you can break through and get a message back home. Try every satellite you can find."

"Roger that, sir. I already have been trying. And sir, those Russians coming in here . . . they wouldn't be the same guys that killed my brother, would they?"

Brent took a deep breath and lied.

The Snow Maiden finished donning her helmet, then made sure Hussein's fit properly. They'd known they'd face resistance and assumed chemical weapons would be used against them, tear gas and other less-than-lethal agents at the very least. Their suits were expertly fashioned copies of the Joint Strike Force advanced MOPP gear prototype number six and not unlike the ones being used by the Americans trying to stop them.

"Where's Chopra's suit?" asked the boy, his voice coming through the helmet's speaker via the open team channel.

"Forget it," she answered, grabbing the kid by the arm as the forklifts rolled into the vault behind her.

Light shone across long metal tables piled high with gold bricks that had been carefully stacked on reinforced wooden pallets. She felt as though she'd entered an ancient Egyptian tomb sans the art and statues, replaced by hedgerows of gold within which you could get lost. The brilliance of all those bricks collected in one place and stretching out for dozens of meters was quite breathtaking, even for someone as stoic as the Snow Maiden.

Chen's men couldn't help themselves either, taking

just a moment to marvel over the bricks and shout a few words of excitement to each other before sliding their forklifts into position to lift and haul away the pallets. Once loaded, the two lifts began whirring out of the vault.

Meanwhile, she and the boy walked thirty meters to the back, where several computers had been positioned in a corner desk area whose walls were covered by old-fashioned paper maps, mostly terrain maps of various parts of the Middle East. She called in two of Chen's men with batteries and a power converter to jump-start one of the computers. They finished their job within a minute, and the computer began to boot up.

She shoved the boy forward, then yanked a data key from her pocket. "Show me what I want and copy it here."

The boy took a seat, pillowed his hands across the back of his helmeted head, then kicked his feet up onto the desk. "All right, bitch, it's time you listen to me . . ."

Before she could react, a voice crackled over the team radio. "Hello, Viktoria, are you there? I know you're busy making a little withdrawal, but I think you and I need to talk."

The Snow Maiden closed her eyes and willed herself to burst into flames. Nothing happened. She looked up.

The kid raised his brows.

Haussler called again: "Viktoria, I've just killed two of your Chinese friends. Don't make me kill any more. I've got this building sealed off. You can't get out."

"Watch me," she growled.

He laughed under his breath. "I know why you're

here and what you're doing. Do you think Izotov can pay me more than what's in that vault?"

"Of course not."

"Then let me help you."

"You're lying. You'll turn me back over to them."

"Come on, Viktoria. You know me. We're both opportunists. Let's you and I seize the day. I'm the only one who can get you out of here. Not this pathetic team they gave you. I have the firepower. And afterward, we can sip champagne—just like the old days."

"We never did that."

"We should have."

She stood there, wanting to call Patti. The Green Brigade was supposed to take care of Haussler. They'd obviously failed, and now she was forced to deal with him. He'd killed two of her men and gained access to their communications, which put them at another disadvantage. She had a decision to make.

The boy looked at her. "Are you going to talk to him or me?"

"Shut up."

"No, *you* shut up! You're going to deal with me. I want a suit for Chopra! If you don't get me a suit right now, I'll smash these computers!"

She removed her pistol and shot him in the leg—

Before he even had time to take another breath and utter another word.

Bang. A bullet had struck the armor plating in his suit and ricocheted off, but the impact would give him a terrible bruise.

He wailed and nearly fell out of the chair.

She turned her scorching gaze on him. "Get on that computer and get me what I want! I *will* kill you!"

He scrambled forward and began typing on the wireless key panel. He slid off a glove for fingerprint authentication, received it, issued a voice command, was identified, then, finally, gained access.

"Oh, no," Riggs was saying as she whirled to find six fully suited Spetsnaz troops standing behind her. She faced forward, where two Chinese troops were doing likewise.

Schleck was screaming, as was Voeckler.

And Brent watched it all happen in his HUD as Juma's driver raced toward the Silver Tower.

The woman Brent remembered as looking so ravishing the night they had gone to the Tour de France party did the only thing she could do.

She opened fire on the Chinese guys, then spun back and fired on the Russians.

She didn't last long. Of the dozens of rounds fired at her, only a few needed to find the seams in her armor. She shouted, "I'm sorry, Ghost Lead. I tried my best."

And then her avatar flashed red and the camera image from her helmet showed the wall. She lay there, unmoving.

The voices came: *We've lost Riggs! We've lost Riggs!* The reports swirled in Brent's head and never took hold, all of them unreal for just a moment and then finally, inevitably, they registered as a cold shock to the system.

Suddenly, Riggs's helmet camera swiveled to an image

of another man, now wearing a helmet of his own; it was Haussler. He was staying a while after all. He muttered something in Russian to a man behind him, then dropped Riggs's head with a thump. The camera shook.

With a finger gesture, Brent closed the window, took a deep breath, and tried to calm himself, his gloved hands balling repeatedly into fists.

That opportunity lasted all of two seconds before the whomping of a Cheetah sounded from behind them, and before Brent could scream his warning, a rocket detonated not three meters behind the SUV, causing the driver to lose control, smash into the retaining wall, rebound, then hit the opposite wall, even as cannon fire stitched a line through the top of the SUV.

A round struck the driver and blood splattered over Brent's visor as he hollered for everyone to bail out.

The SUV had slowed to about twenty miles per hour when he hit the concrete, dropped, rolled, and came up with his rifle.

Lakota was beside him, as was Juma, who took a hard fall but assured them he was okay. The militiaman with the Javelin launcher jogged off, found a position to his liking, then lifted his weapon to the sky. He shouted something drowned out by the din of motors, and then the entire highway turned pure white as the missile streaked away.

Brent craned his head to follow the Javelin's trajectory. The bird homed in on the chopper, but this time the Cheetah's pilot launched electronic countermeasures— white-hot chaff that bloomed like a cloud of metallic confetti. The missile punched into the chaff and streaked on by, losing its lock on the chopper and then flying skyward for a second or two more before heaving into a thundering explosion.

"Come on, let's go!" Brent cried, waving them down the road as the chopper banked at a steep angle, then turned its guns northward and opened fire a few blocks down from the tower.

More flashes came from behind the skyscrapers, and the thought of Juma's men being mowed down by the Euros made Brent's skin crawl.

He and the others were only a quarter kilometer from the ample cover of the high-rises, and they ran hard and fast but dropped Juma quickly. The fat man could not keep up, and Lakota went back to urge him on while Brent and the Javelin guy hit the wall of the nearest skyscraper, the Goldcrest Executive Tower, which stood just beside the Almas.

Shifting furtively and almost not wanting to do so, Brent reached the corner of the building and stole a glance.

The BTR was sitting there like a pit bull on all fours, big guns lowered and pointed directly at him. Two dismounts hunkered down on either side of the vehicle, while the driver sat forward, his hatch open.

Yes, the long way around was through the Silver Tower tunnel, but at least they wouldn't have to face Haussler's buddies.

Brent checked the WAN uplink and dreamed of having Colonel Grey call in an air strike, something, anything, to ward off these wolves.

"Ghost Lead, this is Remus," called Voeckler. "Euros just got orders to provide air cover and escort to any vehicles leaving the tower area, including the Russian BTRs. You believe that?"

"She's got the Euros and Russians working for her. And no, I don't believe it," Brent answered.

Voeckler's camera switched on, and Brent saw that the man had taken up a position behind some kind of maintenance section with large machinery.

"Where are you?" Brent asked.

"I'm moving closer to the vault. We're thinking if I can cut the main power, we can lock her inside."

"Providing they're already in."

"It's worth a shot, sir."

"Do it."

Juma and Lakota came up behind them. Juma paused a moment to take both a radio call and a cell phone call from his men. When he was finished he looked up gravely. "I've already lost nearly half my army. I'm sorry, Brent. But I must call for a retreat—unless you can get us some help."

Brent took a long breath and closed his eyes.

And there, of course, was Villanueva, with his Corvette burning behind them.

The punk shook his head. *"You know, you didn't have to do any of this. No one cares. You didn't make anything right by joining the Army. You thought you could get rid of me. But I keep coming back. You wanna race?"*

"NO!"

"Now you feel bad that you got Juma into a fight you can't win."

"I did."

"What do you want, Brent?"

"I want her."

"No, I mean what do you want in your life?"

"To get rid of you . . ."

Villanueva smirked. *"Joining the Army didn't fix that. And you think getting her will solve all your problems?"*

"I never said that."

"No, but you've been thinking it. Deep down. You've been telling yourself that if you get her, then maybe you're done. You'll just retire. Maybe teach. But you've done enough. Paid your bill. And I'll go away."

"Yeah."

"And what if that doesn't happen? Then what?"

"I don't know . . ."

Chopra lifted his head enough to see the computer screens in front of Hussein. The maps were complex, commissioned and produced by geologists working for the family, while others showed the locations of the hidden oil reserves. Two were aboveground, while a third was submerged within the Strait itself and carefully disguised.

The boy was giving her everything. Had Chopra placed too much faith in the goodness of the world? Probably. But did he have any other choice? Some would argue that he did. Admittedly, he'd listened to his heart. He knew no other way.

"Hussein," he gasped. "What's that smell?"

"Shut up, old man!" cried the Snow Maiden, standing over the boy's shoulder. "You'll go to sleep soon."

"Upload's complete," Hussein said, handing something to the Snow Maiden.

"Let's go," she snapped. "We wait up top until they finish loading."

"No, I'm not leaving," he said. "I'm staying with him."

The Snow Maiden drew back her shoulders, and for a moment, Chopra thought she would shoot the poor boy.

"I told you to come with me."

"No!"

She raised her pistol, thought it over, muttered something under her breath, then took off, running.

"Hussein, come here," said Chopra.

The boy limped over and took Chopra's hand. "I'm sorry for what I did." His voice was muffled by his helmet, so Chopra had to prick up his ears.

"You're hurt?"

"Only a bruise. She shot my armor."

"Listen to me. I want to tell you about the dreams your father had for this country, for our country. We don't have much time, and I want to share them with you."

Hussein began to weep. "I should have listened to you."

"It's not too late."

"She has all the gold. The oil."

"But she hasn't escaped yet. I know they're coming for her. So it's not too late."

"Okay."

Chopra took a deep breath that hurt. "Your father drove me out to the desert one afternoon. We walked one hour away from the car, and then he lifted his hands to the sky and said, 'Manoj, when I close my eyes I don't see the sand anymore. I see an empire.'"

TWENTY-FOUR

Almas Tower
Business District, Dubai

"Ghost Lead, this is Daugherty. I've taken my squad along the south side of the tower, moving toward the Silver one, but take a look at this . . ."

The image appeared in Brent's HUD, and Daugherty zoomed in. Through the somewhat grainy green of night vision came a flash that lit up a group of combatants hunkered down near a small bridge facing one of the Almas Tower's garages. The combatants, about ten or twelve, were dressed all in dark colors and wearing balaclavas. Daugherty panned to show that they were trading fire with one of the Russian BTR crews and two Spetsnaz troopers.

"Can't ID them yet," Daugherty continued, "but they're laying down some nice fire on the Russians."

"Haussler's got somebody on his tail. His enemies are our friends," said Brent.

"And that's not all of them, sir. Two other squads just showed up. Got about thirty or forty of them now."

"Do what you can to make contact. Let's see who they are. Offer to hire them. You know the drill."

"Roger that. Money talks, sir. Just be careful when you come around."

"Brent, did you call for help?" asked Juma.

"No," said Brent. "But they came anyway, come on."

Lakota took point this time, leading them around the other side of the building. When they reached the corner, she checked the area, then gave the signal. They darted across the street, reached the next building, and traversed the shadows beside it, and then Brent leap-frogged past her to the next corner. From there he spied the Silver Tower.

"Ghost Lead, are you there, over?"

"Wait," Brent called as a window opened in his HUD. "I'm here, buddy, what do you got?"

Schleck had tucked himself into a narrow maintenance hallway running adjacent to one of the vault tunnels.

"I'm hidden here," he whispered into his microphone—even though they probably couldn't hear him. "Voeckler's right behind me."

Forklifts weighed down heavily with gold bricks hummed on by, one after another. Brent counted four in all, and he couldn't believe how many bricks they were hauling out of there. Just seeing gold piled up that way was surreal; the pallets might as well be props from a movie set.

"This is the third trip already," said Schleck. "If you guys don't get down here soon, they'll get away with all of it. They're making very good progress, up and down the elevator and back again."

"I hear you, Schleck. Just sit tight, man. You're doing a great job."

"Sir, this is Remus," called Voeckler. "Still no uplink with the satellite but I've just reestablished contact with the *Florida*."

Another data window opened in Brent's HUD. Commander Andreas stood on the submarine's bridge, rubbing his chin in thought. "Captain Brent, are you there? I'm afraid I've only got audio contact on my end. Video is breaking up."

"I'm here, sir, and sir? I could use a favor."

"Better make it a quick one. We're being called out of the strait."

"All right, here's what I have in mind . . ."

The Snow Maiden marched forward with Chen Yi to her right, another of his special forces sergeants to her left. They moved directly toward Haussler, who was approaching with a trio of his own troops, their weapons leveled on her.

"Stop right there," she told him. "Take off your helmet."

"Why, Viktoria, what is this? Don't you trust me?"

She shook her head.

He grinned.

And Lucifer himself had taught Haussler how to smile.

As he removed his helmet, she did the same, and Chen Yi looked at her. The gas canisters that had been ignited by the Americans were still billowing, but they were at the far end of the tunnel. The air was still clean, but not for much longer.

She moved toward Haussler, reached him, grabbed him by the back of the head, and kissed him deeply while reaching around and grabbing his ass. She shoved her tongue down his throat, and the German responded in kind, groaning softly.

Then, as quickly, she ripped herself away. "You get the rest later. For now, you come with me in my trucks. I want all your men. There will be a ship waiting for us at Mina Jebel Ali, far south side of the port. Order your drivers to head back to the airport." She checked her watch. "In about ten minutes a Chinese cargo plane will touch down. You have them drive right onto the plane. I'll make sure it's all arranged."

Haussler chuckled under his breath. "Viktoria, it sounds like you have been planning this all along."

"You always plan two escape routes," she said with a smirk. "What I didn't plan on was *you*."

At that moment, she whirled, and knowing exactly where to aim, she put a bullet in Chen Yi's neck and another in the sergeant's. Both men dropped, gasping.

Haussler's men confiscated their weapons.

She spun back to face the German. "Tell your men to kill the rest of them when they're finished loading."

"So you prove your loyalty."

"And you prove yours. It's me and you. No one else, okay?" She raised a brow.

He grabbed her once more and kissed her again, his breath quickening.

She pulled away. "Let's go."

Without warning the concrete floor began to rumble, and what sounded like a violent earthquake began to rip through the tunnel. A crack splintered up the wall ahead, growing into multiple veins and arteries, and then chunks of rock began falling away even as Haussler cried out to his men and all of them sprinted on wobbly legs.

A pair of thunderclaps struck, followed by another pair, and then she realized what was happening.

Brent, Lakota, Juma, and the Javelin guy, who had since abandoned his weapon, had reached the entrance to the Silver Tower's parking garage—all of ten seconds before the first pair of Tomahawk missiles struck the Goldcrest tower, blasting off huge sections that came raining down in a horrific storm of glass, concrete, insulation, and support struts.

The men in the BTR below never saw it coming.

And as they vanished beneath the massive pile of debris, a second pair of Tomahawks struck the Lake Terrace Tower rising just north of the Almas. The missiles hammered into the skyscraper about two-thirds of the way up and exploded with such force that a portion of the remaining third simply fell away.

And all the while Voeckler was talking to the crew aboard *Florida* as he watched via the team's exterior sticky cams. Because they were all tied into the same tactical network for situational awareness, Voeckler had been able to stream his video of the targets back to the sub's control room. With Park and Noboru's help, he'd passed along four critical points on the buildings that would result in the desired effects.

"That's two, we got two," he told them. "They're buried good; outstanding work, gentlemen!"

The south and north parking entrances to the Almas Tower were now successfully blocked, and two of the six BTRs had been taken out of the fight, buried beneath tons of debris. That was no cause for a victory party, but Brent was damned pleased.

Juma, on the other hand, was outraged.

"I told you I would help you capture this woman and protect my nation's gold, but I did not give you permission to destroy our buildings!"

A half dozen glib remarks came to mind, but Brent softened his tone and said, "I'm sorry, Juma. Better to do everything we can to save the gold, right? The buildings can be repaired. It was the best I could do. Now, can you back us up with a couple of squads? I can't do it without you. Here come my guys now."

Juma didn't look happy, but he finally nodded and turned away to call his men.

Brent waved Daugherty, Copeland, Heston, Park, and Noboru into the parking garage. They gathered around him.

"Destroy the other exits," he ordered. "If she tries to come out through this tower, I want this to be her only way out."

"Have C-4, will travel," said Heston. "We're on it, sir."

"She's still got two other exits via Almas," Lakota pointed out.

"Yeah, but those mystery troops are keeping the BTR crews busy over there," said Brent. He faced Daugherty. "You figure out who they are?"

"I got in close enough to examine one of their dead, pulled his mask, took a picture. But there's still no uplink to run his ID . . ."

"All right, we'll get to that later. But for now, we'll take all the free help we can get."

"Ghost Lead, you better hurry," said Schleck. "They've cleared the vault area. I think the last of the forklifts is in the elevator now."

The boy was talking to him and crying, but Chopra could barely sense him through all the cold. There was no fear, only a growing sense of calm like a soft wind blowing in his ears. He reached out, took his father's hand, and felt the calluses of a man who had toiled all his life. That was what love felt like. His father smiled, and there was pride in that grin.

Chopra smiled now at Hussein, who had made a promise to continue his father's dream.

There was one more breath coming. One more.

Chopra took it.

When they reached the cargo trucks, the Snow Maiden nodded in satisfaction at the sight of the dead Chinese special forces troops. Haussler's Spetsnaz had dispatched them with precision. Had there been any doubt? After all, Haussler's men were Russians.

The bad news was that they'd lost two of Haussler's vehicles. They still had the tank and the four remaining BTRs. She hesitated before climbing into the cab of one cargo truck loaded with gold. "You drive the lead truck. I pull up the rear," she told Haussler. "I'll tell you where to go."

"As always," he said with a sigh.

Just then he got a report from one of his troops: A missile had struck the tank. Now it was out of the fight, too. He cursed.

As did the Snow Maiden. Her original plan had two trucks going to the airport, two going to the ship. The idea was to split the gold so that any opponents would believe that one shipment was a diversion, when in fact both were hot and at least one should be able to escape. She'd never disclosed that to Patti, who, of course, wanted all of the gold, but fifty percent of something was better than nothing.

But, of course, they'd lost a truck and had overloaded the remaining three. The BTRs had room enough to carry the gold and were much better protected, but she feared that wasting any more time to make a transfer might result in their being trapped.

Were she an American Special Forces leader, what would she assume? Well, the smart money had the gold inside the better-protected vehicles. So she had to hope that they'd go after the BTRs. That made sense. Thus, they'd send out the armor first. The cargo plane landing at the airport would also raise suspicions.

"Can you get the choppers outside to cover the BTRs when they leave?" she asked Haussler.

"Izotov has put me in direct contact with the Enforcers Corps commander," he answered. "I've never seen such an efficient piece of blackmail."

"Good. Do it."

"I will, but first, I'm putting those Cheetahs on the entrances. Your old friends from the Green Brigade have become a wart on my ass."

She rolled her eyes. "Thanks for that image."

"Anytime."

With their rifles at the ready and targeting data streaming across their HUDs, Brent and his team hustled their way through the garage and down toward the main tunnel that would take them over to the Almas Tower.

Juma remained up top to meet the two squads he had called over.

When they were halfway through the tunnel, the warlord called to say that the choppers were gunning down the mystery fighters opposite the east and west entrances, and it seemed likely that Brent's target would exit from one of those areas because the Cheetahs were clearing the path.

Brent could hear all the booming above and feel it in his legs. He told Juma to get as many vehicles as he could near those exits. Once the choppers neutralized the mystery force, only Juma's men could slow down the Snow Maiden's escape, while Brent and his Ghosts came in from behind.

Schleck and Voeckler checked in. They'd slipped into the main vault area for a quick recon, and Voeckler's camera picked up a figure wearing an environment suit and kneeling over an old man whom Brent quickly recognized as Manoj Chopra. He used a finger gesture to widen the data box and watch as Voeckler confronted the figure, who turned out to be Hussein.

"We're not here to hurt you," said the Splinter Cell.

"I know," answered the boy, his accent distinctly British. "Where are you taking me?"

"Someplace safe."

"What about him?"

"We'll come back when we can. Later . . ."

"Get him through the Silver Tower," Brent ordered. "I'm charging both of you with keeping him safe. That's royalty right there. Do you guys read me?"

"Yes, sir," said Voeckler.

"Don't worry, Captain," added Schleck. "This kid's got the best bodyguards in town. Moving out now."

"Brent, it's Juma! The choppers are backing off and

the BTRs are coming out! Four of them now, turning up toward the highway. Still small-arms fire from a few stragglers, but they're getting away."

"Schleck, did she load the gold onto the BTRs?" Brent asked the sniper.

"Sir, I'm not sure. She's still got the three cargo trucks, but I'm trying to pinpoint their locations."

"Brent, it's Juma again. One of my teams up near the airport says a cargo plane just touched down. It's military, unmarked."

"She's got the gold in the BTRs, and they're heading to the airport. Everyone, turn around, we're getting the hell out of here! We need to get back up top! Voeckler, is *Florida* still available?"

"Negative, sir."

Brent cursed. "Lakota, still no uplink?"

"Nothing. I've got a loop set to alert us the second we break the jamming."

"Brent, some of the Euro armor is now moving in behind the BTRs, escorting them, and they've got the choppers covering by air. That has to be her."

"Juma, what do you have in between here and the airport? Anything that can stop her?"

"I'm sorry, Brent."

"Can your guys at the airport at least attack the plane?"

"I'll see what I can do."

A new window opened in Brent's HUD: His laser-based radar system (LADAR) had detected movement behind them, about a thousand meters back. The image revealed three contacts growing more distinct: the cargo trucks. Whatever people she'd left behind were probably making their escape as well.

Not five seconds later they came under heavy small-arms fire as headlights wiped into view and reached up the tunnel toward them.

Lakota screamed to take cover.

Brent threw himself toward the wall, dropping down and rolling back up with his rifle to fire on the lead vehicle as it roared by with a man hanging out the cab window and firing a steady stream.

The second truck roared by, and Brent ordered the others to hold fire—

He was blinded for a moment by the truck's headlights, and then his mouth fell open.

He'd just caught a glimpse of the third truck's driver. She might be wearing a suit and helmet, but he recognized those eyes. He'd studied them for too many hours.

Perhaps the gold was being shipped out on the BTRs, but Viktoria Antsyforov, the Snow Maiden, had another escape route in mind.

"Get on!" he screamed.

He and Lakota raced behind the last truck and launched themselves into the air, groping futilely for some purchase. They both tumbled to the ground as the exhaust washed over them.

Lakota rolled up with a grenade, about to throw it, when Brent looked down and saw them.

Four more grenades rolling toward them like baseballs, lobbed by the men in the trucks.

It was all he could do to turn around and throw himself back when the explosions tore through the tunnel, and the blast wave lifted him from the ground.

Chen Yi's men had not reported any more Americans in the tunnel, and the Snow Maiden had felt the breath escape her as they roared by. That Haussler's Spetsnaz troops had dropped a handful of grenades before the Americans could throw theirs was just luck, and as the booms echoed and explosions flickered in her side mirror, she called up to Haussler and told him how lucky they were.

As they reached the uppermost level, he reported that all three exits had been sealed off by explosions and debris, and only one path was available; it would no doubt be defended.

"Call off one of the choppers," she told him. "Wait, no. Don't do that. Just blast on through."

"Are you sure? One of my lieutenants says two squads outside. Looks like only small arms, but we will take a lot of fire, maybe an RPG."

"You're right. Stop here. Call the chopper. Put some fire on those guys outside. Clear us a path."

He pulled to a screeching halt, as did the truck behind him. They were at the far end of the garage, ground level, and out in the darkness she saw the shadows move—militiamen waiting for them . . . or maybe even Green Brigade.

She glanced over at the Spetsnaz troop sitting beside

her, a young, lean, dark-haired man with seemingly vacant eyes. "Where are you from?" she asked him in Russian.

He just frowned at her.

"Do I offend you?"

"We know who you are. You betrayed your country. Our job was to bring you in. Haussler has other plans. My orders are to follow him. So I do. But I do not have to like it, nor do I have to talk to you."

"Get out."

He looked at her.

"I said, *get out!*" She drew her pistol and shoved it into his neck, just below the helmet.

He opened the door, climbed out, jogged to the next truck, and was let inside.

"Okay, three more minutes," Haussler finally said.

"Tell that pilot to hurry up!"

When Brent finally looked up, he saw most of his team lying on the concrete floor. Copeland was already tending to Daugherty and Heston, who'd been nearest to the blasts, their helmets scorched, shrapnel jutting from all over their suits. Noboru and Park were assisting him, but they too looked dazed, covered in shrapnel, some of which had clearly penetrated the more vulnerable sections of their suits.

"Brent, I'll stay down here with them," said Lakota. "That was her, wasn't it?"

"Yeah," he gasped.

"Then you have to go after her. We'll link up with Schleck and Voeckler."

He nodded, "Juma, she's coming your way! Three trucks!"

"I know, I know," cried the warlord. "But here comes the chopper!"

Even as he spoke, Brent heard the powerful whomping in the background. Then gunfire. Explosions. Screams.

"Lakota, Copeland will stay with them. You come with me."

She shrugged.

"I need you, girl."

"We're hurting, Brent. We're hurting real bad. I don't know if there's anything else we can do."

"There's one thing," he said. "We can try. Not give up. Not yet. Come on."

They sprinted through the lingering smoke, rounded the next corner, then raced through the next leg of the tunnel, heading up to the deepest level of the parking garage. Somewhere above came the hum of idling engines.

Lakota slowed, stopped, then raised a finger to the ceiling. "Listen. They've stopped."

He did. Nodded. Then urged her on, just as Juma's voice broke over the channel. "My squads are dying out here, Brent. We have to pull out. Here come the trucks. They're coming now!"

Brent tensed and picked up the pace. This was it. He was going to lose her. Again.

TWENTY-FIVE

Silver Tower
Business District, Dubai

Fires raged through the ground-floor windows of the building where the militiamen had holed up. Those pathetic dolts thought they had a perfect firing line on the Silver Tower's remaining exit, but the Enforcers Corps chopper and its gunner had routinely ruined their plans.

Now Haussler, still at the wheel of the lead truck, hit the gas, and the Snow Maiden followed him. They bounced over the concrete curbing, left the garage, and rumbled onto the street, with the chopper still hovering above.

Within two minutes they were headed southwest along the desolate highway, bound for Mina Jebel Ali, guided by night vision and, well, to be blunt, vengeance and greed.

Patti contacted her over the suit's radio and said that

their ship, the NYK Line's *Leo Leader* out of Panama was pulling into the dock and would be ready within a few minutes to receive them.

"How did the Americans get here? By land? Or by sea . . . if there's a JSF ship out there—or a submarine—this could all be for nothing. Do you understand?"

"Viktoria, there's no need to remind me of that again."

"Well, if you haven't taken care of that, then I can't promise you anything."

"I understand. And *you* should understand that linking up with Haussler was beyond foolish."

"You gave me no choice. Your Green Brigade friends couldn't stop him. So I earned his trust by killing the Chinese. Are you happy?"

"What will you do with the German now?"

She took a deep breath. "I'm not sure."

The Range Rover was parked just behind a pile of concrete rubble on the north side of the tower. Juma turned over the car to Brent and Lakota. He was going back into the tower to find his cousin, who was with Schleck and Voeckler. The rest of Juma's men had sought cover in the Almas Tower, but ironically, the chopper had broken off to escort the telecom trucks. Juma said the convoy was heading south down Sheikh Zayed Road.

Brent took the wheel, with Lakota at his side. He checked the gauges. Half a tank of gas. They had to assume the Snow Maiden was meeting someone. The farther south she drove, the stronger the radioactive fallout became. She might be moving the gold out of Abu Dhabi, but probably not much farther south than that.

"Brent, I just got a call from my men at the airport," said Juma over the radio. "They've been putting some fire on that cargo plane, but one of the choppers is keeping them pinned down."

"See if they can disrupt the convoy of BTRs. That's about all we can hope for now. I'm thinking the gold is with them."

"Okay, Brent."

He turned onto the highway and put the pedal to the metal. One headlight was out, and the engine wailed against his coaxing. He turned off that headlight and used the suit's night vision.

"Ghost Lead, this is Copeland," called the team's medic. "Heston and Daugherty are stable but took some serious shrapnel hits. The suits administered pain meds before I could do anything. Heston's fuel cell is out, damaged by the grenades, and Daugherty's is shot, too. We need to evac a-sap."

Copeland's camera view filled a window in Brent's HUD, and he glimpsed his men sitting up against the tunnel wall, both grimacing.

"All right, hold position till I can get you out of there. Noboru? Park? Go back for Riggs and Schoolie."

There were few jobs more grim than retrieving the bodies of your fallen comrades.

He tossed a look to Lakota. "There's just the two of us, some small arms, and a few grenades. How do we stop a convoy of trucks with a big lead?"

"Somebody told me you drove Corvettes when you were younger."

"Maybe."

"Then just drive, baby, drive!"

He drove his foot deeper into the pedal.

"That's nice!" she cried.

Brent flicked his gaze to the right, saw Villanueva's door just a few feet away, both Corvettes neck and neck now, their Borla exhaust systems thundering as they raced up the four-lane road.

He blinked again and saw Lakota. She looked at him. "Don't worry. I'll make sure we take out those trucks. She doesn't get away this time. Not this time." Her voice did not falter, and he knew she would keep her promise or die trying.

The telecom trucks were running with lights out, so it took both Brent's night vision and zoom lens to finally glimpse them in the distance, range 2.23 kilometers and falling.

"I can't get this piece of crap to go any faster."

"It's no Corvette."

He snorted. "Yeah."

"Whoa. Hold," she said. "We don't have to catch them." She spoke rapidly to someone else on another channel, her voice muted by the helmet.

He tensed. "What?"

"You know the old saying, if it becomes a sensor it has to talk to all of us?"

"Yeah, yeah, that thing about situational awareness, but what's that have to do with—"

"Voeckler's sending stuff to me since he knows you're driving. He's regained temporary contact with *Florida*. Andreas says he's talking to Colonel Grey, passed on word of what's happening. *Florida*'s just launched a predator drone from one of her modified tubes. Drone's in the air now. Check it out."

A window irised open in the upper right-hand corner of Brent's display to stream video from the unmanned reconnaissance drone as it arced high over the road. He spotted their Range Rover and the three trucks gliding like blips in a video game display across the dark road. The drone's camera panned right and focused on a long series of docks. A flashing red label appeared with the words *Mina Jebel Ali*. Another quick zoom revealed a ship. After a pause, a second glowing label IDed her as the *Leo Leader*, a hulking blue cargo vessel with a huge bay entrance constructed at her stern. Ramps were just now lowering so that the Snow Maiden could drive her trucks directly into the hold without stopping.

"All right, I'm confused," Brent confessed. "She might be heading to the dock, but is she taking the trucks because it's just faster?"

"No, because she's also got the gold," finished Lakota. "And the BTRs are just the decoy. We assumed the gold was in the better-defended vehicles, and we played right into her hand."

"She's crazy."

"And so are we."

"Ghost Lead, this is Hawk's Honor, up top at nine thousand feet, over."

A new window in Brent's HUD showed a rotating file image of a JSF Boeing 747 that was operating out of Diego Garcia in the Indian Ocean. The image switched to the pilot, who wore a narrow headset with attached monocle similar to Brent's Cross-Com. A bar below him indicated that his aircraft was equipped with a YAL-1 laser cannon attached to the jet's nose cone. The 747's chemical oxygen iodine laser was primarily an air-to-air missile defense weapon, but the YAL-1 had recently been modified to take out ground targets.

Two smaller windows opened on Brent's screen to show the 747's escort: a pair of carrier-based F-35s operating from the USS *Dwight D. Eisenhower* Carrier Strike Group.

Brent could barely contain his excitement.

He'd already resigned himself to losing her, but now he had a real chance, with good intel.

"Hawk's Honor, this is Ghost Lead," he began, trying to calm down. "I need a strike on those three telecom trucks observed via predator. If you can take out the engines with minimal collateral damage, the beers are on me. I'd like to take my target alive. Also, I've got a cargo plane at the airport. Need that taken out, too, if it's not too much trouble."

"Roger, Ghost Lead. We have your ground targets in sight. Stand by . . ."

Brent switched channels. "Juma, can you get me some people out here? We're going to stop the trucks, but I need help! Pick up my guys at the Silver, then come on out!"

"I'll call my people from the Almas, but we only have two cars left. I can call some more from the north."

"Do it!"

"I will, Brent. And good news. My cousin is okay."

Brent sighed. The Snow Maiden probably could have killed the boy. He doubted she had a soft side. She'd left him alive because that benefited her in some way—but how?

The stench of fuel and burning rubber filled the truck's cabin, and the temperature grew unbearably hot for a moment before the engine began to cough and protest. The Snow Maiden didn't notice the basketball-sized hole in the hood until smoke began wafting from it.

Haussler's truck pulled over to the side of the road, followed by the second truck, and then the Snow Maiden joined them, the engine finally dying altogether.

She was aghast as she climbed out of the truck, glanced at the sky, then got on the radio to Patti. "You told me you jammed their uplinks here."

"That's correct."

"Well, they've taken us out with a laser, melted right through the engine blocks. The gold is sitting here. Either you come and pick me up, or it's over. I still have the oil-reserve data. Time to cut your losses, you hear me?"

"We need that gold, too."

"Get me out, or I'm walking right now!" she screamed.

Haussler ran over to her. "What now? You want us to carry the gold to the ship?"

Several of the Spetsnaz troops slid open the rear doors and hopped down from the truck. They ran ahead of Haussler and the Snow Maiden, then began pointing down the road. One whirled back. "Vehicle coming. Looks like militia."

"I've called for a pickup," said the Snow Maiden.

"I'm sure you have." Haussler turned away from her and began speaking in French to the chopper pilot. He finished, looked at her, smiled weakly, then began speaking to someone else.

Meanwhile, the Cheetah broke away, wheeled around, and headed north toward the oncoming car.

"Okay, so there's a gunship," said Lakota calmly. "Any thoughts?"

"Not really."

"So we just drive right at him?"

Brent squinted. "His rocket pods look empty."

"But his cannons aren't."

"Yeah, you're probably right."

Lakota's voice grew more tense. "Captain . . ."

"Relax. I got this."

Brent took a long breath. She couldn't hear or see what he did on the closed strategic channel. The 747 pilot had cut loose his escorts, and the F-35s were both en route, with the lead jet already locked on to the Cheetah.

The pilot stoically reported that her Sidewinder missile was away.

A shooting star wiped across the sky and descended toward the Cheetah.

Brent's heart beat once. Twice.

He gasped.

The Sidewinder struck the Cheetah top down, and the chopper disintegrated into a fireball that lit up the entire highway. Flaming debris shot from the flames and spread like fireworks to cast a deep glow over the Range Rover's hood.

Brent veered to the left as a jagged piece of fuselage slammed down on the hood and shattered the windshield. Then he rolled hard right, tires screeching, as the fiery hunk of metal sent flames billowing toward his helmet.

The Snow Maiden stood, aghast. Their air defense had just been blown from the sky, and all she could do was breathe.

For just a second, she closed her eyes and told herself no, she wasn't ready to surrender. Not yet.

A blast of air nearly knocked her to the ground.

Suddenly, a pair of jets came swooping down, banked hard, then slowed and turned on their axes as vectoring nozzles switched directions, pointing downward. Both hovered now like choppers, and their pilots cut loose with internal cannon fire, rounds ripping and sparking across the road, sending all of them diving for cover behind the trucks.

The Spetsnaz troops began to return fire, but Haussler hollered for them to keep down. The jets descended even more, and the cannon fire grew unbearable, shredding through the trucks, the gold, and striking the troops huddled down near the tires.

She grabbed Haussler by the arm and ran back toward the embankment, exploiting several feet of cover below the road. The troops were screaming, dying up there in the hell storm of unrelenting salvos.

"This is it, Heinrich," she said. "I guess this is it."

"Did you think I would come here with no backup plan myself?" he asked.

"What do you mean?"

"Wait. Look . . ."

"What am I looking at?"

"A favor from your old friend General Izotov, who would like to see you more than ever—and I've promised that meeting. And so now we are saved."

"I thought we had a deal."

"Unfortunately, your contacts let you down. Mine won't. You'll be coming back to Moscow with me."

He'd barely finished his sentence when both jets blew apart in successive bursts. Wings, cockpit canopies, and landing gear appeared through swelling fires and tumbled end over end to crash down and scrape across the highway. A wedge-shaped piece of fuselage crashed into the telecom trucks, knocking two on their sides and tearing them open. Bricks of gold tumbled out and glittered in the flames, and the Snow Maiden hit the dirt as more bricks thumped to the ground around her.

She reached down, grabbed one bar, and cursed at the top of her lungs.

* * *

Six Russian Federation KA-65 Howlers like the ones Brent had faced near Sandhurst thundered overhead as he approached the shattered telecom trucks.

At the same time, a pair of fighter jets streaked above them, and though Brent received no indication of their IDs, he could only assume that they, too, were Russian and had been responsible for taking out the F-35s.

As he and Lakota bounded out of the Range Rover, a wave of gunfire from somewhere behind the trucks sent them down to their bellies, and not a second later, a grenade exploded on Lakota's side of the truck.

He screamed for her. No answer.

Feeling as though he'd been hit by ten thousand volts, Brent bounded around the Range Rover and dropped down beside Lakota, who was lying facedown near the wheel. Razor-sharp pieces of shrapnel had peppered one side of her suit. He rolled her over, and her eyes slowly flickered open. "Don't let her get away . . ."

His HUD showed her vital signs and that the suit had already hit her with painkillers.

Brent nodded, looked up, and saw that the Russian choppers were just now coming around to escort a larger, slower bird, a troop transport.

And then, from the embankment, he saw two figures dash forward, away from the trucks.

Brent charged after them, and they didn't notice his approach as the rotor wash whipped across the road.

He leveled his rifle on the taller one and cut loose a

triplet of rounds that punched the guy onto his back; however, the rounds failed to penetrate his armor. He was only stunned.

The smaller figure swung back to face him.

It was her.

And as she fired into his chest—one, two, three rounds—he threw himself into the air and knocked her to the ground. He dropped his rifle and pinned her arms with his knees, and his gloved hands fumbled for the latch on her helmet. He found it, threw it back, and, as she fought to squirm free, twisted off her helmet and tossed it away.

He wrapped his gloved hands around her neck and began to choke her. "Do you know how long I've been looking for you?" he screamed in English, knowing she understood him.

"I don't care," she said, groaning in exertion.

With a sudden jerk she rolled, driving her legs up and over his head, boots slamming into his helmet. The power in her legs was remarkable, and she tore him free, forcing his head back with her ankles. He lost his grip on her throat and fell away, reaching out to his right for his rifle.

"Ghost Lead, this is Hawk's Honor, second squadron of F-35s inbound. They'll be in missile range in two minutes, if you can just hang on, over."

He couldn't answer the pilot.

And if he could just delay her for two minutes . . .

Brent sat up—in time to watch the Snow Maiden's boot connect with his helmet, knocking him back down.

He rolled, tried to sit up again, but she stood over him now, aiming her pistol at his head.

"Who are you?" she screamed, her short hair whipping in rotor wash as the transport chopper landed, with Russian troops thumping out beside the door gunner, who swung his machine gun around to face Brent.

The first guy Brent had shot was staggering to his feet and screaming in Russian, waving for the Snow Maiden to follow him.

Was that Haussler?

Ignoring him, she screamed once more for Brent to ID himself.

The weird light in her eyes told him enough. If he kept pushing her buttons, he'd buy more time. "You don't give me orders, little girl."

Voices in his ear now:

"Brent, it's Juma! We're on our way! Almost there!"

"Ghost Lead, this is Hawk's Honor, one minute . . . Stand by . . ."

The Snow Maiden leaned toward him, aiming at his neck. "I can shoot you right here, and you'll die."

"Then do it, you crazy bitch."

"Viktoria!" screamed the other man. That had to be Haussler!

The Russian troops were running forward now, about to surround them.

Brent stole a look back at Lakota, who was now lying on her side, clutching her rifle, and staring vaguely at him.

Then he glanced back up the road, where in the distance he saw two cars, a Ford pickup truck and another

Range Rover SUV about three hundred meters behind. Some of his Ghosts were riding in the pickup, hanging over the flatbed's sides, rifles brought to bear.

The Russian gunships had fanned out, and two were turning toward the oncoming cars.

Brent wanted to call off Juma and his people, but it was already too late.

Lakota began firing at the oncoming Russians, who dropped and returned fire.

At that moment, the Snow Maiden leaned down and began to jab her gun into his neck.

Brent grabbed her arm as the pistol went off.

And then he pulled her down toward him with all his might. She lost her balance and fell. Just as he moved to climb back on top of her, gunfire hammered across his back, and then it came, the sharp, steady pain.

He gasped and fell over, onto his side, as the Snow Maiden was pulled away by the other man, who Brent now confirmed was Heinrich Haussler. He was working for her?

Lakota fired again, and more rounds from the Russians ahead punched into and clanged off their Range Rover.

Rockets ignited above and streaked away from the Russian choppers. Brent turned his head to watch as his people bailed out of the cars only seconds before the missiles struck. Twin explosions swelled into summits of fire, and the screams from his men over the team channel were awful and unbearable. The Range Rover assumedly carrying Juma turned around and headed back in retreat.

"Ghost Lead, this is Hawk's Honor, thirty seconds . . ."

You're too late, Brent wanted to tell him, but a wave of dizziness was taking hold, the ground listing to the left as though he were on a boat.

He knew if he stared hard enough at those flames in the distance he'd see Villanueva, shaking his head in disappointment.

"Ghost Lead, they'll have missile lock in five, four, three, two . . ."

The Snow Maiden glanced back once more at the soldier who'd tackled her. It had been years since she'd encountered a man so fiery-eyed and determined. He seemed obsessed with her, and she took that as a true compliment. She thought of ordering the Russians to grab him, capture him, but she couldn't explain why.

She climbed into the transport, and as they began to lift off, she shoved her pistol into Haussler's neck and fired two rounds, whispering, "I'll never go back to Izotov. Never."

As he started to drop, she slid him aside and tossed him out of the chopper. His body tumbled and slapped across the asphalt, limbs twisted at unnatural angles as the troops standing beside her looked dumbfounded.

She pushed through them, put her pistol to the back of the chopper pilot's head, and shouted: "Okay, now you'll take me where I want to go."

Just then explosions like tiny orange novae woke in

the night sky, and the radio traffic from the gunships grew frantic.

"The Americans are here," cried the pilot.

"Good," she said. "Take me back to the airport."

One of the troops jammed his rifle into her back. "Lower your weapon," he cried.

She glanced back over her shoulder. "I'll kill him! And then we all die, unless you know how to fly this helicopter."

He thought it over, then complied, and in one fluid motion, she turned, put her pistol to the trooper's head, and shot him point-blank. The trooper beside her grabbed her arm.

But before he could get closer in an attempt to seize her weapon, the chopper suddenly pitched forward, and cannon fire tore into the bay. Alarms blared from the cockpit, and the pilot cried, "I've lost power!"

EPILOGUE

Sheikh Zayed Road
Near Mina Jebel Ali
Two Hours Later

A SEAL team had flown in from the *Eisenhower* Carrier Strike Group, and Brent had already been examined by the medics. He was about to be airlifted back to the ship when Juma shifted forward with his cousin. "Brent, I'd like you to meet Sheikh Hussein Al Maktoum. The ruler of Dubai."

The boy, who was still wearing an environment suit identical to the Snow Maiden's, extended his hand. Brent took it. "Thank you, sir, for recovering the gold and helping my country."

"You're welcome. I do wish we could have gotten her." He glanced up to Juma. "Any word yet?"

Juma shook his head. "Her helicopter went down near Al Lisaili, but there's still no sign."

The boy released Brent's hand. "Captain, if there is anything I can ever do for you?"

Brent took a long breath. "Hold that thought. I may come looking for a favor sooner rather than later."

Hussein nodded. "Anything you need. Just let me know."

Two crew members from the chopper lifted Brent's long backboard and carried him away. At his request, they placed him beside Lakota in the helicopter's cramped bay. He reached over, took her hand, then raised his voice over the droning engines. "You did good, kid."

She sighed. "You, too!"

He raised his head and spotted Voeckler and Schleck seated across from him. They were ragged, red-eyed, exhausted.

He took a deep breath. The rest of his team who'd been riding in the pickup truck was coming home in body bags. He closed his eyes and braced himself.

The guilt burned.

And burned. And burned.

Moscow
Four Days Later

The Snow Maiden stood over his bed, watching him sleep. He was a pathetic old man swollen with greed and with a terrible lust for power that had blinded him to the atrocities committed by his government. He had been schooled in the rules of success by a war hero father who'd taught him to crush those in his way, so even from the beginning there had been no hope for him. He was a schoolyard bully with a war machine at his disposal.

Her breath grew shallow as she considered shooting him. Ending it quickly. No words. Just instant gratification. Revenge served coldly, as it should be.

Instead she nudged his head with her pistol until he jolted awake.

She flicked on her penlight and shone it on her face, illuminating herself like some night creature.

"Viktoria, is that you?" he said, lifting his hand and squinting.

"Yes, General. Heinrich said you wanted to talk to me."

"We assumed you were dead. Like him."

"Another friend gave me a ride, although she's no more trustworthy than you."

"If you've come to kill me, then be done with it. I'm sixty-two and much too old to be insulted by you."

"You're fat and ignorant. And even with a gun to your head you still think you can give orders?"

"Viktoria, we didn't kill your husband. Or your brothers. You've constructed this fantasy and turned us into murderers, when we are anything but."

She jabbed the pistol into his forehead, and he groaned sharply. Then she climbed on top of him and began pressing the muzzle deeper and deeper into his flesh. "You don't know anything about me."

She began to tremble.

"Just shoot me!" he cried.

"I should," she gasped, beginning to pant, her face warming with the desire to finish him now. "But I won't. I can't."

"Then what do you want?"

"You're coming with me."

He stifled a laugh. "You're going to kidnap me?"

"Yes. I need your help."

"With what?"

"With killing the president. With bringing down the motherland. And then we will stand back and watch it burn."

"You're insane."

"Yes."

"Okay, Viktoria, whatever you say. Whatever you want me to do, I will do."

She pulled the pistol from his head and set it on the night table. "First you'll satisfy my needs, then you pack. We have a long trip ahead of us." She shoved her tongue down his throat and tore at his pajamas.

**SinoRus Group Oil Exploration Headquarters
Sakhalin Island
North of Japan
Six Days Later**

Igany Fedorovich rose from his desk as the Snow Maiden and Izotov strode into the room. Patti entered from a side door, and all four of them took seats around a small conference table.

"Please forgive the weapons search," said Fedorovich. "But it was necessary. I'm sure you understand."

"I hope this will be brief," said Izotov.

The side door opened again, and the Snow Maiden lost her breath as in stepped Colonel Pavel Doletskaya, along with another woman, smartly dressed and at least ten years younger than Pavel. She seemed strangely familiar.

The Snow Maiden bolted from her chair and crossed to her old colleague and lover. His eyes were already glassy. He rushed to her, took her into his arms, and clutched her tightly, whispering, "There is nothing we have to say. We are together again, that is enough. You don't know how long I've waited for this moment . . ."

Patti cleared her throat, and slowly, they broke their embrace and returned to their seats.

Fedorovich introduced the younger woman as Major Alice Dennison of the Joint Strike Force. She was the *Ganjin*'s mole, nurtured from birth and controlled while her birth parents never knew what was happening.

"My God, woman, what have you done? She works for you?" asked Izotov, his jaw hanging open.

"And so do you."

He recoiled.

"Our plan is to bring a peaceful end to the conflict, one which will be mutually beneficial to us all. We will cut the power lines of corruption in Washington, in Moscow, and in Paris in order to better stabilize the world's economy and foster the health and welfare of all human beings. And when we're finished, the world will, indeed, be a better place."

Izotov began to chuckle. "Good luck with that. I've never heard a more ridiculous and naïve plan."

"When your surgery is completed, you will believe in it as fervently as we do," Patti said, raising a well-tweezed brow at him.

Izotov's smile vanished. "Surgery?"

"It's painless . . . and completely undetectable," said Dennison, her eyes eerily vacant. "And when it's over, you'll feel a sense of freedom you've never felt before."

A chill woke across the Snow Maiden's shoulders. Dennison's tone was unsettling, and the Snow Maiden wondered if Patti and Fedorovich were already controlling her and that everything she'd done this far was part of their master plan and that she'd never had free will. She'd been their instrument from the beginning. No, that couldn't be true. . . . Could it?

"All right, let's talk now about Dubai's oil reserves," Patti began.

The Liberator Sports Bar and Grill
Near Fort Bragg, North Carolina
Two Weeks Later

It was about five P.M., and Brent sat alone in his usual corner booth. He'd been released from the hospital the day before. They'd kept him a bit longer than Lakota to perform a second surgery and had finally removed a piece of shrapnel that had been lodged in his back. He was scheduled to meet with Colonel Grey tomorrow morning, but the meeting was a formality. He was being reassigned to the JFK School, and his days in Ghost Recon were over. That news had come through the grapevine and was no surprise. He told himself he was all right with it.

Thomas Voeckler had been nursing a beer at the bar and finally came over to sit across from Brent. "Didn't see you here."

"And you call yourself a spy?"

Voeckler grinned. "Half-assed. My brother would tell you."

"No, you're top notch. What you did for me was harder than anything your brother ever did."

"I doubt it."

"Did your brother ever finish a mission, knowing that he'd just lost you?"

Voeckler thought about that and shook his head.

"Point made."

Voeckler sighed, sipped his beer, then said, "It's okay that you lied about Haussler being in Dubai. I know why you did it, but you didn't have to worry. Haussler got his anyway, huh?"

"Yeah, and I'm sorry about that."

"Like I said, it's all right. The bastard's dead."

Schleck arrived in the doorway and caught Brent's gaze. The lanky sniper steered himself over and took a seat. "Who do I kill to get a beer?"

Brent shook Schleck's hand. "Hey, man, thanks for coming."

"Are you kidding?" Schleck drew his head back,

dumbfounded, then wiggled his brows at the waitress and ordered his beer.

"Where's Lakota?" asked Voeckler.

"On her way," said Brent. "Oh, there she is now." He rose and rushed to the front door, holding it open for her as she hobbled into the bar, favoring her right leg. She'd refused to use crutches, but Brent gave her no choice when he grabbed her arm and helped her over to the table.

"Hey, guys," she said with a grin. "You clean up nice."

Once they'd dispensed with the pleasantries and each had a beer, Brent got down to the business at hand: lifting their glasses to fallen comrades. His voice cracked. But that was okay. The beer was cold, the sentiments honest. Nothing else mattered.

After an hour, Schleck and Voeckler bid their good-byes and good lucks.

"You still want to hang out with a broken old war-horse?" Brent asked Lakota.

"If you think you're getting off cheap with just beer, think again, mister. I want dinner and a movie."

"At my pay grade?"

"Yeah. And Brent, you're not an old warhorse."

He snorted, glanced away in thought. "You know, I never meant to do any of this."

"What're you talking about?"

"Truth is, I joined the Army because I thought I could take another guy's place. I thought I could live his life and make things right. So everything I've done was to try to say I'm sorry. But it doesn't matter. No one really cares. And I have to convince myself that my life wasn't his but mine. I'm the soldier, not him. I didn't live his life. I lived my own."

"That's right."

"Yeah, I can talk the talk, but the walk is . . ."

"Maybe it's easier if I take your hand." She reached across the table.

He grinned. "Doesn't feel any different. Maybe if you take off your clothes."

She frowned. "Pig!"

He busted out laughing. "Come on, let's go see that movie. We'll get a late dinner. You mind driving? My car's still at the impound."

As Brent rose, his cell phone rang. Unidentified caller. "Hello?"

"Brent? This is Scott Mitchell."

He looked at Lakota and mouthed the name. Her eyes widened and she shifted close to him, putting her ear near the phone.

Brent took a deep breath and answered, "General, what can I do for you?"

"I just got off a call with Sheikh Hussein. He's in the process of having some of his oil reserves moved, but there's an unidentified force, company size right now, moving toward Dubai. He's concerned."

"I understand, sir."

"The sheikh has asked me to appoint you as a special liaison officer for the JSF, acting in that capacity and as a consultant to the sheikh's security forces. In addition, you'd work with his cousin's militia, rebuilding and training that force. Interested?"

Brent took a deep breath. He hadn't asked Hussein for a favor yet, and the kid had already come through. Sure, Hussein had probably been influenced by Juma—you could almost hear that influence in the general's report—but that didn't matter.

"Sir, I'm interested, and I'd like the opportunity to handpick my own staff, with your endorsement, of course."

"You want Schleck, Voeckler, and Lakota to start . . ."

"Well, sir, that would enable me to—"

"You got 'em. Just get me a list before the end of the day. We'll have you in Dubai by the weekend."

"Yes, sir. Thank you, sir."

"We'll be in touch, Captain."

"Yes, sir." He thumbed off the phone.

Brent's life was about to change again, only this time the change would *not* be marked by swelling clouds of smoke and fire.

It would be marked by something very different.

He leaned over and took Lakota into his arms. Without hesitation, he gave her the longest, hottest kiss he could muster. As she hugged him even tighter, he ignored the cheers and applause from his colleagues, surrendering himself to her grasp.

When they finally came up for air, she looked at him and whispered, "To hell with the movie. Take me home."

TOM CLANCY'S GHOST RECON®
COMBAT OPS

WRITTEN BY DAVID MICHAELS

Captain Scott Mitchell and his Ghost Recon team are in the heart of Taliban-controlled Afghanistan, on the hunt for leader Mullah Mohammed Zahed. And after years of government abuse and corruption, the locals trust the Taliban more than any promises from America. With enemy attacks increasing, Mitchell must maneuver his way through a minefield of bloodshed and politics if Ghost Recon is to accomplish their mission.

But one fateful decision may cost Mitchell and his team their honor—and their lives.

M776T0910

Tom Clancy's
SPLINTER CELL®

WRITTEN BY DAVID MICHAELS

SPLINTER CELL

OPERATION BARRACUDA

CHECKMATE

FALLOUT

CONVICTION

ENDGAME

penguin.com

M223AS0610